WHAT THE JAGUAR TOLD HER

For my parents,
Hugo Méndez Ramírez and Vialla Hartfield-Méndez,
who introduced me to the wonders of books
and gave me a beautiful childhood.

This is an Arthur A. Levine book
Published by Levine Querido

LEVINE QUERIDO

www.levinequerido.com • info@levinequerido.com
Levine Querido is distributed by Chronicle Books, LLC
Text copyright © 2022 by Alexandra V. Méndez
All rights reserved
Library of Congress Control Number: 2022931604
ISBN: 978-1-64614-175-3
Printed and bound in China

Published October 2022
First Printing

WHAT THE JAGUAR TOLD HER

Alexandra V. Méndez

LQ

LEVINE QUERIDO

Montclair | Amsterdam | Hoboken

1

Jade couldn't get used to the sounds of the night. There were loud, loud crickets *ch-ch-ch*-ing to one another, and occasional hoots from some other winged thing that sounded either scary or scared, she couldn't decide. And every once in a while, through her new bedroom window, at two in the morning when her parents and Katerina were sound asleep, she would hear a train whistle, like the call of another animal in the dark.

She lay awake, waiting for sleep and wondering about this strange new city and the things that made the sounds. Her black cat, Mortimer, climbed up onto her bed and she reached out, exhausted, to stroke his back.

Eventually, somehow, she fell asleep.

In the morning Jade blinked herself awake and remembered where she was. The new house. Atlanta. The yellow summer light filtering in through the blinds was what had woken her up, not the blaring radio alarm that would knock her upright during the school year. She had that to look forward to—tomorrow. For now, though, it was still Sunday and still summer.

For a moment she watched the dust particles do their slow-motion dance in the slanting light, then pulled herself up out of bed to go have breakfast. The familiar smell of warm tortillas reminded her of Abuela's house. Her mom must be making some fresh.

Mortimer was already pawing at her bedroom door. He meowed when he saw that she was up. He had exceptionally fierce canines for a house cat, but Jade knew she could stick her finger in his mouth and he would only prick playfully at her skin. As soon as Jade opened her door, he dashed off toward the kitchen.

It had already been three weeks since they moved here, but the walk to the kitchen on the other side of the house still reminded Jade how much bigger this house was than their old one. In the old house in Chicago, all the rooms had been next to one another; here, she had to go past a whole extra bedroom—a guest bedroom—and a living room just to get to the kitchen.

Her mom stood over the stove, her movements steady and sure, in her house clothes and the apron that Abuela had embroidered in bright, dancing colors. She held herself with an elegant confidence that never seemed to leave her. Even in her T-shirt and running shorts, she was marking her place here in the new kitchen, leaving no room for doubt. Her sturdy arms didn't stop moving as she made breakfast happen, slipping the spatula cleanly under an egg and flipping it to reveal its lightly golden face, which crackled happily in the skillet. Her skin was much darker than Jade's, and her deep brown eyes were alert, as always, as she glanced up at her.

"Good morning," said her mom, her voice cheerful enough, but perhaps a little tired. "Did you sleep well?"

"I guess so," said Jade, reaching for the bag of cat food in the corner. She still didn't really feel completely awake. Mortimer slipped past her and went to sit by his tin bowl, swishing his tail back and forth in anticipation.

"It's always hard to get used to a new place," her mom said, setting four plates on the granite counter, and Jade wasn't quite sure whether she was saying it to her or to herself. Her mom tucked up one of her flyaway wisps absently into her ponytail. She only ever wore her hair like this in the house. On workdays, she wore it down and curled slightly under in a perfect bob for the TV camera. Even when she stood on a windy street corner giving the latest news to the cameraperson and the people watching at home, her hair always stayed smooth and contained. Jade liked watching her mom on TV when she got the chance, and she was always a little awed by how she kept herself so put together. No matter how her mom wore her hair, though, Jade thought she was beautiful.

Mortimer meowed and nosed the bag of cat food that Jade had begun to open.

"Oh, right. Sorry, Morty," she said. She scooped out a generous amount and let it clatter into his bowl. The cat dove in immediately, cracking the pellets with his ferocious yet dainty teeth. Jade was hungry, too.

Her mom dressed each plate on the counter with a perfect breakfast: a fresh corn tortilla topped with ham and a fried egg, the orange yolk of each one ready to burst through the surface. Huevos rancheros. Her mom transferred them to the low wall that opened out to the spacious dining room, where her dad and her little sister, Katerina, were already at the table. Jade took a plate and went to join them, already anticipating the flavors.

Katerina swung her legs as their dad grabbed a plate for her and cut her breakfast into bite-sized pieces beside her on the table. The blond hairs on his freckled arm caught the sun streaming in through the picture window that faced the big front yard and the house across the street. Jade got her own freckles and blond hair from his side of the family.

"Good morning, Jade," he said brightly, looking up to greet her. He was such a morning person, in a way that Jade could never understand. He liked to wake up with his plants, he said. Sometimes it grated on her—how cheerful he could be in the mornings—but today his voice seemed to match the clear, inviting light that spilled in from the window, and she didn't mind it.

"Morning, Dad," she said. The sunlight filled the room and bounced off all the glistening surfaces—the eggs, the silverware, the small blue-and-white ceramic bowl with fresh red salsa. The reflection of a sparrow hopping among the azaleas in the front yard shimmered on the glass doors of the antique dark-wood china cabinet in the corner that her dad kept impeccably clean. It had been passed down through generations of his family in Nebraska, and now it housed the painted ceramic dishes that had once proudly decorated the Casa Azul, the restaurant in Chicago that her abuelos used to run.

"Hey, Sissy," said Katerina, looking up at Jade as she sat down. "It's hard to sleep without you now."

Instinctively, Jade reached out and smoothed her sister's uncombed black hair. She returned the six-year-old's gaze, looking into her big dark eyes. They used to share a room in the old house.

"I know," said Jade. "I have trouble sleeping, too." She had thought it was just the new house, but now it occurred to her that part of what she was getting used to was not having Katerina in the room, always falling asleep before Jade did, her calm, unconcerned dream-breaths a kind of lullaby.

When her mom came in and sat at the head of the table, she spread salsa on her egg, but her body tensed when she was about to dig in. Holding the fork and knife just above her plate, she said, "Only a few more boxes. Then we'll be moved in. Well—almost."

"Relax, Sol," said Jade's dad, settling in beside her mom and squeezing her shoulder. Her mom looked at him and seemed to loosen up a bit. She sank her fork into the egg and cut her first bite.

"It just feels like it's never-ending," her mom said. "Did we decide about the blinds yet?"

"Let's enjoy breakfast," her dad said softly but firmly, and he shook a few tiny dollops of salsa from the little wooden spoon in the blue bowl onto Katerina's plate.

Jade agreed with that plan. This was the first time her mom made fresh salsa and tortillas since they got here. She couldn't see why her mom was stressing out right at this moment. Taking the wooden spoon, she painted an even spiral of salsa onto her egg, opened the yolk with her knife, and carefully spread the warm, sunny liquid, mixing it with the salsa to get the flavors just right. The deep yellow ran across the plate and swirled with the red.

"Jade, there's one more box you need to unpack," said her mom.

"Really? I thought I was done," said Jade, not looking up. She had a divine first bite ready on the tip of her fork.

"Your winter pajamas are in there," her mom said.

"Oh," said Jade, and ate her bite. "*Mmm!*" she said, relishing how exactly the taste matched what she had expected. "This is delicious." Her dad and Katerina joined in in a chorus of approval. Her mom nodded and smiled, satisfied. Maybe the food wasn't quite as good as what Abuela used to cook, but it was still amazing. It had that smoky taste that Jade loved.

When they had all indulged in a bit of contented silence, her dad said, "Who wants to help me in the garden this morning?"

"Me!" said Katerina, stretching her hand high and spitting out some salsa as she said it.

"Hey—what did we say about talking with your mouth full?" her mom said, but she didn't really seem angry.

Her dad smiled. "Jade?" he said.

"It's too hot," said Jade. "Maybe another day." She didn't mind gardening, but she didn't want to do it in this Atlanta heat.

"All right, bug," her dad said to Katerina. "Let's see what herbs we can grow out back." He touched her mom's arm lightly. "So we can have even more of your delicious food," he said more quietly, just to her.

Her mom smiled, and for the first time since she sat down, she looked fully relaxed.

Jade opened the last box in the middle of her room. She pulled out miscellaneous soft things and put them in a dresser drawer. White underwear with little pink bows that her mom always bought in packs of ten. The green-and-purple-striped pajamas her mom had mentioned at breakfast that, now that Jade thought about it, she hoped she never had to wear to a pajama party. Some light-pink training bras she had replaced by now with real ones, but for some reason still hadn't thrown out.

At the bottom of the box her fingertips struck something hard. Between folded underwear and pajamas, she found a smooth, black stone disc, about the size of her palm. Sitting back on her heels, she ran her index finger carefully along its razor-thin edge. The stone fit comfortably in her hand. Its glossy black surfaces bulged in gentle, symmetrical curves on either side.

Peering closer, Jade saw that it was webbed with smoky veins. She ran her pale thumb over the cool, polished face to make sure they weren't cracks. The blackness had a sheen like a looking glass, and Jade sensed that entire worlds could be contained in the stone's reflections.

"Mom, what's this?" Jade called, not taking her eyes off the disc. She turned it over and then over again, as if one of those flips might reveal its secrets to her. She heard the zip of an X-Acto knife as her mom ran it along the seam of a box in the hallway, then the click as she snapped it shut and came to the doorway. When Jade looked up, her mom was eyeing the mirror in a funny way, like it reminded her of something. Her face was soft.

"Mom?" said Jade.

"It's a mirror," she said, pulling her eyes from it to look at Jade.

Jade looked back at the mirror. She wondered whether her mom saw something in it that Jade didn't—couldn't—see.

She inspected her reflection on the smoky surface. Instead of her long, thin face and dirty-blond hair that she was used to seeing in mirrors, she saw two faces—hers and her mom's—in three different parts of the disc. When she moved it, the light from the window slithered over it and their faces became distorted, big and goofy in some places and impossibly small and elongated in others. The tiny veins in the stone undulated like transparent threads of smoke, veiling the reflection, making it uncertain.

It was a mirror, but it was a strange one.

"I'm not sure what I see in it," she said, hoping her mom might say something that would help her make out whatever it was she was supposed to see.

Instead her mom said simply but firmly, "Keep it." And she walked away.

Jade understood that it was an order. Like so many things with her mom, this mirror was something unexplained but important. She felt around in the box for something to wrap it in, to protect its sharp edges and polished surface. She found a frilly white camisole that would do the job, and wrapped it with reverence. She felt slightly ridiculous, though, because of how silly the white cami looked in contrast to the mirror. But it was the best thing she had. She pushed the wrapped mirror deep into the bottom of the drawer. She stuffed the last clothes from the box on top of it and closed the drawer, its dangling brass handle clattering against the wood.

She stared at the pull handle. Silently, she lifted it and pulled the drawer out again. She reached into its depths until she felt the mirror again through the camisole. Was she making sure it was still there? She wasn't certain.

She shut the drawer again and pulled her eyes away from it.

At last she was moved in. Maybe she would fall asleep early tonight.

When they had first driven into Atlanta three weeks ago, the skyline had appeared before them suddenly, a city of silver and glass against a blue, blue sky at the end of the six-lane highway. All Jade could think of when she saw it was that it wasn't the Chicago skyline. She had always loved seeing those bright, familiar silhouettes etched into the night sky, the step pattern of the Sears Tower with its crown of colored spears, appearing in the windshield after one of the long drives to visit her grandma in Nebraska. The sharp edges and peaks of this new Atlanta skyline were strangers to her.

As they had exited the highway and the car burrowed into the new city, the green of trees and parks and front lawns began to mix with the grays and blues and blacks of metal and concrete. Katerina hadn't stopped talking since the city appeared. She nearly climbed out of her car seat and covered the window of the Honda with little finger-smudges as she pointed to all the new things. "Look!" she said, over and over again, swinging her black braided pig-tails around as they drove past boiled peanut stands, sleek car dealerships, and infinite pine trees. "Look, Mommy! Look, Daddy! Look, Sissy!" And Jade had looked, but said nothing, only patted the mesh top of Mortimer's carrier in her lap. She didn't know yet what to make of all these new things. She just knew that she felt calmer when she kept her eyes on the trees.

Their new house was two redbrick stories tall, waiting for them at the end of a cul-de-sac in a quiet, leafy neigh-borhood. Two houses stood angled slightly toward each other at the end of the wide, recently paved street: theirs, and a blue wooden one that was just as big. The two grassy lawns stretched toward them like freshly unrolled carpets as they approached. Her dad slowed and pulled the car into the driveway beside the flagstone steps that led to the front stoop with its wrought-iron banister.

"Whoa," Katerina said.

The house and its yard certainly were impressive. But what had caught Jade's eye was something else—a neatly kept dirt trail beside their driveway, between the two lawns, that led from the street into the trees behind the houses. She leaned forward to see where the path led beyond that, but it curved out of sight behind a line of pines.

All the houses here had big shady backyards. Beyond that, tall trees grew thickly together. The neighborhood had been cut out of a forest. Since the move, Jade had walked out to the edge of the dirt trail a few times to get away from the mess and confusion of her parents' unpacking and deciding where the furniture should go. A wooden sign at the entrance read WILDCAT TRAIL. Jade had stood at the edge of the trees where the path curved into the woods, wondering where it led. When she looked back at the house, the two sturdy oak trees in the backyard looked like they were left over from the forest. Their shade stretched halfway across the yard.

The people in this neighborhood were different from Jade's neighbors in Chicago. Most of them were white, for one thing—even though it didn't seem like all of Atlanta was like that. People seemed to be always either going to the pool or coming back from the pool—probably the place called Athenian Pools that Jade had seen when they drove in. She often saw the two toddlers who lived in the blue house beside theirs either walking to their family's silver SUV carrying towels that were bigger than they were or climbing down from it, the towels wrapped around them and their tiny heads wet. In the evenings when the family left the blinds open in their living room that faced the street, Jade could see what they were watching on their big TV. Often it was baseball; sometimes it was the news.

On that first night when they arrived, in the strange bed with the strange noises outside, Jade thought maybe she was going to be all right in this big new house. They had moved here because her mom got a new, important job at CNN, and that made her parents happy. Maybe she could be happy, too, in this nook at the end of the neighborhood, protected by trees. But then the warm tears had welled up, and she let them stream slowly down her cheeks, not making a sound. The house was too big, the bed was too soft, and she wished she could ride her bike with her dad and Katerina to Lake Michigan one more time, and feel the cool water lap against her toes in the sand.

When her pillow had grown uncomfortably damp with tears, she heard Mortimer scratching outside her bedroom door. Sleepily, she got up to let him in before sinking straight back into the bed. He scampered up, curled up at her feet, and looked at her, his yellow-green eyes shining in the dark. Jade had returned his steady gaze, and it had calmed her. She hadn't felt like crying anymore. She had thought of the trail outside, and wondered where it led. And with that question floating in her mind and Mortimer's quietly breathing body warming her toes through the covers, she had at last been able to fall asleep.

There was one thing Jade knew she could do to make the tumult inside her settle down, even just for a bit. In the late afternoons when her parents got tired of unpacking and her dad walked through the sloped, wild landscape of the backyard, setting stones here and pots there as he envisioned its taming, Jade stayed inside and sat on her bed in the AC to draw in her favorite green spiral-bound notebook. Through her window came the rip and rustle of her dad wrestling long vines of ivy off the old oaks, and the soft rapping of Katerina's tiny shovel. She drew mindless swirls and many-petaled flowers to fill the whole ruled page, going over her pencil lines again and again, tracing silvery furrows that made the paper curl toward her as if it were alive.

She kept her good paper and pencils stacked neatly inside her desk drawer, along with the other art supplies that her grandma had given her over the years for birthdays and Christmases. She hardly ever touched those. They were so beautiful and pristine that she didn't want to mess them up by dulling the pencil points or drawing a wayward line on the granular white paper that felt almost like cloth beneath her fingertips. She preferred the familiar light blue lines of her notebook paper and her mechanical pencil that had lead points that she didn't mind breaking. She could mess up and it would be fine. She felt freer that way.

After dinner on Sunday, Jade went into her new bathroom that she had all to herself and held up to her body the uniform that her mom had laid out on top of her dresser. She was going to wear this tomorrow for the first day of eighth grade at Our Lady of Hope Catholic School. She had never worn a uniform before, aside from her Girl Scouts vests in elementary school. She had picked these clothes out from the school's catalogue with her mom: a white collared shirt, a blue plaid skort, navy knee socks, and brown leather shoes. The skort was weird, but at least it went all the way around in the back so no one could immediately tell that there were shorts underneath. She liked it better than the pleated skirt option. When she held up the skort to what her mom called her "natural waist"— way higher than anybody her age wore their jeans—it was still so long it hit just above her knee.

If she were in Chicago still, she wouldn't be starting school for another three weeks. It was as if a chunk of the summer had been stolen from her. She laid the clothes back on her dresser and then half sat, half flopped onto her bed. If she were starting eighth grade at her old school, she would have called up Madison and Veronica, and they would have helped one another decide what to wear for their first day at the top of the middle school food chain. Madison always went for something loud and daring, to remind everybody of who she was. Jade and Veronica usually were a little less likely to venture beyond the fitted T-shirts and flared jeans they wore all summer. Jade always liked to walk into school the first day knowing that her friends enthusiastically approved of her outfit. She wouldn't have that tomorrow. But hopefully it wouldn't matter, because everyone had to wear this uniform anyway.

The sky wasn't yet completely dark. For a few more hours, it was still summer. Grabbing her green notebook, she curled up on the bed and began to draw, as the grays of evening overtook the world outside, and her mom typed away in her new office at the top of the stairs.

Jade let her mind wander along the paths that her pencil etched. Back in Chicago, there were things she had either taken for granted or never thought to ask about. She always knew Abuela was just a short car ride away, and she could count on when the summer heat would end and the fall breezes would cool the streets. But here in Atlanta, so far from everything and everyone she knew, in this house where even old things seemed suddenly new because it felt like they were out of place, questions bubbled up inside her. Her mom had insisted so forcefully that she keep that odd, veiny mirror. Why was it so special? And why did her mom want her to have it?

She ran her pencil again and again in the grooves she had made and listened to the typing upstairs. It wasn't such a surprise that her mom hadn't explained all this to her. Her mom was very private, and only explicitly revealed things about herself every once in a while. She also never spoke to Jade in Spanish, and Jade wished she did. Maybe then she would have better understood the stories Abuelo used to tell her before he died—stories of multicolored, fortune-telling birds, of silky blue agave fields that stretched the length of the highway and then some. Abuelo had died years ago, but Jade still remembered acutely the feeling of incompleteness she had been left with, the feeling that she hadn't been listening hard enough. That on those nights when her abuelos had taken care of her so her parents could have a night out, when Abuelo had amused her with bedtime tales in Spanish of life in his hometown of San Juan de las Jacarandas, he had actually been telling her something very important.

The backyard was completely dark now. Mortimer hopped up and settled himself in the window, like he was a part of the night.

Jade thought of Abuelo's angular face in profile against the night sky in the window of their house in Chicago, his playful eyes lit by the moonlight and the streetlamps. In those moments, his eyes had seemed to mirror another world beyond the brick facades and power lines of this one.

When she put her uniform on in the morning, it felt as awkward and stiff as Jade had thought it would. The clothes were boxy, like they didn't really fit the shape of her body, and the waist of the skort was way too high.

At the dining table Katerina was sharpening yellow pencils in the wall-mount sharpener that hadn't yet been bolted to anything, grinding the handle round and round obsessively and blowing loudly at the shavings. The pencils she had finished sharpening were half their original size, and piles of shavings lay beside them in little heaps on the table. Jade fed Mortimer and ate the scrambled eggs her mom had made while she watched her sister tuck her sharpened pencils beside her Hello Kitty notebook in her new ladybug-shaped backpack. Katerina strapped her backpack on and ran to the door, hopping up and down. "Hurry up!" she squealed.

Their mom was already at the door, too. Jade shoved the last bites into her mouth and went to join them.

In the doorway, Katerina looked like a miniature of their mother. They had the same smooth skin the color of rich wood paneling and thick black hair that was hard to tame. Her sister's hair was pulled back in a long braid to battle the flyaway curls that would inevitably take over by the end of the day. Her mom had picture-perfect work-day hair.

Her dad came to the back door and crouched to give Katerina a squeeze. "You be good now," he said, smiling at her. Katerina beamed and twisted a little from side to side, her ladybug backpack sliding back and forth across her back.

He stood up and turned to Jade. "You'll be great today," he said, and patted her back.

"Thanks, Dad," she said, already heading out the door. She didn't want to admit it, but somehow, that was just what she had needed to hear to feel like she could face the day.

She had thought they were headed to the car in the driveway, but instead her mom led them across the backyard to the path marked WILDCAT TRAIL, holding Katerina's hand.

"This is the way to school?" said Jade. She hadn't expected to find out so soon where the path led.

"That's right," said her mom, pressing on.

Jade's new leather shoes bit into her ankles as she stepped after her onto the trail. The heels of her mom's polished black pumps looked especially shiny against the dirt of the path, and Jade wondered if she'd have to clean them afterward. As they passed the line of pines at the edge of the yard, Jade felt a thrill. The trees thickened and offered their shade, and the green of the woods enveloped them on either side of the skinny, snaking path.

The farther they walked, the harder it was for Jade to believe that they were still in a city. The trees were tall and had wide, hefty trunks, and some were overgrown with ivy like the oaks in their new backyard. Along the path, clusters of little pink flowers sprouted atop long stems with wide leaves that grew in upturned pairs like hands making an offering. The ground beneath them was dusted with tiny fallen blossoms. Sprays of long dark leaves with taut green berries tinged with their first purple rose to the height of Katerina's knee. Twitchy squirrels and rambunctious chipmunks rustled in the leaves and something half squawked, half screeched overhead.

The forest comforted Jade. The specific trees and flowers and animals were new, but they didn't feel as strange to her as the new house. Walking along this path felt a little like walking through the paths that her dad had tended back at the Chicago Botanic Garden, only wilder.

A boy about Jade's age rushed by them on a bike, just barely missing them. His white shirt, navy dress shorts, and red backpack flashed past. Jade wondered if he was in her grade. When he disappeared around the next bend, she heard some chatter behind her. Looking back, she saw another mom with a long blond braid holding the hand of a little boy about Katerina's age some distance away. Apparently, this was how a bunch of people went to school. Her mom smiled and waved back at the other mom. The forest felt alive with the morning chirps of animals and people.

They emerged to the sun glinting off shiny car metal in the parking lot of the school. Children large and small spilled out of sparkling sedans, minivans, and SUVs. The youngest were Katerina's age, the oldest Jade's. Jade saw the switch flip in her mother, and she became Mrs. O'Callaghan, smiling and ready to make small talk with any mother who might approach her. It was a version of the person she was on TV. Katerina attracted attention—she always did, and especially so today. Jade had to admit she looked incredibly cute in her plaid jumper and polka-dotted ladybug backpack. But she didn't love it when these moms smiled at Katerina and barely acknowledged her.

As they approached the school, Jade saw that not a single girl her age was wearing blue knee socks or brown leather shoes or a skort. Everyone was wearing white knee socks, box-pleated navy skirts, and shiny two-tone, white-and-black oxford shoes. Jade had gotten it all wrong. Who knew there was a uniform within the uniform?

She followed her mom and sister to the front office, where a woman with short, straw-colored hair curled under introduced herself as Ms. Higgins, welcomed them, and gave her mom some paperwork to fill out. She smiled widely and talked to Jade and Katerina as if they were both Katerina's age. "Are you excited for your first day of school? Oh, I'll bet you are!" She had that lilting Southern accent that Jade had only heard in the movies, only softer and less twangy. She flashed her red fingernails in the two opposite directions that Jade and Katerina were to follow to get to class—one toward the middle school wing, the other toward the elementary school. Jade heard, "Ms. Jackson's eighth grade homeroom, room 107, straight down the hall and to the left," and gave her mom a hasty kiss on the cheek before darting in that direction.

As she headed down the hall, a girl walking in the same direction said, "Are you the new girl?"

Jade started. "Yes . . ." She hadn't expected anyone to come up to her like that, so soon. She hoped this girl was friendly.

The girl's big coffee eyes were rimmed with heavy, grown-up-looking mascara and eyeliner, but Jade could still tell that she was her age. Her skin was olive and her long, straight hair was dark, but she didn't look Hispanic. Jade became self-conscious of her makeup-free face. The girl looked past her at Katerina, who was making a scene and about to cry.

"Is that really your sister?"

"Yes, why?"

"She's so dark and you're so pale."

"I know." Jade had heard this plenty of times before, and was mildly annoyed without wanting to be. She was grateful to this girl for talking to her.

"Okay," said the girl, and she seemed to accept it.

They walked in silence and arrived at room 107. Jade tried to think of how to break the silence, but luckily she didn't have to.

"I'm Chloe, by the way," the girl said.

"Jade."

Suddenly, the girl leaned in and whispered to her: "We have an awesome homeroom teacher. I know her from cross-country."

Jade raised her eyebrows and followed Chloe into the room. Maybe this girl was cool.

The sea of new faces in the classroom was too much for her. Nobody paid her any attention. There were girls squealing and hugging one another. There were boys running around pointlessly—like boys, Jade thought. She saw the one with the red backpack who had biked through the trail. They were clearly all so *used* to one another. After all, most of them had known one another since kindergarten—since they were Katerina's age.

A few girls said hi to Chloe and hugged her, but there were no squeals. Jade watched Chloe position herself at the side of a group of girls and followed her. The girls got quiet when they saw her.

"Hi," said one of them, who had straight red hair and a welcoming face. "I'm Caitlyn."

"This is Jade," said Chloe, and Jade was thankful that Chloe was introducing her, as if she already knew her, so she wouldn't have to do it herself.

"Hi, Jade," they all said.

"I'm Emily." Emily was brown with freckles and curly hair. She had her thumb in a thick paperback. The way she looked up at Jade but kept her place in the book reminded her of Veronica. Veronica always had something in her hands—either something she was making or a book she was reading, her fingers active on the pages as if she were taking the story in by touch as much as by sight.

"Hi," said Jade, giving a little wave from the height of her waist. She suddenly wondered what these girls thought of her hair, which she had simply brushed and let fall around her shoulders. It had already frizzed up with the humidity.

"So, where are you from?" said Emily, smiling and revealing her purple braces.

"Chicago," said Jade.

"Is it cold up there?" said Caitlyn.

"It's hot down here," Jade replied.

"You must be Jade."

She jumped slightly at the sound of her name behind her. Turning around, she saw the teacher, a tall, athletic woman with shoulder-length, dyed-blond hair.

"I'm Ms. Jackson," she said, extending her hand and a big, toothy smile. "Welcome to Our Lady of Hope. We're extremely happy to have you here." Jade wasn't sure who the *we* was. "The bell will ring any moment now, and I'll introduce you to the class, okay?" she said. Jade nodded. She could already feel the tops of her ears getting warm. The bell rang and Ms. Jackson went to the front of the classroom and clapped everyone to attention.

"Welcome back!" she said, flashing that smile of hers. "It's good to see all of you again. I know most of you from social studies last year, and a couple of you from cross-country, but let me introduce you to a new person I just met—Jade, can you come up here, please?"

Jade obeyed and walked to the front of the classroom. She stared at the teacher so as not to look at everybody staring at her.

"This is Jade. She's from—Chicago, is that right?" Jade nodded. "Jade will be joining us this year and I hope we can all give her a very warm welcome. Now, let's get to our desks."

Ms. Jackson took a piece of paper from the pocket of her slacks and began to assign seats, weaving her way through the classroom and touching the tops of desks while she called out names. Jade tried very hard to remember the names but it was too much, so she zoned out and played with the purple-and-green chevron bracelet Veronica had made for her before she left. She missed her.

Ms. Jackson called her name and she sat down. She was pleasantly surprised to see that she was right next to Chloe.

As Ms. Jackson assigned the rest of the seats, Chloe leaned in and whispered, "You're lucky. You're gonna be next to *Peter.*"

Chloe was right about the seating. Peter was assigned to the desk on the other side of Jade, and he was pretty in a blond, Leonardo DiCaprio sort of way. Jade tried to look at him without looking like she was looking at him. She couldn't decide for sure if she thought he was cute, but these days all sorts of boys left her feeling self-conscious and wanting to look in every direction except theirs, and Peter was no exception.

When everyone was seated, Ms. Jackson returned to the front of the classroom and said, "All right everybody, let's start with the Our Father."

Jade instinctively looked to Chloe for help. Chloe made the sign of the cross and Jade copied her hurriedly. She still felt like she messed up—had Chloe made the sign the opposite way from everyone else?

Everyone started saying: "Our Father, who art in heaven, hallowed be thy name . . ." Jade moved her lips but only mumbled something. She had only been to a few Catholic masses before with her abuela, and those had been in Spanish. Halfway through the prayer she realized she had heard Abuela say this prayer, intoning rhythmically along with the rest of the congregation. *Padre nuestro, que estás en el cielo . . .*

Homeroom was okay, but the rest of the day was a bit of a struggle. It took her five tries, with Chloe helping her, to get her locker open. When they switched classes, she followed Chloe. Luckily Ms. Jackson's homeroom went everywhere together. In the morning there was pre-algebra, language arts, and social studies. The teachers seemed nice enough, but it was always hard to tell on the first day.

When the lunch bell rang, everyone bolted. By the time they arrived at the cafeteria, most of the girls had hiked up their skirts. There was a whole technique to this, apparently—something about rolling the waistline and pulling at the shirt until it was bloused out but still technically tucked in. Jade surreptitiously tried to hike her own, but the crotch of the skort made this uncomfortable and kept it from riding more than a few inches above her knee.

She tried to sit next to Chloe but realized with a tightening feeling in her chest that there was no room at the table. She tried to play it cool and started to walk to another table, but Chloe pulled up a chair for her. "There's room," she said.

"Thanks," said Jade, trying not to sound as relieved as she felt.

As Jade unzipped her lunch bag, Caitlyn, the redhead, said, "Did you guys see *Legally Blonde* this summer? I went with my sister last weekend and it was *so* funny."

"Ooh, I wanna see that!" said Emily.

Jade had seen the poster for that movie, but it looked a little too *pink* for her.

"Wait, isn't that about some ditzy sorority girl?" said Chloe, frowning skeptically.

"Yeah, but she's actually really smart," said Caitlyn.

"Wait—did you guys see *A Knight's Tale*?" said Emily.

"Yes!" they all said, including Jade. She had seen it with Madison and Veronica, and all summer Madison hadn't stopped talking about Heath Ledger.

"But the best movie this summer was obviously *Moulin Rouge!*," said Chloe. She sang out the opening line of "Diamonds Are a Girl's Best Friend," and Jade was surprised by how nice her voice sounded. Madison had wanted to see that movie, but none of them had been brave enough to ask one of their moms to take them because it looked so steamy.

Like Jade, Chloe also had a lunch from home. It looked amazing. It was something with a flaky crust that was filled with cheese and other things, and Chloe ate it all in ten minutes. Jade's mom had packed her leftovers from last night and a little note that said *You'll be great! Love, Mom*, which Jade quickly turned over so no one would see it. Everyone else at the table had school lunches.

"Hey, what is that?" said Caitlyn, pointing to Jade's food.

Caitlyn was plainly just curious, maybe even jealous, but still Jade sighed inwardly at the question. How could she explain? It was a chile relleno with some rice and corn and zucchini. But she knew this girl wouldn't understand "chile relleno" so she said, "It's like a pepper with stuff."

Caitlyn nodded and went back to her fish sticks, which for some inexplicable reason she was dipping in her applesauce.

After lunch was Catholics in the World with the soft-spoken Ms. Berenson, then science, which was cool because of all the posters of plants and animals and diagrams. And finally, PE with Coach Porter, a stocky guy who wore a cap that said US MARINES, where Jade at last felt free, outside on the field, dashing from base to base as they played kickball. She didn't have to pretend to know any new rules—kickball was the same everywhere, and she was good at it.

When she walked out to the sunny breezeway by the parking lot at the end of the day, her heavy backpack tugging at her shoulders, she looked around and noticed that everyone looked different. All at once, like the boxes suddenly showing all the letters on *Wheel of Fortune*, everyone's shirt was untucked. Jade hurried to untuck hers in some sort of graceful way.

Her mom was waiting for her and Katerina a little farther down on the sidewalk by the parking lot. She had struck up a conversation with another mom. Jade envied how easily her mom made chitchat with perfect strangers.

She turned to Chloe to wave a shy goodbye, but Chloe wasn't looking. She was talking to Emily and Caitlyn about something to do with cross-country, and they all had sports bags slung over their shoulders. For the first time all day, Jade felt like she was completely on the outside of something. She gave up trying to get Chloe's attention and went to her mom.

"How was school?" her mom said, turning her full attention to Jade and away from the mom she had just made friends with. Jade could tell she really wanted to know the answer, wanted to know if she was okay.

She thought for a moment, but she wasn't sure what to say. "It was all right," she said quietly, shrugging a little. Her mom put a hand on her shoulder but let it fall quickly. Maybe she could tell Jade didn't want or need too much attention in front of all these new people.

Jade looked past her mom, past the shiny cars lined up to pick up kids, to the shady spot at the entrance to the Wildcat Trail, the stretch of dirt leading from the parking lot into the trees. She felt a calm spread inside herself as she watched it—a calm that seemed to quiet the bright, loud sounds of the kids around her. She stepped out into the parking lot, making sure to check for cars, and headed toward the trail. As she stepped onto the soft soil, she heard her mom call out behind her, "Jade, wait for your sister!"

Jade stopped. "Okay!" she called.

She peered down the path at the greens and browns bobbing and twinkling in the afternoon breeze. She thought maybe she could hear running water somewhere close by, but she wasn't sure.

She took a few steps forward. She knew she was supposed to wait for her mom and Katerina, but it wouldn't hurt to go just a little farther.

The ground was soft and inviting under her feet. Buttercups and violets brushed little butterfly kisses on her ankles as she walked slowly past, stepping on the dapples of sunlight that fell patchily through the canopy. A squirrel stood motionless in front of her until she came within a yard of it, then it jumped onto the nearest tree, flicking its tail, and climbed up to disappear into the foliage.

"Sissy!"

Jade turned.

"Sissy, wait for me," Katerina said, running toward her, a piece of red construction paper flapping in her outstretched hand. Their mom was just behind her.

"Look what I made!" Katerina said when she caught up with Jade. She held the piece of paper up as far as her little arms would reach. It was a drawing of a girl with black hair in a triangular dress. Underneath it was written in big letters, uneven but determined: KATERINA.

"It's a nice picture," said Jade. She wasn't quite sure what a six-year-old's drawing was supposed to look like, but it was definitely clear what this was a drawing *of*, and that seemed like a good thing.

"It's not a *picture*," said Katerina. "It's a self-portrait!"

"I stand corrected," said Jade, smiling softly in spite of herself.

Her mom reached them and gestured for them to keep moving. "What a *beautiful* self-portrait . . . !" her mom said, walking on with Katerina.

But Jade lagged behind. She thought she heard something—like a cat purring, but deeper. She stood still and tried to listen. It almost sounded like just another whisper of the forest, but there was something distinct about it, too. She wanted to know what it was. She felt a little like she did in those moments when she knew that

Mortimer was right outside her door, even before he started scratching.

"Come on, Jade!" her mom called.

"Come on, Sissy!"

Jade kept walking, slowly. She didn't hear the sound anymore. But she thought she felt a warm presence in the trees just beyond the trail, a presence as inviting as the forest itself. She couldn't explain it, but she felt like there was something—or someone—in the trees who she had known for a long time, and was keeping her company as she walked.

The sunlight up ahead signaled the end of the path, and Jade was reluctant to leave the forest. As she stepped out into the grass of her backyard beside the driveway and the afternoon heat poured down on her again, she wondered what it was she had sensed.

Maybe it was nothing.

2

Jade's mom didn't normally like to have her family watch her reporting on TV. But that evening after the first day of school, she didn't object when Jade's dad turned the TV on to CNN. They were all seated at the dining table, digging into juicy slices of chicken her mom had roasted with sprigs of rosemary that had just begun to anchor their roots in her dad's new herb garden.

The anchorwoman for the evening news, a woman with straight blond hair, announced that "President Bush's approval of support for stem cell research has been somewhat controversial. Sol O'Callaghan—has the story."

The family got quiet and watched. There was Jade's mom, notepad in hand, interviewing someone in a lab coat at the CDC. Jade was used to seeing her mom on TV—she had been an anchorwoman on the local news ever since Jade could remember—but this was different. The camera quality was better, and Jade knew that people all over the country were watching this. Maybe even the neighbors next door.

This was a big deal for her mom. She had just produced a special on alcohol and drug addiction in Chicago when she got the offer from CNN. Her mom had jumped into her dad's arms and he twirled her around in their little kitchen. There was never a question about it: Her mom had gotten a dream job, and they were all going to move to Atlanta. And Jade and Katerina would go to Catholic school, like her parents always wanted.

On TV, her mom was wearing her trim black pantsuit and the woman in the lab coat was listing out diseases: "Alzheimer's, Parkinson's . . ."

Beside Jade at the dining table, her mom watched her recorded self on TV. Her hands were clasped under her chin, her elbows resting on the table, and her lips were relaxed in a gentle, contented smile.

The scene cut to her mom walking toward the camera in front of a big, curved, green-glass building. "Funding for this research has been hotly contested," she was saying in that confident, informed manner of hers, "but scientists hope that these new experiments will lead to breakthroughs in curing some of the most pernicious diseases.

"Sol O'Callaghan, CNN, Atlanta."

"Yeah!" said her dad, and he started clapping. Katerina joined in, gleeful, and Jade did, too. It was her mom's first story on CNN. She had to admit, it was pretty cool.

Her dad put his muscular arm around her mom. "Well, look at that gorgeous lady," he said. "You're amazing, Sol." He gave her a big kiss on the cheek. Her mom smiled more widely now, looking up at him, and let herself be pulled into his embrace.

"Daddy, I drew a self-portrait at school!" said Katerina, as if time was up for their mom, and not her, to be the center of attention.

"Did you?" her dad said, looking up from Jade's mom but still stroking her arm.

"Yeah, let me show you." She got down from her chair and only then seemed to remember her manners. "May I . . . ?" she started to say.

"Yes, you're excused," her parents both said at once.

As Katerina ran off to get her picture, her dad asked, "How was the first day for you, Jade?"

Her mom reached for the remote and dialed down the volume on the TV.

Jade thought again about how to answer. It hadn't gone quite as badly as it could have, but still she had felt out of step so much of the time. "It was okay," she said.

"Did you make any friends?" said her mom.

Jade nodded. "I think so," she said. "I mean—this one girl, Chloe, seemed really nice." Looking back on the day, she thought it might have been a disaster if it weren't for her.

"That's great, Jade," said her mom, smiling. "Chloe." Jade watched her file the name away in her brain. Her mom's hand was resting lightly on top of her dad's.

Mortimer padded silently into Jade's bathroom while she was washing her face that night. He was the family cat, but really, he was Jade's. He would let no one else pet him, scratching anyone who got too close. His body was stronger and bigger than a normal cat's. His ears were rounded, and his yellow-green eyes had a fierce look about them. Everyone said he was wild and unpredictable, but

Jade had never been afraid of him. She had found him as a kitten when she was about Katerina's age. He had been alone in the park by their old house—a tiny puff of a thing—running frantically back and forth on the street side of the chain-link fence, meowing to her with his little pink mouth open wide, and showing his already sharp canines. Jade had coaxed him under the wire fence and he ran straight into her open palms and sat there shivering. Her parents hadn't wanted to keep him, but when they saw what a fit she threw—a fit that nearly scared Mortimer away—they gave in. Her dad made her promise she would feed him every day and clean the litter box. Jade had readily agreed, not having the faintest idea what she was agreeing to. By now, these chores were second nature to her—Mortimer's needs were like an extension of her own.

The cat ran his tail against the back of her legs as she foamed up her face. He jumped gracefully onto the edge of the counter and stretched out there.

People said she had a way with cats, but Jade didn't think of it like that. She felt she understood them, yes, and cats ran to her on the street hoping for a tummy rub, sure. And yes, there were those admittedly odd moments when she knew without a doubt that there was a cat around a street corner or behind a bush. But there was nothing unusual in this for Jade—she had always been this way. Besides, plenty of people she knew had strange and even extraordinary abilities, too. Her dad, for example, could make any seed grow anywhere, no matter if the plant wasn't meant for the local climate. Her mom had a way of getting people to tell her things that they had never told anyone else. Veronica could look at an origami crane or a lily and figure out exactly how the delicate paper was folded, and make one just like it. It seemed to Jade that probably everyone had some kind of special ability like that—something that was completely natural to them but perplexing and impressive to others.

She rinsed her face and patted it dry. Mortimer yawned and jumped down to stalk silently back and forth behind her.

In the quiet as she dabbed benzoyl peroxide on the spots that threatened to flare into zits, Jade realized that she could hear her parents' conversation in the next room. Their bedroom must be just on the other side of her bathroom wall. She was still getting used to the layout of this new house.

"It's so great, honey," her dad was saying. "I'm so happy you're finally getting what you deserve. America now finds out about the latest developments in national health from the mouth of this gorgeous woman, Sol O'Callaghan."

Her mom giggled softly.

"Seriously," he continued. "You're the young Latina they need."

There was a pause.

"Chris, that's not why they hired me."

"Oh, honey, I didn't mean *that*—"

"It's about experience, knowledge, poise, and delivery . . . not race." Her mom sounded annoyed.

Her parents fell silent. After a moment, her dad said, "I'm sorry, Sol. I shouldn't have said that. That's not what I meant. I just—I'm worried about this job."

"You'll get it," Jade heard her mom say, her tone soft and conciliatory.

"I hope so."

Jade didn't know which job they were talking about— she knew he had applied to several here in Atlanta. He had loved his job at the botanical gardens in Chicago so much. She wondered whether he would find something that would make him just as happy.

Mortimer slipped between her legs and into her room. It was time for bed.

As they sat at their desks in homeroom, Chloe asked Jade, "Why'd you run off yesterday? I was looking for you but you were gone. You didn't even say goodbye."

Jade saw in her eyes that she was hurt, despite her bold, dark makeup.

"I tried to say goodbye but you were talking to people," said Jade. She had thought Chloe cared more about talking to Caitlyn and Emily than talking to her, but maybe she was wrong. She hoped Chloe wasn't mad at her.

"Oh," said Chloe. "Well, I was going to ask if you wanted to go get ice cream. My dad decided to treat me and my brother and whoever else we wanted to invite."

"Oh!" said Jade. Chloe had wanted to hang out with her? Outside of school? "That's—really nice of you. Thanks. Was there an occasion?"

"He was just here for the day. He lives in Charlotte. Sometimes he comes here on business trips. And to see us."

"Oh." Jade was suddenly embarrassed, like she had followed Chloe on some sort of excursion but hadn't brought the proper gear. She knew people with divorced parents, but she still always assumed people's parents were together like hers.

Suddenly, Chloe leaned over and lowered her voice. "You know you don't have to keep that button buttoned," she said.

"What?" said Jade, surprised at the change of subject.

"The top button."

Jade felt for her top button, which was almost at her throat. "But the uniform—" she started to say, remembering all the language in the handbook. *Two inches above the knee, top button buttoned . . .*

"Teachers don't get on your case about buttons," said Chloe, and she gave Jade a little conspiratorial smile.

Jade felt herself smile back. She was glad Chloe was talking to her this way, giving her the unwritten handbook to succeed at Our Lady of Hope—OLH, as they all called it. She looked down at her chest, at her finger on her top button, and suddenly she felt like she was way too covered, especially compared with all the other girls. She wanted to feel cool, to feel *in,* and she didn't want anyone to think she had just stepped out of the nineteenth century or something. She undid the button, leaving a triangle of pale skin bare on her chest. For a second she felt exposed, but the feeling subsided. Now, at least in this one way, she was like everybody else. And that was a relief.

In the afternoon Chloe waved goodbye to her, a blue sports bag slung over her shoulder, and climbed into Ms.

Jackson's red jeep along with Caitlyn and Emily. Jade waved back and figured they must be headed to cross-country practice.

Her mom hadn't arrived yet, but Jade crossed the parking lot anyway and stood at the edge of the woods. She looked down the trail, wanting to enter. The forest was inviting, as always, with its moist smells and its promise of cool shade and a respite from this Georgia heat.

A group of girls approached the entrance, too, laughing together, and Jade recognized one of them as Tanya, who was also in her homeroom. Her straight, blond hair was pulled up in a high ponytail with a wide pink scrunchie. Tanya gave Jade a quick "hi," still smiling at something her friend had just said, and they walked past Jade into the trail. She watched their monogrammed backpacks and navy skirts make their way into the trees.

Did none of the middle schoolers wait for their parents to pick them up? Was she the only one? Suddenly, Jade thought maybe this was another way she needed to be cool, like the other kids. She didn't mind too much walking with her mom and Katerina, but the other kids looked so free.

Her mom came around the bend in the path, dressed in her elegant work clothes, but with comfier shoes this time. She was already in conversation with the mom they had seen the day before, who had walked the kindergartener to school. When her mom caught up to Jade, she said a cheery goodbye to the other mom and gave Jade a little squeeze on the shoulder. "Hey," she said quietly. "Let me go get your sister."

Jade nodded, and they both looked across the parking lot in the direction of Katerina, who was standing on the breezeway surrounded by a bunch of her new little friends.

"Boy, she's social, isn't she?" said her mom.

Jade laughed and looked up to meet her mom's eyes.

"She makes it look easy," her mom added. She shook her head and looked Jade straight in the eyes. "It isn't," she said.

As her mom crossed the parking lot to pick up Katerina and mingle with the other moms, Jade watched her and wondered for the first time just how much effort it took for her mom to be as charming as she was. She was grateful that, at least in that moment, her mom made her feel like it was okay not to be surrounded by a gaggle of friends.

Back at the house, Jade's mom let Katerina in through the back door but motioned to Jade to stay behind on the stoop.

"Let me show you something," she said. She reached into the earthen heart of the blue-green agave potted plant that her dad had set on the stoop, expertly avoiding the pointed burs as she did so, and pulled out a key. "This is to the back door," she said.

"Okay," said Jade.

"You know the way to school now," her mom said. "You don't need me anymore. You're going to walk Katerina there and back, okay?"

A warm feeling welled inside Jade's chest. Her mom was trusting her with this grown-up thing, and she was going to be like the other middle school kids who didn't have to wait for their parents.

"That sounds good," she said.

"Now, you have to make sure you keep Katerina in your sight at all times," her mom said. "Can you do that?" She was looking her in the eyes.

"Yes," said Jade.

Her mom nodded, satisfied. "I'll still pick up Katerina on Thursdays—or Dad will. She has Daisies after school that day, but you don't have to stay for that."

"Okay—got it," said Jade. Daisies was the babiest version of Girl Scouts there was. Jade had gone through Daisies, Brownies, and Juniors with Madison and Veronica, but she quit when she got tired of selling cookies and Madison decided to do horseback riding instead. All at once, Jade wished she had something of her own like Katerina did—a way to make friends and do fun things outside of school.

Jade's mom gave her the key. In her hand it felt small and easy to lose.

"Now, put it where it belongs," her mom said, and she went inside.

Holding the key firmly between her fingers, Jade reached down into the terra-cotta pot like her mother had done and pressed it into the soil at the base of the plant, so that only its flat metal head rose aboveground and was hidden beneath the spiked, fleshy leaves.

Later, as afternoon turned to evening and Mortimer snoozed on her windowsill, Jade sat beside him on the bed and scratched his neck and stroked his back. The cat yawned and twitched his tail, and she felt him begin to purr beneath her hand. She looked out at the pines that separated the backyard from the forest. She loved walking along that trail through the forest, for reasons that she couldn't quite explain to herself. As she petted Mortimer, she watched the gentle orange glow of sunset tint the swaying green sprays of pine needles with the last ruddy colors of the day.

When she stepped out into the sunny breezeway and said goodbye to Chloe after school the next day, she took Katerina by the hand and strode confidently across the parking lot to the Wildcat Trail. At the entrance, Tanya stood deep in conversation with Peter, the blond boy who sat next to her in homeroom. She kept laughing and letting her ponytail fall forward, then pulling at the two halves of it to make it tighter.

Jade's hair would never do that—it was too thick and frizzy. She also couldn't imagine having the guts to flirt like that. She pulled her eyes away from them and stepped into the forest with Katerina.

"Sissy, guess what Ms. McDade gave me today!" said Katerina.

"What did she give you?" said Jade, squeezing her sister's little hand and indulging her.

"She gave me a green card! Do you know what a green card means?"

"No, I don't know what a green card means," said Jade, laughing, and certain it didn't mean what it meant in the grown-up world. A mockingbird flew across the path overhead, the white fan of its tail flashing bright. It alighted on a branch and let its gray plumage fold back onto itself.

"A green card means you got a lot of good behavior points," said Katerina. "A red card means you were bad. Here—let me show you my card." She began wriggling her hand out of Jade's hold.

"Oh—no, it's okay, you can show me when we get home," Jade began. Her sister was taking her backpack halfway off and searching around inside it, and Jade was afraid that all the colored folders and papers stuffed in there were about to fall onto the ground and get dirty, and then she would have to deal with a crying Katerina and that was never good.

"Here! I found it!" said Katerina, pulling out a green index card and holding it up for her to see.

Hallelujah, thought Jade. Crisis averted.

"Look!" said Katerina. "It says 'Good'—good—let me see. Good—job. It says 'Good job.'"

Jade smiled, as much because she was relieved that the entire contents of Katerina's backpack hadn't spilled as anything else.

"That's great!" she told her sister. "Now hold my hand—we're almost home, okay?"

She hadn't expected it, but she was actually enjoying being in charge of Katerina. Sure, it could be a bit of a pain sometimes, but she liked being the responsible one, the one her sister had to listen to. And here on the forest path, she didn't feel alone in that responsibility—other kids' footsteps pattered up ahead, and the woods themselves seemed to give off that old, familiar feeling that she had noticed since the moment she first set foot in them.

Jade's parents weren't home when they arrived, so she let herself and Katerina in with the key from the agave plant, making sure to put it back carefully. She pulled a few chocolate chip snack bars from the pantry and left Katerina on the couch to eat and watch the Discovery Channel, before heading off to her room.

In moments like these, when the house was quiet and the light outside was still bright enough, Jade often liked to draw. But today it didn't feel like that would do the trick to calm what was prickling at her. She sat on the bed and thought of Tanya's high, perfect ponytail and that loud, hot-pink scrunchie. How Peter had stood close to Tanya as they talked at the edge of the parking lot. She thought of Chloe's dark eye makeup, and what she had told her about how no one buttons that top button. She reached a finger to the skin there and ran her fingertip along the edge of her shirt, from the topmost button up to her collar.

She wanted so much to feel like she was one of the OLH girls. Did you have to wear makeup like Chloe did, to be one of them? To be cool? To be pretty? Did you have to straighten your hair and pull it up in a high ponytail like Tanya? Did you have to wear your hair down and flowing around your shoulders and flip it around, like Caitlyn?

Jade wanted to feel pretty. And even though the thought terrified her a bit, she wanted boys to look at her and think she was pretty, too.

She headed to her parents' bathroom, where her mom's makeup was.

It was at the end of their giant bedroom. Jade passed her mom's purses and scarves that hung from hooks along one wall and her silvery-blue papier-mâché owl—her tecolote, as she always called it—that gazed out with its glossy painted eyes from its perch on top of her dresser.

The bathroom was almost as huge as the bedroom. It was the biggest one Jade had ever seen in a house. Everything about it—the wide marble counter with the two sinks, the hair dryer lying unplugged by one of the sinks, the shower with the clear glass—made it feel very grown-up.

Then she saw it: her mom's shiny black tube of mascara, leaning against a hairbrush in a drawer that hadn't quite closed completely. It was just lying there, as if waiting for an expert hand to pick it up, use it, and return it to the drawer with a practiced flip of the wrist. Jade looked at it but didn't dare touch it.

She locked the bathroom door quietly. Her parents weren't home yet, but just in case.

She looked at herself in the vast framed mirror above the sinks and studied her face. The lightest of freckles were spread across her nose and her turquoise eyes reflected the wall tiles behind her. Her skin was pinkish red where old zits had been. Her wavy, dirty-blond hair had a halo of frizz.

What did she look like, beside the other girls at school?

She pushed her very small boobs up and together in the mirror to get the tiniest sliver of cleavage to show in the V of her blouse. She held the pose and tried to categorize herself, tried to decide if she was pretty, if a boy could like her.

The mascara caught her eye again. Maybe if she used just a little bit and put it back exactly where it was, her mom wouldn't notice.

She let go of the pose and picked up the black tube, careful not to disturb anything else in the drawer. It was tapered a bit at each end and stamped with shiny silver lettering. She held its weight in her palm for a moment before opening it.

The bristles shone with black ink. Holding the brush up to her lashes, she began.

It was harder to do than she had expected. She couldn't stop blinking, and as soon as she managed to paint some ink onto her lashes, she somehow got little black dots all over the skin around her eyes, and then smudged them. She had to rummage around in the drawer to find her mom's makeup remover and some round cotton discs to wipe away the smudges. She hoped her mom wouldn't notice how much she had squirreled around in there.

When she was done, she took a step back from the mirror and inspected her work. It was pretty bad. The thick goop made her lashes look like ridiculous black bat wings against her pale face. It was a far cry from Chloe's makeup, applied with a sure, steady hand. As disappointing as the effect was, Jade thought maybe she could do better next time, using a lighter touch and holding her eyes open, even if they watered. Or maybe mascara just wasn't for her.

She tried once more to roll the skort at the waist to shorten it like the girls at school did, but again it bit into her crotch. That silly seam. Maybe she could just rip it out?

She was really going for it now. She found her dad's grooming scissors in another drawer. She would just do it, she decided. Taking off her skort, she sat down on the closed toilet seat to pull out the stitches, one by one, taking care not to tear the fabric. As she did so, she looked at the fuzzy blond wisps on her bare legs and decided to start shaving that very night. She undid the seam methodically, absorbed in her work.

She was almost done when she heard a knock. "Jade, are you in there?" came her dad's voice.

She froze. She hadn't even noticed when he got home.

"Yes—one sec!" she said. Quickly, she pulled on the skort and scrambled to put away the mascara and the scissors.

"You've been in there quite a while, and I've really got to go! That's why you have your own bathroom!"

Jade flushed the toilet and ran the sink faucet as she washed off the mascara and dried her face as fast as she could. When she stuffed the cotton discs back in the drawer, her fingers found her mom's stash of disposable purple razors. Not giving herself time to think twice, she pulled one out and tucked it into the waistband of her skort under her shirt.

At last, she unlocked the door and opened it. Her dad pushed past her and said, "You could've hurried up at least a little!"

"Sorry—number two!" she called as the door closed.

She felt for the razor in her waistband and headed back to her room, hoping that shaving would be easier than putting on mascara.

*

When Jade grabbed her lunch bag from the kitchen counter and headed for the door the next morning, her mom stopped her.

"You started shaving," she said.

Jade came to a halt in the doorway and turned around. Katerina was already outside on the back stoop, ready to go.

"Yeah?" she said, startled. She was surprised her mom had noticed. Was she mad at her for taking her razor? She looked down at her knees and the pale bit of calf sticking out from the top of her knee socks. She had been careful the night before to do it very smoothly, and she had nicked herself only a little on her ankles.

"You know you can ask me for a razor," her mom said, and her voice was warm and gentle, not accusing. Still, Jade felt her face go hot and wondered just how much her mom had noticed. Could she tell that things were out of place in her makeup drawer?

"Okay," said Jade, looking up at her mom briefly and lowering her eyes again. She decided to just be honest with her. "I didn't ask you because—I thought you might say I'm still too young for that."

Her mom reached out and tucked one of her wispy hairs behind her ear. Jade looked her in the eyes this time.

"Clearly, you've decided it's time," her mom said. "I didn't want to pressure you one way or the other."

Jade hadn't thought of it that way. She was glad her mom hadn't ever made her feel like she *needed* to shave her legs.

"See you this afternoon," her mom said, patting her shoulder.

"See you," said Jade, and she scampered out the door to the stoop where Katerina was hopping up and down impatiently.

As they headed toward the Wildcat Trail, Jade wondered whether anyone at school would notice that her legs were smooth. They would have to be looking at her knees. The only time her calves were exposed was in PE, when she swapped her knee socks and leather shoes for ankle socks and sneakers. Maybe people wouldn't notice at all, and that would be the best thing—they would just think she looked really good in kickball as she ran from base to base.

Since it was Thursday and Katerina had Daisies, Jade headed into the forest on her own that afternoon. She liked it this way. She relished the quiet nature sounds, the bird chirps and leaf rustles that were so calming, and so different from the idling car engines and squealing laughter of the parking lot.

As she stepped along the soft dirt path, the soles of her shoes stamping their rubber pattern into the ground, that *feeling* came over her again, the sense someone was there, a familiar, invisible presence moving just beyond the leaves that flanked the path. It was as if someone she knew were beckoning to her, but she couldn't quite see them, much as she peered into the brush. Perhaps it was the forest itself that she was sensing.

She continued down the path, letting herself be cradled by the comforting sensation as she wound through the trees. She let her mind wander with her steps. She thought of her reflection in the giant mirror in her parents' bathroom, and how the mirror couldn't tell her what she wanted to know. It couldn't tell her if she was pretty or what other people thought of her. It couldn't tell her if she would ever be a real OLH girl, who wore the uniform just so and knew how to say the whole Hail Mary.

There was, of course, the other mirror. The small black one that her mom had told her to keep. The reflection in that mirror wasn't clear. You couldn't use it very well to brush your hair or check your teeth. But what if the mirror showed you something else? Not the flat reflection of how the light bounced off your face, but something different, something beyond that? Was it possible that the shiny black stone in her dresser drawer could show her something that an ordinary mirror could not?

There was truly someone in the woods, off the path. Jade had no doubt about it this time. It wasn't a sound that let her know this, just a feeling, a certainty. She turned to look at the brush beside her where she felt the presence, and behind green leaves shining in the late August sun that filtered through the trees, she saw a golden spotted hide.

She froze.

Jade held her breath. The pelt of a large animal moved noiselessly through the undergrowth. A powerful paw stepped out onto the path right in front of her, followed by the whole animal: a wild cat that rose to the height of her waist, solid and warm and filled with a palpable, terrifying energy. Its hide—taut across well-defined muscles—was dotted with the unmistakable black eyelike rosettes of a jaguar.

It was looking directly at her with its solemn, amber-green eyes. Jade was too frightened to scream. She could not think; she could only stare at the muscled jaw and the piercing eyes.

And then she realized that it was not a jaguar standing before her, not a jaguar at all, but an old, old man.

3

The old man was practically made of wrinkles, from his deeply lined forehead to his small, knobbly hands. He was perhaps the smallest man Jade had ever seen. He was shorter than she was by at least a foot and hunched forward just slightly. A simple white tunic was knotted above his right shoulder and hung limply from his wispy frame. The white stood out against his dark brown skin. His folded hands rested in dignified fashion atop a serpentine wooden staff, and his amber eyes looked out at her with a friendly smile.

Jade stood transfixed. She was *certain* that moments before—in place of this tiny old man leaning on his staff—there had been a frightful, powerful jaguar. She had seen the jaguar, in all its fearsome, golden glory. But now, as she took in the old man's comforting eyes, her heart, which had been racing with fear, began to slow. She recognized in this man the familiar presence she had felt on those walks through the forest path. He looked at her with kindness, and Jade knew he wouldn't hurt her.

"You *have* come!" said the man, and his voice was stronger than Jade had expected from such a small, elderly person. He gave a light little chuckle and patted the top of his staff. His accent was from a faraway place that Jade couldn't pin down. It was familiar and new at the same time.

"Wh-what do you mean?" said Jade. Had he been waiting for her? The leaves overhead rustled with a light breeze and a shimmering blue dragonfly glided past them down the path.

The little man laughed again softly to himself. "I was beginning to think it would never happen." He took a few tiny slow steps toward the edge of the trail, planting his staff carefully in the dirt, using it as a cane to steady himself. Jade was afraid he might trip on a root and fall. She almost reached out to help him, but then she remembered how her abuela always gritted her teeth and tried to shake her off if Jade ever tried to help her out of a chair or the car.

"The time has come," the man continued, and he kept walking, slowly but determinedly, into the low brush that grew by the side of the path. Time for *what*? Jade noticed his intricate leather sandals that had been carefully patched in a hundred places. They were every shade of brown stitched together to cradle his feet.

"You don't leave a place unless you must," the old man went on. He was turned away from her now, and his small steps were taking him farther off the trail. Was he trying to leave? After *that* entrance? But he kept talking: "You leave a place when you have to, when someone needs you, when there is a wrong to be righted, a mission that cannot be fulfilled unless you come out from the place you've known and take a journey to a place where everything is different—the words, the flowers, the way the people say hello . . ."

He stopped and turned his head sideways and called softly back to her, "Are you coming?"

His face was silhouetted in profile against the bright slanting sun. With a jolt, Jade realized that he looked a whole lot like her abuelo in profile—minus the mustache.

She looked down the path toward the school, and up toward where her house was. She looked back at the old man. A shadow of disappointment had crossed his face at her hesitation. It was just like the face Abuelo used to make if she told him she didn't want to hear a bedtime story. That look of disappointment always made her change her mind and say, "Sí, Abuelo, I want to hear a story." That's what she wanted to say to this little old man.

"I'm coming," she said, and she stepped out into the ferns and the ivy.

As he smiled and turned his head forward, Jade caught that happy spark in his eye, the same playful glint that used to light up in Abuelo's eyes when he would do a magic trick—like when he'd ask her to choose a lotería card and hold it behind her back, and then he'd guess which one it was.

The man did not walk far; his small, deliberate steps took them just a few yards beyond the trail. Why did he walk this way, so painstakingly, if he could spring and bound through the forest as a jaguar? Jade was sure of what she had seen, but not at all sure of what it meant.

She felt herself being enveloped in the green forest where the air was moist and cool beneath the dense tree shade. She looked back over her shoulder every few steps to make sure she could still see where the path was, as she made her way through the trees and coaxed aside the hanging vines.

They arrived at a narrow, shallow stream, no more than two or three feet wide, that snaked along roughly parallel to the path, bubbling softly and happily over rounded stones. She *knew* she had heard it. The light green lacy ferns grew more thickly here and curved forward toward each other over the water. The stream bank was held up by tree roots that stretched and burrowed into the ground like fingers.

The old man stepped carefully out of his sandals and shuffled down to the edge of the stream. He put his staff out into the shallow water, and Jade watched and held her breath as he stepped cautiously but surely out onto the stones and crossed to the other side, with movements that told her his feet knew these stones and he had done this many times before. As a man or as a jaguar?

When he was on the other side, he turned to her and laughed softly again, the playful twinkle in his eye. He shook his head. "I can't believe it," he said. "You're here at last!" He seemed so pleased, and again Jade wondered what he meant. She watched him from her side of the stream.

"Where do you hail from?" he said, leaning forward a bit on his staff.

This old man sure had a funny way of talking. Jade was taken aback by his question. How could he have been waiting for *her* if he didn't know who she was or where she was from?

"I'm from Chi—" she started to say, but she stopped herself. Wasn't *he* the one who needed to do some explaining? Instead, she said, "Where do *you*—um, hail from?"

She couldn't imagine that a tiny old man dressed in a cotton shift and well-worn sandals had lived his entire long life in this forest.

"Ah!" said the man. "Yes, of course. Where do I come from. Where do *I* come from?" He directed the question upward, as if to the wind. "Well, that is exactly the question. In fact, that is why *you* are here. For me to answer that question. For me to tell you."

Jade was quiet. Was that why he had been waiting for her? So he could tell her his story?

He leaned his staff carefully against the trunk of a tree and picked something up from the ground. At first Jade thought it was just a stick, but then she saw him hold it delicately and purposefully in his hands, as if it were a pen, and she noticed that it had been smoothed all around, and had a tapered point. With it, he began to draw something in the dirt. Jade held her breath, fascinated, and watched to see what he would make.

He was drawing in a cleared-away strip free of ferns and ground cover. It sloped slightly so Jade could see what he was drawing from this side of the stream. He etched what looked like a large semicircle into the dirt, or maybe an upside-down sack or a hill, with smaller hills inside of it around the rim—seven of them. It was open only at the bottom.

"Chicomoztoc," said the man, and before Jade could ask, he said, "The Place of the Seven Caves. The Womb of the World. This is where I come from. And there is a story that was told to me, of how our people left the Place of the Seven Caves, long ago, long before my time."

He looked at her expectantly. A tiny sparrow arrived at the stream bank and began pecking at the ground startlingly close to Jade's shoe. It was as if the little bird had stopped to listen to the story.

Jade's backpack felt heavy. She eased it off her shoulders and set it on the ground, startling the bird. He *was* going to tell her a story. And she wanted to hear it.

She met the old man's expectant eyes, and said, "Please tell me the story. I'm ready."

The man nodded, content, and turned back to his artwork.

"The one who led my people out was a woman," he said. "A goddess. Her name was Itzpapalotl. Obsidian Butterfly." Using quick, smooth strokes, he etched a butterfly with fiercely sharp wings at the entrance to the hill. As he did so, he lifted up tiny trails of moist earth with the point of his wooden pen, like it was ink. The ground he uncovered beneath it gleamed red.

Papalote. Like the kites she and Abuelo used to make out of shish kebab sticks and the comics section of the newspaper. They used to fly them down by the lake on summer Sundays.

"Itzpapalotl was beautiful as a butterfly, swift as the wind before a hurricane, and fierce as knives," he continued. "She wielded a fearsome weapon—a human leg spoked with obsidian blades as thin as leaves that could slice cleanly through any foe."

Jade imagined the Obsidian Butterfly-Woman. She had heard the word *obsidian* before, but she wasn't quite sure what it was. She thought it was something flashy and dark at the same time—not unlike the black mirror in her dresser, she realized. She watched the butterfly the man had drawn and imagined the goddess Itzpapalotl flying with her sharp-edged black wings that glinted in the sunlight and shimmered in the moonlight like a velvet dress. Twirling her leg-weapon in front of her like it was a deadly flag-line baton. What did men think of her when they saw her like this?

"Itzpapalotl's people lived in the Place of the Seven Caves, along with other peoples. The place was protected from the world, like a womb." He retraced the outline that contained the seven caves, making an even deeper line now, as if to separate the place even more strongly from what lay beyond its contours.

"Our people only left the Place of the Seven Caves because our friends came asking for help," he went on. "The land where our friends lived—a place called Cholula—was being taken from them, and our friends wanted help taking it back. Itzpapalotl thought that theirs was a just cause, so she said yes."

Jade had heard stories like this before, of land being taken away, being fought for. It wasn't always easy to sort out who was right.

"The goddess Itzpapalotl led our people out of Chicomoztoc, flanked by our finest warriors, and they set out on a journey to recapture Cholula."

What a sight that must have been. All those warrior men marching to battle with a flying butterfly-woman all dressed in black at the helm.

"Our people learned a great many things along the way," the man continued. "They met many other peoples, each with their own altepetl—their own watery hill. They learned from every part of the journey, from every watery hill they came upon."

"Watery hill?" said Jade, trying to imagine what that might look like. Would it be filled with water? Would water run through it, somehow?

"Watery hill, yes," said the old man. "Or watery mountain, if you wish, if it is very big. You may call it a city, a town. It is a place where people are from, a place where people settle. A place with earth to live on and water to drink from. A mountain or a hill surrounded by water—that is an ideal watery hill. Sometimes they do not take exactly that form, but they are still watery hills."

Jade nodded. It sounded like a watery hill was a place that gave life, where people came together. As she tried to make sense of it, she realized that the old man was drawing more hills across the cleared swath of earth, and that these must be other watery hills. She wondered how many of his people had passed through before getting to Cholula. He drew watery swirls at the base of some of them. They looked like real hills, but also like symbols. Sometimes they were topped with little animals or plants, drawn in a style Jade had never seen before. She was sure that these meant more than just the creatures or flora they represented. She was amazed at the detail the man was able to achieve, and how quickly he made his sure strokes. He wielded his wooden pen as delicately as if it were a painter's brush, at times reaching out his free hand to grab a slim tree trunk to steady himself. One false move, it seemed, and he would slip and fall into the water—but he was too careful to let this happen.

The man stepped back from his drawing for a moment, and Jade watched as he walked deliberately across the strip of ground where he was drawing, sinking his bare feet into the moist earth, leaving footprints that led out from Itzpapalotl and the Place of the Seven Caves. These footprints, too, were more than just his footprints, she realized. They were the footprints of his people as they journeyed.

"At last our people arrived at Cholula," he said. He leaned over and drew in the middle what was unmistakably a city, though the buildings were different from any that Jade was used to. She was pretty sure she had heard of this city before, and in her mind it was an abstract place on a map, like Chicago or Atlanta. The man crowned the city with what looked to be a stepped pyramid, like the ones Jade had heard about but never been to outside Mexico City. This city didn't look quite like the other watery hills he had traced in the earth, but a swirly rivulet ran beside it. With the water and the temple, this must be yet another watery hill—just a particularly special one. Maybe a watery mountain.

"Our people arrived arrayed for battle, Itzpapalotl leading them with her fierce obsidian blades. It was a fearsome battle, and they vanquished the enemies who wanted to take the land. Cholula was returned to our friends."

The way he said it, it sounded like this was the just outcome. He stooped and etched a delicate bow and arrow into the ground beside the city, as if to mark the battle.

"After that, our people were changed," the man went on. "They had won the fight, but they had left the Womb of the World, and they had seen for themselves the hardness of this world."

Jade found herself nodding. As strange and new as the old man's picture was and the story he was telling, she felt she at least understood a little how hard it must have been to leave their warm home and face a world where they had to be on guard, bows and arrows at the ready. Chicago was so warm, cozy, and familiar, and it had been so hard to leave.

"So . . . they stayed there, in Cholula?" she ventured tentatively. "Or did they keep going on their journey?" If this was the story of where this old man and his people were from, was he going to tell her where they ended up?

"Oh, they kept moving," he said. He swept his hand over the other watery hills beyond Cholula that his footprints led to. "Out of gratitude for the help we gave them in winning back Cholula, our friends let our people set out again to settle the lands they wanted."

"Where did they end up?" said Jade. The man kept drawing more watery hills as they spoke.

"They ended up here," he said, crouching to add some details to one of the watery hills. He made it look like one of the caves in the Place of the Seven Caves. Inside it he drew a bird with large wings folded to its sides, like an ornately clad ruler standing sedately. The man gave it sharp talons and a curved beak. It was an eagle.

The eagle was facing something. Jade leaned forward to watch more closely as the old man coaxed its form from the dirt. Was it—a cat? He added tiny spots, flicking up the dark topsoil so they were clay red. Was it a jaguar? The eagle dominated the scene, but still the stocky, spotted creature sat there, staring back at it, the two of them seated regally inside the cave.

This was no ordinary watery hill.

"The Eagle Cave," said the old man. "That's why my people—my father's people—were called the People of the Eagle Cave."

If Jade had named it, she wouldn't have left out the jaguar. She would have called it the Jaguar Cave.

"This is where they ended up," said Jade. "These were their lands. Did they stay here?"

The old man's eyes grew sad. "They stayed," he said. "But they could not keep their land. The Mexica came and took it from them." He pronounced it meh-SHEE-cah.

"The Mexica?" said Jade, trying out the word in her mouth.

"Or the Aztecs, if you prefer," he said with a dismissive wave of his hand. "They had also come from the Place of the Seven Caves. Their great warrior god Huitzilopochtli, the Hummingbird of the South, had told them to settle and build a city on a lake when they saw a sign."

Jade knew this story. It was one of Abuelo's favorites. "A big golden eagle eating a turquoise serpent—on top of a prickly pear cactus," she said. "That was the sign." She thought of the Mexican flag that hung in her abuelos' restaurant, the Casa Azul. The angry eagle wrestling with the serpent and winning.

The man nodded, and he seemed pleased with what she knew. He went on: "But once the Mexica had settled in their own city, Tenochtitlán, they wanted everything. They sent their eagle warriors across the land. They wanted everyone to say yes to them, 'yes, you are our lords,' and to give them gold and people and jade stones and animal hides. They wanted to rule it all."

That didn't sound good at all. Jade had thought of the Aztecs—the Mexica, she now knew to call them—as powerful, but she hadn't thought of them as a group that wanted to take things from people and make them their own.

"When the Mexica came to the Place of the Eagle Cave where our people had settled, it became just one of the many writhing hometowns trapped in the merciless beak of the Mexica eagle." The man drew serpentine lines connecting the watery hills to form a segmented snake. He drew a beak clamping down on the snake's body.

Jade was silent, not sure what to make of all this. The Mexican flag in the Casa Azul was a point of pride, a symbol of what neither the Spaniards nor the gringos could take away from the Mexican people. But here was this little old man, telling her that the Mexica had had a voracious appetite, too, gobbling up land and tormenting the inhabitants. For Jade, the Aztecs—the Mexica—were the people who had been in Mexico when the Spaniards arrived. She thought of them, in some way, as her ancestors, however remote. Clearly, though, there were so *many* different peoples who had been there when the Spaniards came, and before that, too.

"So, what happened to your people when the Mexica took over?" said Jade. "What was it like to live there? Did any of them leave and go on more journeys? Did they meet more people from other—watery hills?" Jade wanted to know all about these people, who had settled in the watery hill-cave with the eagle and the jaguar, which were clearly not just an eagle and not just a jaguar. She wanted to know if they had survived, despite the Mexica, despite everything—and if so, how they had done it.

The old man smiled. "That is a story for another time," he said.

Another time? Did he mean to tell her more stories, draw her more pictures and maps?

"But—" Jade started. She was too curious—she wanted to hear it all now.

But the man was already turning away from her, heading into the thick woods on the other side of the stream with his slow, shuffling gait, steadying himself at each step with his staff as he went.

"At least tell me your name!" Jade called.

The man turned back to her. His eyes were kind and warm. "Itztli," he said. "You may call me Itztli." It sounded like EATS-tlee.

"Itz-tli," she said slowly, testing the new sound on her tongue. It was hard to say.

"And you are?"

"Jade," she said, deciding to trust him completely, because what she felt around him was what she felt at Christmas at her abuelos' house, where tall glass candles with pictures of the Virgen de Guadalupe stood sentinel all around, and fresh, warm, doughy tamales lifted cleanly out of their corn husks, and the painted ceramic nativity was arranged on the hearth beneath the delicate papel picado . . . It was a feeling of calm, of being protected.

"Chalchihuite," said the man, nodding. Chahl-chee-WEE-teh.

Of course. Of course he knew her special name, the one that only Abuela and Abuelo called her. Once again she felt that, somehow, she had known him for a long, long time.

The man began to turn away again. "Ah, and one more thing," he said, already partly facing away. "That is just one way to tell the story. Others will remember it differently. I may even tell it differently myself."

And with that, he jumped into the air.

Jade hardly had time to gasp, afraid the little old man might hurt himself, before she saw that he wasn't a man anymore—he was the jaguar.

The animal flashed golden through the air and disappeared into the green and brown. Jade stood watching the place where he had vanished, until the light shifted and she couldn't see the spot anymore.

All that was left of the jaguar man was the map he had drawn, etched into the side of the stream.

The light was slanting through the trees now. Jade watched the undulating reflection of the old man's drawings in the water. Her mom and Katerina would be home any minute now. She hoisted her backpack onto her shoulders and, with a final glance at the map, turned back toward the path. She retraced her steps, pulling aside vines and stepping over thorns, until she reached the trail again and scurried toward home.

4

The moist dirt of the trail was soft beneath Jade's quick feet. The path made twists and turns that she was beginning to learn and anticipate. She imagined it following the contours of the stream that she now knew lay just to the side of it, beyond the thick of the trees.

She wondered if the old man's map would still be there tomorrow or the next day, if the stream and the birds and the chipmunks wouldn't wear it away. She wondered if she would be able to find the spot again. If she would have to, or if the jaguar man—Itztli—would find her again, like he had today. He had left her hanging, the story unfinished.

The trail opened up and her backyard and the driveway came into view. The tiny points of crushed sand that made up the black, newly laid asphalt of the driveway glinted like sharp jewels in the afternoon sun beside the soft grass and moss of her hilly backyard.

The sharpness of the light bouncing off the dark pavement beside the gentle rise of the hills made her think once more of her sharp mirror made of black polished stone. How it caught the light in such unpredictable ways. *Was* it made of obsidian, like the wings or blades of the Obsidian Butterfly?

She stepped out of the trees into the bright slanting light, slowing her pace as she walked in the grass along the edge of the driveway, toward the house. It seemed almost impossible that the hot asphalt to one side of her, and the houses in the cul-de-sac, could share space with the forest and the stream she had just come from. She thought of Itztli's map, how he had drawn footsteps and waterways and towns that were hills. Humans had been building things forever, making the contours of the earth fit their needs. Maybe the challenge was to find a way to build a home, a city, that worked *with* the land, and what it offered. Her parents might have had this in mind when they chose this house so close to the trees. One of the great oaks in the backyard was close enough to the house that its roots reached to the corner of the back stoop and its lowest branches nearly scratched the top of the roof. In the sunnier part of the yard, tiny young sprouts poked their heads up from the clay and soil her dad had broken and massaged. He had told her that these sprouts would grow to be cabbage, cilantro, and parsley for them to eat, and she liked that what they ate inside the house came from the land it was built on.

A small bird flew from the top of one of the pine trees by the trail to perch on the corner of her house and chirped. The bird was the same gray-blue slate color of the roof, and it appeared to delight in modeling against it, matching it. Jade admired the ease with which the little bird traveled from the living canopy of the forest to the unyielding square corners that humans had chiseled. The bird had made their roof its perch, just as much as her family had made this patch of land their home.

Mortimer appeared from behind a peak of the roof, and the little bird, terrified, flew up and away. The cat leapt gracefully down onto the wrought-iron railing of the back stoop and then to the ground. He looked at Jade fixedly with his yellow-green eyes as she approached. When she crouched to scratch his neck and pet him, he pulled away, like he smelled something on her.

"Come on, Morty," she whispered, and held the back of her hand out to him. The cat sniffed and then accepted; he pushed his nose into her knuckles and Jade scratched behind his ears and stroked his back.

"There you are!"

Jade looked up and saw her dad coming around from the front of the house, dragging the hose.

"Where have you been?" he said. "I thought you'd be back by now." His tone wasn't accusatory—it was just a question.

"Hey, Dad," said Jade. "Yeah, I, um . . ." Part of her wanted to tell her dad what had happened. But she didn't know what to say. How could she tell him what she had just experienced? "I had . . . stuff," she said, and headed quickly for the door so she wouldn't have to answer any more questions. She needed to figure things out for herself first, starting with that mirror. The story Itztli had told her, and his map etched in the dirt and in her mind, kept making her think of it. And even though all she had seen in the mirror before were strange reflections, maybe now it would show her something more.

When she got to her room, the jangle of keys and Katerina's excited chatter announced the arrival of her sister and her mom at the back door.

Opening the drawer where she had stowed the mirror, she reached in among the soft clothes and felt for the hard stone. She was relieved once again to find that it was still there, wrapped in the thin white camisole where she had left it. She didn't always keep good track of her things, and it felt even more important now to keep the mirror safe. She pulled it out and unwrapped it like it was a living thing—maybe a turtle with its head tucked in. Cupping it in her palm, she ran her free index finger carefully along its sharp edge. The mirror's black sheen caught the light that filtered lazily in through the blinds of her window. No matter how still she held it, the reflections danced around, flitting in and out among the smoky veins, like they didn't want to be caught.

She wanted to find the meaning of this mirror. But it refused to let her in.

"Jade!" her mom called from the kitchen. "Do you want a snack? Your sister is having string cheese."

Jade looked at her bedroom door that she had left cracked open just slightly. Mortimer silently skinnied his way in. String cheese sounded inexplicably delicious right now, but she couldn't think how she could face something so ordinary just yet.

"I'm okay!" she called back.

She could just ask her mom about the mirror, about the jaguar, about it all. But no—that was impossible. How would that conversation go? Her mom was the most no-nonsense person Jade knew. She was all facts, facts, facts. Journalistic rigor, getting to the truth of the matter. The truth of *this* matter might be more complicated.

She wrapped up the mirror carefully and put it back exactly where it had been. As she closed the drawer, she felt almost annoyed at it that it wouldn't reveal its secrets to her or explain something about what she had just seen in the forest, which felt connected. Maybe another time.

Grabbing her green spiral-bound notebook and a mechanical pencil, she settled onto her bed, belly down. She didn't bother to turn on the light—she positioned herself so that the rays from the window slanted brightly onto the lined pages. Mortimer hopped up and settled into her side in the puddle of warm light.

At first, Jade tried to re-create the map that the old man, Itztli, had drawn. She mouthed the sound of his name, *Itztli*. It was a strange new word, and she didn't want to forget it.

She wanted a copy of his map so she could go back to it and remember it, and the story he had told her. She tried to hold her pencil the way Itztli had held his wooden pen, and make the sure strokes she had seen him make. She drew as many of the details on the watery hills as she could remember, the animals and plants sprouting out of them, and the regal spotted jaguar facing the eagle inside the cave where Itztli's people had lived.

But she was disappointed by her rendition. She couldn't evoke the ink-trail effect that Itztli had created, nor the subtle yet firm imprints of his feet. Itztli's map was very different from any others she had seen. It told very little about where things were. Instead, it told about the places and the journeys between them.

Itztli had said his people left the warmth of the motherly womb they were used to and burst out into the hardness of the world. Maybe it was always like that, she thought, as she drew a winding road that curved like the forest path between the watery hills. Maybe leaving where you came from was always something that tore you from the rock of what you thought you knew, something that hurt somewhere deeper than your body, something that changed you.

Mortimer burrowed more deeply into her side. Jade pressed her nose into his fur for a moment, grateful for his company. Much as she tried to keep the feeling tucked away, it hurt that she couldn't go down to the lake anymore with Madison and Veronica and run barefoot with them across the sand into the cool water. At least she still had Mortimer here with her, and she could press her face into his purring side.

She sat up and turned the page, deciding to start anew. This time, though, she would draw her own map.

In the top left-hand corner, she drew a watery hill filled with endless fields of agave, like the ones Abuelo used to tell her about. Further on, she drew another hill with delicate papel picado strung across its entrance, like the Casa Azul at Christmas. She made smoke curl out the top of it. And on the far edge of the two-page spread she drew a hill that encircled a brick house with a black cat guarding the entrance. Mexico, Chicago, Atlanta.

Mortimer stepped his two front paws lightly onto the pages, wrinkling them slightly, and inspected her artwork.

There were so many missing pieces. The hills had empty space in them that Jade didn't know how to fill. There was no road between them, only the gaping white and the light blue lines of the paper. And a break at the middle, where the ridge of the tight spiral spine and the three-hole punches on either side made what seemed like an insurmountable interruption, and threatened to split the whole picture in two.

"Sissy, what are you drawing?"

Jade snapped her notebook shut, and Mortimer scrambled to get his paws out in time. Katerina was standing in the crack in the doorway, pushing at the door with her shoulder and eating string cheese out of its plastic wrapper. She was still wearing her sky-blue vest with colored badges on it from Daisies.

"A picture," said Jade.

"Can I see?" Katerina stepped into the room.

Jade slid the notebook back into its slot on her bookshelf. "Maybe later," she said. She turned around and saw the pouty look on Katerina's face. She hated it when Katerina was moody—no one had a fun time of it. "Maybe later you can help me color it," she offered, searching for something to say that would soothe her.

"I want to see it! Let me see it!" her sister said. She reached up for the notebook on the bookshelf with her string-cheesy hands but she wasn't nearly tall enough.

"It's not done yet!" said Jade, more loudly than she had meant.

Katerina got quiet. "Will you show it to me when it's done?" she said.

"Sure," said Jade. "Yes, I'll show it to you when it's done."

Katerina nodded and sucked on her string cheese like it was a pacifier.

"I promise."

*

When Jade came out to the kitchen to grab a snack for herself, her mom had the corded phone that was mounted to one of the cabinets tucked under her ear, and she was taking notes on one of her index-card-sized reporter's notebooks. She was still wearing the crisply ironed blouse and pencil skirt from her workday. She gave Jade a distracted nod and said, "Aha," into the phone and kept taking notes.

Jade opened the fridge and tried to figure out who her mom was talking to. She wasn't using her reporter voice.

"But is this the first time Mamá has had one of these episodes?" her mom said.

It had to be Tío Carmelo, who was still in Chicago. For a long time Abuela seemed to be doing perfectly fine living alone in the house she and Abuelo used to share, but lately her mom and Tío Carmelo checked on her a lot more.

"Ya, pero, what did she seem like? . . . Mmm . . . Aha. Okay."

Jade decided on apple slices and peanut butter, her go-to.

When her mom got off the phone, her dad came into the kitchen and raised his eyebrows, his way of asking what was up. Jade listened to them over the low wall as she ate her snack at the dining table. Katerina sat across from her and colored carefully in her favorite coloring book, an Audubon-themed one with birds and leaves and flowers. For a six-year-old, she was pretty good at keeping between the lines. She sometimes chose surprising colors, so that a leaf was purple and a flower was lime green, but she chose them deliberately, with care and conviction, and in the end made it seem like insisting that a leaf was supposed to be green would be an exceedingly narrow-minded proposition.

"Mamá had an episode," her mom told her dad softly.

"What kind of an episode?"

"I don't know—it's hard to tell. Carmelo took her to the doctor and they're trying to figure it out. Like she fainted or something. Maybe she was dehydrated. She seems fine now, apparently." Her mom sounded like she might be trying to convince herself of it. She wasn't a doctor, but she knew an impressive number of medical terms from reporting on health topics, one of her main beats for years. It couldn't be easy for her mom to have such limited information on Abuela's condition.

Her dad rubbed her mom's back. "I hope she's okay," he said.

Katerina kept coloring and Jade kept eating, and they said nothing. These were grown-up things. She and Katerina weren't excluded from the conversation, but they weren't invited in either.

Jade hoped Abuela was okay. But she tried not to get worried and just trust her parents—to worry about it, to do whatever needed to be done. Jade had done that for such a long time—entrust the grown-ups with the pricklier parts of life, the parts she knew she couldn't do anything about, the parts they whispered about and only ever told her bits of eventually, when they *had* to. She had been fine with that, and it was nice, in a way, to sink into the cozy comfort of being a kid and have a good excuse not to deal with the heavier things.

But a part of her also wanted to be let in more. She *wasn't* actually a kid anymore—not like Katerina, anyway.

She could handle more. After all, she was walking Katerina to school now. Who knows—maybe Jade could even help, if she knew better what was going on.

Right now, though, it was still easiest just to keep being a kid, and not ask to know more. It was easiest to try not to shoulder the worry and let her parents take care of that.

Her mom was stressed and distracted all through dinner. The rice didn't have enough salt, and the ground beef mixed with corn and zucchini came out dry and rubbery. Her father quietly turned off a burner on the stove that her mom had left on. Her parents hardly exchanged a word as her dad loaded the dishwasher and her mom grabbed a binder from the kitchen counter and headed upstairs to her new office. The only time her mom worked at night was when she had a big project. Back in Chicago, she used to work at the kitchen table with papers and notes heaped around her, and she would wave everyone away, saying, "I'm working on a story."

Jade brought her social studies book out to the dining room table. It had a flying bald eagle with an American flag rippling behind it on the cover. She was supposed to read about the Pilgrims. Some things were exactly the same in Illinois or in Georgia. Why did they learn every single year about the religious persecution and the Puritans and the *Mayflower* and Plymouth Rock? Why did they see those same pictures over and over again, of the white bonnets and the beaver hats? This was a tale of a journey from here to there that she had heard so many times, it was hard to focus enough to actually read the words. She knew what was coming.

Itztli had told a story of a journey from here to there that she had never heard before. How many more stories were there like that one?

"Ah-ah, don't go up there, bug," her dad said to Katerina. "Mommy's working."

"But I want Mommy to read me a book!" said Katerina, at the bottom of the stairs.

"I'll read it to you, bug," he said, drying his hands.

Jade flipped through the chapter, not reading it. She wondered what her mom was working on. Her last big project had been the series on addiction in Chicago, and the process had lasted months. The series was the reason CNN had offered her the job. Jade had watched part of it, although her parents hadn't really wanted her to. Katerina had been strictly forbidden from seeing it. Her mom interviewed all sorts of people in it, some of whom were blacked out and had their voices distorted. Teenagers who sounded like they had gotten caught up in something that was far bigger than they were, parents and siblings who were trying to make sense of a gaping hole that had opened up in their families when they'd lost someone. But mostly she interviewed doctors and nurses, and emphasized throughout that addiction was a public health concern. The producers chose a blocky, black-and-white banner and suspenseful true-crime music for the interludes, all of which her mom hated. "It's a *health* series," she would say, shaking her head at the TV.

Her mom had been interested in health topics ever since Jade could remember. Tío Carmelo once told her that her interest had started when he and her mom were teenagers and Tío Efraín, their youngest brother, died after a car crash. Jade didn't know many of the details, but she knew that Tío Efraín had been in the hospital for days, unconscious, while the family prayed for him at home. In the end, the doctors hadn't been able to wake him up. Sometimes Jade thought that her mom's obsession with medical terms, with getting to the bottom of exactly what was going on with a patient or a drug trial, was her way of trying to wrap her arms around the problem and get a firm grasp of it, as if maybe if she held on tight enough, she could keep the facts—and maybe even people—from slipping away. Years ago, when Jade fell off her bike and busted her knee open on the blacktop and had to go in for stitches, Jade saw her mom grill the nurses and doctors, speaking their language, making sure they gave her the best care. In the car on the way home, Jade had asked her why she hadn't become a doctor, if she knew so much about medicine and hospitals and the struggle against illness and death that doctors fought every day. "Because if I were a doctor, I would never have time to listen to people's stories," she had told her. "And I would never get to tell their stories either."

This was her mother's way of wielding obsidian blades. Fighting to listen, fighting to be heard, fighting to tell a story that needed to be told.

Jade never could get the story straight from anyone in her family about how exactly Tío Efraín had wound up in that hospital decades ago. She knew he was very young when he died, maybe fifteen or sixteen. Abuela had a phrase she would use to reference his death: "Cuando Dios me lo llevó." *When God took him from me.* Tío Carmelo would say, "When Efraín left us," as if his little brother had up and decided to leave the house one day. And Jade's mom would hardly talk about it at all, saying only, "After Efraín was gone" or "When Efraín was around." She would reference the before and after, but never the event itself, as if that were too huge to mention. Still, Jade had been able to puzzle some details together: The car crash had something to do with a friend of his and a drunk driver. An accident on an icy night in November, when the rain was just turning to snow. That was all she knew.

When her mom got the offer from CNN and accepted it, after the initial excitement had died down, her mom said to her dad, standing in their kitchen with the stapled pages of the contract, "I've been reporting on health in this community for years. Only now that I've talked about addiction and Mexicans—drugs and Mexicans—*now* they pay attention."

She took the job anyway, of course, and now they were here.

The phone rang. Jade's mom was upstairs working and her dad was reading Katerina a book in her room.

"Jade, can you answer it?" her mom called down the stairs.

Jade stared at the phone. It rang again. She really didn't want to. She hated talking on the phone.

"Jade!"

Jade hurried to the phone and picked it up. Whatever awaited her on the line couldn't be worse than her mom's exasperation. "Hello?" she said.

"Jade, is that you?"

It was Chloe's voice.

"Chloe!" she said, brightening. "Yeah, it's me."

"Who is it?" her mom called from upstairs.

Jade covered the receiver and called, "It's Chloe!"

"Who?"

"Chloe!"

Her mom was coming down the stairs now.

"Sorry about that," Jade said into the phone. "Um, what's up?"

"Oh, I was just calling to see if—" Jade detected some shyness in Chloe's voice for the first time. "Do you wanna come over tomorrow?" said Chloe, in one quick breath. "There's no cross-country tomorrow, so I figured—"

"Yeah, I want to come!"

Her mom was at the entrance to the kitchen now. "Let me speak to her mother," she said to Jade.

"Hey, um, Chloe?" said Jade. "Can our moms talk?"

"Yeah, of course!" said Chloe. She sounded relieved. Jade heard her call out, "Mom!" Then to Jade, she said, "Okay, see you tomorrow. Tomorrow is Friday and my mom always makes rice pudding on Fridays, so you can have some. Okay, bye!"

"Hello?" a woman's voice said.

"Hi, Mrs. . . ." Jade realized she didn't know Chloe's last name. She felt the tops of her ears go hot and red.

The woman laughed kindly. "You can call me Eleni," she said.

"Okay—um, here's my mom!" said Jade, and held the phone out to her mother, not wanting to have anything to do with it anymore. As her mom took it, Jade let out her breath, relieved.

She watched and waited as her mom got all the details straight. Chloe's mom would pick them up from school. When the conversation was over, her mom said, "You're going to do some homework there, right?"

"It's Friday, Mom," said Jade.

"Right," said her mom, smiling to herself. "Of course. I'm happy for you!"

Jade nodded and headed back to the dining room. Her mom was acting like it was a feat to be celebrated that she had made a friend. Did she think Jade wasn't capable of making friends?

But the truth was, making friends at Our Lady of Hope—where everybody had known one another since forever—actually *was* super difficult. Jade was caught off guard by how much she was looking forward to hanging out with Chloe. She used to get this excited about seeing Madison and Veronica, but now she was excited to spend time with her Atlanta friend. She wanted to see Chloe's house, see who Chloe was outside of school. And she wanted to show Chloe who *she* was outside of school, too. She wanted Chloe to know that she was cool.

5

Chloe's mother drove up after school in a rather dinky-looking minivan that resembled a flabby whale amid the shining muscled SUVs in the parking lot. Jade brushed a few snack crumbs from a seam in the cloth upholstery as she climbed into the back seat with her friend. Chloe's mom took off her big sunglasses with their flashing gold arms and twisted around in her seat to greet Jade. She was lean and beautiful. Her black hair fell in a long side-braid in front. She wore tasteful mascara to make her big black eyes look even bigger, and Jade saw that Chloe was trying to make her eyes look like this, too.

"So nice to meet you, Jade," she said, holding out her hand. "Chloe says you're the nicest girl she's met at OLH."

Jade shook her hand and glanced with surprise at Chloe, who was looking out the window and pretending not to hear.

"Nice to meet you, too, Mrs.—um, Eleni," said Jade. "Thanks for picking us up."

"Oh, no problem at all!" Chloe's mom turned back around and maneuvered out of the parking lot. "You're from Chicago?" she said.

"Yes," said Jade, but that answer didn't feel like enough to her, so she added, "but my family is from Mexico, and also Ireland, if you go way back."

"O'Callaghan certainly sounds Irish," said Chloe's mom. "But Mexican—I wouldn't have guessed that."

"I know." No one ever did. She decided for the moment not to let it bother her.

"We're from Greece, you know."

"Oh, really?"

"Yeah." Chloe's mom looked at Jade in the rearview mirror. "We moved to Charlotte in ninety-four. I came to Atlanta with the kids two years ago."

"I had no idea," said Jade. She looked at Chloe, but Chloe was still looking out the window.

That meant Chloe hadn't known everyone at school since kindergarten either. Jade was starting to realize how much she didn't know about Chloe. But then again, she hadn't told Chloe much about herself either. She hoped that would begin to change this afternoon.

They were driving through a part of Atlanta that Jade hadn't seen yet. On Chloe's side of the road, dark green box-cars were parked on train tracks. Brush grew on either side of the tracks, and behind it rose the forest—those thickets of trees that seemed to be everywhere in this city. The forest was all around, like it was the natural state of the place, despite the straight-edged buildings and the hot concrete streets that curved with the contours of the land. A chain-link fence separated the tracks from the road. On Jade's side of the road she saw a car wash, a climbing gym, and an auto repair shop with a big blue-and-yellow rendition of Rosie the Riveter pushing her shirtsleeve up and showing her muscle as she challenged the cars driving by with her gaze. The image read: MY FAVORITE MECHANIC IS A WOMAN.

Further on, a pile of fresh reddish dirt rose beside a muddy yellow bulldozer where something big was being built. Already they had erected what looked like plywood scaffolding on one end of the lot. The Latino men working on the scaffolding reminded her of the men from her abuelos' neighborhood. What were they building, and who were they were building it for? Who would live there, if it was a home, and would the inhabitants look anything like these men who were building it? The plaintive trumpets and lively beats of banda music pumped from a radio as they worked.

They approached a row of narrow brick town homes, and Chloe's mother pulled the van into the parking lot.

As soon as Chloe's mom opened the door to their place, a familiar warm scent of cinnamon and vanilla hit Jade. It was an intimate smell that reminded her distinctly of the arroz con leche that her family had at Christmas and Easter. She was startled to find this aroma here, but she was drawn to it. It propelled her forward into the cozy two-story apartment. The place felt a bit like her old house in Chicago, and she was surprised at how quickly she had gotten used to the larger space of their new house. She and Chloe set their backpacks down by the couch in the living area while Chloe's mom spooned rice pudding into two bowls from a big pot on the stove. She sprinkled a little cinnamon on top of each glistening heap.

"Thank God it's Friday!" Chloe half sang, skipping into the kitchen to grab a bowl. She had already kicked off her shoes. "Rizogalo," she said to Jade. "You're gonna love it."

Jade liked this Chloe, the one that was emerging now. Here, in the kitchen, shoving rice pudding into her face, she was more like a kid, under all that makeup.

She kicked off her own shoes and let the scent pull her to the other bowl. She said thank you hastily to Chloe's mom and dug in. The first bite was as sweet and melty as she had anticipated. But there was also something different about it that she couldn't quite place. It wasn't quite the arroz con leche that she was used to. But the more she ate and the more she savored it between her tongue and the roof of her mouth, the more she liked this version of it, too.

"It's good, isn't it?" said Chloe's mom.

Jade nodded vigorously with her mouth full.

"Well. You girls get the very first bites of the batch." She began transferring the pudding into a large plastic tub. "The rest goes out to the restaurant. It's our Friday dessert special."

Jade swallowed her bite. "The restaurant?" she said.

"Oh, Chloe hasn't told you? Our restaurant is on Lawrenceville Highway. It's called Ajax House. You've probably passed it at some point."

Jade had no idea where Lawrenceville Highway was or even that it existed, but it was probably one of those wide, busy avenues that crisscrossed the city. "No way!" she said. "My grandparents used to have a restaurant."

"Really? What was it like?" said Chloe, her mouth full. Her mom shot her a look, like the one Jade's own mom would give her if she talked with her mouth full.

"It was . . . like a little hole-in-the wall place," said Jade. "Everything was blue and white, inside and out, down to the cups and bowls." She tapped the bowl she was holding. "Everyone always spoke Spanish there." She ran her finger along the outside of the dish, remembering the sense of understanding and not understanding at the same time what people were saying around her. "When I was little it was my favorite place to go." She got excited, remembering it. "They had these little square tables, angled like diamonds, with tablecloths that my abuela embroidered. She made something very similar to this, too"—she pointed to the remains of the rice pudding sticking to the bottom of her bowl—"but only on special occasions." She ate the last bite in her bowl and made sure to swallow. "It only closed a couple years ago when my abuela couldn't keep it up anymore." And when her mom and Tío Carmelo had insisted on it for Abuela's health—but she didn't mention that.

"That's too bad," said Chloe. "It sounds like an awesome place. I like ours, too," she said, glancing at her mother. "I hate the strip mall and the parking lot on the outside, but once you get inside, it's cozy."

Jade imagined it might feel similar to this town house, warm and welcoming, with its quirky, distinct dishes and a lived-in feel. A refuge from the concrete parking lot and the noise of cars and construction outside.

"I better go get ready," Chloe's mom said, glancing at her watch. "The Friday night rush!" She headed upstairs.

Both their bowls were empty now. Chloe silently spooned another small helping for each of them from the top of the full tub, putting a finger to her lips and smiling mischievously. Jade returned the smile, and the two girls brought their bowls to the couch and ate quickly and quietly.

The walls of the living area were decorated with family photos and framed newspaper clippings. Jade took them in. There was a series of Polaroids taken on a beach somewhere. One of them showed a close-up of a tiny girl who must have been Chloe when she was three or four years old, squinting at the camera and flashing a dimply smile. It looked like she was on someone's shoulders, but you couldn't see the person's face. In another one a little boy, maybe Katerina's age, with huge dark eyes and long lashes, smiled proudly up at the camera. He was holding out a pile of seashells that was about to spill from his small, sand-encrusted hands.

"Who is that?" she asked.

"Oh, that's Nikos, my brother," said Chloe. "Do you want to watch something?"

Jade pulled her eyes away from the Polaroid and saw a small TV that was set into an antique cabinet in the corner. Chloe turned it on and flipped through channels. She paused a moment on a soap opera in Spanish. An unshaven man was holding a woman's hands and saying something Jade didn't quite catch, but it had the word *amor*. Tears brimmed in the woman's eyes as she looked up at him. At last she said something, too, breathily, and they kissed.

Jade watched but she felt awkward about it. The kiss was really long and the music kept swelling. The two girls sat in silence.

At last the credits started to roll.

"I don't get it," said Chloe quietly.

"Don't get what?" said Jade, turning to her.

"Like, how does it happen?" Chloe half whispered. "How do they go from not kissing to kissing?"

Jade breathed out and didn't feel awkward anymore. "That's exactly my question!" she whispered back. "Like there's this *moment*, in between when they're not kissing and when they start kissing, and it sort of just"—she clapped her hands together, interlacing her fingers—"the moment just disappears."

"Yeah, it's like there's some kind of magic code or something," said Chloe. "It's like they both just *know*."

"Yeah!" said Jade. "It's like—it's like this show I saw on *Nova* one time." She remembered watching it with her dad and Katerina on the couch in their old house. The pulsating neon diagrams against a black background. "It talked about quantum leaps," she told Chloe. "Where a particle jumps from one state of being to another, but there's nothing in between. Crazy. And kissing looks just like that!"

"Exactly!" said Chloe.

Jade smiled into her empty bowl. Apparently, Chloe didn't have it all figured out either.

There were footsteps, and Chloe's mom appeared at the bottom of the stairs, this time in a fitted black dress and dangly gold earrings. She snapped the giant lid onto the tub of rice pudding and said, "I'm headed back to the restaurant. You girls be good now!"

"Bye, Mom!" said Chloe.

Chloe's mom headed out the door, balancing the tub against her body with one arm. Jade watched in awe as she did all this *in heels*, managing the door with her free hand. Before she closed the door, she called something out to Chloe in Greek.

"Okay, Mom!" said Chloe.

"Your mom is impressive," said Jade, when the door had closed.

Chloe laughed a little. "You wanna see my room?" she said. She had already switched off the TV and was headed for the stairs.

"Of course!" said Jade. She was curious about it. Maybe she would get some decoration ideas, too, since she hadn't bothered to decorate her own room much since the move.

Chloe's room was just big enough for her twin bed and a little desk jammed in the corner by the window that looked out onto the front parking lot. On top of the desk were a couple of spiral-bound notebooks that looked a lot like Jade's, a hand mirror, and a mascara stick. A well-worn fluffy teddy bear had been propped carefully against the pillow on the purple bedspread. Jade wondered how many times Chloe had placed him like that, lovingly, mechanically, in the groggy morning hours. There was a silver boom box by the bed with a karaoke mic attached to it, and beside that, an impressive collection of CDs stacked in neat columns. Chloe had broken into song at lunch that first day, but Jade hadn't realized Chloe was this into music.

Posters and magazine cutouts of singers were taped to the walls. Some of them Jade recognized, like Shakira, with her dark eyeliner and bell-bottoms, or the Spice Girls in their shiny leather and spangles, looking out from the glossy poster with parted lips. But others Jade had never seen before. Some of the posters had words in Greek written across them. They were all of fierce-looking women striking sinuous silhouettes. It must be something, to wake up to all those women who seemed so sure of themselves.

"Let me show you something," said Chloe.

She opened the door to her closet. OLH uniform clothes rubbed shoulders with brighter-colored regular ones— camis and T-shirts, flared jeans. At the bottom, Chloe's blue sports bag was crumpled against sneakers that were caked with dried reddish mud and sharp, fresh flecks of grass. If the trails the cross-country girls ran on were anything like the Wildcat Trail, Jade thought, the runners would kick up the moist dirt of that top layer to reveal the brick-red underlayer that Itztli had uncovered when he drew the map. Maybe the whole of Atlanta, this forest-city, was like this, covered with a soft, inviting blanket that was drawn over its red, living core.

Chloe kicked the shoes aside, spraying flakes of dirt on the floor, and pulled her sports bag out to get to something else. She knelt and pulled out a large black box and set it on her bed.

"What's that?" said Jade.

"A record player."

"Wow, that's hard-core." Jade had never seen a record player before in real life, only in movies. Chloe opened it up to show her the big round black turntable. There was not a hint of dust on the surface. Chloe lifted the slim metal arm on the side with two fingers and let the needle hover just above the edge of the platform where the vinyl would go, as if readying it to play an invisible song.

"My parents fought furiously over this when they got divorced," said Chloe, still holding the needle gently aloft, as though waiting for something. "They managed to figure out how to split up everything else—including us. But this was the last thing they couldn't decide on.

"I remember they were in the kitchen at our old house in Charlotte." Chloe lowered the arm carefully back down to its resting position. "They were screaming, and I was afraid that in all that commotion they were going to break it. They used to play songs on it all the time, mainly after dinner. These Greek oldies, you know. Romantic songs. Sometimes they would even dance. I was so afraid they were going to break it. It felt to me like if they broke it, then . . ." Chloe was staring at the turntable now but it didn't look like she was seeing it. "Then *everything* would be broken," she said quietly. She shook her head and seemed to come back to reality. She looked up at Jade and said, "I was so scared of that. I was more scared of that than I was of interrupting my parents' fight. So I went into the kitchen and I sort of screamed, '*Let me have it!*'" She laughed a little and Jade did, too, picturing it.

"And they just let you have it?" said Jade.

"Yeah, they kinda looked at me like 'Oh, there are other people in this world!' and then they sort of calmed down and said yeah, sure, take it." Chloe closed up the record player and stroked the top of it. "I think I solved that problem for them," she said. "But I still keep it in my closet, you know. I used to keep it out, but every time my mom saw it she would get this sad look on her face, and I just got tired of that."

"Yeah, I bet," said Jade. "I would, too."

Chloe slid the black box gently back into the closet and closed the door, kicking the cross-country gear in as she did. Suddenly she jumped onto her bed. It creaked a little and the teddy bear hopped and fell on its side. Chloe let her legs dangle. It looked like she had something to say.

"You know, I didn't know anyone at OLH when I started in sixth grade," she said. "My friends were basically my mom and Nikos, and Mom was super stressed out all the time, trying to get the restaurant up and running. My parents had just finished their divorce, you know . . ."

Jade listened but wasn't sure what to say, so she stayed silent. She almost didn't want to imagine what that might be like, to have your parents break away from each other. It must be so difficult to watch the threads come apart from a fabric that you had thought was one tightly woven piece, and try to find your own place amid the new folds and frayed edges. And to have that happen and move to a new place, all at once—that sounded so hard. For Chloe it had been really hard, and yet she didn't seem totally broken by it. After all, she had taken it into her own hands to rescue the record player and keep it looking new.

At Jade's silence, Chloe patted the bed beside her. Jade sat down and faced her, sinking a little into the covers. Chloe had more to say, and Jade wanted to hear it.

"All the other kids—they've known each other since kindergarten, you know?" said Chloe.

Jade nodded. She definitely knew. All the other kids seemed to know one another so well. Until this afternoon she had sort of assumed that Chloe did, too, but now that she thought about it, she wasn't so surprised that wasn't the case. In homeroom the other girls would talk to one another and not always include Chloe, and now Jade understood better why. Chloe just hadn't been there forever, like the rest of them had.

"Thank God for cross-country," said Chloe. Jade looked over at the closet where Chloe kept her running gear. She wished she had something like cross-country. "Emily and Caitlyn and I run for the middle school team of the high school, Saint Stephen Martyr," Chloe continued. "We run with some girls from other middle schools in the archdiocese. I'm closest to Emily and Caitlyn, though. And they're cool. But they're not—I don't know. I don't feel like I can *talk* to them."

Jade nodded, and her gratitude to Chloe for feeling like she could talk to *her*, for opening up to her this way, spread like a warmth in her chest. It made her want to open up to Chloe, too.

She wasn't sure there was anybody she could really talk to these days. Who could she tell about the story Itztli had told her and the map he had drawn, for example? Or the mirror that was in her dresser drawer, with its smoky veins that held so many secrets?

Chloe had invited her into her room, let her in on her feelings. Jade didn't know how to talk about everything that was on her mind, but she decided to let Chloe in as much as she could.

"Everything is different here in Atlanta," she said. "I'm not used to anything yet. Even the ground is different."

Chloe nodded and hugged her knees to her chest. "I know the feeling," she said.

They let the sounds of traffic and construction fill the room for a moment.

"Sometimes I feel like—like there are things that the grown-ups in my family just won't tell me," said Jade. "Important things, about where we come from, and how we got to be *here*." She gestured vaguely, trying to signal Atlanta, OLH, and all the buildings and asphalt that were carved out of the woods and were still being built by those men she saw earlier, the ones playing banda songs from a radio set. "And now—something's happening with my abuela. I don't know what's up, but something's not okay. I know my mom is worried." She realized as she said these things how much they were bothering her. "Do you ever feel like that?" she asked Chloe. "Like there are so many things they won't tell us?"

Chloe nodded slowly. "All the time," she said. "Like why my parents left Greece. They always tell me something different. But mostly I wonder why they got divorced. I mean I saw the fights—well, I heard them mostly—but I still don't get it. Why?" She shook her head and covered her ears, as if to drown out an obnoxious noise. "And they won't tell me," she said, lowering her hands. "And I feel like maybe Nikos knows something but he won't tell me either." She picked a piece of lint off the bedspread and flicked it to the floor.

Suddenly there was a loud commotion outside—the unmistakable sound of skateboard wheels scraping against pavement.

"Speaking of the devil," said Chloe. She went up to the window and looked out onto the parking lot. "Oh—*Justin* is here," she said almost breathily.

"Um, who is Justin?" said Jade.

Chloe snapped around. "Only my brother's hottest friend," she said.

"How old is he?" said Jade, sitting up straight and realizing all at once that the boys outside must be *high school* guys. She had no idea how to act around older guys. She always tried to play it cool but it never seemed to work.

"Not sure," said Chloe, grabbing the mirror from her desk. "He's in my brother's grade and Nikos is a sophomore." She turned to Jade. "You can't tell Emily I have a crush on him."

"Why would I tell Emily?" She barely knew Emily, the curly-haired cross-country girl with light brown skin and freckles and a friendly smile.

"Because he's her brother," said Chloe.

"Oh—got it," said Jade. She motioned zipping her mouth shut.

"I just can't help it," said Chloe. "I saw him first at one of Nikos's soccer games last year . . ." She fanned herself dramatically with one hand. "He's on defense because he's so tall. Oh my god, I can't wear this," she said suddenly, looking down at her uniform. She went to the closet and brought out flared jeans and a tiny black tank top and held them up for Jade to see. "What do you think?" she said.

"Ooh, nice!" said Jade. Chloe would look great in those clothes—she had the curves to pull off the look. Unlike Jade.

They both looked at Jade's starchy uniform skort. Were they thinking the same thing? As much as Jade wanted Chloe to rock her cute outfit, she knew she would look pretty frumpy beside her friend if Chloe changed.

"Wait—I can get you something to wear, too," said Chloe.

Jade looked at her, grateful, but knew that wouldn't work. She and Chloe were more or less the same size, except Chloe actually had boobs and hips, so there was no way her clothes would fit Jade. She didn't know how to tell Chloe this.

"Never mind," said Chloe, as if reading her mind. "I don't have to change."

"No, you should!" said Jade.

But Chloe was already stuffing the cute clothes back into her closet. Back at her mirror, she carefully rolled her shirtsleeves up so the top curve of her arms just before her shoulder would show. "Come on!" she said. "Let's go. I want your opinion." She gave Jade a conspiratorial smile.

The front door downstairs opened with a hermetic squeak, and the house was filled with teenage-guy voices. They were really here now.

Jade followed Chloe down the stairs, trying to roll up her own sleeves at the same time, and watched her friend undergo a transformation. Chloe stood tall, swung her hips, and stuck out her chest. She pulled her purple scrunchie out as she descended the stairs, letting her dark hair fall around her shoulders and flicking her head so that it whipped around. But the girl with the teddy bear who had scarfed down rice pudding wasn't gone either.

Jade could still see her underneath it all, even now. Still, she marveled at Chloe and wished she could be half as cool as her.

The cinnamony smell still wafted up the stairs from the kitchen. The girls got to the bottom of the staircase just as the boys burst from the kitchen into the living area—three high school guys carrying chips, Gatorade, and whatever other snacks they could fit in their arms. The space, cozy just a little while ago, now felt cramped, overcrowded with tall boys and movement and the pop and crunch of snacks. The boys were sweating and breathing heavily from skating in the August heat. Their faces wore that look of tired relief that people get when they are hit by much-needed AC. They all had on the uniform of Saint Stephen Martyr High—oxford shirts religiously untucked from khaki pants that sagged at the ankles where the dust and dirt of the day had collected.

They were tracking dirt all over. Only one of them had taken off his shoes and was padding around in sock feet. The cut of his body and the way he moved it—easily, with sure steps—drew in Jade's eye.

He was tall, strong, and lean, maybe fifteen or sixteen. He walked around the living area like he knew it well, shaking his longish black hair out of his eyes every so often. His olive complexion was the same as Chloe's and her mom's—he had to be Chloe's brother. He carried a Gatorade and a bag of chips toward the couch.

Someone had turned on the TV. A woman on the screen slammed a door and walked out onto a street, looking very proud of herself and very *done*.

"Seriously, Chlo?" the guy said. "You're watching *this*?"

"Is that the last bag of chips?" said Chloe.

"There's a perfectly good Champions League game to watch," he said, reaching for the remote.

Jade watched him, more and more curious and taken with him, as he flipped through the channels. He was skinny like the boys in her class, but his torso seemed more solid under his white button-down shirt. His jaw was square and just barely dotted with stubble. Jade had hardly ever really interacted with any guys who had facial hair.

He found the soccer channel. A red team was playing a white team. Normally, Jade would have immediately wanted to know who was playing, which team to root for. But what was happening in the room right now was too distracting for her to pay much attention to the game.

Suddenly, Chloe's brother looked up and saw Jade, and his dark eyes locked with hers.

Her heart jumped, and she realized she was staring at him. She hadn't moved since she had seen him.

"This is my friend Jade," said Chloe. "This is my brother, Nikos. Please excuse his obsession with Real Madrid."

"Please excuse my sister's obsession with David Beckham!" he retorted, not taking his eyes off Jade.

"Not true!" Chloe called, walking over to one of his friends who was near the kitchen.

Jade and Nikos said nothing. Jade couldn't move. She was caught off guard by what she was feeling, a tremulous sensation in her chest that she couldn't quite put her finger on, and that she hoped didn't show. And yes, she was still staring. But so was he.

Those eyes. So dark, the lashes so long. Commotion whirred all around them but they both held still, held the gaze. Jade wondered how long this could last. It had only been a few seconds but still it was significant. She didn't want it to end. A boy was looking at her. A *guy* was looking at her. A guy was looking at *her*. A *high school guy*.

At last she looked away. She just had to. She was afraid if she kept watching him she would completely lose control and make a fool of herself by farting or something. She twisted the untucked hem of her shirt around her finger and looked around for Chloe.

Chloe was playing with the purple scrunchie on her wrist as she talked to Nikos's friend. This must be Justin—his face was light brown with freckles like Emily's, and he was indeed very tall. His uniform shirt was unbuttoned and his white undershirt clung to his sweaty torso. No wonder Chloe was into him. It looked like he enjoyed watching Chloe as he leaned against the kitchen counter and sipped his Gatorade. If she were just a few inches taller, Chloe could look like she was in high school. Justin's eyes kept finding the shadow where Chloe's top button held her blouse together.

"Come on, Raúl!" said Nikos, egging on the player in white who was dashing toward the goal, his legs like a motor with the ball. Their moment—whatever it had been—was definitely over.

Chloe came over to Jade with a little smile. *That's Justin*, she mouthed, with her back to the boys. Jade nodded and smiled back.

"Noooo!!!" The boys were blocking the screen, so Jade couldn't see what they were upset about.

"That was for sure a penalty!" said the third boy, a blond guy with a mop of curly hair. He looked slightly younger than the other two guys and seemed almost small in comparison with his tall, muscular friends.

"Red card!" said Justin.

For a moment, Jade and Chloe watched the guys watch the game. It was amazing how quickly the boys' attention could shift.

Chloe pulled her scrunchie round and round her wrist. Then, decisively, she walked over to the pantry in the kitchen and pulled out a tin of chocolate Piroulines. She nibbled off just the top, taking her sweet time to do it, trying to catch Justin's eye.

It didn't take long. With a glance at Nikos, who seemed to be absorbed in the game, Justin sauntered over to Chloe and took a bite of the same twirly chocolate wafer, which Chloe was offering him.

"You want one?"

Jade jumped. It was Nikos. She looked at him as if he had just spoken to her in French.

"Do you want one?" he repeated, holding out the bag of chips.

Jade looked over at Chloe. She was trying to grab the chocolate stick from Justin and giggling softly.

She looked back at Nikos. Did this mean he liked her? Or was he just being polite?

She managed to shake her head in robotic little jerks. Nikos stuck his veiny forearm down into the bag and ate a chip, still looking at her. He licked his fingertips and Jade watched his tongue. Supposedly, people kissed with their tongues, but in movies you could never really see people's tongues because they were inside each other's mouths.

"Jade, right?" said Nikos.

"Yeah," said Jade. For the life of her she couldn't think of anything else to say. "Nikos, right?" she said eventually.

"Yep," he said. He wiped the chip grease on his pants and made a funny movement with his hand like he was going to offer it to her, but then slipped his hand into his pocket instead.

"So, um, you play?" said Jade, gesturing toward the TV. Her voice sounded a lot steadier than she felt.

"Yep, offense," he said, flicking his hair back. "I'm a starter on varsity."

"Cool," she said. It would be fun to watch him run, score goals. She imagined his hair feathered back in the wind.

"Do you run with Chlo?"

She shook her head. "I wish," she said. "I guess I—draw."

"Cool," said Nikos, but she couldn't tell whether he actually thought it was cool or not.

She looked down at her feet and hoped he would think of something to say. Hoped there was something else he *wanted* to say, maybe ask her. But he just kept standing there, and she couldn't bring herself to meet his eyes again.

She looked over at Chloe, who was looking at Nikos with mild annoyance. Jade hoped she wasn't annoyed with her, too. This made two of them, she realized—now she and Chloe both had crushes on one of their friends' older brothers.

"Halftime!" the blond boy announced loudly, throwing his arms up and looking around in front of the TV, making sure no one missed his announcement. "I'm ready to skate again," he added. For a moment Jade felt sorry for the boy, whose friends had left him to watch the game alone.

Justin and Nikos acted on cue, turning their attention away from Chloe and Jade. The boys all headed out the door again for another round of skateboarding. In their wake they left bits of chips and a sudden silence, papered over by a peppy commercial for Axe. Jade and Chloe looked at each other from opposite sides of the space that now felt large without the boys.

Jade wasn't sure what to say. Chloe had for sure noticed her and Nikos. She checked her watch. "It's already almost six," she said quietly. "My mom should be here any minute now. She's always really punctual."

Chloe shook her head as if to shake away whatever nonsense Jade had just said. She moved quickly to the couch and motioned for Jade to sit, hitting mute on the remote as she did so.

"Isn't he *cute*?" Chloe said, half whispering in case the guys outside could hear them.

Jade nodded. "Uh-huh," she said. Was Chloe just going to ignore what had just happened, or was she just really absorbed in her thing with Justin?

"I am *so* happy that he and Nikos are friends," Chloe continued.

"Do you, like, want to go out with him?" asked Jade. She didn't really know what that would mean. Madison had gone out with Luke Thompson last year for three and a half weeks, and all they'd ever done was hold hands in the halls.

Chloe pulled at the scrunchie on her wrist. "I mean yeah, I guess," she said. "But how do you do that? Like, do I try to get him to ask me to go see a movie? Do I—I don't know—do I try to get him to ask me to go to the homecoming dance at the high school?"

Jade was relieved that she wasn't asking her about Nikos. She wouldn't have known how to respond, anyway. She leaned back into the comfy couch. "I have no idea, Chloe," she said. "But I don't think any of that is going to happen with your brother around." And nothing was going to happen between her and Nikos if Chloe was around. Not that she was even sure what she wanted with Nikos.

"Ugh, you're totally right," said Chloe. "It's a lost cause."

"I don't know," said Jade. "I mean, I think he's into you."

"Really?"

"I mean, the way he looks at you . . ." That was how you could tell, right?

"I hope so," said Chloe. She shook her head. "He's just *so cute.*"

Jade nodded. Justin definitely had a lot going for him. But Nikos—now he was *incredibly* cute.

The doorbell rang and it was over. Jade was reluctant to get up from that comfy, lived-in couch. Veronica and Madison had known her forever, so it was natural that they could tell one another all sorts of things. But Chloe had only just met her, and already she had welcomed her into her family home and let her in on some of her rawest, closest secrets.

"*So* nice to meet you," Jade's mom said to Chloe when she opened the door. She was wearing her skirt suit and playing the part of Mrs. O'Callaghan. Jade wished she would let go a little. There was no need for all that in front of Chloe. "Thank you so much for having Jade," she said. "I'm so sorry to take her away from you, but it's dinnertime."

"No problem. We should do it again."

"Yeah, at my place!" said Jade.

She hugged her friend tightly goodbye, and Chloe hugged her tightly back. In that embrace, starchy uniform to starchy uniform, Jade felt like she could trust her.

That night as she lay in bed, Jade stared up into the indistinct darkness of her room. Mortimer, curled up on the quilt at her feet, petted her softly with his tail. The rhythm lulled her mind to numbness.

She thought of Nikos's eyes. She slipped her hand under her shirt and held it on her heart, feeling the warmth there, skin to skin.

She replayed it over and over again in her head. How he had offered her chips. How his back and butt had looked from behind when he headed out the door to go skateboarding. How he had looked at her.

She wanted to feel that again. She wanted to be looked at again.

There was something inside her fighting to get out. She pressed her palm harder into her breastbone, fingers outstretched against the budding curves that rose on either side, as if to contain whatever it was that lay beneath—but also to feel it, to get to know it. It was as if there were a warm, soft animal inside her that had been tied down and was waking up and straining against its bonds. If it broke loose, Jade thought, she wouldn't be able to hold it back.

6

Jade felt more self-aware than ever as she walked into the girls' locker room for PE. She pretended not to watch everyone else as she changed into her PE uniform, not to wonder what everyone else's boobs looked like. She wished for the first time that she had a sports bra. Not because she needed one, really—her regular one with the tiny bow in the middle did just fine—but because then it would look like she knew what she was doing with herself. She made a mental note to ask her mom for one. Her mom had said she could ask her for a razor; she should be able to ask her for this, too.

Out on the field, the early sun already pricked. Jade longed for the cool shade beneath the swaying leaves of the forest that lay just beyond the chain-link fence. The field was a rectangle of grass and clover across the parking lot from the Wildcat Trail. There was no barrier to the parking lot, which was quiet now during the school day, bright and hot under the piercing blue sky. Balls often bounced onto the pavement and went rolling away across its painted lines, sending someone chasing after them. But a chain-link fence separated the field from the forest edge on the side perpendicular to the pavement, and from a shaded thoroughfare with cars that rushed past on the side opposite the parking lot. The brick side of the gym enclosed the field on the fourth side.

Coach Porter waited in the middle of the field for them to gather, in his Marines cap, as always, with a whistle around his neck. He was stocky and strong and at least fifty, his graying hair buzzed short. He had the arms and chest of someone who lifted weights. He led them through a few stretches, and Jade was already sweating as she did the lunges.

The coach sorted them into teams for a relay race and had them put on red or blue mesh jerseys over their gray uniform T-shirts. Jade was on the red team; Chloe was on the blue team. The jerseys vaguely stank, and as she pulled hers on, Jade tried not to think about all the other kids who had worn it since it was last washed.

She got into position in a corner of the field, facing the trees. She concentrated, her leg muscles preparing, twitching, as she watched her classmates run. Cars whooshed past. She watched the cross-country girls in particular—Chloe, Emily, and Caitlyn—and tried to gauge just how fast they were. How good did you have to be to make it onto the team?

Chloe was running now. She handed the baton off smoothly to Emily, like they were one girl running. Chloe seemed barely out of breath as she slowed to a walk.

A boy on Jade's team was running toward her with the baton. It was Benjamin, a guy with floppy brown hair.

It was Jade's turn next. Benjamin was fast on his long legs but puffing hard. His blue eyes were trained on her. She met his gaze and watched him closely, hardly blinking. He was almost there . . .

She grabbed the baton and bolted. Peter was up ahead on the blue team, his legs pumping in a whir beneath his basketball shorts, the little blond hairs on them glinting. Jade sped up and dashed past him.

She loved it.

She loved being faster than Peter. She kept running as fast as she could to hold her speed and keep her lead. She loved the soft, quick bounce of her feet against the grassy earth. She loved how the wind rushed past her ears and through her ponytail. She loved how free she felt—free to let go and move how she wanted, free from any one place.

Caitlyn stood at the corner, knees bent, her freckled arm reaching out for the baton. All at once Jade was practically there. She managed to hand off the baton without slowing down, slamming it into Caitlyn's palm just as Caitlyn took off in a flash of her orange-red ponytail. The fence was up ahead. Jade put her hands out to stop herself but still she crashed into it, smashing her cheek into the wire diamonds that separated her from the trees. Looking back, she saw that Peter was only just now reaching the next handoff point. Tanya grabbed the baton and ran, but it was already clear that Caitlyn would get to the finish line first. The red team—Jade's team—was going to win.

Caitlyn dashed through the finish line and threw the baton up in celebration, sending it glinting and twirling silver through the air. Everyone on the red team cheered. Jade joined in, raising her voice as best she could through her heavy breathing. Tanya reached the finish line and threw her baton on the ground in frustration.

Jade was pumped now, and even though she was winded, didn't want to stop. She walked to the middle of the field to hear what Coach Porter would have them do next.

"Same teams, hurdles," Coach Porter said. He asked for volunteers, and when Chloe raised her hand to help set up the hurdles, Jade did too.

Chloe's eyes were big and eager as she approached Jade, and in them Jade recognized some of the bubbly excitement she had seen in her friend the other day in Chloe's room.

"You're really fast," Chloe said when she reached her. They began walking side by side across the field, spacing the hurdles out evenly in two rows.

"Oh—thanks," said Jade. Chloe must have been watching her, too, just as she had watched Chloe. "You're *super-fast*, though," she said to Chloe.

Chloe shook her head. Up close like this, the layer of liquid foundation on Chloe's cheeks glistened with beading sweat—but her mascara held admirably. "That was a wild sprint," Chloe said. "I didn't know you could run like that."

"Honestly, I didn't know either," said Jade. Her breathing was still heavy. "I mean I've always liked running, but I've never run like *that* before." There was something different now. She remembered being Katerina's age and racing her dad along the lake. He would always let her win. But by the time she was about ten, it became clear that he was actually putting some effort into it, and when the contest became sort of fair, it petered out. They didn't race anymore. She had always enjoyed those runs, and the cool lake breeze, but she had never felt like *this*—like there was something inside her that was driving her forward, something that had maybe always been there but was just now waking up and spurring her on.

"You know what—" said Chloe.

"What?" said Jade, but Chloe had already started off toward Coach Porter, leaving a couple hurdles still lying in the grass, her task unfinished.

Jade put up the rest of the hurdles in her row and watched as Chloe talked to Coach Porter. She couldn't hear what they were saying, but they kept looking over at her. She didn't love being talked about, but she also trusted Chloe. Coach Porter's eyebrows were slightly furrowed— whether at what Chloe was saying or against the sun, Jade couldn't tell. Each time he and Chloe looked over at her, she looked away. To do something with herself, she finished setting up the hurdles left in Chloe's row.

At last Coach Porter nodded and Chloe ran back. But she didn't stop. She just said *thank you!* to Jade and kept running past her and across the parking lot.

Coach Porter clapped his hands and told them all to get in positions for the hurdle race. Jade got in line absently, watching as Chloe entered the school building.

There was no time to wonder what she was up to, though. Soon it was Jade's turn to run and jump high to clear the hurdles.

She concentrated and glided over them all, tumbling with each landing toward the next jump. She grazed just one, the tallest one, with her toe, and lost her rhythm only slightly. Peter, running beside her, cleared it just fine. His legs were much longer—that wasn't fair, Jade thought.

When Jade went to get in place in line again, Chloe was back on the field. Jade caught her eye and raised her eyebrows at her. Chloe poked her chin in the direction of the parking lot. Ms. Jackson, their homeroom teacher, was standing on the edge of the field in her high heels and flared slacks, arms crossed, watching Jade.

Jade looked back at Chloe. Chloe smiled ever so slightly at her.

Jade understood. This was her chance.

Three of the hurdles were already down—that would make it easier to run fast and gain speed. She bent her knees, left leg in front, and rocked gently on the balls of her feet. When it was her turn, she dashed forward and tore across the grass, her steps swift, light strokes on the ground that propelled her forward and faster. She sprang as high as she could and cleared the tallest hurdle that was left, and as she landed she kept running in a single motion and blew right through the last hurdle, knocking the beam down with her knees as she barreled into it. She didn't care.

She bent forward and held her knees to catch her breath, hair falling into her eyes. She looked up at Ms. Jackson. The teacher had a hand on her hip and was looking at her with her head cocked to one side.

"We still won, even though you knocked down that last hurdle epically."

Jade stood up. It was Caitlyn. "Sorry . . . ?" she said.

Caitlyn shook her head. "We would've lost without your wild sprint," she said, smiling.

Not far away, Emily and Chloe were high fiving and saying, "good game, good game."

Jade wanted so badly to be one of them.

Coach Porter blew his whistle, and everyone headed to the locker rooms, pulling their jerseys off over their heads as they went.

Ms. Jackson stopped Jade as she approached the gym. "Let me talk to you for a minute," she said, like it was nothing. She walked steadily out onto the field despite her heels.

Jade nodded and followed. As Chloe and Emily passed them, Emily smiled at her and Chloe mouthed, *Good luck.*

When everyone had disappeared into the gym, Ms. Jackson said, "Do me a favor and run a lap around the field."

"But—" she started to say. She didn't know if she had it in her anymore. She had just given her all in the hurdle race and hadn't gotten her breath back yet.

But then she saw the look Ms. Jackson gave her. Her blue eyes were steely and her pink-lipstick mouth was set. "But what?" she said.

"Nothing," said Jade.

Ms. Jackson nodded. "Good." She was holding a stop-watch. "Go ahead, start here." She pointed, and Jade got into position. "On the count of three. Three, two, one, go."

Jade took off. Her legs burned; she felt she could barely breathe hard enough. But then the thing that was inside her roared to life and she broke through something, and now she was just running. She was running like the running would take her somewhere. Like there was no fence, like she could blow past it into the forest, into the trees, over the stream . . . She zipped past the trees, past the gym, past the cars zooming by.

She was approaching the place where Ms. Jackson stood, stopwatch in hand. "Keep going!" Ms. Jackson called to her. "One more!"

Jade sped up. She was loving it now and didn't feel tired at all. All she wanted was to keep going. In no time she made the loop again, and as she neared Ms. Jackson the second time, she dashed past her and only slowed when she realized she was going to slam into the brick wall of the gym. She put her hands out and cushioned the impact, scraping her palms a little.

"Thirty-one seconds," said Ms. Jackson. She walked over to Jade. "Gotta figure out how to stop, don't you?" she said.

"I—" Jade panted and tried to catch her breath. Her heart was pounding and suddenly her legs were hurting again. "I don't want to stop," she managed to get out, looking up at her.

Ms. Jackson nodded. Her straight blond hair and pearl earrings were nearly blinding. "Did you run in Chicago?" she asked.

Jade shook her head.

"You're fast but you've got to learn some control," said Ms. Jackson. "And some endurance."

Jade nodded.

"Here, let's walk," she said. "You'll get cramps otherwise."

Jade followed her along the edge of the parking lot. Was Ms. Jackson going to say something more? She hardly dared hope.

"Tryouts were in the summer," Ms. Jackson said as they walked. She was impossibly steady on her heeled pumps in the grass that brushed against the hem of her slacks. "We can't normally take people on the team this late," she continued, not looking at Jade. "But we have a chance at the state championship this year, and we need to give it all we've got." Suddenly, she turned and looked directly at Jade. "Do you want to run cross-country for the Saint Stephen Martyr middle school team?"

Jade looked at her. Now that it was real, she wasn't sure what to say.

"Do you want to be on the team?" Ms. Jackson repeated.

"Yes," said Jade, with an exhale that felt like a long-awaited release.

Ms. Jackson nodded and gave just the slightest hint of a smile. "Good. That's what I needed to know." She slipped the stopwatch into her pants pocket and pulled out a folded piece of paper and a pencil. "Talk to your parents about it, see what they say," she said. "Tell them they can always talk to me if they have any questions. And let them know that if you need a ride, I take Caitlyn, Emily, and Chloe to the high school where we practice Monday through Thursday, and I have room for you, too."

Jade nodded. She couldn't believe it. This school had seem so closed to her at first, with its funny uniforms and unwritten rules. But now all these people were warming to her, extending her invitations that felt like lifelines thrown casually from solid ground out to the moving sea where she wavered on a wobbly raft. Maybe, maybe, she would be able to find her place here after all.

"Thank you," she said, finding the words. "Wait—the high school?"

Ms. Jackson nodded. "Mm-hm," she said. She was writing on the piece of paper.

If practice was at the high school, would she see high school boys practically every day? Would she see Nikos more often?

It was too many thoughts at once. She shook her head to drive them out.

Ms. Jackson handed her the piece of paper. It was a release form, and her phone number was written in a corner. "You'll need to start ASAP," she said. "This week if possible. Now go ahead and get changed."

The teacher turned and walked back toward the parking lot, her long, pointy heels marking soft divots in the ground.

Jade clutched the piece of paper to her chest. She looked over at the trees that rose above the fence and imagined the trails she'd get to run on. This little sheet of paper could free her from that fence. With it she could dash through the fallen leaves and ivy, over gnarly roots and along streams. She wanted so much to run through the patches of light and dark in the forest, quick and light, maybe even climb up into the trees . . .

"Jade!"

She turned. It was Coach Porter, motioning for her to go inside.

She hurried toward the gym. The bell would ring any minute now and she still had to change out of these sticky, stinky clothes.

When she got inside, almost everyone had already spilled out into the hall, and they stood in their regular uniforms with their backpacks on, waiting for the bell to ring. But inside the locker room, Chloe, Emily, and Caitlyn were waiting for her.

"What did she say?" said Chloe.

"She wants me on the team!" said Jade, holding up the piece of paper.

Chloe squealed and stomped her feet, and Caitlyn and Emily said, "Woo-hoo!" and did some jumpy, matching dance moves.

Chloe trapped Jade in a sweaty hug. Jade hugged her tightly back.

"Bobcats for life!" she heard Caitlyn say. Apparently they were bobcats.

"Thank you," Jade said quietly in Chloe's ear, still hugging her tightly, and she felt Chloe nodding into her shoulder.

7

The sun was still toasting the parking lot when school let out that afternoon, and Jade stepped onto the breezeway with Chloe and Emily. Blinding shards of sunrays exploded on car hoods, and the little kids who sat down to play on the sidewalk jerked their hands away from the ground when the concrete stung their palms.

"Sissy!"

Katerina was running toward Jade, pushing through the crowd of kids, her ladybug backpack sliding back and forth.

"Look!" said Katerina. She held out her fist and opened it for Jade to see. A shiny, curved red bean rested in the center of her cupped palm. "We planted these today, and Ms. McDade let me have one!"

"Good for you!" said Jade. Emily and Chloe were watching Katerina, amused. Katerina took note of them and became quiet and serious.

"Katerina, these are my friends Chloe and Emily," said Jade. "Can you say hi?" She was secretly proud to show her sister that she had friends, too.

Katerina said nothing and only looked at them with her big eyes, then looked away toward the parking lot. "Daddy!" she said. She forgot her shyness, waving her free hand as high as she could and hopping.

Jade's dad emerged from the Wildcat Trail across the parking lot, wearing reflective sunglasses and a big smile. She hadn't seen him this confident in a while—not since they had moved here—and she wasn't sure why he was picking them up from school.

"There's Coach Jackson," said Chloe. "I gotta go." She gave Jade a quick hug. "You'll be coming with us too as soon as your parents sign that form!" she said with a grin. Jade smiled back and waved as Chloe headed off. The release form was carefully folded in her backpack, and she was going to tell her parents as soon as she got the chance.

"How's my bug?" her dad said, approaching them. Katerina jumped into his arms and he hoisted her up. Jade remembered when he used to do that with her, not so long ago. That time had passed; she wasn't a little kid anymore. It was easier to be so outwardly loving with someone as tiny and adorable as Katerina.

"Daddy, today we planted beans!" said Katerina.

"No way!" he said, and Jade followed him as he started walking along the breezeway, toward the entrance to the trail. He looked over at Jade. "How about you?" he said. "How was school today?"

Jade was about to tell him what had happened, that she had been fast enough to make it onto the cross-country team. She wanted him to be proud of her, and to pay attention to her and not just Katerina. But first she wanted to know why he had come this afternoon. "School was great, actually," she said. "But, Dad, why are you picking us up?"

"Because," he said, grinning, "I have news for you girls!"

"What? Tell me!" said Katerina, squirming around in his arms.

"Okay, Katerina-Ballerina, you're going to have to get down," he said, lowering her to the sidewalk to cross the parking lot.

"What is it? Tell me, Daddy!" Katerina said as soon as her Mary Janes hit the pavement.

"Your daddy got a job!" he said, and he looked over at Jade for approval.

So that's why he looked like he'd just won the lottery. "Congrats, Dad!" she said.

"Yay, Daddy!" said Katerina, clapping her hands.

Getting a job didn't sound particularly exciting to Jade—it sounded like work—but she knew it meant a lot to her dad. He carried himself with ease now, nodding and smiling with quiet pride at the teachers on after-school duty, and she felt like she had gotten a part of her dad back that she hadn't even known she was missing.

When they reached the entrance to the Wildcat Trail, the rough concrete gave way to the softness of the moist dirt underfoot, and the tree limbs reached out to shelter them and invite them in. Jade stepped onto the path, her dad and Katerina close beside her. Jade let out a breath of relief, glad to finally exchange the fierce sun and whiffs of gasoline for the delicate green parasol of the canopy and the earthy scents of bark and stream-bathed spreads of moss. She couldn't see the moss, but she smelled it and knew it was there, behind the trees, crowning smooth stones by the stream where Itztli had told her his story. Had she always been able to smell the moss? Could she catch its scent now because she had seen it, had sat on the stream bank and inhaled its earthy odor as she watched Itztli draw his map?

The path curved gently out of sight up ahead, but she remembered how it bent, the course it charted through the trees. How wonderful it would be to leave her backpack behind on the steaming asphalt and run along the path, unencumbered, the wind cooling the patches of sweat that had begun to form under her backpack straps. Running cross-country, she would learn what it felt like to dash through paths like these.

Her dad held Katerina's hand a few paces ahead of her. Seeing how tall he stood, how easily but firmly he held her sister's hand, Jade brought herself back to his good news.

"So, what's your job?" she asked, catching up to them. Even though she was itching to tell him about cross-country, she didn't want to upstage him—he was so happy right now.

"Chief horticulturalist at the Museum of Art and History," he said. The title came easily, like he had practiced it. "It's nearby—over by the college."

Jade nodded. She still could hardly tell where anything was in Atlanta, but she did remember the pink-and-white-stone entrance to the college at the top of a hill beside one of those many-pronged intersections not far from their house.

"Will you be taking care of plants like you did before?" said Katerina. That was how their dad always used to describe his old job at the botanical gardens in Chicago: taking care of plants. His job wasn't just planting them or growing them—it was coaxing them into standing tall, making fragrant flowers, or bearing juicy fruit.

"Absolutely," he said. "I'll be taking care of plants again. Different ones this time. Lots of them have been growing in these parts for centuries."

Jade watched the bushes and groundcover as they wound along the path. Dense ivy crawled around sprays of dark green grass and climbed the trunks of thick trees, clutching at the bark as it snaked its way up. Bushes with prickly, glossy leaves and little green berries stood at intervals along the path, and low, thorny stems reached their three-leaf clusters out into the walkway. Every once in a while, a bright, papery purple flower with a velvety heart of burgundy thrust itself into view around waist height, demanding to be admired. Each pop of color, each waving leaf, added its own textured brushstroke to the landscape.

Around the bend a startled squirrel eyed them from the middle of the path with its dark, bright eyes, sitting on its hind legs, its bushy tail an S against its back. It held a large, half-nibbled acorn in its tiny handlike paws. When it saw that they kept coming, it twitched its tail once and scurried into the brush.

"Daddy, what is that?" said Katerina. She was pointing at one of the light purple flowers with the regal-red hearts. Its petals were thin and delicate as papel picado.

"Hollyhock," said their dad. "This is a hardy one that found a little patch of sunlight in all this shade."

"What about that one?" said Katerina, pointing to an even taller flower crowned with a burst of little pink flowers. Katerina was going on one of her spates of asking questions.

"That's ironweed," said her dad. "They love streams. There's a tributary of Grapevine Creek that runs through here somewhere . . ."

Her dad was right, of course. Jade listened carefully for the softly rushing water that she knew was there, just beyond the vines and brush and the thick tree trunks.

"Ironweed," said Katerina, closing a fist. "It sounds strong."

Jade had to admit that she was enjoying this, too—this wasn't just a case of Katerina asking annoying questions. She was glad to put names to the plants, to the many shades of green speckled with bright colors here and there.

A tall dark spray of grass with green berries brushed Jade's calf.

"Monkey grass," her dad said, before Katerina could ask.

Katerina giggled. "Monkey grass!" she said.

"Like a monkey I know," said her dad, smiling and tickling Katerina's side. Katerina squealed with glee.

"What about these trees, Dad?" said Jade, motioning toward some that were especially thick. "They're mostly oaks, right?" she said.

"That's right, mostly oaks," he said. "White oaks, live oaks. That big one over there is a live oak that might be nearly a hundred years old."

He was pointing to one that was as thick as two or three normal trees and had an army of roots anchoring it into the ground among the ivy. It was set back a bit from the path, and Jade peered at it from behind the skinnier trees in front of it. The great oak's branches looked like they had been twisting into their dancing shapes for ages. Its weathered bark made it look like it had borne the brunt of a thousand storms, and would stand tall amid many more.

How long had Itztli lived in this forest? Had he been here as long as this oak? How long was that? Was it a time you could measure in years, like the rings of a tree stump? Or was it a time that was measured in the more slippery units of memory, like the handfuls of seasons her abuelo used to conjure with a gentle arc of his hand in the air when he told her stories?

She heard the stream now, whispering along the smooth stones. Perhaps Itztli was nearby, keeping them company from behind the shelter of the oaks and the ironweed.

"Dad, why does a museum need a horticulturalist?" said Jade. "What kind of a museum is it?"

"I'll have to take you girls there sometime," he said. "They have ancient art from different places, including right here in Georgia. And they have a garden that's like a mini-botanical garden, with species from all over, but they have this major focus on plants from Georgia. You'll like it."

It sounded like she would. When Abuela had taken her and Katerina to the art museum in Chicago for the Día de los Muertos festival a few years ago, Jade had enjoyed taking in the colors and lines of the paintings in a setting that didn't feel like school. Abuela had let her and Katerina follow whatever caught their eye, whether it was a canvas with a woman weaving or luminescent blue stained-glass windows.

She was almost more excited about her dad's new garden, though. She and Katerina had loved going to the Botanic Garden in Chicago when he worked there. The star of the show had always been the model train, of course, and the miniature landscape that it chugged through. The scaled-down tracks and train cars made the bendy, twiggy shrubs resemble trees, and the slight hill with the tunnel appear to be a mountain.

They were approaching the end of the trail now. The light sloped in through the trees more strongly. Jade wasn't in a hurry to get back out into the fierce sun's glare.

Just before the path opened out into the backyard, she was certain she heard Itztli softly, not far away. It sounded like he was purring, but also like he was calling to her. She kept walking but peered through the trees, trying to see him. Right before she stepped out onto the grass, she caught a glimpse of his golden hide as he slipped noiselessly through the foliage and disappeared.

She stood there a moment at the edge of the yard watching the spot, her dad's and Katerina's voices soft in the background.

He had appeared again, like the glowing tail of a shooting star that's gone as soon as it's seen. He had flashed before her, beckoning to her once more.

The sweet-savory smell of onions, serranos, and tomatoes cooking with cilantro picked fresh from her dad's garden curled up from the crack beneath Jade's bedroom door. She sat on her bed, looking out the window and scratching Mortimer's tummy as he stretched out on her covers. The sun had softened now and was glazing the lamb's ears and the spritely black-eyed Susans in the backyard the color of browned butter.

Itztli had something more to tell her, and she wanted to know what it was. She looked toward the threshold where the forest began at the edge of the yard, but all she saw was the row of tall pines, their brushlike needles feathered high against the blue sky, and below them the short green shoots from seeds her dad had planted.

They were having a celebratory dinner for her dad, so of course they had to have fresh salsa. When Jade got to the kitchen, her mom immediately asked her to start forming tortillas out of the balls of masa. She looked more relaxed than usual as she stood over the sizzling, crackling comal in her embroidered apron. Her work blouse was untucked and her face was soft as she turned the tomatoes and chiles on the stove with tongs, making sure they blackened on every side but didn't burn. The good news about her husband's job seemed to have settled like a calm around her shoulders.

Jade instinctively laid a ball of masa on the iron tortillera that her mom had prepared with Saran Wrap so it wouldn't stick, and pressed the moist dough softly so it cracked apart just slightly at the edges. She brought the iron top down on its hinge and bore down on the handle to flatten the tortilla between the two layers of metal. When she opened up the tortillera again, there was the tortilla, ready for the stove.

When Jade was very little, in the kitchen of the Casa Azul, Abuela had shown her how to press firmly but not too firmly, to get the tortillas to just the right thickness so they would puff up like proud children as they cooked on the stove, their two thin layers separating from each other to form a dancing pocket of heat. The flattening of the masa with the tortillera was the only step that Jade did. Abuela always made the masa herself, mixing the harina nixtamalizada—the finely ground corn flour—with just enough warm water to get the perfect consistency. She would knead it together with strong knuckles and quick fingers. When she cooked the tortillas on the stove, she would lay them out on the big restaurant griddle and flip them over with her fingertips at just the right moment. She somehow never burned herself as she did this, even when her eyesight started to go.

Abuela hardly ever made tortillas anymore. Now Jade's mom did the steps Abuela used to do, but somehow it was never quite the same. There was simply nothing quite like Abuela's tortillas.

Katerina skipped into the kitchen. "I want to help!" she announced.

Jade didn't know what to tell a six-year-old to do in the kitchen. She kept at her rhythm—place, press, lower, press. The metal creaked and thudded in time to her motions.

"You can make the guacamole," her mom told Katerina. Quickly, dexterously, her mom sliced open an avocado and took out the pit. "Here." She handed Katerina a small fork and a blue-and-white bowl and pulled up the step stool so she could reach the counter.

"Yay!" said Katerina, hopping up onto the step stool. Immediately, she grabbed the fork and went to smashing the ripe avocado.

Their mom was going all out tonight—tortillas, salsa, guacamole, and chicken strips sizzling in a skillet.

When it was all ready, Jade fed Mortimer and she and her dad set the table, her dad whistling softly to himself. Her mom brought out two cold glass bottles of amber beer and popped them open, releasing their smoky wisps of fizzed air out into the room like twin spirits.

With the family seated, her mom raised her beer and said, "To the man who can make anything grow!" She smiled sideways at Jade's dad. Her parents clinked their bottles together and drank up, looking into each other's eyes with that playful, slightly mischievous look they gave each other sometimes.

"Sissy?" Katerina was holding out her glass of apple juice. It was an invitation. Jade clinked her own glass of Sprite with Katerina's glass, and the ring sounded unexpectedly nice. She glanced at her sister in pleasant surprise and Katerina grinned as the sound lingered in the air.

The meal tasted even better than usual—or maybe Jade was just hungrier than usual. The salsa and tortillas were infused with the smoky singe of the comal. Her mom had slipped extra tomatoes into Katerina's portion of salsa to make it milder, but Katerina asked for the "grown-up sauce" and swallowed, watery-eyed but determined to enjoy it. Jade's parents were in such a good mood that they didn't scold Katerina for talking with her mouth full or for leaning forward and dipping the ends of her pigtail braids in the salsa.

"I have some news, too," said Jade, when she had satisfied her hunger enough to slow down a bit. She figured she wouldn't be upstaging her dad anymore at this point if she told them her good news.

"Oh yeah, what is it?" said her mom.

Jade felt her lips twitch up in a smile as she said it. "The coach wants me on the cross-country team," she said.

Her parents stared. For a second they were silent, then in unison they began congratulating her.

"That's great!"

"That's amazing!"

"How did it happen?" said her mom.

"I *knew* you were fast!" said her dad.

"Good job, Sissy!" said Katerina, wanting to join in.

Jade returned her parent's beaming smiles. "I ran around the field twice in half a minute today after PE," she said. "Ms. Jackson timed me."

"What? That's *so* fast!" said her dad.

"So fast," echoed her mom. "Ms. Jackson is your homeroom teacher, right?"

"Yeah. She takes the cross-country girls to practice at the high school in the afternoons, Monday through Thursday. Chloe's on the team—"

"Oh!" Her mom looked at her dad, and they nodded, apparently in agreement. "That's just wonderful," her mom said, turning back to Jade. "Do you *want* to run?"

"Yes!" said Jade.

"Well," said her dad, after a moment. "Where do we sign?"

"I'll go get the form!" said Jade. The happiness bubbled up inside her, gold and fizzy like her parents' beer. She could hardly believe it. She was going to run with Chloe and Emily and Caitlyn. She was going to be one of them now!

She dashed to her room. Behind her, Katerina whined, "She has to be excused!"

"I'm coming right back!" Jade called out.

With the release form in hand, she raced back to the dining room. Her mom had sat back against her dad's arm, and he was rubbing her shoulder with his thumb contentedly as he savored his last bite of the meal.

Jade set the form on the table and watched her parents peer over each other's shoulders to read it, her mom's hand hovering over it with her reporter's pen. All at once the fizz of excitement bubbled over inside her. "Thank you!" she burst out.

Her parents looked up and laughed, and with a flourish her dad took the pen, caressing her mother's hand as he did so, and inked a signature that ran all the way across the page.

When the dishes were done and the counters wiped off, Jade's parents parked themselves on the couch and sprawled in each other's arms to watch a comedy show. Her mom was taking a rare break from the work she did in her upstairs office most nights these days.

Jade was too excited to concentrate on her math homework. She couldn't wait to give Ms. Jackson the release form in homeroom the next day and ride in her red jeep to practice with the other girls.

The phone rang. She heard her dad dial down the volume on the TV, and her mom's quick steps as she reached the phone in the kitchen.

"Hello?" There was a silence. "Oh."

That didn't sound good.

Jade went to her door and opened it just a crack so she could hear better. Katerina had stepped into the hallway, too, silent and serious. Bad news had a particular sound and feel to it—a brokenness, something out of order—that even a kindergartener could pick up on. Jade couldn't catch exactly what was going on, but it had something to do with Abuela.

When her mom got off the phone, Jade heard her dad ask, "What is it, Sol?"

"Oh, Chris," she said. There was a funny silence that made Jade wonder if her mom was holding something back. She looked at Katerina. Her sister's eyes were wide.

"Mamá had a stroke," her mom said finally. The words came out in one quick breath, followed by a heavy sigh, like the whoosh of leaves rustled by an ominous wind.

"How bad?" her dad asked.

"I don't know." Her words were muffled now, and Jade thought she must be saying them into their dad's shirt. "But I have to go see about her."

Katerina stepped toward her. Instinctively, Jade pulled her in. They held on to each other like that a long time in silence.

If their strong, firmly planted mother had bent like a sapling in a storm, at least they had each other to sway with in the gathering winds.

8

The cozy scent of coffee greeted Jade as she emerged into the hallway of their house the following morning, Mortimer at her heels. Her hair had poufed up with all this Georgia humidity, but she needed to get to school and there wasn't much she could do about it right now.

Jade never drank coffee herself, but she loved the earthy smell, the way the plumes of steam rose in a lazy dance from her parents' breakfast cups on early yellow mornings. She liked how the shifting haze just above the surface of the cups turned the world behind it into a soft, pulsating blur, until the smoky plumes reached up and disappeared into the air. Today there was something different about the smell that cut through the usual warm tones. Something sharper, sweeter, stronger.

In the kitchen her dad stood beside a skillet with steaming scrambled eggs and spooned coarse brown sugar into two thick painted ceramic mugs. Katerina stood by his pants leg like she was his shadow and watched their mom with her big eyes.

Their mom was taking up all the space. She had the phone cocked between her ear and shoulder and was pacing around, pulling the cord with her as she walked, her small reporter's notebook and a pencil in hand. In her polished pumps and gold-stud earrings she looked even more put together than usual, if such a thing was possible. Her hair didn't move at all; she must have used hair spray today. Her heels clacked as she moved in a whir of activity that Jade could barely take in this early in the morning.

"Aha," she was saying. "A layover—how long? *All night?*" She shot an exasperated glance at Jade's dad.

Jade made as little noise as possible as she fed Mortimer, not wanting to do anything to disturb the swirling, gathering tempest her mother emanated.

"Well then, get me the earliest direct flight you have in the morning," her mom said into the phone, and it came out like a sigh. Her tone was civil but firm, and Jade didn't envy the person on the other end. Her dad reached out and touched the top of her mom's back lightly with his fingertips. He meant to calm her, but she hardly seemed to notice.

They sat down to breakfast without Jade's mom and ate in silence, the only sounds their mother's taut voice, her furious pencil, and that incessant clacking of her heels on the tile floor.

At last she hung up. The storm was contained, for now. There was still no stray hair out of place, no wrinkle in her blouse. She slapped her pencil down and came to sit with them. Talking quickly between bites of egg, she said, "I have to call the doctor. And the insurance. And Carmelo—I have to see if he can be there tonight."

Hospitals, diseases, treatments—these were her mom's *thing*. But this wasn't some news report. This was Abuela.

Jade wasn't quite sure what a stroke was. Veronica's uncle had had one when they were in fourth grade, and Veronica had called it "a heart attack of the brain."

Jade's questions piled up against each other inside her. Was Abuela able to talk? Did the doctors speak Spanish? Did they have her hooked up to a machine with a screen and zigzag lines? Was this all just a passing thing, or had the stroke left Abuela changed for good?

"Carmelo can handle things," her dad told her mom. "Have some coffee."

Jade wished her parents would say something to her, too. Beside her, Katerina was still quiet as a shadow. The two of them were on the outside of their parents' conversation, as if separated by an invisible wall. But this discussion affected them, and they were here at the table, too.

Her mom put another bite of egg in her mouth, swallowed hard, and looked at her dad. "Carmelo can handle *some* things," she said. "But Mamá needs *me*. You know that."

"Sol." Her dad took her mother's hand, steadied it on top of her napkin. The gray-blue owl embroidered on it stared up at them. "Have some coffee." Her dad said it so quietly it was almost a whisper.

After a moment, her mom pulled her hand out from under her dad's and cupped the mug in both her palms. Swaying tendrils of steam rose from it. Her mom's finger traced the raised, glossy designs that Jade had seen so many times—sunny flowers, curling vines, plops of glaze for berries.

"It's just there's the New York project, too," her mom said, watching the mug, but still not drinking from it. "I'm supposed to go next week."

The New York project? That must be the story her mom had been working on all those late nights recently.

"Then postpone the New York trip," said her dad. "Don't worry about it." He was speaking with the calm and authority that had been restored to him ever since he heard about his job.

"I can't push it back, Chris," she said, looking up at him. "I have everything lined up. I'll fly to Chicago tomorrow morning and be back in just a few days so I can head out to New York again in time for the trip."

That sounded like a lot. No wonder her mom was worked up.

"Sol," her dad said. "Drink the coffee."

Katerina silently twirled a single tiny piece of egg with her fork.

Her mom lifted the mug and took a sip, the steam swirling across her face. "Ahhh," she said, and closed her eyes, setting the mug back down. "You put cinnamon in."

That was the difference in the coffee smell today. It had cinnamon, like the café de olla her abuelos used to serve with pan dulce at the Casa Azul.

"You needed some comfort food," her dad said, patting her mom's shoulder as he stood up to clear the table.

Her mother sat there, quiet at last, running her fingers over the painted mug and sipping the cinnamon coffee. She stayed planted in her seat, and Jade's dad saw them out the door.

*

Jade gave Ms. Jackson the signed release form in home-room, but she still needed a doctor's note before she could actually start going to practice. Her dad was taking care of that. When school let out and Caitlyn, Emily, and Chloe gathered to get into Ms. Jackson's jeep, Jade gave Chloe a quick hug and told her, "I'll be there next time. Promise."

She couldn't wait to start. Especially now—with her house full of things unsaid, silences she had to step around—she craved that freedom of running, of pushing through the burning in her legs to revel in the whoosh of the wind, of letting it all fall away.

Before Chloe climbed up into the jeep, with one foot on the pavement and one foot on the doorstep of the car, she turned to Jade and said, "You okay?" She said it in a matter-of-fact way that Jade appreciated. The question surprised her, though. Was it written across her face that something was off, that there was a little storm cloud at home that threatened to burst open and unleash a deluge at any moment? Had Chloe seen this on her face all day?

Jade clutched her backpack straps and pulled them for-ward, and said, "Yeah, I'm okay. It's just—my abuela, you know. Apparently, she had a stroke. Whatever that means. And my mom is leaving for a few days, and I don't know what's going on, and—" She stopped because she could feel herself talking faster, her voice getting higher.

"Gotcha," said Chloe, nodding slowly. "Call me if you want." She stayed there a moment longer, her head tilted slightly, before climbing into the jeep and closing the door. As they pulled out of the parking lot she waved at Jade, and Jade knew she had meant it.

Jade held Katerina's small, warm hand all the way home through the Wildcat Trail.

"Mommy's not going to be gone very long," said Katerina. She said it like a statement, but also like she wanted Jade to answer her. Up ahead, a couple of middle school boys a little younger than Jade were kicking a soccer ball between them in zigzags across the dirt.

Jade wanted to reassure Katerina, but she didn't know how. It was comforting to know that she and her sister were in this together, with some of the same things on their minds, even if Katerina was little and didn't understand as much.

She squeezed her sister's hand and said, "That's what Mommy said."

She breathed in the forest air, and the sturdy oaks comforted her. She wondered if the mirror in her dresser drawer could answer some of the questions she had. Could its smoky veins reveal something that the grown-ups wouldn't tell her?

They emerged from the trail out into the bright wideness of the backyard and the driveway, and Jade's dad opened the back door like he had been waiting for them.

"You're going to love the snack I got for you," he said, when they reached the back stoop.

Jade and Katerina hurried inside.

The surprise was on the kitchen counter: a huddle of ladybug-shaped chocolates with shiny red-and-gold wrappers, and a tall, hexagonal box of Chocolate Abuelita. The strikingly pale abuela on the side of the box was raising a porcelain cup of hot chocolate and smiling out over her glasses. Jade and Katerina slid their backpacks off and headed straight for them—Katerina to the ladybugs, Jade to the Chocolate Abuelita.

"Thought it was time for some comfort food for you girls, too," her dad said.

Opening the box, Jade drew out the top tablet. She pulled off the crackly paper wrapper and smiled at the familiar pattern of triangles on the hexagonal bar. This was hands down her favorite chocolate. It was supposed to be for making hot chocolate, but Jade preferred to eat it solid.

"I thought these were only for Christmas!" said Katerina, unwrapping her first ladybug. They were just like the ones their grandma in Nebraska always arranged on the mantel in her house at that time of year, so it looked like the ladybugs were making a pilgrimage to see the Nativity. She said they reminded her of her days as a college girl traveling in Switzerland.

"I got this on Buford Highway," her dad said to Jade, pointing to the bar of chocolate she was holding. "I'll have to take you girls soon. They have all kinds of food—Mexican, Vietnamese, Indian . . . They even have pan dulce."

Jade bit into the hard chocolate with her molars and gnawed. It had that perfect, cinnamony flavor, and the sweet shavings melted as she chewed. It tasted a lot like the coffee from this morning smelled—but so much better than coffee actually tasted.

"This is awesome, Dad," she said.

Katerina took a bite and did a little dance. "Thank you, Daddy!" she said. She raised her arms and their dad scooped her up into a hug.

Jade took her chocolate outside to the back stoop. Abuelo once told her there was a chocolate factory not far from San Juan de las Jacarandas, the town where he and Abuela had grown up, and that if you drove by during work hours, even with the windows up, the sweetness would come and inhabit your car and make it smell like chocolate for miles.

Abuelo had described the cacao trees, too. And he had told her that Mexicans invented chocolate. But he had used so many lush words—words that Jade didn't know—to describe the trees and their power-packed pods, that she hadn't quite been able to form an image in her head. What she did understand from Abuelo was that by the time a piece of chocolate arrived in eager hands, people often forgot about the Mexicans—the ones who had invented chocolate and who sometimes still made it behind factory walls.

The golden light undulated behind the row of pines. All at once, Jade realized that it wasn't the light. It was the jaguar, pacing elegantly behind the trees, his spotted hide coming in and out of view between their trunks.

Jade wrapped the uneaten half of her chocolate in its paper wrapper and set it beside her on the stoop. She glanced inside the house through the screen door and saw her dad and Katerina absorbed in a puzzle. Katerina was sorting pieces by color and trying to eat her ladybug chocolate at the same time.

Jade looked back at the trees. She was sure of what she had seen, but she couldn't see the jaguar's golden fur anymore. He must have headed into the thick of the forest.

She knew for certain now that if she wanted to hear what the jaguar had to say to her, if she wanted to learn the things the grown-ups wouldn't tell her, she had to find him.

She headed for the trees.

She saw a flash of Itztli's golden fur when she reached the edge of the forest and stepped into the dark green brush beneath the pines. She hurried forward and was almost ashamed of how much noise she made. The jaguar forged ahead soundlessly, his gait assured, his ringed spots darting in and out of sight through the trees. Jade tried to imitate him, stepping lightly through the ivy and over twisting roots. She pushed aside tall stalks of ironweed with their wide leaves and their delicate pink crowns, and her shoes brushed the purple flowers and green berries on the monkey grass. It was even cooler here, under the dense canopy, than it was on the trail. It was nearly September now, and at last the August heat was waning.

All at once the stream opened up before her. It was the place where he had led her before. The jaguar came into full view on the other side and looked at her with his amber eyes. All the woodsy activity around them—the chattering squirrels, the calling cardinals, the startled cooing doves—seemed to stop for a moment, as if in reverence of the great cat, who stood with sureness and majesty beside the stream.

Despite his fearsome frame, Jade recognized the friendly, inviting twinkle of the old man's eyes, which seemed to smile out at her. She began to smile back, to return his greeting, and as she did so she saw that in fact he *was* the old man now, in his knotted white tunic, leaning augustly on his serpentine staff.

"So, you have come again," he said, smiling softly. His dark, wrinkled hands were folded calmly atop the staff, just as before. "I have much to tell you," he said. "But, Chalchihuite." Jade drew her breath in at the sound of her name—the name that he and her abuelos had for her. It was still a surprise, coming from Itztli. "Something is troubling you." His brow furrowed and he peered at her with his bright black eyes, as if trying to discern what it was with his gaze. "Tell me," he said. "Tell me what is troubling you."

This was the second time today that someone had asked her that—first Chloe and now Itztli. Both times it had caught her off guard and jolted her out of the habit she was in, of trying to keep these thoughts inside. Abuela's illness, what needed to be done, and what would happen next—these were grown-up concerns, right? She wasn't supposed to worry about them, right?

Even as she had these thoughts, Jade knew they weren't quite true. More and more she had to admit that she was no longer content to let her parents and the adults do all the worrying, and all the *doing*. Jade wanted to do something, too. She didn't want to be left out anymore. She wanted to help. But she didn't know how.

Itztli lowered himself carefully down to the soft stream bank and sat with his legs folded beneath him. Jade understood that she was supposed to sit, too; it felt strange, disrespectful, to remain standing while he sat. So she found a seat among the roots and ferns on her side of the stream and lowered herself to the bank, letting her legs dangle just above the quietly chattering water.

She might as well answer him honestly if it was written all over her face. She watched the smooth brown stones in the stream as the water hopped and swirled over and around them. She tried to put words to what was bothering her—"troubling her," to use Itztli's phrase. He sat patiently, expectantly, across from her, his hands folded over his white tunic, and Jade felt that she could open up to him, could accept his invitation. She had a hunch that he was a grown-up who would understand, who wouldn't ask her for explanations, and who would tell her things that others wouldn't say.

"I guess what's bothering me is that—I'm afraid," she began. Her words surprised her even as they left her mouth. She hadn't said this to anyone—not even to herself. She wasn't sure how to continue. She looked up at Itztli. He was watching her with his calm, concerned dark eyes and with a patience that assured Jade that he would wait as long as it took for her to get her words out.

"I'm afraid of what might happen to Abuela. And my mom," she said at last. She let the words flow out over the stream, settle onto the stones, get lost in the current. "No one has told me how Abuela is doing," she went on. "I don't even know if she can talk or not. And when Abuelo died, no one told me back then either, that anything was wrong. Not until the day he died."

She remembered going with her mom to her abuelos' house in Pilsen on what she now knew was one of the last days of Abuelo's life, and seeing only Abuela in the sitting room. Her mom had been pregnant with Katerina then, and she kept stroking her bulging belly in the floral armchair where she sat, as if to protect it from something. It was a small room with family photos of people Jade knew and people she didn't know, crowding one another on every inch of the walls. As she and her mother sat there that afternoon, Jade had felt as if all those people were watching them.

Abuelo had stayed in the bedroom the whole time they sat there talking. An unnamed tension permeated the room, the way her mom and Abuela spoke in hushed tones, the way Abuela gave Jade little half smiles every once in a while, the kind where her eyes stayed sad and didn't crinkle at the corners.

"I get it," Jade told Itztli. "I get why no one told me back then. How do you tell a six-year-old that someone is about to die? How do you even explain what that means?"

Itztli nodded slowly.

"But I still wish I had gotten to say goodbye," she said. She flicked a tiny twig beside her knee into the creek and watched the current sweep it away. The little stick got caught for a second between two pebbles, but the inexorable stream quickly pushed it through, and it continued to rush away, out of sight.

"When I saw Abuelo's body in the casket at the funeral, I knew that wasn't really him anymore," said Jade, looking up at Itztli. "By that time, Abuelo was already gone."

She had been holding her mother's hand when she walked up to see the open casket, her mother's great belly, pregnant with Katerina, preceding them. The church had been packed; it seemed like the whole neighborhood was there. Jade had felt that all these people were almost like intruders. Who were they to witness Abuelo resting like that in his final sleep? But these strangers each greeted Abuela and seemed to know her intimately, and Jade marveled at how many people Abuelo's life had touched who she had no idea about. Jade never once saw Abuela cry that day, but she did see her clutching her wooden rosary beads and never letting go.

"They had marigolds on the casket," Jade went on. She had stood on her tiptoes to peer inside.

Abuelo's hair had been combed and his mustache waxed, fixed in place. The body had been yellow. Jade had stared in fascination, squeezing her mother's hand tighter and tighter until her mother pulled her away.

"There was just no way that was him," she said to Itztli. "The Abuelo I knew was gone." The Abuelo she knew pulled on his mustache when he was thinking, when he was searching for the right word, even if he knew she might not understand it. The Abuelo she knew showed her how to play with a balero, how to swing the wooden colorfully striped cylinder just so and catch it on the rod attached to it by a long string. The Abuelo she knew didn't lie immobile, waiting for people to gawk at him, mutter prayers over him. The Abuelo she knew was gone.

"He used to tell me all these stories," she said, "and I didn't know . . . I didn't know one day they would end." Of all the stories Abuelo told, not a single one was about the steel mill outside Chicago, where he had worked most of his life in the US before he and Abuela opened the restaurant. Jade's mom had explained to her later, in matter-of-fact tones over a cup of strong coffee on the gray morning after the funeral, that it was the steel mill that had pounded him slowly into the grave.

"And your abuelo," said Itztli, "where was he laid to rest?"

"In San Juan de las Jacarandas," said Jade. "In Mexico." She plucked a small handful of dirt from the ground and let it fall between her fingers, remembering how Tío Carmelo and five other sturdy men had borne Abuelo's casket down the aisle at the end of the funeral, a corrido playing from the speakers. The song told them to bury Abuelo in his beloved, beautiful Mexico, even though he died far away.

Outside the church, a yawning hearse received the body and carried it to the airport.

"My mom told me that he's buried beneath a double headstone," Jade went on. "Abuela's name is written on the other side."

There it was now, the reality of it, out there floating over the stream. She hadn't quite said it, but it was clear: She was afraid that Abuela was going to die. Most of all, she was afraid that she was going to die like Abuelo had died, suddenly, and Jade wouldn't have a chance to say goodbye to her either. And there was another fear, too, one she couldn't bring herself to say at all. She was afraid that if Abuela died, the stories would be gone for good. Whatever stories she couldn't quite remember that Abuelo had told her, whether because she was too little or because she hadn't understood the Spanish or because she hadn't known to listen closely, surely Abuela still knew them. But if she was gone, too . . .

Tears stung her eyes and threatened to come forward, but she blinked them back.

"Chalchihuite," said Itztli. "Your abuelo's body may lie in San Juan de las Jacarandas. But *you* can keep his memory alive."

Jade nodded, but she wasn't really sure what he meant. She didn't look directly at him, afraid the tears would flood forward and rush down her cheeks at any moment. She concentrated on a very drab, very small brown rock in the stream just beside her left shoe.

"And your abuela—ha!" He gave a little sound that surprised Jade, because it was almost like a laugh. She looked up. "She is still alive!" Itztli said, spreading his arms wide. "She has not yet given up her last breath!"

Jade wondered whether the old man was talking about himself, too. He was smaller and more wrinkled than any grown person Jade had ever seen, and yet here he was, sitting calmly by the sun-dappled stream, his arms wide like a heron about to take flight, listening to her.

"And you, Chalchihuite," he said, bringing his arms down and folding his hands again. "There are a great many things you can learn. A great many things I wish to tell you. But you must listen." His eyes were kind but serious, his voice firm like when her mother told her to do something.

Jade straightened her back. She was ready. "I want to learn, Itztli," she said. "Please tell me a story. I'll listen. I promise."

Itztli's face softened, and his friendly, familiar smile eased itself onto his lips again.

He reached for something to his side; it was a small ceramic bowl. It looked like it was made of the red earth that was just beneath the dark brown surface in these parts. A fine blue powder glinted inside it, and the bowl fit perfectly in Itztli's cupped palm. More artist's tools were laid out with care on the ground as well—a paintbrush made of a slim rod of elegant golden wood tipped with fine bristles and a smooth stick that had been whittled to a polished roundness at one end. Perhaps Itztli had had more time to prepare, since this time he had known she would come.

Jade took in the tools with the same thrill she used to feel when she looked in the window of the art supply shop on the way to the lake in Chicago. She loved the *potential* of these instruments, the infinite possibilities of what could be made with them. But mostly she loved how beautiful the supplies themselves were, the oil pastels with their tips not yet worn down, the wooden paintbrushes of every size with their metal bands not yet encrusted with paint. Sometimes she had lingered at that shop window, watching the tools and colors mingle with her own reflection in the display glass.

A large strip of bark was propped against the trunk of a young oak, its pale, curved underside that was nearly as white as paper facing out. Would that be Itztli's canvas today? The forest had already dusted smooth the dirt and clay where he etched his map that first day. She leaned forward and tried not to blink; she didn't want to miss any of this.

Cradling the small bowl gently in his palm, Itztli dipped its ceramic lip into the stream and let a single curl of water swirl in, like broth into a ladle. With the smooth stick's round end, he blended together the sparkling blue dust with the stream water. The blue danced slow circles in the water until the liquid turned a deep, dark blue, nearly purple. It reminded Jade of how Abuela mixed salsa made from dark red chile de árbol after boiling it and scraping out the pulp, how she ground the pulp and the water together in her three-legged molcajete that she had once told Jade was made of red-hot lava turned to rock.

The liquid in the bowl now looked like fine ink. Itztli dipped his brush in it, and in his hand it was as delicate as a fountain pen. He began painting on the bark, and as he painted, he spoke.

"I grew up knowing a secret," he said. He painted a long, sure stroke in an inverted arc. The bark drank up the blue ink.

"I grew up in a small town near Lake Pátzcuaro. I grew up with many languages around me, many peoples, each with their own story of where they came from. I grew up knowing that the mighty Mexica, the Aztec Empire, were sworn enemies of our people—my mother's people—the Purépecha."

Jade remembered what he had told her the first time they met—that the Aztecs, the Mexica, were every bit as much of an iron-fisted empire as any. "Are these the same people you told me about before?" she said. "The ones who settled in the cave with the eagle and the jaguar?"

Itztli shook his head. "Those are my people, too. But my mother's people, the Purépecha, were another people, with another language." He kept painting, making the curved swath of blue wider and wider on the bark. "The secret was that my father, who died before I was born, was Mexica."

He paused for a moment, examining the bark. The freshest lines he painted were dark and thick; the first ones were paling as they dried. Jade tried to see his face, but all she could see was part of his profile as he examined his work.

"My mother told me this," he went on, "and because of where we lived, it had to be a secret. But my mother also told me"—here he turned to Jade, holding his blue-tipped paintbrush aloft—"that I must never *ever* be ashamed of this secret."

Jade nodded because it felt like he was telling *her* to never ever be ashamed of something—though of what exactly, she wasn't sure.

"In many ways it was hardly a real secret," he said, shrugging a little. He dipped his paintbrush back in the ink again and swirled it around slowly. "I had a Nahuatl name—Itztli—not a Purépecha name. A strange name, and the other kids made fun of me for it. My mother told me that she named me Itztli—'Obsidian'—because on the night I was born, the lake shimmered black and beamed back to the stars their shifting, rippling reflections."

Itztli. *Obsidian*. Like Itzpapalotl, the Obsidian Butterfly-Woman. And like the mirror she kept in her dresser, which she was certain had to be obsidian, too.

"My mother always told me, *Your father was not just Mexica, just like you are not just Mexica, or Purépecha, like me, or anything else. Your family comes from many places.*" Itztli turned to Jade. "My father was Mexica, but his people were also the People of the Eagle Cave."

"How is that?" said Jade.

"Do you remember how the Mexica took over the lands of the People of the Eagle Cave?"

"Yes," said Jade. She had been so surprised to learn that the Mexica, too, had taken lands from people.

"Well, my father grew up there, in the lands of the Eagle Cave, but under the Mexica rule," said Itztli. "His family came from both peoples. They all spoke with the same tongue. When people live together in the same place, it is hard to keep everyone separate."

Jade thought she understood. People sometimes tried to pin down where she was from, as if there should be one answer and that should be it. She always felt this when she had to pencil in the ovals beside race and ethnicity on the standardized tests they had to take at school each year. None of the options ever felt exactly right. She didn't enjoy filling in those ovals, solidly and completely, staying inside the lines, but she did it anyway.

"In the evenings before I went to bed, my mother told me in whispers about my father," said Itztli. "He was a jaguar warrior for the Mexica. He was the most courageous of them all, she told me. He stood at the side of Moctezuma, the emperor, when the strange bird came, with the mirror for a head, and the ruler peered into it and saw that the Spanish were coming. My father was there when the Spaniards arrived in Tenochtitlán, when they came in on their horses on the causeway into the island city, the Tlaxcaltecas just behind them. The Tlaxcaltecas had joined the Spanish because they wanted to overthrow the Mexica, like so many other nations who writhed like the snake in the beak of their empire."

Jade tried to picture it all, but it was hard. A strange bird with a mirror for a head? Was it an obsidian mirror, like the one she had?

She remembered that first drawing on the ground, how Itztli had etched the beak of the Mexica eagle clamping mercilessly down on the snaking paths among the watery hills.

"My father was there when the Spaniards attacked the people in the temple when they were dancing," Itztli went on. "He led the warriors who drove the Spanish into retreat. And he was there, in front, when the Spanish came back again with the Tlaxcaltecas and their other allies from the nearby lands, and they took the city for good, bloodying and muddying the gorgeous lake city and its minutely tended island gardens. It was then that he died, his great jaguar headdress bouncing to the ground as he fell."

Itztli set the paintbrush down in the inkwell and folded his hands. "Or at least—that is what my mother told me," he said.

They were quiet for a moment, letting the ever-traveling water fill the silence. Itztli wasn't painting right now, and

Jade wished he were, so she could see better what he was telling her. That curved swath of blue was all he had painted so far.

Itztli's story made it sound like his father was a great hero, who was there at all the major moments when the Spaniards and their allies came to take the Mexica capital. Was that really what had happened?

"Do you believe what your mother told you?" said Jade. She didn't want to question what he thought he knew about his father, who he had never met. If stories were all Itztli had of him—not even memories—then they must be very precious. But she also wanted to know if he believed it all.

Itztli didn't answer right away. "This is what my mother told me," he said at last. "Whether it is true or not—or whether the story can be told another way—that is another question. My mother told me these stories at night, just before I fell asleep, and sometimes I fell asleep and the story continued, and I didn't know if I was dreaming or still hearing what she was telling me."

He looked into the inkwell, as if he saw something more there. Suddenly he shook himself, and the paintbrush.

"These were our secret stories, between my mother and me," he said. "But my mother's people, the Purépecha, we were never conquered by the Mexica. Not once did we let that eagle clamp its beak on us." He held his brush proudly aloft.

What must it feel like, to be part of a *we* that rejected something you knew was a part of yourself, too?

"Even when the Spaniards came to my mother's people, and they submitted to their rule—even then, we did not lose

ourselves—not completely," Itztli continued. "The Spaniards stripped so much from us, but go to the mountains of
Michoacán today, and you will hear our language still."

Jade wondered what had brought him here, so far from
his homeland.

"My mother made sure to tell me the story of us
Purépecha, of our god, Curicáueri, and our goddess,
Xaratanga, of where we came from," he went on, and he
turned back to the pale bark, the blue-inked tip of his
brush poised just above its surface.

The new words he was saying sounded different from
the words he had been using just now, and in his first
story. They were not from the same language. There was
an ease and gentleness to how he said these, like they were
words he had known forever. Jade listened closely to try to
catch them all. She knew she wouldn't be able to, but she
wanted to try anyway. She was glad to see that he was
painting again.

Beside the curved blue swath that had already dried, he
painted a tall form. Was it an oak?

"My mother told me about the oak trees that let us con-
nect with the gods," he continued, "and how you must use
wood from an oak to keep the fires alive in the temples to
Curicáueri."

Above and behind him, Itztli was surrounded by oaks,
the same ones she and her dad had talked about on their
walk yesterday. Maybe Itztli had chosen this spot because
of them.

"The god Curicáueri and the goddess Xaratanga
appeared to our rulers ages ago and told them that Lake

Pátzcuaro and the lands that hugged its shores were theirs to rule. The gods appeared to them in their sleep and told them this."

There were two oaks in the painting now, one on either side of what looked like a bend in a flowing stream, like the one she and Itztli were sitting on either side of now. Jade marveled at how quickly he made forms bloom on the bark. He was painting people now, gathered near each of the oaks. Jade watched him ink their seated forms, their hair, their faces, with the fine tip of his brush. She took note of the way he held his wrist, the way he gripped the brush firmly but lightly in his worn, practiced fingers.

Some of the people in the painting had their eyes open, and some had them closed. There were men and women, and many appeared to be resting. Their forms outlined against the pale bark reminded Jade of the designs on the blue-and-white ceramic bowls at home that were from the Casa Azul.

Itztli lifted his brush from the painting, and Jade leaned in and peered more closely.

"What do you see?" said Itztli.

Jade looked up at him, startled. He was gesturing with his palm open toward the bark and the blue forms he had just painted there with brushstrokes that were beginning to dry.

She took a deep breath. His eyes were kind and he was smiling softly; she tried not to think of this as a test. Looking back at the painting, she tried to read it.

"Two of the sleeping people are bigger than the others," she said. "Does that mean they are more important?" she guessed.

Itztli nodded, his smile broadening a little, and folded his hands. Encouraged, Jade went on. "The only people who are standing instead of resting look like they're talking to the bigger sleeping people, because they are pointing to them. These people standing—are they the gods?"

Again, Itztli nodded. This was going well so far.

"There is a stream—and land," she said. "And there's a hill." It was in the inner elbow of the bend in the stream. "It looks like a watery hill," she said. She looked at the people and the land together. The larger sleeping people held their heads in their hands, but it almost looked as if their hands were also cupping their ears, to hear the gods better. "These people . . . ," she said, not knowing how to explain what she was thinking. The people in the painting, resting and listening, seemed to be somewhere between wakefulness and sleep, as if they existed on another plane from this landscape. "It's like they're *in* the landscape—but also somewhere else, at the same time," she said, and she looked up at Itztli to see if she had gotten it right.

Itztli's smile was content and satisfied, but even so it didn't quite reassure Jade that she had gotten it right. Maybe there was no right answer. Maybe it was like he had said—there were so many different ways to tell a story, even the story of a painting.

Itztli repositioned himself on the ground so he was seated with his back resting against the oak that his painting was propped against. The entirety of his slight body seemed to have relaxed.

"You read very well, Chalchihuite," he said.

Jade smiled and tried not to look too proud of herself. Itztli's painting was unlike any she had ever seen before, and she had been able to read it, with his help. Now she wanted nothing more than to be able to paint one like it.

"Itztli, where did you learn to paint like this?" she said.

Itztli chuckled and turned back to his painting. With quick strokes he made little footprints at the side of the bark-page that walked right up to the edge, as if the story didn't end there, but instead kept going, off the page. "There is a long, long tradition of painting in Mexico," he said, "even though the Spanish burned most of our books. And I began to paint when I was very, very young. In fact, I was so good that when I was of age, I went to Tzintzuntzan, the Purépecha capital on Lake Pátzcuaro, and they asked me to paint a history of the Purépechas."

He looked over his shoulder at Jade.

"Of course they did," she said, grinning. How could anyone see him paint and not want him to paint for them? "So, you painted a history?" she said. She had so much to add to her green notebook. She wanted to draw a picture like this one, where people were both bound and not bound to the physical space around them. She had felt like that when she ran for Ms. Jackson—like she was connected to the place where she was, but also at the same time like she was inhabiting another space somehow, beyond her immediate surroundings.

"Absolutely," said Itztli. He inked a final footprint deftly onto the bark and pulled away from his painting to examine it. He looked proud, but also pensive. His dark eyes shone. He rested his paintbrush in the little clay bowl. "I painted the history that my mother told me," he said.

He put a hand on his knee and reached for his staff to stand up.

It was always hard to watch him move like this. No matter how dexterously he painted, he was still such a creaky old man, and Jade was afraid his small bones might snap if he made a false move.

She took his cue and stood up as well. She felt as if he had welcomed her into a lush sitting room lit by amber stained-glass windows, and she didn't want to overstay her welcome.

"Thank you, Itztli," she said. "But, I want to know—how can I paint a history, too?"

Itztli stooped and gathered his bark painting in his hands. Jade saw how fragile and brittle it was, and her heart leapt suddenly at the thought that he might drop it and have it shatter on the stream bank, its pieces sliding down and away with the current.

"You must first listen to the stories, Chalchihuite," he said. "Only then can you paint them."

He tossed the painting toward her over the stream. Jade had no time to think—she reached up and caught the bark midair, careful even in the act to grasp it lightly in her fingers so it wouldn't break.

When she looked back, she just barely caught sight of Itztli's golden tail as he disappeared into the thick behind the trees.

She held the painting aloft, stunned, and listened to the happy gurgling whispers of the stream as the slanting light played on the eddies.

9

The bark painting caught the honey-colored light that came through the trees as Jade held it gingerly between her fingers. The outside was rough on her fingertips in contrast to the papery smoothness of the painted inner side, which curved slightly with the memory of the contours of the tree it once protected. Jade had seen a few trees with bark like this near the Wildcat Trail—tall, elegant trees dressed in gray and white. She was pretty sure they were called sycamores—her dad would know for certain. Up close, she could better appreciate the fine details of Itztli's brushstrokes: the undulations of the stream, the calm yet alert expressions on the sleeping faces.

With Itztli gone, the animals took over the forest once again. A chipmunk scampered and disappeared into its hole, and Jade heard what might have been an owl hooting, its gentle call low and resonant. She spotted a small rabbit—maybe a baby one—near the chipmunk's hidey-hole. It stood still in profile, its ears straight up, watching Jade, as if by staying still it would make itself invisible.

Jade hurried back to the house, picking her way through the forest and holding the painting out in front of her, making sure not to brush anything with it. She remembered which way to go, even though the trees were dense and the amber light filtered ever more obliquely through the leaves above. She felt she knew the ground, and that she was finding her way to the line of pines by smell, almost, as much as by sight. Up ahead she recognized the tessellated gray-brown bark of the pines, before stepping out into the grass of the backyard.

Her chocolate was still right where she had left it, half eaten in its wrapper on the stoop. She scooped it up as she entered quietly through the back door. Her dad's and Katerina's voices floated softly to her ears from the living room. They were still matching colors and snapping puzzle pieces in place—they hadn't noticed that she had been gone.

Jade tiptoed carefully to her room so they wouldn't hear her. Itztli did it so well, moving silently through the trees and only showing himself when he wanted to. Jade wanted to be able to do that.

She closed her bedroom door and Mortimer meowed. He jumped down from his perch on top of the bookshelf and landed lightly on his soft paws to trot over to her. He watched the painting intently and meowed again.

"I know," said Jade. "I've never seen anything like it either."

She stepped out of her shoes, set the chocolate on her desk for later, and propped the painting carefully on her bookshelf at eye level. She wanted to display Itztli's work properly, at a height where she could scrutinize it, memorize it, and maybe even try her hand at making a picture like it.

It was the first piece of decoration she had put in her new room. She thought of Chloe's room, how the walls shone with the glossy sheen of her posters of singers. Jade didn't have a theme for her room yet, but she liked this as a start.

Mortimer hopped onto her desk and then to the shelf and sniffed the bark, brushing it lightly with his whiskers, as Jade grabbed her notebook and her pack of colored pencils and stretched out on the bed.

She needed to draw—she didn't yet feel prepared to try to paint quite the way Itztli had. For that, she would need better tools. There was no way she could achieve such fine details or make the water seem to ripple on the page with just her colored pencils, with their plasticky exteriors and noisy points.

Still, she wasn't ready to move on from her trusty pencils. She knew what lines she could draw with them, what colors and blends she could make. For now, she would stick with what she knew.

She opened the notebook to the two-page spread where she had last drawn, in shiny pencil, the three watery hills connected by a road of footprints—one for San Juan de las Jacarandas, one for the Casa Azul in Chicago, and one for this house in Atlanta. The lines were begging for color. Forest hues would be best—dark and light green, brown, goldenrod yellow—to fill in the space around the house in Atlanta. With the points of the pencils she drew intricate vines, the outlines of leaves, tree trunks, and branches. She did her best to move her hand with smooth control like Itztli, and to draw long, sure, curving lines that alternated with quick, sharp accents. To be anywhere near as good as Itztli was, she would need to practice a lot.

As soon as the point of her dark green pencil began to dull, she reached for the little wooden sharpener on her desk. Her dad had gotten it for her from the art supply store on the way to the lake in Chicago when he had noticed her lingering in front of its colorful display. Her pencil points needed to stay sharp so she could make lines as fine as those Itztli had painted with the tip of his brush. The curly shavings drifted to the floor beside her bed.

With blue and touches of violet, she drew a snaking stream below the house that stretched to the edges of the page. Tilting the pencils low, she stroked the paper softly with the flat of the color to make overlapping bands like the ones she had seen Itztli paint. The stream cradled the forest. She flecked tiny dashes of bright green onto the stream, too, so it would look like a turquoise jewel glinting in the sun.

Next up, the lake in Chicago: broad blue line upon broad blue line, so that the lake appeared to have many layers, just visible on the rippled surface. It didn't look like Itztli's painting, but maybe an echo of it. Jade was bumping up against the limits of what she could draw with her colored pencils, and she wanted to feel that outer edge, the very most that she could do with them.

Now came the people. She looked up at the bark on the bookshelf. This would be the hardest part.

The most important people were the biggest in Itztli's painting. But who was most important? That was relative. Itztli had made the human rulers larger than the gods.

Abuelo and Abuela, they were certainly important for Jade's map. They should be large on the page.

She hovered a light brown pencil over the watery hill of the restaurant in Chicago for a moment, then changed her mind. Abuelo and Abuela belonged in San Juan de las Jacarandas.

But how to draw them there? She didn't know what their life had been like. When she tried to think of what should go in this space on the picture, her mind grasped at snatches of colors, unfinished shapes. Her heart leapt a little with the fear she had confided to Itztli, that she might lose forever the stories she needed to fill in this part. Her memory held only snippets, like fragments of a ceramic vessel whose complete form she didn't know.

"Jade, I told you not to track in mud!"

Jade jumped and snapped her notebook shut at her mother's voice. She hadn't realized she was home.

The door opened and her mom came in.

"Mom, the door was closed" was the first thing that came to her mind to say.

"Do you see your footprints?" said her mom, pointing to the floor. She was still in her work clothes, but her blouse was untucked and her hair had loosened itself a little from the grip of the hair spray. Jade liked her hair better that way—wavier, freer.

She looked down at the floor where her mom was pointing. There they were: reddish-brown footprints in the shape of the soles of her school shoes.

"Sorry, Mom," she said. "I'll clean it up."

"You've been drawing," her mom said in a softer tone. She was looking at the little pile of forest-colored shavings on the floor by Jade's bed. Jade always felt like her parents weren't quite sure how to encourage her drawing, but they liked that it was something she did. Her grandma was the only one who ever made a big deal out of her liking to draw.

"Yeah," said Jade. Instinctively, she put a hand on her notebook, in case her mom tried to snatch it and see what she had drawn. She wasn't sure whether her mom was still upset with her or not.

Her mother's eye fell on Itztli's painting on the bookshelf. Mortimer was sitting next to it, studiously licking his paws.

Jade watched her mom look at the painting. She hadn't put it there on display with the thought that anyone else might examine it. But she realized she didn't mind. She almost wanted her mom to ask her about it. Even though she knew her mom had so much on her mind right now, Jade wanted her to pay attention to her, too. Maybe they could talk about some of the silent things that neither of them was saying right now.

"Sweetie, get me the mirror," her mom said, her voice still soft, her eyes still on Itztli's painting.

Mortimer glanced up mid-lick, his little pink tongue still halfway out of his mouth. He almost looked as astonished as Jade felt.

Was this really happening? Jade had nearly assumed her mom was never going to bring up the mirror again. That she would have to unlock its secrets without her help. But now here she was, asking her for it, and looking at Itztli's painting nearly as intently as Jade had. Was she going to explain more to her now, about the mirror, and how it might be connected to Itztli and his stories and paintings?

Not wanting to disrupt the moment in case her mom changed her mind, Jade went to her dresser and pulled it out. Her mom kept watching the painting as she did this, and Jade was grateful for this small privacy that her mother allowed her—the privacy of where she kept it. Her mom might barge into her room unannounced as if Jade were still a little kid, but she let her keep some things to herself. And the mirror was hers now.

"Here, Mom," she said, holding it out.

Her mother turned to look at it and Jade thought she looked comforted by the sight of it. Her mom took it in her hand and rubbed her thumb over it, just the way Jade had so many times, in a kind of reverential caress.

Not taking her eyes off the mirror, her mom sat down on Jade's bed. Jade pushed her notebook aside and sat beside her. Her mom had invited herself fully into her space at this point, but Jade decided now was not the time to try to tell her that she would prefer it if she knocked first and asked if she could sit on the bed. She was too curious to hear what her mom might tell her.

She watched her mom, waiting. Mortimer was waiting, too. From far away on the other end of the house, she heard Katerina say, "Does this piece go here, Daddy?"

"Abuela gave me this when I was your age," said her mom, still looking at the mirror in her hands. "She told me that it's made from thick lava that ran fast as a water-fall from the erupting summit of the volcano near their town, lava that cooled just as quickly to glass before it reached the bottom."

The volcano. Abuelo had described it to Jade one time. How it still smoked sometimes; how it was so tall that you could always see it in the distance from the agave fields; how when it was awake and grumbling, the smoke rose even above the clouds that encircled it.

Jade had never heard her mom talk about this volcano—or about San Juan de las Jacarandas at all, for that matter. But now she was telling Jade how this mirror was made from a burning river that had been expelled from the entrails of the earth where her family was from—just like the molcajete that Abuela used to crush chiles and blend them into salsa and mole.

"That happened ages ago," her mom said. "Four hundred or five hundred years ago. That is how obsidian is made."

It really *was* obsidian.

"Mamá told me that when she was a girl she saw the mountain belch one time, and it was like the earth letting off steam and reminding everyone not to take this solid ground for granted," her mother said. She turned the mirror over and this time she looked at it as if watching something reflected in it.

Jade was still, afraid that if she moved she might interrupt the flow from whatever font had come untapped inside her mother that made her talk like this. She had so many questions she hoped her mom would answer without her having to ask. Where did Abuela get this mirror? How did she know what it was made from? How long had Abuela had it? How long had her family had it?

"Not long after Mamá gave it to me, I met the owls," her mom said.

"Um—*what?*" said Jade. This was too much. Had she met owls who were like Itztli? People who were also animals? Was that what happened when you got the mirror?

"I met the owls," her mom repeated, looking at her. "Well, the tecolotes."

Jade nodded, even though there was still so much she didn't understand.

The word *tecolotes* in her mother's mouth surprised her almost as much as the mention of the owls. Her mom hardly ever said anything in Spanish to her, as if it was the domain of the abuelos, as if the language wasn't quite hers to share. The word made Jade think of more than just the owls outside that hooted softly in the evenings from their unseen perch or that sailed gracefully from tree to tree with outstretched wings. It made her think of the gray-blue papier-mâché owl perched on her mother's dresser that watched the room with bright eyes painted like starbursts, ever alert. It had been such a fixture for all of Jade's life that she had never thought to wonder where it came from. Her mom only ever referred to it, very occasionally, as her tecolote, never as her owl.

"There were three of them," her mom said, looking back at whatever she saw in the mirror. "Gray spotted owls, as large as hawks, with big, round, friendly faces. I was in the park on the corner by the abuelos' house—the one with the swings, you know?"

Jade knew the park, the one near the bright mural of the people gardening, across from the grocery store in Pilsen.

"They swooped in from three directions, low and silent," said her mom, "and perched in the tallest tree and waited for me. Those owls"—she stopped for a moment, left something unsaid—"they understood me," she said. "And I understood them."

Jade was still and silent as the rabbit she had seen in the woods. Her mom was all facts and no-nonsense journalism. Not in a million years could Jade have imagined her mother having adventures and communing with spotted owls. But then again, she could never have imagined that she would have met a jaguar who was also an old man in the forest behind her house either.

"Were they—just owls?" Jade ventured, hoping her question didn't interrupt her mom's story.

Her mom shook her head. "No, they weren't just owls," she said. "They were"—she cocked her head a little to the side and looked at Jade—"they were guides."

Jade nodded again, even as many more questions swelled inside her. If the tecolotes were guides, what had they guided her about, or to? And was Itztli Jade's guide?

"Mamá got really worried," said her mom, smiling into the mirror like she was remembering. "She looked all over the neighborhood for me. Eventually she found me, of course. Sitting in a low V in the branches of the oak tree at the edge of the park, with the tecolotes."

Jade looked into the mirror, too. She tried to see whatever her mom was seeing. All she saw were their two faces reflected in it, sliding around on the smoky surface.

Jade had been so certain that what she had experienced with Itztli was all her own. And maybe it still was. But now she was sure that if the mirror had brought about her mother's encounter with the tecolotes, it must have brought about her own encounters with Itztli, too. What she had seen and heard by the stream in the forest behind her house was bigger than just her. How long had the mirror been passed down? How many other guides had lent their wisdom to her family, in how many different forms?

"The owls are *my* business," her mom said suddenly, straightening her back as though returning to her normal self. "And what the mirror does for *you*, Jade, that is yours."

Jade felt her eyes go wide. It was one thing for her mom to talk about her own experiences, and that was shocking enough, but it was quite another for her to mention Jade's.

Her mom handed her the mirror, pressing it decisively into her palm. It was still warm from where she had held it. Jade clasped her hands around it and understood that this was the end of that part of the conversation. That was all her mother was going to tell her.

Jade pressed her palms against the smooth surface of the mirror to contain its warmth. "Mom?" she said. She wanted to ask her something—but not about the owls.

"Yes, honey?"

"I know you're going to see Abuela tomorrow."

"Yes." Her mom blinked a long blink.

"Is she—can she talk?" said Jade. "Do you know?"

"Yes. I talked to Tío Carmelo today, and he said that she can talk. That it's very difficult for her and tires her out, but she can talk. The doctors say it will take a long time for her to recover fully, but yes, Jade, she can talk."

Jade let out a long, windy breath. "That's good," she said. She had been so afraid that she might never be able to speak with Abuela again, might never be able to hear her stories.

"Thank you," her mom said, and all at once she was standing up.

"For what?" said Jade.

"I needed to see the mirror," she said. "I didn't know it, but your painting reminded me."

They both looked at Itztli's painting again. It seemed to belong there on her shelf.

"I don't know where you've been, but you need to clean up that mud," said her mom. She was pointing with her socked foot to one of Jade's muddy footprints and pulling her navy blazer together in front as she did so. As she headed to the door, her mother's gaze found the mirror again for just a moment. Then she was out the door.

Jade stared after her. She couldn't believe how quickly her mom had gone back to her normal self. She said, "Yes, Mom," softly, even though she was already out of earshot. Mortimer jumped down from the bookshelf and onto the bed and curled himself up next to her, on top of her closed notebook.

Jade shook herself and stood up. She tried to think what would be best to clean the floor with. Some old towels in the bathroom might do the trick.

She was still holding the mirror in her palm and she caught sight of her distorted reflection, her poufy hair, and her light eyes. Itztli's painting was reflected, too, and the people in the painting seemed to float and move behind the smoky veins.

If Itztli was supposed to guide her, he was already doing that. He was showing her how to paint stories, and he was helping her see that her abuelos' stories did not have to be lost.

Itztli had said that Abuela was still here. And her mom had said that Abuela could still talk.

Jade *had* to talk to her. She had to ask for her stories. Abuela had never been the talkative one—Abuelo was. Abuela always called him parlanchín—chatty. But Jade needed to know. She needed to fill in her map in her notebook, to draw the story of Abuelo and Abuela in San Juan de las Jacarandas, in their early days in Chicago. She couldn't accept that it had all been lost forever when Abuelo died. And she needed to know more about this mirror.

Abuela was still alive, and she could still tell her these things, even if she was miles away in Chicago and recovering from a stroke under merciless hospital lights in a white room with gowns and beeps and cords.

Jade had to know her story.

10

Standing next to her dad on the back stoop in the drowsy morning before school the next day, Jade found it hard to walk away from the house, knowing that in the evening her mom wouldn't be there. Through the screen door she watched Katerina whine at their mom, telling her *Mommy, please don't go,* her little hand bunching up the starchy fabric of her pencil skirt and wrinkling it. Jade was waiting for her turn to say goodbye, but Katerina was taking long enough that they might be late for school.

Their mom was dressed as if for work, but today it was because she was going to be on a plane. Every time she flew for a news story she got dressed up like this, and Jade had come to anticipate the smell of her fresh shampoo and the satiny brush of her mom's nicest blazer against her cheek as they hugged goodbye before a trip. "It's so they treat me right and don't make faces," her mom had told her once. Jade had a hard time imagining how anyone wouldn't take her mother seriously and treat her with respect, but the way her mom had said it, Jade knew she was speaking from experience.

"I won't be gone long," her mom promised Katerina in a lullaby voice, looking down into her dark, shining eyes and smoothing the top of her hair. "It'll be just a few days. You won't even miss me! You'll see. Sh-sh-sh-shhh . . ."

Jade looked away, toward the driveway. Katerina could say what Jade couldn't say. Jade was thirteen years old—she was supposed to be completely fine with her mom leaving for a few days. But she didn't really want her mom to leave her, and she was a little jealous that she got to go back to Chicago. Atlanta, this forest city, was beginning to feel like home now, and Jade didn't want to miss her first cross-country practice. Still, it would be so comforting to see her old neighborhood, and Abuela, even though she was in the hospital. The things happening to her in Atlanta now—Itztli's paintings, the obsidian mirror with its veins like ghost-memories of the lava that had formed it—kept sending her thoughts back, back, back. Back to Pilsen and the bright murals on the sides of the buildings and the parks. Back to the Casa Azul and its smells, the sound of easy chatter as people lingered at the small, square tables, sipping beer or coffee even after they had cleaned their plates. Back even to San Juan de las Jacarandas, a place she had never known and could see only in pieces, remembering what Abuelo had told her.

"Hey, Katerina-Ballerina, you're going to be late for school!" said Jade's dad. "You want to get there in time for the morning songs with Ms. McDade, don't you?"

Somehow, that was what convinced Katerina to loosen her grip and stumble out onto the stoop to take her father's hand.

"Jade," her mom said quietly, holding open the screen door. Behind her the kitchen still held the cozy smell of their hasty breakfast.

Jade stepped forward into her mother's warm hug and put her head on her shoulder like she always did, breathing in the smell of her shampoo.

"You're going to be fine," her mom said, softly enough so only she could hear.

Jade squeezed her back. Before she let go, she said, "I can't go with you, right?" She knew the answer, but she felt she had to ask anyway.

Her mom pulled away from her gently and rubbed her shoulders, looking into her eyes. "No, honey," she said, shaking her head.

"When will I get to see Abuela?" said Jade. "Or at least talk to her?"

Her mom shook her head again. "I can't tell you that, Jade," she said quietly. "But you will get to. I promise." She squeezed Jade's shoulders.

Jade nodded, satisfied enough. She understood that her mom was telling her more than she would tell Katerina, that she was letting her in, even just a little. She wasn't giving Jade the kind of assurances she might have wanted to hear, and it unnerved her a little that her mom wasn't hiding her uncertainty. When Jade was a little kid—or even not that long ago—she had wanted to believe that her parents could be certain about almost everything. She had known that wasn't true, of course—no grown-up could control everything—but a part of her still wanted to believe it, even now.

"Bye, Mom," she said, and she shrugged her shoulders out of her mom's grip and turned around before it got harder to say goodbye. As she headed down the steps to the flagstone path in the grass and hurried after her dad and Katerina toward the Wildcat Trail, she decided to trust what her mom and Itztli had said. She didn't know *when* she would get to see Abuela and hear her stories, but she knew she *would* get to. And she would do everything she could to make sure it happened.

In homeroom Chloe broke away from her conversation with Emily as soon as she saw Jade walk in. Jade hoped Chloe wasn't upset because she hadn't called her, after she had offered. But Chloe didn't look offended, just concerned.

"Is everything okay with your grandma?" said Chloe.

"Um . . . I mean, it's not *okay*, but—I'm okay," said Jade. "Sorry I didn't call. I just—there was a lot going on . . ."

Chloe shook her head and waved it away.

"But—I was thinking," said Jade. "Maybe we could hang out again soon?" A smile began to spread across Chloe's face, and Jade went on. "Maybe my dad could take us to the museum where he works? It sounds pretty cool."

Chloe's face fell a little, and Jade remembered that the words *museum* and *cool* didn't often go in the same sentence together. "They have a garden, too, with all these native plants from around here," Jade added. "That's actually where my dad works." There was no way Chloe could know this, but her dad's love of gardens was infectious. He had a way of leading you through them that made you feel like you were being invited into a hushed, private outdoor room.

"Okay . . . ," said Chloe.

"I don't know, I just feel like it could be fun," said Jade. "My grandma took me and my sister to this museum in Chicago a couple years ago, and we had such a good time."

"You've been thinking a lot about your grandma," Chloe said.

"Yeah," said Jade. "I guess I have." She and Chloe slid into their seats beside each other, and Jade lowered her backpack to the floor.

The day Abuela had taken her and Katerina to the museum for Día de los Muertos, Abuela had pointed out some painted ceramic vases from Mexico and tried to tell them something about them. But Jade had been more interested in other paintings and sculptures, and Katerina had been taken with the colorful swirling skirts and rhythmic footwork of the dancers who swept through the halls.

Chloe wasn't yet on board, but Jade was determined to convince her. This was something they could do while her mom was away. And Jade thought it might make her feel close to Abuela, somehow.

"When my grandma took us to that museum in Chicago," she told Chloe, "at one point I just stood in front of this stained-glass window that looked like the sky with all these galaxies, and I tried to figure out how the artist had made all those shapes in the glass—"

Chloe was smiling now. "Yeah, you *would* geek out on that stuff," she said playfully.

"What makes you say that?"

"I've seen your drawings," said Chloe. "I know you like—art, that kind of thing."

"Wait—you've seen me draw?" Jade hadn't shown her green notebook at home to anyone.

"Of course!" said Chloe. She nudged Jade's backpack with the toe of her shoe.

"Oh! You mean my *doodles*?" Chloe must have seen what she penciled in her school notebooks during class. She filled the borders of the lined pages with swirling organic figures as if illuminating one of those old medieval manuscripts.

"Your *drawings*," Chloe insisted, still grinning. "I'm in! Let's go see this museum. And those plants."

Jade reached over and hugged Chloe. "Thank you!" she said into her neck. Chloe had let her in on her world of delicious rice pudding and an old record player full of memories. Now Jade wanted to let Chloe in on *her* world— one that she herself was piecing together, bit by bit.

Jade's first day of cross-country practice was going to be on Tuesday, the day after Labor Day, and she made plans to go the museum with Chloe the following weekend. By Friday her dad had gotten everything in order for her to run, including after-school for Katerina on the days she didn't have Daisies. He would pick her and Chloe up from practice that first day.

Jade's mom called every evening for the next few days. Jade kept her bedroom door open while her dad took the calls in the kitchen. He mostly listened. Katerina often wandered into Jade's room, and the two of them waited together for their turns on the phone. Jade curled on her bed doing homework or drawing floral and woodsy designs in the blank pages of her green notebook, while Katerina played on the wooden floor with her set of farm animals, a gift from their grandma. The floor became strewn with small, rigid plastic horses, cows, and curly-tailed pigs, like their bedroom floor in the old house in Chicago. Jade had to watch where she stepped, but she didn't mind too much. The toys felt familiar, and she liked how they kept drawing her sister back into her room.

When their dad called out to them and handed them each the phone in the kitchen, it was always first to Katerina and then to Jade. Jade could tell her mom was being chipper with Katerina; she let her daughter chatter on about whatever popped into her head. But when Katerina inevitably started asking when she was coming home, their dad would gently intervene and pass the phone to Jade.

With Jade, her mom didn't pretend not to be tired—and she sounded *so* tired. When Jade asked how Abuela was doing, her mom told her that she was out of the hospital and doing better, but she still needed a lot of care, so she was in a rehab center now. There, nurses in white were helping her do exercises to coax her left leg and arm into working properly again, into lifting them as high as her brain commanded them. Her lips, too, needed practice, and when she smiled, it came out crooked.

"Does she talk much?" Jade asked on the first evening, gripping the phone tightly.

"Yes," her mom answered. And after a pause, "But it just takes her some time, and she gets tired, and sometimes her words sort of blur together."

Jade nodded, even though she knew her mom couldn't see that through the phone. It was hard to be patient; she wanted Abuela to get better right away.

She asked her mom the same question again every night, just when she could sense that her mom was about to say goodbye and ask her to hand the phone back to her dad. On the third night her mom said, "Her words are clearer now. She's going to be fine." Again, Jade decided to trust her. Maybe Abuela wasn't fine right now, but eventually, at some point, she would be.

Nearly every day her mom was away, it rained starting around lunchtime, cloaking the world in a soft gray. By the time school let out, the rain cleared up or waned to a misty drizzle that the sun shone through. When Jade walked Katerina home, their steps squelching in the muddy trail, the nearby stream rushed more loudly than ever before. The mud inked the soles of Jade's shoes with a wet, rust-colored coat. She made sure to brush them off onto the bristly floor mat on the back stoop before stepping inside, and she made sure Katerina did this, too.

On Monday evening Jade found her dad in the kitchen leaning against the countertop, his brow pensive.

"What's up, Jade?" he said softly, straightening up as she came in.

"I know Abuela is going to be okay," said Jade.

Her dad nodded.

"But what does that mean? After a stroke, do you just— go back to being normal?"

Her dad crossed his arms and leaned back against the counter. "Often, the answer is no," he said, looking her in the eyes.

Jade didn't like this answer.

"Sometimes when a person has a stroke, the damage is lasting," her dad went on. "Sometimes it never really goes away. Maybe it's a droop in the face, or a leg that refuses to move quite like the person tells it to. Sometimes it's the words that never fully return."

Jade drew in a sharp breath. "The words?" she said.

"Yes. It's like—a set of gaps that appear in the person's vocabulary, that they try to walk around or cross over as best they can. And the people listening to them have to try to guess what they mean, what might be in those empty spaces, the slid-over words, the names out of place." As he said this, his hands moved like they were tracing a meandering path. How could he speak so specifically about it?

"Is that what happened to Grandpa?" she asked. Jade had no memory of her grandfather, but there was a picture of her as a laughing baby in his arms, her hands clasped together in glee and her grin showing two whole teeth.

"No, Grandpa had a heart attack," he said. "My uncle Charles was the one who had a stroke, a long time ago. But, Jade, there's no telling exactly how it will be for Abuela."

Jade nodded. She tried not to imagine what Abuela would be like when this part was over. "Thanks for telling me," she said.

"Of course."

Jade walked back to her room and tried to tell herself to wait, to just be patient and see what happened. *Then* she could talk to Abuela. But staying patient and just waiting was very hard to do.

She went to her dresser to choose what to wear for cross-country tomorrow. She wanted a distraction from her thoughts, and she wanted to wear exactly the right thing for her very first practice. She had to look cool, like she knew what she was doing, like she belonged with the other girls. Besides, practice was at the high school, so there was the distinct possibility that she might see some high school boys—maybe even Nikos.

As she rummaged, her fingers found a splash of purple, and she pulled it out.

This was it. This was what she would wear.

It was the shirt Abuela bought for her at the Día de los Muertos festival at the museum. It had a big skull made of purple flowers printed on it. That day, Jade had pulled it on over her outfit as she decorated sugar skulls and ate pan de muertos in the museum courtyard. Katerina had twirled beside her, imitating the dancers who performed nearby—the women radiant in their full, whirling skirts, the men dashing in their black-and-silver charro suits.

Jade tried on the shirt in the bathroom mirror, turning to look at herself in profile and sticking her chest out. She liked that her boobs had grown just enough so that the shirt was starting to look tight on her. She rolled up the sleeves like she had seen Chloe do. This shirt would work fine, but when her mom got back—and hopefully that was soon—she was going to ask her to go shopping for some actual running clothes.

When Ms. Jackson's red jeep pulled up to the breezeway the next afternoon, Jade nearly leapt up onto the seat beside Chloe. Packed in with Caitlyn, Emily, and Chloe,

Jade didn't have to say much to feel like she was a part of their flowing banter. By now she recognized most of the names they mentioned, and she laughed along when Emily mimed how Benjamin had used the dissected pig's eye as a bouncy ball in science. It was gross when he'd done it in class, but it was funny watching Emily pretend to do it.

Ms. Jackson was pretty strict in homeroom, but she didn't seem to mind the girls talking loudly over one another now. She drove with the windows down and let the refreshing breeze rush over them. It was a perfect day for running—little puffs of clouds floated in the sky, and the September sun had lost its August bite.

A little stuffed yellow jacket with the letters GT stamped on its side dangled from the rearview mirror. It was curled and indignant, as if poised for attack, but it was also sort of cute with its giant eyes and bobbling antennae. Jade had been in Atlanta just long enough to guess that GT stood for Georgia Tech. She wondered what Ms. Jackson would be like as Coach Jackson, who wanted them to go as far as they could in the state championship, and maybe even win it.

Ms. Jackson stepped on the gas as she merged onto the six-lane highway and maneuvered the jeep between the speedy cars over to the nearly empty HOV lane. As they passed the cars beside them, she turned up the radio loud enough for it to be heard above the wind that now flapped in thunderously through the windows. Caitlyn, Emily, and Chloe raised their voices in a collective "woo-hoo!" as they recognized the song and began to sing along.

It was one of the hits Jade had heard all summer, in stores and on the radio. She didn't know the words very well, but these girls knew the whole thing perfectly—they had done this before. Ms. Jackson didn't sing, but she bopped her head and tapped a finger on the steering wheel. The lead singer's voice rang out, loud and brassy, her tone daring anyone to cross her. The girls belted along, and when the chorus came around, Chloe was the loudest one, calling on all the women who depended on no one but themselves to raise their hands up in the air. And the girls all put their hands up—including Jade, a beat late. She watched how Chloe imitated the singer, and she thought her friend was actually pretty good. Chloe bounced in her seat and made dramatic faces like those on the posters in her room. Jade nodded to the popping beat, too, and when the chorus came around again, she sang out with them.

"Who sings this?" Jade asked Chloe when the music had switched to a country song and Ms. Jackson turned the radio down a bit.

"Destiny's Child," said Chloe. "Beyoncé is the lead singer. *Such* a good voice." She shook her head in admiration.

Ms. Jackson shifted out of the HOV lane and made her way across the lanes to take the exit on the right. She glided the car smoothly across the highway, as if it were an extension of her body.

As they pulled off the highway and the jeep slowed, Jade took in a part of town she hadn't yet seen. They passed shopping centers with wide, bright parking lots and signs in many languages. A green sign at the intersection read BUFORD HIGHWAY—where her dad had gotten the

Chocolate Abuelita. And the people in this neighborhood did look like the people who lived in Pilsen.

A group of wiry teenaged boys was walking up ahead, and one of them wore a green Mexico soccer jersey. The boys looked up at the girls as they drove by. The one with the soccer jersey was kind of cute, and Jade turned her neck to watch him, hoping at the same time that he couldn't see her. They rounded a curve, and the boys were out of sight.

The high school came into view ahead: a flat, wide array of low brick buildings with a huge parking lot and two or three fields. Imposing and new, it looked nothing like the houses and apartment complexes surrounding it. They were building something next to the football field; a large red mound of dirt rose beside cone-shaped piles of wood chips. The construction workers operating heavy yellow machinery and walking around in hard hats were brown like the people in the neighborhood, like the workers she had seen at the construction site near Chloe's house. Jade couldn't imagine what else they might need to build for the school—it appeared to have everything already.

At the entrance to the football field stood an iron statue of a slit-eyed, pointy-eared bobcat, crouched and baring its long fangs, its jaws open in a silent roar. Jade thought it looked almost *too* aggressive, as if the sculptor had focused too much on the fierceness of the beast and not enough on its quiet grandeur.

Ms. Jackson drove into the parking lot at a crawl, avoiding the high school students who were milling about or driving around like they were walking instead of driving. A line of skateboarders ripped past way up ahead, and Jade sucked in her breath as she recognized Nikos.

She knew she might see him, but still, she hadn't expected it in that precise moment. The wind pressed his white uniform polo to his lean torso and tossed his dark hair back as he sped along. She felt a jolt even stronger than what she had felt the first time she had seen him. The confidence written in every sure movement of his body, the way he let the wind wash over him—it was all so *smooth*. From this distance she could barely see Nikos's features, but they jumped to her mind immediately, in sharp detail, as she remembered their encounter at Chloe's house.

Jade lost sight of him behind a tall silver SUV that closed in like a wall. Ms. Jackson was pulling into the parking space beside it. Jade turned to Chloe, wondering whether she had noticed her brother, but Chloe was unclicking her seat belt and gathering her backpack and blue sports bag. She looked at Jade and Jade realized that she had momentarily frozen. She shook herself and got into action—she had to get out of the car so Chloe could. As she gathered her things and popped open the door to step out, the excitement of the afternoon took her over again, driving thoughts of Nikos back out into the corners of her mind like a cat chasing birds into the sky.

The songs from the radio echoed in her head as her shoes hit the pavement. The brick-colored lanes of the track field encircled an expansive oval of too-green grass that smelled freshly mowed. Behind the field stood those ever-present Atlanta trees marking the mulchy edge of the city forest—tall pines, thick oaks, and smooth, white, peeling sycamores, the curled strips of their fallen bark pale against the dark ground. Blond wood chips blanketed the wide skirt of a path that narrowed from the manicured field into the trees and disappeared into the dark greens and browns that soothed Jade far more than the sunny grass the color of her lime-green pencil.

She gathered her hair up into her turquoise scrunchie as she walked across the parking lot with the other girls, her sneakers tied to her book bag bouncing against her back with every step.

She was ready to run.

The gym where they got changed was grand and echoey. Some high school girls were practicing basketball in the main, open part, their hair tied up in ponytails and sweatbands, shoes squeaking against the shiny floor. On one wall was a giant mural of a leaping bobcat in black and gold. This one Jade liked better than the statue outside; it emphasized the pumping muscles of the animal, the way they all worked together to make the giant leap.

Jade followed Chloe, Caitlyn, and Emily into a blue-and-gray locker room where she met the other girls on the team: Shannon, Devon, and Samantha, all from different schools in the archdiocese. Shannon and Devon had light complexions like Jade, and Samantha had dark, bouncy ringlets that curled against her face. Jade watched the OLH girls merge with these girls, setting their sports bags down among them as they started to change.

She watched the other girls to see what to ask her mom to buy. The thing to wear seemed to be a flowy tank and short, breezy shorts. Jade marveled at how easily the team all changed in front of one another, how comfortable they were around one another's bodies, which were all different. She hoped she would feel that way around them soon. When she pulled on her T-shirt with the skull of purple flowers, she rolled the sleeves up all the way over her shoulders to make it look more like a tank.

Out on the bright green field, Ms. Jackson—*Coach* Jackson—greeted them in a deep blue tracksuit with white stripes down the sides that flattered her.

"Everybody welcome Jade!"

Jade looked straight at Coach Jackson like she had on the first day of school in homeroom, so she wouldn't have to look at the others as they turned to look at her.

"I know she's new, but she's one of us now," Coach Jackson went on. "Remember the shot at the state championship I talked about?"

They all nodded.

"We won't be able to make it unless we all work together as a team, okay? All right. One! Two!"

She began doing jumping jacks, and the girls mirrored her. Jade joined in eagerly, glad to be one of many bodies in motion. She badly wanted the other girls to like her. They all looked so strong, so easy in their tanks and shorts. Jade was fast, she knew that. But would she be able to keep up with these girls? She hoped so.

They ran a few laps back and forth on the green oval; this wasn't a race. Right now they were running just to have fun, to get their muscles warmed up and used to moving. The more she ran, the more Jade enjoyed it. She had been looking forward to this for so long. When she got going fast enough, she could almost forget about everything—how Abuela couldn't yet completely smile, how her mom was away . . .

The sparse clouds offered a welcome veil from the sun, but Jade eyed the forest and wished to run into it, where she knew it was cooler, and the air pungent with the smell of moist earth, fresh wood chips, and the first pine cones.

"Last one and then the trail!" Coach Jackson called out. Instinctively, Jade sped up. She ran the lap and was panting when she got back to where Coach Jackson was standing. She got there first; Chloe and Emily ran up just a few seconds later.

"Try not to use your energy all at once, Jade," said Coach Jackson quietly, just to her, as the rest of the team arrived. "We've barely started."

Jade nodded. It was true—she was already starting to get a little out of breath.

"Okay, we'll do the first loop only, and we'll do it twice, got it? On the count of three. One, two—"

"Follow me," Chloe said in Jade's ear, brushing past her. Jade let Chloe get ahead just a few paces and took off after her. The team narrowed into a pack, roughly two by two, as they dashed off the field, running fast for real this time, and onto the path that led into the forest. Their sneakers crunched on the wood chips and kicked them up, uncovering the red-brown earth.

The bright light of the field quieted as soon as Jade crossed the threshold into the trees. Her eyes adjusted quickly—more quickly than she had anticipated. The path grew wilder as it twisted into the forest. Long, sturdy roots reached across it, and she leapt over them like they were tiny hurdles. Her shoes splashed in red mud every once in a while where rainwater had pooled, sending thick, wet flecks onto the backs of her calves. She heard clearly the rise and fall of the last of the crickets' strumming as they called to each other from either side of the trail. As the path curved deeper through the trees, a smell so sweet it verged on putrid hit her nostrils. It rose up from purple grapes in the path and she instinctively leapt over these, too, as she ran, not wanting to splatter their juices.

She reveled in the bounce of her sneakers on the wood chips, the light brush of tender leaves on low branches against her sides, the way her breathing kept time with her fast, light steps and it was all one continuous motion.

She heard water, the soft rush of it over stones. There was a fork in the path coming up, and the water was to the right. She bore right—

"Jade! This way!"

Chloe was calling to her from up ahead, looking out for her.

Jade was already practically at the fork. She switched directions just in time, at the last second, to head left with the other girls, away from the water, away from the stream that she knew was there. She wondered if it was the same stream that ran behind her house, where Itztli told his stories.

They looped back out into the sun and then into the forest again for the second lap. Coach Jackson was right, she needed to learn to conserve her energy. It was going to take time for her to get used to running as part of a larger, many-footed body, and not just sprinting ahead and breaking away.

She ran well until they reached the fork again, when suddenly she felt the effort. The other girls hurtled forward as Jade's legs became heavy. The air that just moments before she had relished smelling, sniffing, with its slightly spicy earthen smell, at once became palpably humid, a force she had to battle through. By the time they broke out onto the field again, her legs ached and a cramp had developed in the side of her stomach. Whatever it was that had made her run so smoothly in the forest, as if she were a part of it, was dropping away now.

She watched Chloe's ponytail bobbing in front of her and decided to pick up her feet for the last stretch across the field. With painful effort, she caught up with Chloe and together the two of them reached the place where Coach Jackson was standing with her stopwatch, tall and brilliant in her deep blue tracksuit. Jade and Chloe were the last ones—though not by much—and Jade was pretty sure Chloe had slowed down for her.

Jade walked in squiggly circles for a bit, her legs feeling almost as if they were detached from the rest of her.

"Good run, Jade," Coach Jackson said, coming up to her. "That's good—keep moving till you catch your breath."

Jade nodded and didn't try to say anything. Coach Jackson kept moving, too, walking among the other girls who were beginning to do cool-down stretches, giving them words of encouragement. Jade was grateful that Coach Jackson was treating her like one of the team. Still, she didn't quite feel like she actually *was* one of them yet.

At last she steadied her breath enough to copy the other girls. She sat down on the bright green grass with one leg outstretched and the other tucked into her knee and leaned over to tug on the rubbery, muddy toe of her sneaker. The poufed-up puff of her ponytail hung down in front of her.

She did love to run, but she had a long way to go before she could dole out her energies as well as these other girls did. Maybe then she would start to really feel like part of the team. Until then, she had Chloe, who stuck with her even when she nearly scampered off the trail.

11

Gold was just beginning to brush the tops of the trees as the girls waited on the curb for their rides. Tired and flushed from practice, they leaned against their bags with their legs outstretched. A few yards away, some high school kids had claimed the few benches.

Shannon shared her Cheez-Its with everyone, and Jade made a mental note to bring a snack next time. She leaned forward and loosened her shoelaces to let her feet breathe, and she closed her eyes and exhaled as a welcome breeze blew gently through her hair and cooled her damp socks. The red-brown mud was already caking on her sneakers.

Devon and Shannon were talking about some laser show they had been to last weekend at a place called Stone Mountain. She wondered vaguely—was there a mountain around here?

Cars drove up one by one and picked up the girls. Most of them had plenty of siblings, all dressed in the untucked uniforms of the various schools in the archdiocese.

Samantha's dad drove up, and Jade saw where she got her ringlets—he had dark curly hair like his daughter. She wasn't surprised when he called out to Samantha and said her name in Spanish, "Samanta."

Jade wondered, as she often did, how things might be different if she herself looked a little more like Samantha, or like Katerina. What would it be like if people assumed when they first saw her that she was Mexican, or at least generally Hispanic or Latina? What would it be like if the Mexican part of herself weren't something that she always had to reveal or explain to people? She wished for that sometimes.

It didn't always work in her mom's favor to look the way she did—otherwise she wouldn't have to dress up so much just to go to the airport. That irritated Jade and made no sense because to her, her mom was the most beautiful of any she had ever met.

She sighed and closed her eyes, and the strong afternoon sunlight warmed her lids so she saw yellow behind them. When her dad picked her up, with his blond hair and freckles, these girls who she had just met would probably assume something about who she was that was only partly true. Eventually, at some point, that *moment* would come, as it always did, when they would realize there was more to the story.

Opening her eyes, she blinked in the light that sloped ever more horizontally through the trees lining the edge of the parking lot. They separated the high school from the busy street and the Latino neighborhood beyond it, like the school was the Vatican City in Rome—its own separate country, distinct from its surroundings.

Itztli had told her that he had grown up with a secret about who he was—a secret that his mother told him never to be ashamed of. Her mom's huevos rancheros, the memories she had of Abuelo, the stories she remembered him telling her that swam around in her head like designs worn thin and translucent with time, their brushstrokes fading—these things were not a secret, but they weren't obvious to others, or even, sometimes, to Jade herself. Under the shelter of the trees, listening to Itztli's stories, the brushstrokes of her memories had thickened, begun to take on a more definitive form, and she called them to mind more often. Even the things in her house— the ceramic dishes, the bright papier-mâché tecolote on her mother's dresser, and of course the obsidian mirror— she seemed to see more clearly now, to take notice of as if for the first time, like when she had gone to Madison's house for a sleepover in third grade and learned that not everybody had a stack of tortillas in their house at all times.

She looked up at the gilded tops of the trees that formed a veil, their leaves dipping and fluttering over one another in the breeze, making ever-changing peepholes to the sky and road behind it like eyelets in a drapery of lace. Behind the trees the cars zoomed by, their metal flashing through the branches.

A tall high school boy was approaching them on the curb. It was Justin. Beside Jade, Chloe sat up straighter and pushed her chest forward in her purple tank top, and Jade saw Justin's eyes flick over to Chloe for a moment, before he looked away again.

"Dad's here," he said quietly to Emily, keeping a couple feet of distance between himself and the knot of sweaty girls, as if they had cooties or something and he didn't want to be seen associating with them. Jade exchanged a silent, knowing glance with Chloe. Chloe pulled her hair slowly out of her scrunchie and shook her head dramatically so that her hair settled around her bare shoulders. Jade was amazed at how good her hair looked, even after all that running. There was no way Justin couldn't notice.

"Justin." It was Emily, who had stood up and had her backpack and sports bag hoisted onto her shoulders, ready to go. She had caught Justin staring at Chloe. He looked away and started walking off, as if nothing had happened. Emily rolled her eyes and followed after him.

They said goodbye to Emily, and it was just Chloe and Jade on the curb. A few of the high school kids were still hanging out on the benches several paces away.

"Jade, do you think he's still into me?" Chloe said quietly, as soon as Emily was out of earshot.

"He was for sure looking at you," said Jade, grinning. "I saw it."

"Really? I felt like he was ignoring me. He didn't say anything to me."

"I mean, he wasn't going to do anything in front of Emily," said Jade.

"I guess you're right," said Chloe. "It's just so hard for me to tell. He's over at my house a lot, but my brother is always there, you know."

A pulse of electricity shot through Jade at the mention of Nikos, but she nodded calmly and tried not to let Chloe see what she was feeling. It was one thing to think about him, and another thing to hear Chloe refer to him out loud.

"I have to tell you what happened on Friday," said Chloe, leaning closer. Jade leaned in, too. "Nikos was upstairs, right? And I was in the kitchen drinking this huge glass of water. I was really chugging it, you know, loudly, because I was so thirsty. And I get done with the water and I'm like *ahhh* really loudly, you know. And I look up, and there's Justin, at the bottom of the stairs! Like he's been watching me the whole time. And I had no idea he was there."

"That's . . ." Jade wanted to say that was weird, but she didn't.

"Oh, it was weird for sure, I know," said Chloe, and Jade felt her face relax into a smile. "So there I am, with my mouth open, you know, *ahhhh*, and I just stare at him because I don't know what to do, and then—you won't believe what he said."

"What?" said Jade. Chloe was clearly enjoying telling this story, and Jade felt like the special one Chloe had chosen to tell it to.

"So I'm standing there with my mouth open, right, and he goes, 'Chloe. You have pretty eyes.'"

Jade raised her eyebrows. That was a major, major statement. But at the same time she couldn't help feeling that it was also so—*boring.*

"He *said* that?" she said.

Chloe nodded up and down, her eyes wide, smiling.

"I mean, then he for *sure* likes you," said Jade.

"I know, but '*You have pretty eyes*'? I mean, who *says* that?"

Jade laughed loudly. She loved how she and Chloe were so often on the same wavelength, even when she wasn't sure they would be.

"Yeah, couldn't he have found something better to say?" said Jade. "Something more original?"

"I know! And then he just went upstairs. That was it! I'm standing there with my mouth still wide-open, and I'm, like, *what was that?*"

They laughed together, and Jade shook her head thinking of Chloe standing there in the kitchen, watching the spot at the bottom of the stairwell where Justin had just been. It cracked her up. "He *likes* you," she said singsongy.

"No but seriously," said Chloe, and she did in fact look serious all of a sudden. "I think I really like him."

"Yeah?" Jade stopped laughing.

"Yeah." Chloe looked down and tugged at one of her shoelaces. "I know we barely talk, but I just—I *feel* something when I'm around him, you know? It's like he's a magnet, and I can almost feel this tug in my body toward whatever direction he's in . . . I don't know, that sounds ridiculous."

"That does not sound ridiculous," said Jade. She wouldn't have used the same words, but what Chloe was describing wasn't far off from what she felt when she met Nikos.

"I mean, I've liked people before, obviously," said Chloe. "Like Peter, for example." Jade smiled. Of course. Peter was pretty cute. "But it's never been like *this*," Chloe went on. "I mean—I almost don't even have to see Justin. I just have to know he's around, in the house or something, and I get all fidgety. I can even just think about him and I'll start to feel sorta—tingly. And I think about his face *all—the—time*. Like I'll be watching Ms.

Colby graph an equation on the board, and suddenly I'll see his face. And when he really is near me, like just now? Oof, Jade, it's wild. It's like he's the only thing I can think about."

Chloe tugged a little harder on her shoestring and the bow came undone and slumped against her shoe. "I feel like I *want* something, Jade," she said. "But I don't know what it is."

Jade knew what Chloe was talking about. Lately, though, there had been so many other things to think about . . .

The parking lot was largely empty by now. Jade wondered what was taking her dad so long. By the edge of the trees a high school girl not much older than Jade was leaning back against a car and giggling, while the guy she was talking to kept stepping closer. Jade and Chloe watched them in silence.

Jade had to admit that part of her was jealous of Chloe's moment with Justin. She wished Nikos would say something like that to her—even something as unoriginal as *You have pretty eyes.* That would be amazing.

"Do you want to kiss him?" said Jade. She had thought about kissing Nikos, but only in the vaguest way. It was more of a curiosity about what it would feel like for another person's lips to touch hers, to press against them.

Chloe thought for a moment, her head cocked to the side. "I mean, I guess so," she said at last. "But only because— that's what you're supposed to want, you know?"

"Yeah," said Jade. "I totally get what you mean." Even though she really liked Nikos, she wasn't sure that what she wanted was for him to kiss her.

They kept watching the pair of high schoolers at the edge of the parking lot. Were they going to kiss? Were they going to go somewhere to kiss? Had they already kissed before?

"Your turn, Jade," said Chloe, poking her lightly in the side. "Who do *you* like? I'm sure you like someone."

Jade smiled and pulled away a little. "I don't know—"

"Come on," said Chloe. "I'm sure you think *somebody* is cute."

Jade looked away. She hated that she couldn't tell Chloe. For a second she thought about telling her anyway, as weird as it was, because she had this feeling that she could share anything with Chloe, but she stopped herself. After seeing how Emily reacted when she saw her brother looking at Chloe, she didn't want Chloe to react like that with her. Their friendship was way too important—she wasn't going to risk it.

"Never mind, it's fine," said Chloe, when Jade had been silent a moment longer. Chloe waved her arms as if to push the question away. "I wanted to ask you, is your grandma okay?"

Jade stared at her. She had not expected the sudden change of topic, but she was grateful for it. That was exactly the question she was running away from and the question she inevitably always came back to. It was the question she felt like her parents still wouldn't quite answer for her, even though they were beginning to. And here was Chloe, asking it, because she could tell, even now when Jade was trying to keep it tucked away, that it was on her mind.

Jade twisted the bottom of her T-shirt into a coiled clump around her finger. "My mom says she's going to be okay, but I don't really know what that means," she said. "No one seems to really know. I mean, I'm sure she'll be mostly okay in the end, but I don't know how long that's going to take." She let the T-shirt go and watched the fabric unfurl in wrinkles like an old map. "I just want her to be able to still talk to me," she said.

"What makes you say that?" said Chloe.

"Because—I have to ask her some things. I have to ask her about the town where she and my abuelo grew up. I have to ask her about when they moved to Chicago. She's the only one who can tell me. My mom knows some of this stuff, but she doesn't tell me much." Her mom had opened up last week about the tecolotes, but she also pretty much closed that door as soon as she opened it. Jade knew she couldn't ask her to tell her much more. "And I want to ask my abuela soon because . . ."

She looked at Chloe but left it unsaid.

Because she needed to fill in the picture in her notebook. And because if she waited too long, who knew—it might be too late.

"Maybe I can talk to my abuela on the phone when she's feeling well enough," she said, considering it as she said it. "But she usually doesn't say much, and you have to really convince her to tell you things." That would not be easy to do over the phone. It would be so much easier if Jade were in Chicago right now. She couldn't stand all this waiting. Her parents were starting to give her some information, more than they would have before, but she still didn't feel like she had control over the situation. She couldn't make decisions the way the grown-ups could. But she had to do this—listen to Abuela.

Chloe carefully retied her shoe, making a perfect, flat bow. "I'm almost jealous," she said.

"Why?"

"Because. I never really knew my grandparents. I mean, I have some really fuzzy memories of my yia yia, but that's it. I was really little. I can sort of remember sitting on her lap while she did something with her hands. Maybe she was shelling beans or something. And I remember her singing to me. Nikos remembers more because he was older." She hugged her knees to her chest and rested her head on them, looking at Jade. "I'm jealous because you can still talk to your grandma."

Jade nodded. She *would* be lucky, if she got that chance.

"But I feel like I know my grandparents pretty well anyway," said Chloe, "even though I don't have many memories of them."

"Then how do you know them?" said Jade.

Chloe shrugged, still hugging her knees. "My parents have told me lots of stories," she said. "And my mom is always making food at home or for the restaurant, and it's all my yia yia's recipes. So I feel like I know what her cooking must have tasted like."

"That rice pudding was delicious," said Jade.

"Oh, that's one of the best ones. Yia Yia was so cool." Chloe shook her head and looked out at the parking lot without really seeming to see it, as if she were actually remembering her grandmother, not just the stories she had been told. "My yia yia came up with her own songs," she said, and looked at Jade for a reaction.

"That's pretty cool," said Jade. "So she was a musician?"

"Well, she was," said Chloe, "but only we know that. She didn't actually write down any of her songs. My mom can sing most of them, but she just hums some of the words sometimes, because she has forgotten them. I want to record my mom singing them, but my mom doesn't like it when I try to do that because she doesn't think she has a good voice."

"Well, does she?"

"I mean, she doesn't have my yia yia's voice, but I think it's not bad. She's just shy about it."

Jade thought of how intensely Chloe had thrown herself into her singing when she belted out the song on the car ride here. She must have gotten her voice from her grandmother. What Justin really should have said was *Chloe, you have a pretty voice.*

"I started writing down some of the songs," said Chloe, tucking her hair behind her ear. "Just the lyrics. I have some of the tunes down, too, but that takes longer."

"That's a great idea," said Jade. It wouldn't be enough just to listen to Abuela's stories. She needed to record them, too, so they wouldn't be lost. She needed to write them down, to put them in the drawing.

"Chloe, how do you think I can convince my abuela to tell me stuff?" she said. "I think she's going to be shy about a lot of it, too."

"I don't know," said Chloe, extending her legs again. "Maybe—maybe tell her why you want to know. Then maybe she'll understand."

Jade nodded and leaned against her backpack. They sat in comfy silence for a few moments, the bright, faraway voices at the edges of the parking lot mixing with the muffled, even hum of traffic.

She thought about Chloe's advice. Why *did* she want to know?

It was more than just curiosity. She wanted to know Abuela's stories because it felt like they were important. Like they might help her understand her family, and maybe even who she was. She wanted to listen and hold on to what Abuela told her because she didn't know who else would.

She thought about the story her mom told her about the owls, her guides, that the mirror had brought to her. Of how deliberately her mother told her this, and how long she had waited to tell her. Of Itztli, of the care and detail he put into each of his brushstrokes, of how he told his stories playfully but always with a note of solemnity underneath.

There was something weighty about these stories that Itztli and her mother had entrusted her with. It was as though a set of small stones, smooth as the ones just beneath the surface of the stream, had been pressed into her palm, and the stones were heavier than they looked. She knew Abuela's stories would be like that, too—weighty pebbles that she needed to be prepared to hold.

That was a big responsibility. But maybe what Itztli had been telling her, and the way she was learning to draw stories, were preparing her for it. If she could push through the burning in her legs to make that last dash out of the forest and onto the field, she could do this.

She sat up a little, lifted the weight of her sweaty back off the backpack.

At last her dad drove up in her family's blue Honda sedan. He rolled down the window and took off his sunglasses as the girls stood up.

"You must be Chloe," he said, stretching out his hand.

Chloe shook his hand and said, "Nice to meet you, Mr. O'Callaghan."

"Please—you can call me Chris," her dad said.

Jade opened the back door. Katerina was in her booster seat in the middle wearing her Daisies outfit, and Jade climbed over her so Chloe wouldn't have to. The AC felt incredible.

"You stink, Sissy," said Katerina.

Chloe laughed and got in the seat on the other side of Katerina. "Sorry, but you're going to be riding between two stinky girls!" she said, setting her backpack and sports bag at her feet.

Katerina pinched her nose and scrunched up her face. Chloe pulled the door shut and Jade's dad drove out of the parking lot.

"How was practice?" he said, watching Jade in the rearview mirror.

"It was cool!" she said. She almost asked what had taken him so long, but she decided to wait until they had dropped off Chloe.

"Chloe, how did Jade hold up today?" her dad said playfully, beaming at them in the mirror from behind his sunglasses.

"Oh, Jade is great," said Chloe. "Superfast. I'm just glad she's on the team now!"

She and Jade exchanged a grin. Jade could tell that even though Chloe got along fine with the other girls, she didn't go deep with them like she did with Jade.

"Is Mommy coming home soon?" Katerina said suddenly.

They were all quiet.

"Actually, bug, she is," said Jade's dad. "She's coming home late Saturday, probably."

"Oh wow," said Jade. It was Tuesday, and the weekend felt soon and far away at the same time. It would be nice to have her mom back. Did this mean Abuela was doing better?

"Yay!" said Katerina, throwing her arms up in the air.

"Wait—Saturday is when we're supposed to take Chloe to the museum," said Jade, looking over at Chloe. She wanted her mom back home again, but she didn't want this to spoil her plans to hang out with her friend.

"We'll still do that," said her dad. "Did you think I'd forget?"

Chloe smiled. Jade glanced back and caught her dad's smile in the rearview mirror, too. Of course he hadn't forgotten. This was his thing.

"You should see the marigolds that are in bloom," he added.

Marigolds. The flowers on the casket at Abuelo's funeral.

"Now, I have a question for you and Katerina," her dad said, his voice serious now.

Jade watched him intently, first in the mirror, then at what she could see of his face in profile from her seat. She felt a little sorry for Chloe, who had to be in the middle of this family conversation. But she didn't mind if Chloe heard. She would probably tell her about anything important later anyway.

"I just spoke with your mother for a while," he said. "How would you feel if Abuela came to stay with us? I don't know how long, maybe just a few weeks or so—"

"Yes!" said Jade. Her dad's eyebrows arched in the mirror. "I would *so* want Abuela to come here and live with us!" she said.

She caught Chloe's eye. Chloe looked at her pointedly and gave her an almost imperceptible thumbs-up with her hand behind the buckle of her seat belt.

"Yes!" said Katerina, and Jade wasn't quite sure if she meant it or if she was just copying her.

Jade's dad was quiet.

"Is that the plan?" said Jade.

He sighed. "I guess so." He didn't sound super excited about it. "It's not going to be easy," he said. "She's still incredibly weak. We'll have to fix up the guest bedroom for her, hire some people to help out . . ."

They were gliding along the open highway now, and he was driving with his usual smooth, calm assuredness. He sighed again. "Well. If you girls don't mind it, then—it'll happen. Your mom will come with Abuela on Saturday evening."

Jade watched her father and let it sink in. Her dad must have been late picking them up because he had been talking to her mom, figuring out the plan.

She looked over at Chloe, who was smiling at her again. Jade thought about what an epic day Saturday was going to be. She was going to hang out with Chloe, and her mom and Abuela would be there that night.

This was her chance.

Beyond Chloe, out the window, the trees rushed by in a whir of greens and browns, all bathed in the amber sunlight of the ending day.

Jade leaned back in her seat and thought about what colors she might use to paint Abuela's stories.

12

Each time Coach Jackson's red jeep pulled up next to the breezeway that week to drive the cross-country girls to the high school, Jade pressed forward eagerly beside Caitlyn, Emily, and Chloe. She was still so excited that she got to ride in this car with them, with the windows down and the music turned up. Practice was hard, but she was getting the hang of it, getting to know the forest paths, and regulating her energy more so she could keep some for the end when they burst forth from the trees and ran out onto the bright field. The sun was more merciful now; she no longer felt like it threatened to scorch her scalp.

Her mom's phone calls in the evenings were now mostly to make plans with her dad. When she talked to Jade briefly, she sounded more like herself now—less tired and more driven, with a purpose.

The main preparations were in the guest bedroom, where Abuela was going to stay. Little by little, it became a place where Jade could imagine Abuela sitting up, making herself comfortable on the poufy bed. Her dad bought a gray bolster pillow, but Jade thought it didn't quite look welcoming enough for Abuela. From the couch she grabbed a couple of small cushions that Abuela had embroidered with tiny red flowers dotting skinny vines, and placed them on either side of the bolster pillow. She was satisfied with how the colors popped against the gray.

On Friday afternoon Jade saw that her dad had put a walker in the room, near the entrance to the bathroom. It was the four-wheeled kind that only very old people used, with brakes on the handles and a faux-leather seat covering a wire basket.

Jade couldn't picture Abuela using that walker. She had never even used a cane—she had too much of a sense of style for that. Would she give in and use this walker? How much did she really need it? Jade didn't want to think that she would need to use it. But if her dad had gotten it and put it there, it was probably necessary.

Abuela and her mom were arriving tomorrow. But first, the museum. Before she went to bed, Jade laid out her clothes on her dresser: jeans and a green shirt that people always said matched her eyes.

Chloe bounded up to the car when they drove up to her place the next morning. She was wearing jeans, like Jade, with an elegant little black purse strung across her, and pleather ankle boots. She looked like she could be in high school.

Chloe pulled on the door handle before Jade's dad had a chance to unlock it. Jade loved when Chloe was like this—when she didn't mind showing how excited she was about something, didn't care if she looked a little silly. It usually happened when no one else from school was around or when she was surrounded by people she seemed to trust.

She got in and greeted them, and as they drove off, Chloe asked, "So what is this place again?" She was clutching the little purse in her lap. It looked entirely too grown-up for her, with its elegant silver clasps, and Jade thought it must belong to her mom.

"Well," said her dad, glancing at them in the rearview mirror, "it's a big house, really, with plenty of land, from before the Civil War. Now they've converted it into a museum and gardens. The man who owned it for a while was—well, he was a rich person who liked to collect things. They have this funny smattering of objects. You'll see."

Jade wondered what this eccentric rich man from long ago had decided to get his hands on.

"They hired me to grow their native plant garden," her dad added.

He turned and the museum came into view. It was indeed a very large house, two stories tall, with a wrap-around porch and a grassy lawn in front. Fiery marigolds bloomed at the feet of perfectly rounded hedges that lined a brick walkway leading to the stairs at the entrance. Her dad was right—the flowers' explosions of color stole the spotlight.

Jade knew immediately, though, that her dad didn't work in these gardens. Despite the exuberant marigolds poking their feathered heads out over the grass, these gardens were too trim, too contained. Her dad's special talent was his ability to coax plants to grow as tall and as curly or stretched out as they wanted to. He liked to wait patiently and see what a flower or a vine was capable of, and then give it little nudges along the way. He didn't beat back his plants to make them look a certain way, and he only ever trimmed them if it was to help them grow again.

Sure enough, when they had parked, her dad headed toward a winding dirt path to the side of the house.

Jade started to follow after him and Katerina, but Chloe lagged behind, fiddling with something in her purse, and Jade waited.

"I have to tell you something," said Chloe softly, when Jade's dad and Katerina were a little ways away.

"What's up?" said Jade.

Chloe opened her purse for Jade to see inside. She looked in and saw a couple of Maxi pads. Jade had seen them in the store before and in people's bathrooms, but she had never seen any so close up. Her mom used tampons that came in yellow paper wrappers, and the mechanics of how they worked were a mystery to her. The pads looked much more straightforward.

"Do you have yours yet?" Chloe said. "Mine started last night."

Jade shook her head. She knew theoretically that at some point she would get her period, but she hadn't ever really stopped to think about what that would actually be like.

"What's it like?" she asked.

Chloe shrugged. "Weird," she said. "I'm paranoid it's going to show through my jeans."

They both smiled a little. Jade was sort of glad she didn't have to worry about that right now, but there was a part of her that was also slightly jealous of Chloe—it seemed to her that if a girl got her period, then she was officially not a kid anymore.

"I'll let you know if it starts to show," said Jade. "I got you."

Her dad was waiting for them at the top of the path.

"Come on, let's go," said Jade, and they headed off toward the trail.

The path led past a line of great trees with trunks as thick as any Jade had ever seen. One of them, a tall, gray beech with smooth bark marked with half circles that reminded her of eyes, had a sign that said it was from before the Revolutionary War.

Her dad unlocked a low wooden gate and held it open for the girls to step through, exchanging a nod and a friendly smile with the young guard who was patrolling near the trees.

Brilliant colors greeted them, and boughs jutted slightly out into the pathways, ready to brush a knee or a calf. Dirt paths forked and snaked through the beds like meandering rivers, and between the beds, emerald carpets of moss rose and fell on the hilly ground, shining in the morning sun. Aside from an older couple ahead of them, they had the gardens to themselves.

Katerina skipped ahead, pausing briefly at the brightest flowers at her eye level, and continuing on. She was wearing a blue dress Abuela had embroidered with red flowers—the same cherry red as on the cushions Jade had chosen for Abuela's bed.

Katerina stopped at some sprays of tiny bluish-purple flowers that were just her height. A bumblebee was crawling excitedly over the blossoms to collect their nectar, and a small, elegant black butterfly with shimmery gold accents sped away from the delicate stalks when Katerina's finger got too close.

As she walked along the path with Chloe, Jade's eyes fell on a bush that looked like it had been decorated with little pink-and-red ornaments. The spiky, round, pink part of each berry opened out to reveal bright, Christmas-red beans. "Wow. Dad, what is this?" she said.

"That's a strawberry bush," he said, approaching her on the path. "It's native to here." Chloe came closer. "It grows best in shade," her dad went on. "That's why it's at the foot of these trees. But not everything is that easy to grow." He headed a little farther down one of the paths, and Jade and Chloe followed him.

Around a bend of the gardens a tiny field of corn appeared, the green stalks as tall as Jade. She had only ever seen corn growing like this on trips to Nebraska to visit her grandma.

"Corn needs humans to keep existing," said her dad. "They need people's hands to spread their seeds." He reached out and gently cradled one of the green husks in his wide palm. "This one will be blue when it's ready," he said. "And this one will be red," he said, softly touching another. "And this one"—he put his hand on the last one— "will have many colors."

Jade thought of the bright, dried, multicolored cobs that Abuela always hung on her door around the end of October, leading up to Día de los Muertos. Jade wondered whether Abuela would have the strength to mark the day this year.

Katerina walked toward them, carefully holding two ladybugs cupped in her hands. She must have gotten them from one of the flowers. Their red matched the embroidery on her dress.

"What about this flower?" said Chloe. With her index finger she held up a small violet blossom in a cluster on a dark green plant, as if she were lifting the flower's chin to see its face better. It looked like a fluttery heart or a butterfly open in mid-flight. Similar leafy plants with pink or violet flowers grew beside it.

"Those are indigo," said Jade's dad. He rubbed one of the dark, oval leaves between his thumb and forefinger.

Indigo. It sounded like the color of a jean wash from the Lands' End catalogues that her dad got in the mail.

But she thought she had heard the word somewhere else, too. Was it one of the colors that Abuela used to use for her embroidery?

"You can make dye with these plants, right?" she said to her dad.

"Absolutely," he said. "Some have even been used to make pigment for ceramics, for paints," he said. "In fact, there are some examples in the museum."

Jade felt her eyes widen. Ceramic? Paint?

Her mind flashed to the shimmering blue powder that Itztli had moistened and thickened until it became ink. Did his ink come from this plant? From indigo?

None of her colored pencils made the same blue on the pages of her notebook as the blue that Itztli had painted on the bark—the blue that reminded her so much of the dainty birds and flowers on the bowls and plates in their house from the Casa Azul. Could these pink flowers and deep green leaves make a blue like that?

She looked toward the brick side of the museum. Now she desperately wanted to see whatever was inside it that had been painted with indigo.

Chloe was looking toward the big house, too. Jade followed her gaze to a window. The sun's glare made it hard to see inside, but she did make out an earthenware vase.

"You girls ready to see the museum?" said her dad, seeing them.

"Yes!" Chloe and Jade said in unison.

"Look, Daddy, I got five of them!" Katerina said suddenly, raising her cupped palms to show him. Jade didn't know how, but she had indeed managed to collect five ladybugs that were strolling around inside her hands like it was their home.

"That's amazing, bug!" said Jade's dad. "Now let's say goodbye to them and give them back to the plants so we can go inside, okay?"

Jade headed back up the path with Chloe close behind her, while her dad helped Katerina coax the tiny creatures out of her hands and onto the indigo leaves.

Inside the museum the floorboards, warped from over a century of changing seasons, creaked beneath their feet. The older lady at the front desk smiled at them over her red glasses when she saw Jade's dad and waved them in.

The entrance room was set up with plush chairs and a coffee table, like an old-timey parlor room. Beyond that were narrow halls and staircases that spiraled up into obscurity.

As they entered the first room beyond the entrance, Jade found herself surrounded by pottery and tightly woven baskets with colorful designs in glass cases. In the center stood a wide-lipped red-clay bowl with a hook-beaked bird painted on it in glossy black and yellow swirls. The label said it was Native American, "possibly Creek or Cherokee." There was nothing on the label about how the rich man had gotten it. Jade tried to guess what tools the artist might have used to make the curling designs glazed on it.

They followed a young couple into the next room. It was the room Jade and Chloe had seen from the garden. Pale stone statues stood watch over ceramic vases with tall necks and stately handles. Bands of symmetrical designs framed intricate scenes in black and terra-cotta on the vases.

"This is Greek," said Chloe, leaning forward to look at one of the scenes on the ceramic.

"Ew, he's naked!" said Katerina, pointing to the uncovered pelvis of one of the statues. It was of a muscular naked man who was standing, stark-naked indeed, with one knee bent, about to throw something. Jade tried to look without it looking like she was looking.

Chloe studied the vase. Whether she was truly absorbed in it or just trying not to be seen looking at the statue's privates, Jade couldn't tell. Her dad was shushing Katerina and trying to explain something to her about how the ancient Greeks thought about art.

Something green and shimmery caught Jade's eye just beyond the next doorway. Above the doorway, the sign read: ART OF THE AMERICAS.

She followed the green shimmers through the other doorway. As she stepped into the room, she saw better what they were: small, green, polished pebbles that reminded her of those in the stream by the Wildcat Trail, only much brighter, encased safely behind glass.

Light poured in from windows that backed up to the edge of the garden, where it met the woods. The small stones reflected the bright morning sun and almost seemed to give off their own glow.

As Jade walked closer to the case, she saw that each stone was intricately carved with boxy and curly designs. She saw animals and faces. Fangs, tails, coils, grimaces. A whole forest of animals was carved into the smooth green surfaces of the rounded pebbles. She wanted to reach inside the glass case and pick one up, hold it in her hand, feel its heft, rub its carved lines with her thumb so her skin would memorize them.

She peered more closely at one that felt familiar. On it was etched the face of a creature in profile, showing its teeth. It had a short nose and rounded ears, and its eyes were wide and watching.

It was Itztli.

She looked more closely. She couldn't explain it, but she felt something like what she felt when she looked into the obsidian mirror that her mother had given her, and that

Abuela had given her mother. Like the stone was trying to tell her something, but she didn't know what.

JADE, read the label. MESOAMERICA.

It felt right somehow, seeing her name there.

She looked back at the stone, at its uneven brilliance. She stared at it, the way she sometimes stared at the smoky mirror, as if daring it to reveal its secrets to her.

Abuela always wore a bracelet of small jade beads on her wrist, even when she was kneading masa to make tortillas. The flashes of green as she worked her hands, cooking or embroidering, were a part of her. Jade had never really looked at them up close, but now she wondered if the beads were like these in the glass display. She would take a good look at the bracelet this time, if Abuela was still wearing it when she got here.

Beside the jade beads, in front of another big window, stood three cylindrical tan vases with red bands around the top and bottom. Scenes were painted on them in swirling black ink, making the clay look almost like a scroll.

They were just like the vases she had seen a few years back, with Abuela and Katerina, at the art museum in Chicago.

She leaned in closer and tried to read what was painted on the vases, the way she had read Itztli's bark painting to him. It was hard to do, though, without a guide like Itztli. She tried to make sense of the scenes—the people offering things to each other, what looked like battle scenes, people floating or falling in midair. There were symbols, too, whose meanings she couldn't guess.

What had Abuela wanted to tell her about these vases?

A bright splash of blue on the intricate headpiece of an important-looking person grabbed her attention. The blue was as bright as the sky above Lake Michigan on a clear summer day.

Was *this* the blue?

"You found it!" her dad said, behind her. He had walked in with Katerina. "The vase with the blue made from indigo," he said.

Jade felt herself smile.

She was surprised. What else did her dad know about this vase and the other artwork in this room?

She looked back at it. Did Itztli use this blue? The color looked different here than it did on the bark, but both had a brilliance that Jade had rarely seen.

It was hard to imagine that the plant outside with the light pink flowers and the dark oval leaves could make a blue like this one on the vase. A precious blue.

Chloe came in the room and stood next to Jade. "This vase is very cool looking," she said, "but I have no idea what's going on in the picture."

"Me neither," said Jade. "I wish I did."

"Back there, in the other room, I saw the coolest vase, and I knew what the story was."

"Oh yeah?" said Jade.

"Yeah, it had this guy with curly hair playing a stringed instrument, and he was looking backward at this woman, and she was reaching out to him but she couldn't touch him. Like she was stuck, like the leaves behind her were holding her back. Orpheus and Eurydice!" Chloe's eyes flashed, like she was proud of herself.

"What?" said Jade. She had never heard of that story.

But before Chloe could respond, Katerina said, atop her perch on her dad's head, "Sissy, can you draw like that?"

She was pointing to the vase with the indigo, and they all went quiet, waiting for her response.

"I don't know," she said, looking up at Katerina and feeling self-conscious. "I can't draw like that now, but—maybe someday?"

Below Katerina, her dad looked at her with curiosity, as if hoping she would say more.

Maybe her parents *would* understand about Itztli, if she told them. Her mom had said that whatever happened to her because of the mirror was hers. Hers to experience, and hers to tell—or not—if she wanted to.

She *did* want to learn to draw and paint like Itztli and like the artists who had made these swirling figures on the vases, ages ago. She wanted to paint stories of long, long ago like those that Itztli told her.

But she also wanted to draw and paint the stories of her own family, and Abuela was the one who could tell her about the objects Jade had grown up seeing all her life—the glazed clay mugs, the embroidered pillows, the flashing jade beads.

"I'm hungry!" said Katerina.

"Well, it's lunchtime," said her dad. "Here, you're going to need to get down, wiggle-worm!"

As they walked out, past the Greek art and the Native American pottery, Jade could hardly believe that Abuela would be here that very night.

"I bet you could draw like that," Chloe said quietly beside her, her boots sounding softly on the creaky wooden floor.

Jade raised her eyebrows at her. It was such a nice thing for her to say. "Um, thanks," she said. She hoped one day it would be true.

As they stepped out into the bright day again, the noonday sun upon them, Jade thought that maybe Chloe, her dad, and Katerina understood her even better than she had thought.

13

That night they had barely finished eating the dinner Jade's dad had cooked and seasoned with rosemary and thyme from his garden when Jade watched him stand up, walk his plate to the kitchen, and reach for the car keys hanging from the hook by the back door without even putting the plate in the dishwasher.

"You girls be good now," he said. "I'll be back soon with your mom and Abuela."

"Wait—Daddy, can I come?" said Katerina.

"Yeah, you weren't just going to go to the airport without us, were you?" said Jade. Her dad was in a rush to get to the airport, but Jade wanted to see Abuela as soon as she could, too. Why should she have to wait—and take care of Katerina on top of that?

Her dad flipped the keys over in his hand, watching them. "Okay," he said. "You can come."

"Yay!" said Katerina, and Jade smiled at her.

"But remember," her dad said, "Abuela is very weak and tired, so we have to be gentle with her. Give her some space, don't talk too much. She'll be here for a while. There will be plenty of time to talk later on."

Jade and Katerina nodded. Jade knew it would be hard not to talk to her right away, but she would do her best.

"I just want to see her, Dad," she said.

"I wanna see Mommy!" said Katerina.

The drive to the airport took them toward the heart of the Atlanta skyline and back out onto one of its infinite highways. The last glow of sunset faded to darkness on the horizon as her dad merged into the speedy six-lane traffic. In the darkening sky above the overpasses that criss-crossed the view, the crescent moon began to show itself faintly.

As they approached the airport, Jade watched as planes taking off or landing flew thunderous and low over the highway, their lights flashing against the night. When her dad pulled up to the curb, the airport lit everything up like day.

Her dad pushed the radio on while they waited. It was turned to the news station. Jade tuned in for bits and zoned out for others. There was something about the Taliban in Afghanistan, but she couldn't quite catch what. And President Bush had invited the president of Mexico for a fancy dinner at the White House, with fireworks and everything.

Her dad turned down the radio. Jade followed his gaze out the window. Under the garish airport lights her mom was emerging through the wide sliding doors, pushing Abuela in an airport wheelchair. They had both dressed up to fly. Her mom had on a dark skirt suit, and Abuela sat with her hands folded over a long, flowy skirt in rich tones of coffee and ochre set off by her bright white blouse. Abuela looked tired, and her thick silver hair was a little mussed from the flight, but she held herself upright. Her bright eyes shone a color Jade could only think to call negro azabache. Abuela determinedly searched the curb for them in the line of cars.

Her dad popped the trunk and hopped out of the car, and Jade and Katerina practically tumbled out, too. Jade saw the recognition light up Abuela's eyes.

"Abuela!" Jade called.

"Mommy!" Katerina called, almost at the same time. Katerina began to run toward them, but something must have reminded her that she was supposed to be careful with Abuela, and she stopped just before she got to them. Abuela smiled at her and Jade, but she didn't move. Her smile was slightly crooked, with one side drooping a little, as if that side of her face were more tired than the other.

Her mom put the brakes on the wheelchair and scooped Katerina up, squeezing her and kissing the top of her head. When she put her down, Katerina reached out and hugged Abuela's neck from the side of the wheelchair.

"Jade, honey," her mom said, her arms outstretched.

Jade walked into those arms and squeezed her mother back, burying her face in her shoulder. She had missed her. And now that she knew what the mirror had brought to her mom, it felt like they shared more than before. Even if they didn't say anything about it.

When she let go of her mom, Jade leaned over the wheelchair and Abuela smiled up at her—that same, sleepy smile. Jade reached out, took her hand, and rubbed it.

"Hola, Abuelita," she said. Abuela always liked it when she called her that. Abuela rubbed her hand back, and the motion felt tired but warm, like her smile.

Something cool and smooth brushed against Jade's palm. She looked down and, with a thrill of recognition, saw Abuela's jade bracelet. The tiny stones shone in a dazzling array of green under the floodlights, from the pale yellow green of a fall leaf that was just beginning to turn to the bold blue green of a parrot's wing. The colors were as varied as those she had seen in the jade stones in the museum, if not more so.

"You're still wearing it!" said Jade. It was still on her wrist, despite the stroke, and the hospital . . .

Abuela nodded, still with her tired smile, but squeezed her hand and let it go, as if to say, *Another time.*

Jade nodded and pulled away. She would ask her about the bracelet later.

Her dad drove them back toward the Atlanta skyline on the wide black highway studded with red taillights. The city was lit up in all its glamour now against the night sky, and for the first time, seeing that skyline made Jade feel like she was headed home. Abuela dozed in the front seat and Katerina leaned sleepily against their mom in the back beside Jade. When her dad got off the highway and they passed the weighty metal sign with the cutout of Martin Luther King's face glinting copper under the streetlights, Jade knew they'd be arriving soon.

Back at the house, Jade's parents didn't let either her or Katerina anywhere near the guest bedroom as they got Abuela situated. Getting her settled into the room was a whole ordeal. Jade was surprised at how little Abuela protested at all the attention that was being poured onto her, all the help she was being given. She didn't complain at all as Jade's mom told her where she was going to sleep and didn't put up a fight when her dad offered her the walker.

Abuela walked very, very slowly, leaning heavily on the walker, Jade's mom close beside her. It unnerved Jade to see Abuela like this, and she could tell that Katerina wasn't sure what to make of it either. Her sister hung back with Jade and watched, silent and wide eyed.

When the household began to quiet for the night, Jade padded toward the kitchen in her pajamas and socked feet to fill up her glass of water. She stopped in the hall when she heard her parents' voices in the kitchen.

"Are you sure you can't get someone else to go instead?" her dad was saying.

"No, Chris, this is a big opportunity for me. All the major health organizations are going to be there—I can't miss it. This is my beat."

Jade stood very still, trying to breathe as silently as she could. Like Itztli, who could step silently through the forest, not rustling even a fallen leaf.

"I know this is really important, Sol," her dad said, "but it's just—you've been gone for so long already. The girls need you."

Jade remembered now that her mom was supposed to leave again. That work trip to New York.

"The girls are fine," her mom said. "Look, I know they've missed me, and I've missed them, too. But I can't pass this one up."

Jade *had* missed her mom. She didn't like the idea of her leaving again anytime soon.

"I get it, Sol, but—"

"Chris, I *know* this is a lot to ask of you."

"That's not it, honey. It's a lot but I'm happy to do it."

"Then what is it?" Her mother sounded exasperated.

"It's about *you*, I'm worried about *you*," he said. "You've stretched yourself thin already, and now you're going to turn around and leave again tomorrow? I just don't want you to get burned out."

Tomorrow? Jade hadn't even had time to get used to the idea that her mom was back.

"I know, I know, but I'll be back on Tuesday," said her mom. "The girls will hardly miss me, and I barely have to pack a change of clothes. I'll just be gone tomorrow night and Monday, and then I'll be home on Tuesday. I'll be here in time to pick Jade up from practice if you need me to."

Her parents were silent for a moment.

"I got it, Sol," her dad said after a while. "This is important for you. And it's no problem for me to stay here and take care of things."

Jade heard a crunch and was pretty sure her mom had bitten into a piece of chocolate. She was surprised at how clearly she could hear it.

"The physical therapist will be here tomorrow," her mom said, with her mouth a little full. "The sitter might come, too." Her mom swallowed. "And we can meet them together."

Mortimer came out silently to see what Jade was up to. She crouched and scratched behind his ears, watching his eyes narrow to contented, yellow-green slits.

"Chris, thank you so much for everything that you've done already," she heard her mom say.

Her dad mumbled something, and then she heard no more words—but from the noises she did hear, she was pretty sure they were making out.

That wasn't something she wanted to eavesdrop on. As quietly as she could, she tiptoed back to her room, with Mortimer at her side, petting her ankles with his tail.

She had to admit that there was something strangely comforting about knowing that her parents were kissing in the kitchen. It meant that her family was back together again, and that was something special that not everyone had. Chloe didn't have that anymore.

She filled up her glass with tap water in her bathroom while Mortimer traced figure eights around her feet.

Jade didn't see much of Abuela the next day either. It was a bright, lazy Sunday. Abuela only came out for meals, shuffling slowly with her walker. Jade's mom stayed close by her side, and they spoke softly with each other in Spanish. Jade caught floating words of their conversations. *Mamá, coma esto. Gracias, mija. Tome. No, yo lo hago.*

Her mom answered the doorbell in the early afternoon fully dressed as Mrs. O'Callaghan. Jade drifted into the living room, curious, and sat in the recliner, her finger marking the page of the Revolutionary War novel she was reading for language arts. Katerina drifted in, too, and dropped to the floor beside the mostly done puzzle. In the part of the puzzle that Katerina and her dad had finished, a cat as black as Mortimer peeked over the shoulder of a woman whose black hair was tied up and decorated with butterflies. The leaves of many greens in the background weren't finished yet.

"Oh, you're both here, thank you so much," Jade's mom said, when she opened the front door. "I really appreciate you coming here on a Sunday." She held the door open for two women who stepped in wearing scrubs.

The first had ebony skin and wavy black hair, and she looked a little younger than Jade's mom. Her makeup was as perfect as Chloe's mom's. She carried a doctor's bag at her side, and the way she held herself made Jade think of Coach Jackson.

The shorter woman who came behind her was older and had the build of someone who had worked many years. She had a round caramel face and graying black hair pulled back into a wispy, loose bun. Jade's mom ushered them into the dining room.

"So, you're—Mrs. O'Callaghan?" said the younger woman, with a hint of incredulity. "That's right," her mom said, extending her hand. With a smile, holding her head high, she pressed past the woman's surprise. Jade had seen her mom do this many times. "You must be Dr. Johnson," her mom said.

"You can call me Crystal," the young woman said, returning her smile and shaking her hand.

"And you must be Ms. Gutiérrez," her mom said, turning to the older woman.

"Dolores," she said, and holding out her hand. Her mom clasped it in both of hers.

"Please, sit," her mom said, motioning to the dining room table. She waited for them to sit first.

Jade only half paid attention to what she was reading while they talked business at the table. Her dad came in as they were wrapping up the paperwork.

"This is my husband, Chris," her mom said, "and these are our girls, Jade and Katerina." She gestured to the two of them in the living room. Jade waved at the two women and suddenly felt as shy as Katerina.

Her dad greeted Dr. Crystal in English and Dolores in Spanish, saying, "Mucho gusto." Dolores seemed to appreciate this, responding in Spanish, too. Her dad's pronunciation was good. He always did that—he would say something in Spanish to any Spanish speakers he wanted to be friendly with, even when her mom stuck to English. On her mother's tongue, English was professional, and Spanish was private.

Her mom took Dr. Crystal and Dolores to meet Abuela in the bedroom. When they had disappeared behind the door, Katerina asked, "Daddy, who are those people?"

"Dr. Crystal is a physical therapist," he said, dropping to his knees to help her fill in the puzzle. "She's going to help Abuela gain her strength back in her left side. And Dolores is a sitter, and she's going to make sure Abuela has all the things she needs."

"How much are they going to be around?" said Jade. She wasn't quite sure what to make of having these new people in the house, and she wanted to know what to be prepared for.

"At least one of them will be here every day during the day, for the next few weeks. As long as necessary." Jade thought she heard some weariness in his voice. He didn't look up from the puzzle.

Jade went back to her book. She didn't yet know how she felt about having them around. She just wanted her mom.

When her mother said goodbye again in the early evening, Jade held back in the kitchen as Katerina protested. Her sister was only consoled when their mom promised, for the third time, that she would be back on Tuesday. Tuesday—it was hardly more than a day away.

Jade only gave her mom a quick hug at the last second. She didn't want to make a big deal out of her leaving, because she didn't want to think about her being gone again.

"You'll be back Tuesday," Jade said as she pulled away from the hug.

"Of course, honey," her mom said. Jade could feel her trying to catch her eye, but she only met her mom's eyes briefly and scurried back to her room. Dolores and Dr. Crystal had left, and Jade was supposed to take care of Katerina until her dad got back from driving her mom to the airport. Jade knew that if she flopped down on her bed with her book, Katerina would eventually come in with her animal toys to play on her floor. That would make it easier to pass the time.

Mortimer hopped up onto the bed with Jade and nuzzled against her in a puddle of golden light on the covers. She reached out to rub his neck and back with one hand while she held the book open with the other. The story was starting to get interesting—the girl was falling for the neighbor, whose big, strong hands were sooty from smithing, and they were about to finally spend some time alone together, without any "chaperones." A thick amber ray fell diagonally across the page, casting thin curled shadows of her flyaway hairs onto the soft pages.

She heard the back door close, and like clockwork, Katerina pattered in. Her sister sighed and plopped herself down to play with her toys.

Jade heard a sound. She looked up from the book. At first she thought it might be the cry of an animal outside her window, but then with a jolt she realized it was Abuela calling.

Not stopping to think, she tossed the book onto the covers and raced down the hall to the guest bedroom where Abuela was staying. The door was closed but she opened it in one swift motion without hesitating.

"Abuela?" she called into the dim room. She listened over the pounding of her heart for a response.

"Chalchihuite, pasa, pasa."

Jade stood in the doorway, her hand still on the knob. She let Abuela's strong voice calm her. She had said her name—Chalchihuite—the way she and Abuelo had always said it, the way Itztli now said it, too.

Abuela was sitting against the bolster in the middle of the bed, the colorful embroidered pillows on either side of her, with her hands folded on her lap like before. A loose white dress that she had also embroidered around the collar billowed up around her. She was still wearing her jade bracelet, and the way the waning sun hit the small green stones, they could almost be amber.

"What is it, Abuelita?" said Jade. She was slightly out of breath from the sprint.

"Tráeme un tecito de manzanilla, por favor, Chalchi-huite," she said.

That was it? She just wanted a cup of tea?

"Is there anything else, Abuelita?"

"No, nada más," she said.

"Are you all right?"

"I will be when you bring me that tea." She said it with that sleepy smile.

"Right."

Jade left the door slightly open and dashed to the kitchen, practically skidding to a stop in front of the pantry. As she scanned the shelves for chamomile, Katerina came in and said, "Is Abuelita okay?"

Jade found the chamomile and filled the kettle. "Yeah, she's fine," she said. "Go play with your animals." She knew as soon as she said it that that was one of the worst things you could say to Katerina. She never wanted to miss out on the action.

"Can I play with them in Abuela's room?" she said. She was holding a toy horse.

Jade was a little startled that Katerina was treating her a bit like she was their mom. All of a sudden, Jade was caring for Abuela. Now she was supposed to set the rules for Katerina?

"No, you're not allowed in there," she heard herself say, as she put the kettle on to boil. Really, she wasn't allowed in there either, but that rule was out the window at this point. "You can play with them in the hallway," she said. "Right outside Abuela's bedroom." Those words surprised her too as they came out of her mouth. Abuela's bedroom?

It was the guest bedroom. But for the moment, it was Abuela's.

To Jade's astonishment, Katerina didn't ask any more questions, and instead carried her horse into the hallway.

As Jade waited for the kettle, the evening darkened, sharpening the even blue flames of the gas burner. In her mom's family, chamomile was to "calmar los nervios"—to calm the nerves. She might need some herself.

She chose a painted mug with a small, crouching animal that had big ears. Somehow it felt like the right mug for Abuela. She poured the tea and carried the steaming cup and a small plate for the teabag back to Abuela's bedroom, stepping carefully past where Katerina was playing.

As she set the tea down on the bedside table, she took in the room that she hadn't been allowed into since Abuela got here. The fading sun cast a reddish glow from the window and stained pink the wooden rosary that dangled from the lamp on the table. Abuela looked patient and almost regal in her brightly embroidered white dress. Jade wondered if there was any way Abuela could ever look undignified.

"It has to cool," she told Abuela.

"Gracias," said Abuela. "Prende la lámpara, ¿no?"

Jade turned the lamp on, even though it wasn't necessary for her own eyes. Lately she could see just fine even in low light. It was strange, in fact, how clearly forms appeared to her in the fading light, not as shadows, but as what they were.

The walker stood beside the bed. Jade lowered herself onto its flat cushion and pulled herself up close to the bed.

"Abuelita . . . ," she began. She knew she wasn't supposed to talk much to Abuela—she was supposed to let her rest.

But it was hard not to ask. She wanted to know about Abuela's bracelet. And she wanted to know about this mug, and the little blue animal that was painted on it. Who had made it, and how? And what blue was this? It looked more like the blue that Itztli had painted than the blue from indigo that she had seen on the vase in the museum. Perhaps it was another blue entirely? Or an echo of other blues?

"Abuela," she said, "I know this mug came from the restaurant. But—where did you and Abuelo get it?"

Abuela closed her eyes and leaned her head back against the cushion. "They are from our hometown," she said.

"San Juan de las Jacarandas," said Jade. It wasn't the first time she had said the name of the town out loud, but it was the first time she paid attention to how it sounded. She liked the open vowels, how soft the words felt in her mouth.

"¡Exactamente!" said Abuela, her dark eyes flashing open and catching the lamplight. "So you know about it?"

"A little," said Jade. "Abuelo used to tell me stories."

Abuela closed her eyes again. "Ernesto," she said, as if his name were a prayer. "There used to be a market there, that appeared on the streets every Sunday," she said, opening her eyes a little. "They probably still have a tianguis there. It was still there the last time I went back there, to bury Ernesto."

Tianguis. It was a word Jade knew from somewhere deep inside her, a word that Abuelo must have used.

"I used to sell my clothes there, you know," she said, with a proud smile that was only a little crooked. "Everyone wanted my embroidery. Mis bordados. Blusas, rebozos, vestidos de novia . . . And I got good money for them, too." She held up her index finger and looked straight at Jade, to make sure she got this part.

Jade nodded. She had no doubt that Abuela had made good money selling her bordados. It was no secret that Abuela's great business sense had kept the Casa Azul going for so long. Besides, Abuela's bordados were the most intricate ones that Jade had ever seen, and the bright animals she embroidered always looked as if they were about to jump to life. The little green-and-blue hummingbirds that lined her collar this evening looked as if they would speed away at any moment in search of a flower.

"My sister Flor painted dishes like these," said Abuela, pointing to the mug.

Tía Flor? Jade looked at the mug and watched the steam wave gently just above the surface. She had never met Tía Flor, but she knew the name. Tía Flor still lived in Mexico. At Abuela's house there was a picture of her with Abuela, her arm wrapped around her, the two teenaged sisters leaning against each other and smiling at the camera.

They had a painter in the family?

Jade pulled the teabag out and cupped the raised painted surface of the mug in her palm. It was warm, but she thought it would be cool enough to sip.

Abuela accepted the mug from her slowly, deliberately. Her left hand was a little unsteady and seemed to lag behind her right hand, but once she clasped the mug, it steadied. She sipped cautiously, blowing lightly on the surface first. After the first sip she said, "Ahhh," and closed her eyes, and Jade wished she had made some for herself.

She couldn't wait any longer. "Did Tía Flor paint this mug?" she asked.

Abuela tilted her head and inspected it.

"I don't think she painted this one," she said. "Her specialty was birds. She was great with birds. Owls, eagles, hummingbirds . . ." She took another sip. "When I needed plates for the restaurant, I called up Flor and told her. But when I told her how many I needed"—Abuela shook her head—"she told me, 'Luz, estás loca. ¿Tantos platos?'" She laughed softly. "So, Flor made some of them. But her friends made many more. And we had them shipped all the way to Chicago."

Abuelo had told Jade about the market. About the leather saddles and the musical instruments and the candy. But he hadn't told her about the ceramics or the bordados.

The beaded jade bracelet slipped a little down Abuela's wrist. Jade was itching to ask her about it, but with an effort, she contained herself. Abuela looked as if she were about to fall asleep.

Abuela's eyes started to close. "Abuelita," said Jade. She reached for the mug, and Abuela's fingers relinquished it to her.

"Gracias, Chalchihuite," Abuela said, almost inaudibly. "Ahora sí, puedo dormir."

Jade set the tea down. She was glad Abuela would be able to sleep now.

Abuela began to scoot herself down the bed, using mainly her steadier right arm to try to get her head onto the pillow and turn in for the night. Instinctively, Jade reached over and carefully moved the bolster out of the way and pulled the covers up so Abuela wouldn't be cold.

"Buenas noches, Abuelita," she whispered.

"Buenas noches," said Abuela, and it sounded like she was already asleep.

Jade could almost hear Abuelo's voice from years ago. He had said the same thing so many times before, after a bedtime story, just before tucking her in for the night. She had never dreamed she would be tucking Abuela in like this.

She traced the little blue animal on the mug with the tip of her finger and breathed in the comforting smell of the chamomile.

There was a painter in her family.

She watched her pale reflection in the darkened window, taking in this information.

Abuela had fallen asleep completely. It was time to let her sleep undisturbed. Jade stood up as silently as she could and gathered up the tea from the table. As she headed out, she decided to leave the lamp on, in case Abuela needed to get up and use the bathroom.

She nearly tripped over Katerina in the hallway. She had forgotten she was there.

Katerina stood up from her toys and followed her into the kitchen.

"Is Abuelita okay?" Katerina said.

Jade leaned against the counter. "You already asked me that," she said.

Katerina just stood there with a spotted cow in her hand, waiting for an answer.

"I think Abuela just needs time, and rest—and tea," she said. "Then she'll be fine."

Headlights lit up the kitchen. Their dad was back.

Jade felt her stomach relax. Her mom wasn't back yet, but her dad was, and she could be a kid again.

14

Cross-country on Monday afternoon was much harder than it had been the week before. Coach Jackson ran alongside them on the forest paths in her deep blue tracksuit and high ponytail, shouting encouragements to get them to run faster. "All right, Bobcats! Faster! We gotta beat Christ Savior!" She never took her eyes off her stopwatch for long. Jade knew the idea was to beat your own PR—personal record—and Coach Jackson was tracking each and every one of theirs. But Jade pushed that out of her mind—she knew she ran best if she tried to fall in step with her teammates and make herself one with the pack.

"Christ Savior?" she managed to ask Chloe, panting.

"Biggest rival," said Chloe, breathing hard. "They always win."

They ran far deeper into the woods this time, along winding trails that sidled up close to the creek and pulled away from it again. Jade could hear the softly rushing water as they approached it, no matter how faintly it whispered, no matter how loudly Coach Jackson shouted or the girls' sneakers beat against the dirt. Through the trees on the sides of the path she caught brief glimpses of the ever-changing surface of the water that flashed as it captured the drops of afternoon light falling through the canopy. Once, the trail crossed the stream, and Jade glanced down at the water as she scurried over the wooden bridge that was missing most of its slats. The water danced, playful and dark, like the surface of her obsidian mirror.

Jade was enjoying herself, but the longer they ran, the farther the distances between the girls stretched out, and Jade soon realized she was lagging a bit. She made herself push forward. She didn't want to lose the sense that she was moving as a vital part of a whole. She ran through the burning in her calves and tried to drink in as much of the forest air as she could with each breath. She gulped in the spicy scent of pine bark, the moist aroma of the dark, soft dirt they trampled underfoot.

The woodsy smells comforted her and made her feel stronger. She let them propel her forward.

At last, they finished the loop and Jade made a final sprint toward the bright green field. Out on the trimmed grass beneath the flooding sunlight, she slowed and allowed herself to focus on the pain again. She wanted to crouch down in the prickly grass with her nose close to the silent, traveling ants, but she made herself keep walking upright, hands on her hips, breathing, breathing. Chloe did the same. When she came close to Jade, she held her hand up for a high five. *For what?* Jade thought. Just for surviving, maybe. She high-fived Chloe and kept walking, kept moving. She was afraid if she stopped the aches in her sides would flame up and turn her rigid.

Coach Jackson led them through some cool-down stretches, and at last Jade caught her breath. She could still smell the forest on her clothes as they walked to the parking lot.

Chloe's mom picked them up this time. Jade and Chloe had barely sat down on the curb to lean against their backpacks when she pulled up in the minivan.

"Hi, Ms. Eleni," Jade said as she and Chloe climbed into the back seat. Chloe's mom turned in her seat to smile at her. She was wearing sweats but it looked like her face was done up for the restaurant.

"Hi, Jade—so good to see you again!" She turned to Chloe. "Is your brother coming?"

Jade's heart jumped a little and she felt her ears get hot. Luckily, she was already flushed from running. She had almost forgotten about Nikos's existence. She had a crush on him, she remembered all at once. Or at least she thought she did.

"Oh, God knows where he is," said Chloe. "Let's just go home."

The car rolled forward slowly and Chloe's mom scanned the parking lot for her son. When they neared the exit, he flashed across in front of the car on his skateboard. He kicked up the board and yanked on the front door handle until his mom opened it.

"Jesus, Nikos, you can't just skate in front of cars like that!" his mom said as he got in.

"Mom, you were going like two miles an hour," he said. "Chlo, I know you have Oreos." He turned to the back seat, and his dark eyes fell on Jade. "Oh. Hi," he said.

Jade said nothing and felt herself blush even more deeply. She wondered if she might be turning a shade of purple. She felt immobilized by his gaze, pinned to the corner of the minivan.

But then he looked away from her and back at Chloe, and the moment was gone. Chloe did indeed have Oreos, and they all eagerly reached for them when she pulled them out.

Jade focused on chewing her Oreo and tried not to look at Nikos. She wondered what Chloe would do if this were Justin. She would probably pull the two sides of the Oreo apart and lick the sweet white inside slowly, seductively, while keeping her eyes locked with his. Jade didn't have the guts to do that. Besides, Chloe was right there.

But she kept watching him, the part of his face and shoulder that she could see from her seat. She wanted to memorize even more thoroughly the way his feathery hair pushed at the tops of his ears, the sharp outline of his forehead, his nose, his lips, against the gold-tipped leaves that whirred by on the side of the highway.

She reached for another cookie and saw Chloe watching her with an odd little smile on her face. Jade must have been staring way too long at Nikos. There was no way Chloe hadn't noticed this time, without Justin there to distract her.

Crap.

Jade munched on her second Oreo and watched Chloe apprehensively. Her friend pulled a purple binder and a mechanical pencil from her backpack at her feet and wrote something on a page of notebook paper.

When Chloe handed it to her, it said, *You like my brother, don't you?*

Jade stared at Chloe. Chloe was smiling. Was she really going to be okay with it?

Jade picked up the pencil, but she didn't write anything.

Chloe took the pencil from her and wrote underneath: *Come on, just tell me! You can tell me anything.*

She gave the pencil to Jade.

Jade took a deep breath. She wrote: *I guess so.*

Chloe read it and laughed out loud, then covered her mouth.

"What are you girls laughing about back there?" her mom said.

"Nothing," said Chloe.

Jade was smiling too, now, out of nervousness as much as anything. Chloe was writing something else, and Jade waited impatiently for her to finish. When she passed the binder back to her, Jade read: *That's totally fine. I know my brother is hot.*

Jade raised her eyebrows at Chloe. Chloe took the paper back and quickly scrawled more and handed it back to her.

But he's also a total drag, Jade read. *Not worth it. Trust me.*

It was Jade's turn to laugh and cover her mouth. She took the pencil and quickly wrote: *Don't worry. I completely forgot he existed until today.*

She passed the binder back to Chloe, and they both gave little laughs into their hands. It was fun to have a little secret between them.

Nikos turned around and tried to snatch the binder from Chloe. Jade's heart jumped again, out of fear this time. He got his hand on the page but Chloe snapped the binder closed, pinning his hand. All at once he reminded Jade of the most annoying boys in their grade.

"Seriously, what are you guys laughing about?" he said.

Jade found that she couldn't stop giggling. What if he got the piece of paper?

Chloe managed to get the page out of his clutch and out of his reach, even though he snatched at it.

"Kids, please!" their mom said.

Chloe held the paper high above her head and ripped it to tiny, illegible shreds and let them fall like confetti over her. She smiled at Jade, and this time she was full-on beaming.

Jade stopped her nervous giggling and just smiled back. She was so relieved. And in that moment she realized that she had way more fun passing notes back and forth with Chloe than watching Nikos skate and wishing he would look at her. Chloe was probably right—he was just a skinny kid who liked to tease his sister.

He was still hot, though.

Katerina was "helping" their dad in the front yard when Chloe's mom drove up to the house. She was kicking up dirt with her little red shovel at the edge of a new flower bed that their dad was preparing. It was soft and dark with freshly turned soil and manure. Her dad was leaning against his own normal-sized shovel, having a conversation across the cul-de-sac with the neighbor, a tall guy with sporty sunglasses. The slanting sun gilded their faces, and their long shadows spilled out on the grass behind them.

Jade hugged Chloe goodbye, holding the embrace a little longer than usual, as if to say, *thank you.* Chloe was sweaty but Jade was sweaty, too, and she didn't mind. She hopped out of the car, and as the minivan drove off, she waved hi to her dad and her sister and went in the house.

She slowed as she passed Abuela's door. It was slightly ajar. She wanted to push it open just a little and say hello, but the silence stopped her. Dolores and Dr. Crystal must have already gone home for the day, so Jade wouldn't be interrupting them, but what if Abuela was sleeping and she woke her up? She decided it was best if she waited to be invited in, like before.

Mortimer scurried up to her, meowed his greeting, and followed her into her room. She could tell from the edge in his meow that he wanted her to feed him. "It's not dinnertime yet," she told him, setting her backpack down. She kicked off her sneakers, rolled her sweaty socks off, and wriggled her toes, relishing the freedom. She reached for her notebook and colored pencils instinctively and flopped down on her belly on the bed. She was so tired from practice—all she wanted to do was let her mind wander, and draw.

She stared into space and zoned out a little, tapping her grass-green pencil against her lips. Her eyes focused and she was staring at Itztli's bark painting—at the fine blue lines and the undulating swath of the water.

She looked down at the blank lined page and hovered her pencil above it, thinking of the water beneath the bridge at practice today, its dark, sparkling surface. Of Abuela's bracelet.

Touching the light green pencil to the paper, she stroked the page softly, making the color come out just barely. The tip of the pencil sounded like a feather brushing the page. She drew a ring of beads like Abuela's bracelet. At the edge of each one she pressed harder, trying to get the opaque sheen that would curl the page.

The beads came out the eye-aching green of the track field. Jade did what she could to give them more life with blue, yellow, and dark green. But the familiar frustration set in, only deeper this time: There was no way she could evoke the glistening turquoise and amber of the stones with her old colored pencils.

Maybe now was the time to try out the better materials, the art supplies her grandma had bought for her that she had never used.

She went to her desk and opened the drawer where she kept them: the sketchbooks with the fancy pages, the elegant pencils of many colors with gold lettering stamped on the sides, the pastel-colored chalk with the corners still sharp. And sitting flat on top of the sketchbooks, the tin case of watercolors her grandma had given her a few Christmases ago.

Jade pulled out the narrow tin box and held it in both her hands, before setting it carefully, quietly on her desk. Not taking her fingers off it, she sat back in her desk chair, still not opening the box. The sunlight streaming in began to warm the metal.

She looked at the window. Mortimer was lying on the windowsill, lazily soaking up the late afternoon sun. She looked past the soft black arch of his back to the pine trees that lined the yard. She needed help to get the colors right and to draw stories the way she wanted to. And Itztli was the one who could guide her best.

What could he tell her about the small jade stones she had seen in the museum, as well as the ones on Abuela's wrist? Could he show her how to paint them, how to get the color right? Could he help her know what to say to Abuela, how to ask her about her bracelet, about the market where she used to sell bordados? And could he tell her more about the mirror—more than her mom had already begun to tell her? Right now, Jade wanted nothing more than to escape back into the pine-scented shelter of the woods. The shadows of the pines were already long, but these September afternoons lingered for a while before reddening to sunset and the first hushed grays of dusk.

Tiptoeing swiftly and silently on her bare feet, Jade headed to the back door and out toward the forest.

Blades of grass pressed gently into her bare soles. She liked the feeling of the moist earth beneath her toes as she stepped across the striped shadows of the pines. When she came to the edge of the trees, she kept walking. The twigs and bristles of the forest floor prodded her, but she didn't mind. She pressed on. She knew Itztli was somewhere here, somewhere nearby, even though she hadn't yet seen his golden fur.

Something made her stop. The ground was more damp here—she figured she was close to the water. She closed her eyes and heard it—the happy little gurgle of the stream skipping over the polished pebbles, rounding the bend where Itztli told his stories.

She thought perhaps she heard his purr. A deep rumbling that she felt more than heard.

She peered through the trees but saw nothing.

A burst of sun gold and obsidian black flashed before her. It was Itztli. He must have leapt down from the tree directly above her.

"Itztli!" she said. She was so glad to see him—even more than she had thought she would be. The sight of his majestic fur, his sparkling, playful eyes that matched the colors of the afternoon forest, set her at ease, made her breathe slow and calm.

"I have so much to ask you," she said to him. The jaguar blinked, steady and assured. Jade saw once more how strong the animal was, how powerfully fearsome his paws.

With a graceful, dignified swish of his tail, Itztli turned, and Jade understood that she should follow. On his padded feet he stepped faster through the trees than she did, and she lost sight of him for an instant. Then she was at the bend in the creek, and he was on the other side, his old man self, leaning forward on his serpentine staff and smiling kindly at her.

"You have come again," he said.

Jade nodded and felt herself smiling back. Itztli looked even older than he had before, if that was possible. There was a curve in his back that she hadn't noticed last time, and he was leaning so heavily on his staff that it looked like he would surely fall without its support.

"Itztli," said Jade. She wanted to ask him one of the many questions that had been bumping around inside her. But seeing him standing like that, ever so slightly hunched, with his calm, wrinkled hands folded atop his staff, she remembered her manners and thought she shouldn't just launch into a fit of questions, the way Katerina sometimes did. Itztli was the oldest person Jade had ever known, and he deserved great respect and recognition.

"Thank you, Itztli," she began instead. "For—reminding me that I can still talk to Abuela. She's here now, in Atlanta, and she's getting better. She's still very weak, so I can't talk to her much, but—she has already told me some things."

Itztli's eyes brightened, and he smiled softly and patted the top of his staff. "I am glad," he said. A lone bird called its full-throated, falling whistle from the treetops—a cardinal, somewhere unseen.

"You said you had something to ask me?" said Itztli.

"Yes," said Jade. She had so many questions to ask, but she couldn't ask them all at once. Abuela's bracelet leapt to her mind most insistently. She thought of the jade beads dangling from her wrist and resting on the bedspread in the bedroom that was now hers. How the colors of the small stones seemed to shift continuously with the light, like the water in the creek. How she wanted to draw or paint these colors, but she didn't know how.

"My abuela has a bracelet made of jade," she told Itztli.

"What is it like?" he asked, his brow inquiring.

"It has rounded beads," she said, "and the jade comes in all these shades of green that are constantly changing."

"Are the beads carved?" he said.

She shook her head. "No, but I've seen some like that," she said, thinking of the small stones in the museum.

"Itztli, is there a reason to carve jade specifically? Or to make jewelry out of it? Was it used a lot—in your time?"

"Yes, Chalchihuite," he said. "Jade is a precious stone, and those who carved it were among the most revered and sought-after in my time, as were those who could locate the mother stones."

"The mother stones?"

"Great boulders with veins of jade, in all colors, from which the smaller stones were extracted. In my time, there were people said to be able to find these mother stones, wherever they lay. They could tell where they were from a tiny curl of smoke that rose from the place, a tendril of mist released into the air like a breath let out." Itztli raised one hand as he said this and opened it toward the sky. Jade imagined the great mother stones, exhaling from their place of rest.

"Jade is more than just a pretty stone," said Itztli. "I knew some people who put jade beads in the mouths of their loved ones when they died, to catch and hold their last breath." He clasped his free hand shut, like he had just caught something that he must not let go of.

Jade drew in her own breath and let it out slowly. Had her parents known all this when they'd named her Jade?

Perhaps this was part of what she was meant to do, what Itztli was guiding her toward. She knew that listening to all these stories, and holding on to them, was important. Maybe this was how she would fulfill the promise of her name.

Itztli shifted on his feet, and again Jade was reminded of how old he seemed—how much more so this time than before.

She was about to suggest that they sit, but before she could, Itztli said, as if he were thinking something similar, "I am getting older by the minute. We all are. I am glad you came now. There is much I need to tell *you*, Chalchihuite."

Jade said nothing. She had thought so much about how *she* needed Itztli and his stories, this space away from her house, away from school, away from everything, but she hadn't thought about how Itztli might need her. And that perhaps there was an urgency to that need.

"I'm here," she said at last, and she tried to concentrate on being all *here*—all of her. She worked her toes into the mud at the edge of the creek bed, as if to plant herself there.

"Good," said Itztli.

He straightened himself and walked gingerly over to what looked like a dark wooden book, wider and more square than an ordinary book. Jade held her breath as he walked, hoping he wouldn't slip into the creek. In slow motion, not letting go of his staff and making sure to keep his back in line, Itztli lowered himself and sat cross-legged beside the book. As he reached for the book, Jade lowered herself, too, crossing her legs beneath her like he did. Her body still ached from running. She wondered whether Itztli was about to read to her from the book. She felt a little too old to be read to, but there was also no way she was going to pass up listening to one of Itztli's stories.

As she watched the book in Itztli's ancient hands, waiting to see what he would do with it, she knew she had to be patient and wait to ask the rest of what was on her mind.

And Jade had a feeling that what Itztli was about to tell her might answer some of her questions anyway.

"It's difficult to know who you are, isn't it?" he said, and he looked at her as if he really wanted her to respond.

Jade thought about it. Yes, it was difficult. Especially now, when it felt like so many things were changing so quickly. She was trying to figure out who she was, and that was part of why she was here. It was clearer to her now why she was so intent on asking Abuela for her stories. It was not only because she wanted to know about Abuela and Abuelo and their life in San Juan de las Jacarandas, or because she wanted to gather and fit together as many of the missing pieces of Abuelo's stories as she could. It was also because she wanted to know who she was.

"It *is* hard," she said to Itztli.

"Indeed," he said.

For a moment, they listened to the stream rush by.

"Itztli, last time you told me you grew up knowing a secret," said Jade. "You said you grew up knowing you weren't just . . ." She could hear the word in her head, but she couldn't form it in her mouth.

"Purépecha," Itztli said patiently.

"Pu-RÉ-pe-cha," Jade repeated slowly. "You knew you weren't just . . . Purépecha." There, she'd gotten it. "You knew you were also Mexica," she went on. "How did you figure out who you were?"

Itztli's eyes flashed bright, and he didn't look quite so old anymore. "That, Chalchihuite, is the story I wish to tell you today," he said. "The story of how I came to know who I am." He patted the book affectionately. "Well. One of the stories."

It was always like that with Itztli. There was never just the one story.

Jade settled in, prepared herself to listen.

"When I was still a young man, a pestilence swept through our town. It was the same sickness that had descended upon Tenochtitlán, the Mexica capital, and had taken so many Mexica. A sickness brought here by the Spaniards. It made painful red welts rise up all over your skin. It killed slowly, and the afflicted moaned for days on their reed mats."

Jade was still. She could barely imagine something as terrible as that—or what it must be like to remain alive, to survive while those you knew struggled in vain against their painful deaths.

"My mother succumbed to it," said Itztli, lowering his eyes to the book.

"Oh, Itztli," said Jade. "I'm so sorry." She didn't know what else to say. It sounded like such an awful way to die. And Itztli had said he was still a young man when it happened.

Itztli nodded. "Tlazocamati," he said softly. Jade knew he was expressing gratitude.

He took a deep breath and went on. "When my mother died, it felt like the world broke. I was at a loss. As we were burying her, dressed in all her favorite clothes and jewelry, I realized that with her I also lost everything she could tell me about who I was." He looked into the stream, and Jade wondered if he was seeing it all again there, in the undulating waters. "I couldn't bear it anymore in my town, without her. In those days I spent most of my time in Tzintzuntzan, the Purépecha capital on Lake Pátzcuaro.

I was becoming something of a celebrated painter there, after I had worked on the history they asked me to paint." He said this with a little squaring of his shoulders that let Jade know he was proud of this. "But I wanted to know more about my father and his people. My mother was no longer there to tell me what she knew, so I set out to find out everything I could on my own."

Jade nodded. She understood.

"I set off for Tenochtitlán," said Itztli. "The land of my father. I hoped to offer my services as a painter, and learn more about the great art of painting—how to be a tlacuilo." Tlah-KWEE-loh was how it sounded.

"Tlacuilo?" said Jade. She said it carefully, but she got it right, and she liked how it sounded. She enjoyed how the *l*s leapt vivaciously off her tongue.

"Yes!" said Itztli, and a smile broke across his wrinkled face—the biggest one Jade had ever seen him give. "A tlacuilo. A writer, a painter. A writer of pictures. A painter of stories."

That was the word! It made her so happy that there was a word for it, for the people who painted the stories. She said the word again softly—*tlacuilo*—and made up her mind to remember it.

"It is a long, long tradition," said Itztli. "And I wanted to learn from the very best."

"And the best painters lived in Tenochtitlán?" said Jade.

"Many of them, yes." He twirled a pen in one hand above the book. It was the same wooden pen he had used that first time, to draw in the ground on the stream bank. She leaned closer over the narrow ribbon of the stream to get a better look at it. It was hollow and pointed, as if it had been cut from a tall, sturdy grass.

She looked around for the rest of his tools, wondering if he would paint or draw this time, and if he would use that brilliant blue again. She felt a surge of excitement as she saw a neat set of small clay pots like the one he had used before lined up beside the book. A paintbrush lay beside them as well, its bristles soft and clean, waiting to be used. From where she was seated across the creek, Jade couldn't see what colors the clay pots held. She would just have to wait and see what Itztli made with them.

"The painters of Tenochtitlán painted the walls of the new houses that the Spaniards built for their god," Itztli went on. "And they painted books. Histories. They painted the way the master tlacuilos had painted before them, for generations. And they took what they wanted from the Spanish pictures, too. Moctezuma's old library was gone, but there was a school that the Spanish had set up, and it had a library full of books that the Spanish had brought with them. Beautiful books, many of them, bound in leather, with gold edging and filled with woodcut prints." He picked up the wooden book and ran his finger along the edge of it. Again a wave of curiosity pulsed through Jade. She wanted so much to know what was inside the book.

"The school taught the Bible and Latin, but there you could learn the old traditions, too," Itztli went on. "The ways of the Mexica—my father's people. As long as, of course, you never took a false step into heresy."

Jade knew vaguely about how frightening the church used to be, how heretics had been sought out and persecuted.

Even killed. It must have been difficult to walk that fine line, to tell your own stories and never come down on the wrong side of things. A tough balancing act, a dance on the edge of a knife.

"So you went to that school," said Jade.

"Yes," said Itztli. "Santa Cruz Tlatelolco. I wanted to learn everything I could. And I was lucky, because I met a tlacuilo there who had known my father. His Christian name was Martín. Ay, Don Martín." He looked down the stream, and seemed to see farther down it than was possible because of the trees. "Don Martín took me in, let me stay with him for a time. He made no fuss that I was raised Purépecha. He said, 'Itztli, your father died defending this city, its people, and its splendor. How else can I receive his son, except to welcome him into my home and treat him as my own?'" He looked back at Jade. "That was the kind of person he was."

"Did he tell you what you wanted to know about your father?" asked Jade.

Itztli nodded slowly, and the way he lowered his head and blinked was just the way he had as a jaguar, when he had first greeted her that afternoon.

"The way Don Martín spoke of my father, I thought perhaps my mother was right about the stories she told me. He told me that my father became a jaguar warrior because he could pick out a man far away among the trees and the spears he hurled with atlatls landed with deadly precision. He could scale a tree in an instant and watch, unnoticed from above, and he could dash swiftly up and down the mountains and through the forests, hardly stirring a leaf. Don Martín told me that my father was trusted to choose well when to hurl a spear, and when to sit still. He was a jaguar because of his powers to create and to destroy."

Itztli's father sounded very powerful. Jade wondered what it must be like to know someone like that was your dad.

"I wanted to know everything, of course, about my father, about his people," said Itztli. "The Mexica, and the people of the Eagle Cave. I lived for the stories that Don Martín told me in those days. He used to stand in the entrance of his house and point to the mountains that surrounded us, the volcano in the distance that sometimes smoked like a simmering pot. He told me how these mountains were sacred, how Tenochtitlán was a great watery hill that echoed them. He told me how the great temple that had once stood proudly at its center had itself been like a watery hill, and he told me the stories of the gods that were venerated there. I went to sleep at night telling the stories to myself over again, memorizing them." He ran his fingers along the book cover, following the contours of the wood grain. "It was Don Martín who told me the very first story I told you," he said, looking up at her. "The story of some of my father's people, the people of the Eagle Cave."

"I remember," said Jade. "The people who the Mexica eventually conquered—and mixed with."

"That's right," said Itztli, and he sounded content that she had remembered this. "But most of all," he said, and here he raised his pen in the air to make his point, "Don Martín taught me to *paint* it all."

At last, Itztli opened the book.

Jade held her breath and watched in wonder as Itztli opened it out. This was no ordinary book. It didn't open at the spine with the pages fanning out. Instead, Itztli pulled the two wooden bindings away from each other, and bright pages burst forth, unfolding like an accordion.

He set the opened-out book down gently on the soft earth beside the stream. It was almost as long as Itztli was tall. Jade stared in awe at the fine white squares arrayed on the ground like a tiny, low mountain range.

The most surprising thing of all, perhaps, was that the pages were blank. Pristine and white, they reflected the glowing sunlight and were patterned with the swaying shadows of the leaves. She watched as Itztli dipped his hollow grass pen in the first clay pot, tinting its tip with black ink. He positioned himself carefully beside the last page of the screenfold and held the pen poised just above the page.

Jade had seen him draw and paint before, but was he going to paint an entire book now?

Itztli grinned at her. "You've never seen a book like this, have you?" he said, with a hint of the same pride she had detected before.

"No, never!" said Jade. But then again she had never before seen almost anything that Itztli had shown her.

"It's an amoxtli," he said. *Ah-MOSH-tlee.* The soft consonants crowded together and made the sound of a freshly fallen leaf sweeping the ground.

Jade whispered the word. "Amoxtli." She thought she got it right, but somehow when she said it, it didn't quite sound like it did when Itztli said it.

She wondered how an amoxtli worked. Did you read it from left to right? Was it all one picture, one story?

Itztli had begun to draw. With the fine black ink, he drew a lake with watery hills around it. In the center of the lake he drew two islands, a temple, and some houses. Jade understood that it was Tenochtitlán. From the edges of the lake inward to the islands, he penned narrow causeways. With the very tip of his pen he inked tinier islands, dispersed about the lake, which seemed to be sprouting. He painted with a swift dexterity that left Jade with her mouth hanging slightly open. His skill and artistry, Jade thought, was that of someone who had been painting for hundreds of years.

"Don Martín taught me all this," said Itztli as he painted. "He taught me all the old tlacuilo ways. How to paint time passing, how to write the dates, the places, with hills and water and rabbits and dots—and curling tongues for speech. He taught me how to find all the right colors, and how to mix them into paints."

Jade wanted to know more, but she found she could only watch in silence, drawn in by the painted lines.

"When I arrived, Tenochtitlán was not what it once was," Itztli continued, adding minuscule details to the tiny sprouting islands. "The school where Don Martín taught me to paint was here." He tapped the smaller of the two larger islands in the middle of the lake. "Tlatelolco."

Jade scooted forward on the stream bank so she could see the details better.

"There used to be a market there, where they sold everything you could think of," said Itztli. Jade thought of the tianguis in San Juan de las Jacarandas that Abuelo and Abuela had told her about. "Painted bowls, embroidered tunics, feather paintings."

"Feather paintings?" said Jade, astonished at the thought.

"Oh yes!" said Itztli. "Did you think that paintings were only made with ink?" The light played in his eyes. Jade tried to imagine what on earth a feather painting might look like. Did the artist nudge tiny feathers into place to form a carpeted mosaic? Would it shimmer like the wing of a bird mid-flight?

Itztli turned back to his artwork and tapped the temple. "This was the great temple that Don Martín told me about, that I only saw the ruins of when I got there." Jade looked more closely and saw that the temple had two small peaks. Itztli pointed to the first one. "This is the shrine for Huitzilopochtli," he said.

Huitzilopochtli. Jade remembered the name from the first story he had told. "Was that the Mexica warrior god?"

"Yes!" said Itztli. He looked pleased with her. "The Hummingbird of the South, who led the Mexica people to Tenochtitlán." His demeanor changed, darkened a little. He shook his head, dipped his pen absently in the same inkpot. "Huitzilopochtli, the warrior god of the sun, who could blaze forth and drive out even the total darkness of night. A fearsome god, indeed—and you must remember, I was raised to resist these Mexica and their warriors who set out to conquer all of us."

Jade wriggled her toes in the dirt and considered this. It must not have been easy at all for Itztli to reconcile who he was. How do you accept that you're the son of a

celebrated Mexica jaguar warrior, and at the same time
love those who raised you to resist what he stood for?

Itztli tapped the other peak of the temple. "The shrine
to Tláloc," he said. "The rain god." He painted two bulging circles for eyes. "The one who makes the sproutings of
the earth possible. But also the one who destroys with
lightning and floods."

Above the temple he drew a cross. "By the time I got to
Tenochtitlán, the temple had been destroyed," he said.
"Some of the very same stones that had once formed the
temple, that had been carved and placed with great reverence, were used to build the cathedral to the Spanish god,
in the same city square. The Mexica warrior god and the
god of torrential storms and gentle showers—they were
defeated. They existed still only in memory and in the
stones that now were made to serve another purpose, and
in the few painted stories that survived, or the ones that
were painted anew, from the memory that was beginning
to fray and wear thin like an old huipil."

Huipil. Jade had heard Abuela use this word before,
maybe once when she was talking about her bordados.

She thought about these stones and painted histories
that held the memories of the gods and their stories. She
understood a little of what it felt like to try to pin down a
remembered story and somehow keep it alive. There was
no way the new painted stories could be just like the old
ones—that wasn't possible. Still, though, they could hold
memories.

And if the stones held memories, but they were strewn
about, torn away from the temple where they had been so

carefully placed—what happened to the stories? Did they get broken apart and mixed up, too?

Itztli's painting folded time over onto itself, she thought. There was the temple, and there was the cross, the two existing at once.

Her eyes fell again on the tiny islands that seemed almost to float on the lake. "What are those small islands, Itztli?" she asked, pointing to them.

"Chinampas," he said, brightening once more. "Gardens. Ingenious inventions and feats of irrigation." Again his brief excitement dimmed. "They, too, were destroyed by the time I got there. Along with the lake."

That was a terrible before and after.

Now Itztli was outlining an intricate man, who was seated and wore so many clothes and jewelry, Jade figured he must be royalty.

"Moctezuma," Itztli said, as if in answer.

Moctezuma was nearly as large as the city. He was that important. Near his mouth, just a little above it, Itztli inked what must have been one of those "curling tongues for speech" that Don Martín had taught him to paint. It was as if to indicate that Moctezuma was a ruler and a speaker.

Beside Moctezuma, Itztli painted a giant bird. But it was no ordinary bird. Then again, nothing was ordinary about this painting.

It had a mirror for a head.

"You told me about this!" said Jade, almost rising from where she was seated. "You told me that your father was there when Moctezuma looked into it and saw that the Spaniards were coming."

Itztli smiled and nodded at her like a teacher who was pleased with the progress of his student.

He stepped slowly, carefully, over to the other end of the amoxtli, leaning again on his staff. Swiftly he painted ships, a shoreline, and a man at the top of a hill, pointing out in the direction of the sea.

"Those are the Spaniards, right?" said Jade. She was amazed at how quickly Itztli had made the picture come to life. His painting reminded her of the animated designs in Abuela's bordados. The man pointing on the hill seemed almost to be in the continuous act of reaching out his arm and hand, and the boats looked as if they might float off the paper and away down the stream.

Almost. Maybe if he added color, they would.

"Yes," said Itztli. "Those are the Spaniards arriving." His black-on-white painting was spreading onto other pages now. A path with footsteps and watery hills snaked from the sea to the great city. The picture was familiar to Jade by now.

"The Spanish made their way over days and days from the coast all the way to Tenochtitlán," Itztli went on. His path joined the main causeway that led across the lake to the big center island. "But they did not conquer Tenochti-tlán alone," he said, and he raised his finger to her to make his point, just like Abuela had the day before. He shook his head. "They had the help of the Tlaxcaltecas."

"Right," said Jade, remembering what he told her last time, that the Tlaxcaltecas had allied themselves with the Spaniards to overthrow the Mexica.

"They were in some ways a people like mine, like the Purépechas," he said, smiling. "A people who resisted the Mexica. A people who resisted the empire."

It was hard to see why this group of people would help the Spaniards, who ultimately destroyed so much. But maybe—if Jade were in their place and the temple still stood, a monument to the empire's dominance, if the garden islands hadn't yet been drowned in bloodied, muddied water, if so many people hadn't yet died of the sickness that Itztli had talked about—then maybe, maybe, it might have made sense to help the Spaniards overthrow the Mexica.

The painting looked complete now, a map spread across the accordion pages. Before and after lived on them together all at once—the Spaniards arriving in the ships, the ships in the mirror on the strange bird's head, the footsteps arriving on the causeway. It was all painted there.

But right as Jade settled in to contemplate it as a finished work, Itztli splashed bright blue onto Moctezuma's headpiece. He was using the paintbrush now. She had been so occupied watching the picture appear on the pages that she hadn't seen him dip a brush into one of the other inkpots. The lake, the sea, the curling bases of the watery hills, he painted blue. It was the same blue he had used before, on the bark painting. The wet paint shimmered in the light that filtered through the leaves.

"What is that blue?" asked Jade.

"Texotli," he said. "From indigo."

Jade clasped her hands together and brought them to her heart. The same blue from the museum! The one from the plant in the garden that her father tended, with the dark green oval leaves.

"And if you mix in a little yellow," said Itztli, reaching for the third inkpot, "you get this." With the very tip of

the brush, he filled in the fine string of beads that Moctezuma was wearing with an incandescent green.

Just like Abuela's bracelet.

"What is this color?" she said, standing now. She was
too excited to sit. She stepped down into the shallow edge
of the stream to get a closer look. The cool water swirled
over her bare feet and lapped at her ankles.

"Quiltic," said Itztli, and he kept painting.

"Quiltic," she repeated. The jade green that the indigo
made, too.

Now the painting was complete. The shining blues
and greens gently drying in the falling sun shone like
jewels.

Suddenly Jade noticed how slanted the sun had gotten.
It flashed sideways through the trees now. For the first
time since Itztli had started painting, she took note of the
cool shadows on the paper again.

"I need to get home," she said, stepping back out of the
stream. "Thank you, Itztli."

He looked a little startled, but then he saw the shadows, too. "You are right," he said. "But I have one more
thing to tell you." He dipped his brush in the stream and
let the current wash it out. The green streaks faded to yellow and then clear. "As I listened to Don Martín tell me
about my father, as I learned about his ancestors and his
traditions, I also learned that, like my father, I was jaguar,
just not in the same way."

"How so?" said Jade. A gentle breeze whispered in the
leaves and cooled her ankles. Her hearing seemed to
sharpen as she listened carefully for his answer. She heard

distinctly the cardinal's warble overhead and the silky rustle of a freshly fallen leaf underfoot. It felt like Itztli was telling her something important.

He gave a soft little chuckle. "My dear Chalchihuite," he said, "that is a story for another time."

All at once Itztli was the jaguar again, and his fur was a shimmering dance of sun and shadow. With a flick of his tail he bounded away through the trees.

Jade felt something nudging at her toes. She looked down, and with a rush of elation, she saw the small ceramic pot of green ink.

A gift.

She stooped to gather it up, brought it to her chest, held it close. She would paint with it.

She looked back once more at the amoxtli painting on the other side of the creek. As it dried, the colors did not fade; they only darkened and became more solid.

It was really time, now.

Clutching the inkpot close, she ran, her wet feet picking up dirt and making it into mud as she went. As she dashed out of the trees and past the two tall oaks in the backyard, the muddy soles of her feet stamped footprints in the jade-green grass.

15

Jade heard Katerina and her dad coming in from the front garden just as she made it to the back door, scaling the steps lightly. She brushed off the muddy soles of her feet on the mat, its bristles rough and tickly on her bare skin, and heard the hollow clatter of their dirt-caked shoes as they shed them in the foyer. She tiptoed silently to her room, still clutching the inkpot to her chest.

She stood in the middle of her room and examined the little clay pot. It was squat and rounded, and fit perfectly in her hands. The rough ceramic sang softly against her palms like sand when she rubbed it. It was earth that hadn't been polished, a vessel meant to be used. The paint glistened and sloshed gently inside it, leaving a faint green rim.

The paint would dry out and lose its luster, she figured, if she left it out like that, uncovered. She wondered if the lid of one of the ceramic pieces in the house might do the trick. She set the pot down carefully on her desk to go look for one, and the soft thud of clay on wood was satisfying.

She hurried to the dark-wood china cabinet in the dining room. Something in here should work.

Her gaze landed on a colorful teapot. Its thin handle bent to its waist like a woman with her hands on her hips, and its long, elegant spout reminded Jade of the neck of a blue heron she saw once, when Abuelo took her down to the lake, back in Chicago. Bright animals of many colors ran across the teapot, jumping over one another and looking back at one another mid-leap. Jade had seen the teapot many times, but this time she looked at the animals more closely and saw that they were lean hares and spritely deer. On the small dome lid, tiny rabbits chased one another in a circle. Jade wondered if it was one of the pieces that Tía Flor had painted. She remembered similar teacups in her abuelos' house that she thought might be a matching set. They sat on a high shelf, as if they were too special to be used.

Carefully, she unlatched the glass door and reached in to grab the lid. It looked like it might be the right size.

She took it back to her room and, sure enough, it fit the inkpot perfectly. Satisfied, she set the pot on the bookshelf beside Itztli's blue-and-white painting. Now, at last, she had what she needed to paint Abuela's bracelet properly, to brighten her drawings of the stories that Itztli and Abuela told her with the missing color.

She knew it wasn't the only thing missing. And maybe, as with the artists who painted the stories of Tenochtitlán after it fell, some things would be lost forever. Itztli had learned so much about his father from Don Martín and from the painted stories. But he'd never actually met his father. No matter what, there must have been things that were always missing from the picture.

She wanted to try out the green paint, but now was not the time. She was too tired. Soon, though.

She walked over to the dresser drawer where she kept the obsidian mirror and stroked the wood there. Something Itztli had just told her floated up into her head: *Like my father, I was jaguar, just not in the same way.*

What did it mean to *be* jaguar? And did he *become* like that, or had he always been that way?

Mortimer pushed his whiskers into the crack in the doorway and stepped elegantly in. Jade crouched to pet him and heard her father's voice in the hallway. He was telling Abuela what he was thinking of cooking for dinner—roasted veggies and chicken thighs, a classic Dad meal—and was that okay with her, Doña Luz? Jade was pretty sure he didn't really have a backup plan if Abuela said no, but he consulted her as if she had the final word on the matter.

Suddenly Jade caught a whiff of her own armpit. She stood up and smelled herself—sweat and dirt and pine bark. The odor surprised her—she didn't remember ever smelling quite like this before. She didn't really mind it, but she was pretty sure she would never hear the end of it from Katerina if she didn't shower before dinner.

Before heading to the bathroom, she ran her finger lightly over the tiny rabbits on the lid and made a mental note to ask Abuela about them. Not tonight. She was too tired for that. And she wanted to wait until Abuela was feeling well enough to tell her the whole story.

The next morning Jade could feel that something inside her had relaxed. It was Tuesday, and her mom would be back from New York that night. Homeroom had an easy feel to it: Coach Jackson nodded to her as she walked in, and it seemed like everybody said hi to her, starting with the cross-country girls. She felt distinctly pretty, too, like somehow the running had made her that way.

The buoyant feeling carried her through first-period pre-algebra and into second-period language arts. But during language arts, something began to change. Something she couldn't quite put her finger on. It was as if the vibrations in the air had switched frequency, become more tense.

Ms. Franklin was trying to get them to talk about the Revolutionary War novel they were reading, but the class was being particularly unresponsive. There was a lot of quiet chatter, but no one would answer her questions. Jade had read past where they were supposed to, because she wanted to see the girl get the boy with the soot-stained hands. But she didn't dare raise her hand. That was another level—she still wasn't quite comfortable enough with her classmates to do that.

"Okay, what is it?" said Ms. Franklin, addressing them with pursed lips. She was a young redheaded woman who wore a skirt suit every day and acted older than she looked. She always meant business, and everyone knew you had to read for her class, just in case there was a pop quiz.

No one answered her.

"That's what I thought," she said. "Now. Can anyone tell me a theme that we see in chapter eight?" She squeaked the cap off her dry-erase marker expectantly.

Silence.

A theme that Jade remembered from chapter eight was how the smith boy would heat up the iron to mold it and let it cool again, then heat it up again some more. She liked thinking of his strong hands as he did this, the firelight leaping on his face. But she was pretty sure that wasn't what Ms. Franklin was going for.

"Do we remember what a theme is?" she said, and it sounded like she was trying to come across as patient. Benjamin raised his hand. "Yes, Benjamin."

"In the hall I heard Coach Porter say that New York is blowing up," he said.

A wave of gasps and mutters rolled over the class and subsided. Jade sucked in her breath. New York? It couldn't be.

This was the boy who had bounced a pig eyeball on the floor during a dissection in science class the other day, so maybe she shouldn't take him quite so seriously.

Ms. Franklin was taken aback for a moment, but she composed herself almost immediately. Tucking a strand of hair behind her ear, she said, "Benjamin, could you answer my question?"

Ms. Franklin moved the class forward, explaining the theme to them, something about light and dark, warmth and cold. Jade thought maybe she hadn't been so far off about the smith boy after all. But it was hard to pay attention. Was there something bad happening in New York? What were her classmates whispering about? Once again she felt left out, like she had at the beginning of the school year just a few weeks ago, and she couldn't wait to talk to Chloe over lunch.

When they got to the cafeteria, Jade realized that something was definitely wrong. All the adults wore worried looks. Caitlyn was missing from their lunch table because her mom had come to pick her up early.

"What's going on?" Jade said to Chloe, leaning across the table.

"I don't know," said Chloe. "I asked Ms. Reynolds, the lunch lady, about it, but she told me, 'Don't worry about it, sweetie.' I don't like that no one's telling us what's going on."

"Me neither," said Jade. "My mom is in New York right now," she added. "She's supposed to come home tonight." She wished Coach Jackson were around—an adult she could trust to tell her the truth about what was happening. She was pretty sure she wasn't going to get the full answer from Benjamin, and besides, it would be awkward to ask him what he had heard.

In Catholics in the World that afternoon, the soft-spoken Ms. Berenson started class as usual by leading them in the Prayer of Saint Francis. *Lord, make me an instrument of your peace* . . . At the end of the prayer, before making the sign of the cross, she added that "today we're praying in particular for those who are suffering."

Jade could barely contain herself. Who was suffering, and why wouldn't anyone tell her straight? Most of all, was her mom all right?

She thought about what Itztli had told her, that his father had fallen in a fierce battle to defend Tenochtitlán, fighting bravely in a wounded city. She pushed the thought from her mind. She didn't want to even think that something bad might have happened to her mom, in a city Jade had only seen in movies.

For the rest of the day she felt jittery and distracted. She drew intricate leaves and flowers in the margins of her notebooks to try to calm herself, to get absorbed in something. When the announcements came on over the intercom at the end of the last period, the prayers went on for longer than usual, and they included ones Jade had never heard before. The most important announcement was that all sports practice had been canceled. There would be no cross-country that afternoon.

When the bell rang at last, Jade shoved her books into her backpack helter-skelter, slammed her locker shut, and dashed out to the parking lot, hoping her dad would be there.

The parking lot was quietly chaotic. A tense hush had enveloped it, as if a cottony blanket had fallen down from the sky that was muffling everything. There were more cars than ever, and many of the moms—they were almost all moms—had left their cars parked and come right up to the breezeway to find their kids and snatch them away in a hurry. Even the moms who normally left their kids in after-school were there.

Chloe's mom was one of them. She gave Jade a distracted wave and took Chloe away quickly. Chloe waved back at Jade and disappeared into the parking lot.

That only made Jade more nervous. She saw Katerina coming out of the elementary school building and made her way quickly to where she was. Instinctively, she pulled her sister in close. Katerina didn't protest, only stood there pressed against her leg, scrunching up the tail of Jade's shirt with her fist.

There was her dad. Finally. He was walking toward them quickly across the parking lot. When he got to them, Katerina let go of Jade and latched on to him instead. He grabbed Katerina to him and gripped Jade's shoulder tightly, steering them away from the crowd of kids and moms and toward the Wildcat Trail. His jaw was set and his eyes and forehead were serious. His hand on Jade's shoulder was firm and steady.

"What's going on?" said Jade. She wasn't going to wait for someone to decide to tell her this time.

Her dad said it in her ear so Katerina wouldn't hear. "Two planes flew into the Twin Towers in New York. It made two huge explosions, and the towers came crashing down."

Jade tried to take it in. Apparently, what Benjamin had said hadn't been entirely off base. "Is Mom okay?"

Her dad nodded. "She's okay," he said quietly. "She's covering it now. She was one of the few reporters they had on the ground in New York when it happened."

"When the planes—" She lowered her voice for Katerina's sake, following her dad's lead. "The planes—flew into the buildings?" It sounded weird coming out of her mouth. Planes didn't fly into buildings.

"That's right," her dad said.

Jade couldn't believe it. Her mom was supposed to be getting home today—but instead she was on TV reporting on—*this*? Whatever *this* was.

"Um—the Twin Towers?" she said. Katerina was looking up at them, silent, and Jade could tell she was trying to figure out what was happening.

"The World Trade Center," her dad answered.

"The what?" said Jade.

"A very important pair of buildings in New York, where a lot of people work. Worked." He took a deep breath, ran his hand through his hair. "A lot of people died. Are dying."

Jade said nothing. She had never heard of this place, but clearly it was something big. She tried to imagine it, but it was hard to think of skyscrapers falling to the ground when the cool, leafy forest they were walking through felt so calm.

"They also attacked the Pentagon," he said, "in Washington, DC. The headquarters of the Department of Defense. And it looks like they tried to get to the Capitol or the White House, too, but that plane crashed somewhere in Pennsylvania."

Washington, DC was being attacked, too? What was happening? She had only ever seen the White House on TV, and the Pentagon sounded vaguely familiar.

"When is Mom going to be back?" she said.

"Yeah, is Mommy coming home today?" Katerina chimed in.

Her dad made a grimace, sucked in his breath. "Soon," he said to both of them. "I promise she'll be back soon. But I can't say when." To Jade softly, he said, "They aren't letting any planes fly. Not yet."

Jade was glad her dad was treating her like she could handle it. It was the way Itztli always treated her. But this was a lot, and a part of her almost wished she could be like Katerina, and not have to know about it all.

*

Jade heard the TV as soon as they walked into the house. Her mom's voice, tired, but professional as always. She went to the living room immediately to see. Dolores was there, standing in the doorway and watching.

There was her mom, on TV, like Jade had seen her so many times. She looked tired in a way that no makeup could hide. She stood with New York City's skyline in the background as dark smoke billowed, dirtying the clear sky over the blue-gray buildings. She was saying something in her reporter voice, but Jade could only watch her tired eyes. She wished so much for her mom to be here, in the living room with them right now. Instead, her mom was stuck at a disaster scene.

"She can't get close," her dad said quietly behind her. "It's too dangerous."

"Mom told you that?" said Jade.

Her dad pointed. "On TV," he said.

Jade nodded. That was yet another thing that was very weird.

Katerina wandered in behind her dad. Jade looked back at the TV and watched her mom say, "It looks like another building in the World Trade Center may be about to collapse."

This destruction wasn't over yet.

The blond anchorwoman in Atlanta took over and switched to the president giving a speech. Jade felt relief for her mom—it looked like she really needed a break.

The president stared out at the reporters for a second, the American flag hanging on a post behind him. He launched into his speech and the cameras flashed loudly.

With his squared shoulders and his voice that wavered less and less as he went on, he was trying to reassure people. Her dad watched with his arms crossed, and Dolores watched from the doorway with her hand over her mouth, not moving.

It was a short speech, and afterward the anchorwoman announced they were going to show a replay of the second crash. As soon as the clip started, her dad pulled Katerina into him to keep her from seeing.

The tall rectangular buildings stood side by side, twins indeed, except the first one was maimed, the top of it giving off ugly billows of black smoke. A jagged, cavernous hole gaped where the building had been torn through. And there was a plane, white, angular, and very fast against the blue sky, and—the explosion. The ball of fire bursting from the second tower, the second twin. The smoke rising, multiplying, filling up the sky. The plane was nowhere to be seen, engulfed in the flames.

It was such a jolting, unnatural thing to watch. The plane flying low and fast in the middle of a city skyline. The big skyscraper standing, then suddenly on fire.

"That's enough," her dad said, and he switched off the TV.

Jade stared at the silent black screen. At the edge of her vision, she saw Dolores make the sign of the cross.

The smoke looked terrible. Ugly, dirty, belching forth from the fire that kept burning and burning. Something from the worst nightmare.

Suddenly, she noticed that Abuela had come into the living room, too. She was leaning on her walker, her wooden rosary dangling from her fingers. Dolores said something to her quietly in Spanish.

Jade's dad cleared his throat. "Dolores, do you want to be with your family?" he said. "I know we talked about you staying until five, but you can go home now if you need to be with your family," he said.

Dolores thanked him and went to Abuela's bedroom to gather her things.

"Come on, bug," her dad said to Katerina. "Let's get you some string cheese." Katerina followed him into the kitchen.

Abuela was trying to lower herself onto the couch, and Jade walked over and held her arm. Abuela smiled at her and sat down. "Gracias, Chalchihuite," she said softly.

Jade sank into the couch beside her. Dolores came back with a light sweater and her bag, and squeezed Abuela's hand. "Su hija es brillante," Dolores told her, pointing to the TV. *Your daughter is brilliant.* She flashed a quick, warm smile at Jade and headed out the door.

"Es cierto, tengo hijos brillantes," Abuela said. *It's true, I have brilliant children.* Jade wasn't sure if she was saying it to her, or just to herself. "Sol, Carmelo." Abuela paused. "Efraín . . ."

Tío Efraín. The brother her mom never wanted to talk about.

Abuela reached over with her good arm and took Jade's hand. Her touch was light but firm. Jade knew it must have taken an effort for Abuela to shuffle into the living room on her walker, but she seemed strong.

"So many are going to be missing the people they love," Abuela said, looking directly at her.

Jade thought of what Itztli had told her. *When my mother died, it felt like the world broke.*

"You miss Tío Efraín," said Jade.

"Of course," she said. "He is more than just someone who died, you know."

Jade said nothing. She didn't really know. Her mom had never really told her anything about him.

"He was the fastest runner on the soccer team in high school," Abuela said. "A striker. Un *gran* goleador. You should have seen him out there on that soccer field, with those bright lights on him, dribbling between the players, fooling everyone." She moved her good hand through the air like a fish darting through water. "And then—*pam!* He would always score. You should have seen it."

Jade smiled. She had no idea there were other runners in her family. She could imagine the thrill of it, of outrunning the defenders and scoring the goal. She was certain Abuela would have been cheering loudly for her son, shouting to everyone who would listen, "¡Ése es mi hijo!" *That's my son!*

"If it weren't for that party, he would still be here," said Abuela, her face suddenly long. She rested her hand on Jade's again.

"What party?" said Jade. Was she finally going to hear the full story of what had happened to him?

"The soccer team," said Abuela. "They threw a big birthday party for one of the boys. Con chupe y todo." *With drink and all.* "And that boy drove him. His best friend." Abuela squeezed her hand tightly, so tightly she drove the bones of Jade's knuckles together. "But he never came home."

Jade looked up at Abuela, but she had her eyes closed.

"The thing about Efraín," Abuela said, her wrinkled eyelids pulling even further shut, "was that, when he was running toward that net, dancing that ball with his feet, you *knew* he was going to make the goal. Because he had determined it already." She opened her eyes and looked at Jade.

Jade didn't know what to say, but she didn't get the sense that Abuela actually wanted her to say anything. Abuela had had something to tell her, and she had told her. Slowly, she loosened her grip on Jade's hand and reached again for her rosary. She began praying, breathing Ave Marías, her lips moving in a silent mutter as she polished the beads between her fingertips.

Jade felt like she was intruding. She decided to leave Abuela with her prayers and go find her dad and Katerina. She couldn't bear the feeling of being alone right now.

All sorts of things could prompt a story about the past, it seemed. A bracelet, a painted mug—or something as awful and strange and scary as what was happening now. Something in the present that prodded the wheels of memory into motion and sent them tracing new paths as they turned.

In the kitchen Katerina was standing in front of the fridge stringing her cheese bit by bit, staring intently at it, and not eating it. Her dad was at the counter coaxing a wad of dough into having a shape.

Jade sat down on the floor beside Katerina and pulled her into her lap, hugging her close. Katerina let herself be gathered in and took a bite of her cheese. Jade felt safer like this. It was how she used to feel when she and Katerina shared a room and went to sleep at night.

Mortimer came up and tried to sniff the string cheese, but Katerina shoved him away. Jade's dad looked over at them but didn't stop kneading the dough.

"Daddy—nothing's gonna happen to us, right?" said Katerina, breaking the silence.

Their dad pulled his hands up from the dough, brushed the flour off his wide palms, and came over to them. He squatted so he could be at their eye level.

Jade waited. He was deciding something, making up his mind.

At last he looked straight at Katerina and said, "That's right, bug. Nothing's gonna happen to us."

Katerina jumped up and hugged his neck, and he lifted her as he stood up, hugging her to him while she finished her string cheese.

Jade couldn't decide how much to believe him. She knew he was being sincere, and already she could feel some relief washing over her. But still, as she watched him set Katerina down and continue working at the bread he was making, she could tell from the tension in his forearms, the way he kept his fingers busy and never stopped moving them, that he was worried.

Mortimer stepped into her lap where Katerina had been and settled himself there. Jade petted his soft, lean body for a long, long time, listening to his soft, even purrs, until her dad slid the bread pan into the oven and the cozy, golden scent reached her nose.

16

The American flag was the first thing that caught Jade's eye when she stepped out of the Wildcat Trail and into the parking lot the next morning. She had never paid much attention to it before, but today it stood out to her because it hung at half-mast from the pole at the school entrance, just above the height of her head.

Homeroom was a buzz of chatter, and Coach Jackson didn't even try to get them to be quiet or sit still at their desks. Everyone was comparing shocked stories. It was almost as if they were all trying to one-up one another. *Did you see the plane, the way it crashed into the building—BAM! Did you see the smoke, how the fire just went on and on and wouldn't stop? It's still going! Did you see the people jumping out of the windows? Did you hear about the man who went back to save his friend, and then he died? Did you hear about the woman who fell asleep on the train and missed her stop and didn't go to work?*

For her classmates, the disaster was so remote, it was almost exciting. They were all *living through something.* Something big enough and deadly enough that it would get written into the social studies textbooks. The girls talked with big eyes and a kind of breathy thrill, and the boys made explosion noises with their mouths.

Jade knew that her mom had delivered much of this news to them, many of these stories. Not with the pop and pitch of gossip, but with the measured, even tones of journalism. No one seemed to realize it was her mom, though.

She couldn't join in, get swept up in the frenzy of *Did you see?* It didn't feel remote for her. Her mom was safe and sound, but she was still stuck there. And her way of getting back home—by plane—was, for the moment, an impossible proposition.

Beneath the breathless chatter, Jade sensed fear. She got the feeling that her classmates were trying to be bigger than their fear. She felt some of it herself. It wasn't fear of what had happened. It was fear of how the adults were reacting. The grown-ups were afraid, and that was scary.

Chloe walked in and headed straight for Jade. "Is your mom okay?" she said. "We saw her on TV."

Jade just looked at her. Somehow it sounded different when someone else asked it. Instead of responding, she just reached out and hugged Chloe. She closed her eyes. She didn't want to see anybody, didn't want anybody to see her.

Chloe hugged her tight and rubbed her back a little, then released her.

"Are *you* okay?" she said.

Jade opened her eyes, blinking, and willed back the buds of tears that had welled up. "I miss having lunches that my mom made," she said.

It sounded like such a stupid thing, but Chloe didn't react that way. She just said, "When is she supposed to get back?"

Jade shook her head and shrugged. "As soon as the planes can fly again, I guess."

Chloe nodded. "I can't believe a plane can just—turn into a bomb," she said.

"Yeah, me neither," said Jade.

The first bell rang. Jade hoisted her backpack on one shoulder, and as they headed to pre-algebra, she was grateful for all the normal things—the insistent bell, the weight of books, the walk down the hall with Chloe.

Practice was canceled again, but hopefully there would be cross-country tomorrow. Her dad picked them up like yesterday, but the way he walked didn't seem quite as tense as before.

"I talked to your mom today," he told them as they emerged from the trees into the backyard.

"Is she coming home?" said Katerina.

"Looks like she might be able to fly tomorrow, but we'll see." The way he said it, he sounded relieved. Something about the phone call must have reassured him. It reassured Jade, too, to hear him like that.

The TV was on again when they walked in. From the voices Jade heard, it sounded like either Dr. Crystal or Dolores was in the house seeing about Abuela.

In the kitchen she shrugged off her backpack and tore a fistful of bread from the loaf her dad had made. She bit into the bread and chewed it for comfort. It was the perfect balance of flaky and doughy, and there was a nuttiness to it that she only ever tasted in her dad's bread.

She went into the living room where the TV was. No one was watching it—the news just droned on like background noise. Her mom was interviewing a firefighter in an ash-streaked suit. They were standing beside the rubble, both wearing hard hats. The burnt and twisted remnants of steel beams behind them looked like the skeleton of a drowned ship. It was very strange to see her mom like this, the hat squishing her perfect hair. The firefighter looked like he felt at ease with her. He was talking freely, almost as if it were just the two of them there and the cameras weren't rolling. Jade always marveled at how her mom got people to open up like that.

The firefighter was telling her mom about how they had been climbing and crawling all day among the crumbling slabs of ruin where the skyscrapers had been. How he had pulled out bodies—most of them dead, very few alive—including the bodies of fellow firefighters.

A look of concern was stamped on her mother's face as she listened. Knotted creases that wouldn't leave her forehead.

Jade didn't like to see her like that. She hoped that look wouldn't last.

Her mom looked into the camera and tossed the programming back to headquarters. They showed it again—the planes crashing into the towers one by one, the tall rectangles cascading down with frightening speed, crumbling as they went, disappearing into those awful clouds of smoke. The moments that had turned the bright morning black, split time in two.

Jade was glad her dad was keeping Katerina occupied in the kitchen. She herself couldn't take much more of it. She switched off the TV.

Dr. Crystal came into the living room with her black doctor's bag. She had on scrubs and bright white sneakers, and her geometric earrings were a bold, earthy bronze that stood out against her dark skin and caught the light from the big picture window.

"This must be so hard for you," she said to Jade.

Jade didn't know what to say.

Dr. Crystal pointed to the TV. "Your mom is amazing," she said. "All that calm, in the face of all that . . ." She shook her head.

"I guess so," said Jade quietly. "But it's TV. I mean—she has to be like that."

Dr. Crystal cocked her head to the side. "Not everyone can do that, though," she said. Then she smiled. "But knowing your grandma . . . she's a fierce woman!"

Jade smiled a little, too. Abuela *was* a fierce woman.

"Thank you so much, Dr. Johnson," said her dad, coming into the room and holding out his hand.

"Please, it's Crystal, and you're so welcome," she said, shaking his hand. "Your mother-in-law can be . . . a little stubborn, but she's also determined, and that's a good thing. She's actually making great progress. She's stronger today."

"My wife will be happy to hear that," he said.

Jade was glad to hear it, too. When Dr. Crystal left, Jade went to the kitchen and cut two more thick, even slices of her dad's bread—one for Abuela, and one for her. If Abuela was feeling stronger today, maybe she would be up for talking.

She remembered how urgently Abuela had asked for chamomile tea just a few days before, and how much she had enjoyed it. Maybe Abuela would be more willing to talk if she had some.

She set the kettle to boil and got out two mugs. When the tea was ready, she carried it all on a tray to Abuela's room. Knocking lightly, she pushed the door open just a little, hoping she would find Abuela sitting up and feeling strong enough to talk.

"Ah-ah, Abuela needs to rest," her dad said, appearing in the hallway.

"Está bien, she can come in, Chris," Jade heard Abuela say.

Jade pushed the door open farther. Abuela *was* sitting up, and to Jade's surprise, she beckoned her in with the hand that the stroke had slowed. It was a small motion, her wrist resting on the bedspread, but still.

Jade's dad crowded the doorway beside her. "Do you feel like visitors, Doña Luz?" he said.

"I always feel like visitors who bring me manzanilla," she said, smiling. Even her smile looked less crooked than before. Jade felt herself smiling back.

Her dad raised his eyebrows, but stepped away from the doorway and gave Jade a little acquiescent tilt of his head. "Don't tire her out too much," he said softly, and he gave her a quick pat on the back before heading away down the hall.

Jade stepped into the room and set the tray down on the bedside table beside the window. The steam from the tea danced upward in the angled shafts of sunlight. "My dad made the bread, and it's the best," she said, purposefully loud enough that her dad would hear it from the hallway.

Abuela reached out with her unsteady hand, as if testing it, and rested it on Jade's arm. Her grip was light, but

Jade was amazed that she could do it at all. Maybe Abuela *would* recover fully. She was almost afraid to hope it.

"Crystal helped me do that," said Abuela.

"That's great!" said Jade. She didn't know what Dr. Crystal had done, but whatever it was, it was working. She covered Abuela's hand with hers and sat on the side of the bed. Abuela's hand slipped a little, and Jade held it gently as Abuela lowered it to the covers.

"It's tiring," Abuela said. With her good hand she pointed to the mugs. "Are we going to have some tea?"

Jade handed her the mug. Abuela took it in both hands like before, but more steadily this time. She brought it close to her face, putting her nose in the steam, and closed her eyes.

Jade copied her. Already, just breathing in the familiar scent, she felt calmed. She took a deep breath over her tea, cupping the clay in her palms, and felt her shoulders relax.

"I know it all seems terrible, Chalchihuite, but it will pass," Abuela said. "Like everything. Things will change, like they always do. It won't be the same, but the moment will pass." She took a first, tiny sip of the tea. "But you will always remember," she said. "And the trick is to know how to accept the new, but also hold on to what you cherish from before."

At first, Jade had thought she was talking about what had just happened, about the plane crashes and the incinerated buildings. But the more Abuela talked, the more it sounded like she was talking about something else, too. How were things going to change now? Jade had the sense that she was living through the turn of a terrible before and after, but she didn't know what *after* looked like. And what was she supposed to cherish from *before*?

She took a sip of tea and waited for Abuela to go on. It seemed like she wanted to tell her something. As the tea spread through Jade, it warmed her from the inside out, and she let out a sigh.

"Está bueno, ¿no?" said Abuela.

"Yeah, it is good," said Jade. She felt her stomach unknot itself a little. Her insides had been tense.

"Abuelita," she said, "Abuelo used to tell me about San Juan de las Jacarandas, where you guys grew up. I miss that."

"Oh, Ernesto," she said. "He loved telling you stories. Do you know why he told you so many stories?"

"No." Jade had never really asked herself that before.

"They weren't just for you," said Abuela, laughing softly. "We missed our home very much when we came here. And telling those stories was Ernesto's way of holding on, of not forgetting. He loved spending time with you, remembering. That's why he told them to you in Spanish. He wanted to remember it all in his own language."

Jade drew in a breath. It had never occurred to her that the stories had been as much for Abuelo as for her. It seemed like it was that way with Itztli, too.

"There was another way to hold on to our home, too," said Abuela. "By bringing some of it here."

"Like your bordados?" said Jade.

"Like my bordados, yes." She rubbed the embroidered collar of her dress between her fingers.

"How did you learn to make them?" Jade found herself asking.

Abuela took a careful sip of tea. "My mother taught me and Flor," she said. "We were girls, and we had the little worm to make art. When we were very little, we used to draw things with sticks in the dirt in front of the house. Flowers, birds, all sorts of creatures. We didn't even know what all the creatures were, but we didn't care. You should have seen our pictures. Big flying cats, wolves with turtle shells . . . and we got so mad when the boys came outside and trampled our pictures, kicking a soccer ball across our carefully drawn lines." She laughed. "My mother would bring us inside and beat our skirts with her hands to get the dirt off, and she would put a stretched cloth and a pencil in our hands, and tell us to draw."

Abuela smiled and shook her head and took another sip. "At first, I didn't think it was as fun as playing in the dirt," she said. "But that changed when my mother gave me a needle and let me choose from her drawer of thread spools. The drawer was in a little vanity by her bed, and it was bursting to the brim with those balled-up colors. She let me pick out which one I wanted—but I was not allowed to drop it. Because if I did, the spool would roll and roll, all the way out of the room and out the front door, becoming just a long, thin line." She drew the line with her finger across the bedspread.

"Flor was still too little to be trusted with needles. But I loved the needles from the first time I held one. My fingers were almost too small to hold it—it was as long as my palm was wide—but I managed to poke the bright red thread through the cloth that was the color of a corn husk, and I loved how the red rose up as if born from the cloth, until it was taut in my hands. I pricked myself many times but I didn't mind, because my mother taught me how to blend the colors, how to lay them side by side, make them surprise one another. She taught me how to make the lines I drew come alive." Her dark eyes flashed.

"Flor never wanted to have anything to do with the needles," she went on. "My mother wouldn't let her touch them until she was old enough, and she always resented it when she watched me embroider. So, when she was old enough, she never took the needles. And that's how she came to painting. My mother gave her a tiny paintbrush and let her paint on the cloth. Flor would sit still for hours and hours with her feet folded underneath her until they fell asleep, and she would stand up and walk funny. She painted on everything she could find. And when she started painting on the walls of our room, our mother didn't even try to stop her."

Jade loved the thought of the two girls, Luz and Flor, making colors jump to life in a painted room.

"The bordados were how I got your grandfather," said Abuela, and on her lips a tiny smile danced, mischievous.

Jade raised her eyebrows. "How?" she said.

"Well, you know, Flor and I started selling our pieces at the tianguis when we were teenagers—a little older than you," said Abuela. "We would go early, at the first rays of sun, and set up our blue tent and our table. We would put out our most colorful, detailed pieces up front. We always displayed our work together. I might set out a tablecloth and napkins, and Flor would set up her painted dishes on top of that. We tried to make our stand feel like a little house with a welcoming entrance. We would sit behind the table and chat with the other girls at their stands, and I would thread colors into animals with my needle, and Flor would sketch her designs."

"And Abuelo used to come to the tianguis?" said Jade.

"Oh yes, he sold things there, too," she said. "His little wooden things."

"What do you mean?" said Jade.

"Like the nacimiento—you remember that, right?"

"Yes!" said Jade. Of course she remembered the elaborate wooden nativity that Abuela set out on her hearth every year, with its tiny carved shepherds and wise men, and the Virgin Mary in blue, praying over the baby Jesus that was wrapped tightly in striped cloth like a tamal. "Abuelo *made* those?" said Jade.

"Of course he did!" said Abuela.

Not for the first time, Jade wished she remembered more of him. She thought of the kites they had made together out of shish kebab sticks and newspaper, how they could make them ride the wind for hours by the lake.

"So, that's how you met him," said Jade.

"Well, he was off on the other end of the street, with the leather and the woodwork," she said. "And he wasn't even always there. Often it was one of his brothers instead. They took turns. Ernesto had *so* many brothers. So, we didn't see each other much, in fact." She tapped her mug lightly with one finger. "I knew Ernesto for a long time, but I never really gave him much thought. But then"—a smile spread across her face—"one day, when I was sixteen, he came walking down the street, dressed in his Sunday best. Todo perfecto, boots polished, shirt pressed. His mother had sent him to buy linens for Navidad. Pretty ones."

"With bordados," said Jade.

"Exactly," said Abuela. "And here he comes down the street, taking his time, looking at all the linens, trying to decide. And all the girls flirting with him—oh, you should have seen them!—I mean *every one* of them. He had just come from church, and he was wearing his riding boots and his fedora . . . Oh! Chalchihuite, you should have seen him. And he comes up to my stall, and he takes one of my men's kerchiefs in his hands—a very nice one, with a discreet red threaded around the edges, and he says, 'Vaya, ¿quién es la señorita que hizo este pañuelo tan fino? ¡Que me caso con ella!'"

Jade burst out laughing, and Abuela, too. Her grandfather had declared he would marry someone just because of a beautiful handkerchief. That handkerchief must have been pretty impressive!

"So, of course," said Abuela, "I tell him, 'Soy yo la señorita que hizo este pañuelo, así que usted tendrá que casarse conmigo.'" *I'm the girl who made this kerchief, so you'll have to marry me.*

Jade laughed even harder now, so hard she almost spilled her tea. "And that's how it happened?" she said. "That's how you and Abuelo got married?"

"Algo así," said Abuela, smiling almost to herself behind the tea. *Something like that.*

"Why did you guys leave Mexico?" said Jade. Why would someone want to leave a world of painted walls and threads of color that attracted well-dressed men?

Abuela held out her mug, and Jade took it. She set it on the bedside table, and Abuela's hands fell to the bedspread in slow motion.

"We left because we had to," she said. "Ernesto had so many brothers, so many sisters—there was a new one born every year, it seemed. His family needed all the help they could get. And Manuel had already gone to Chicago, and he was sending good money back."

Tío Manuel, Abuelo's brother. Jade had known him only a little. She remembered him as a strong, compact man. He had been a pallbearer at Abuelo's funeral, carrying the casket down the aisle of the church while the brassy music played and the stained-glass windows tinted his lined face pink and gold.

"The hardest part was leaving Flor," said Abuela. "She told me she was going to be okay, that she would set up the stand herself, sell her ceramics. But we both knew it wouldn't be the same."

Jade wouldn't have been able to leave Katerina. Sure, her little sister got on her nerves sometimes, and she didn't love it when she had to watch her. But when something happened like what had happened yesterday, the awful crash of the planes, all she wanted to do was hug her sister to her. She didn't know what she would do if one day she couldn't do that.

"That's why I made the Casa Azul that way," said Abuela.

"What way?" said Jade. It stood out to her that Abuela said "I made." People in her family talked about the restaurant as belonging to Abuelo and Abuela, but the way Abuela said it, she made it sound like it was mostly hers.

"Like a little . . . casita," she said, shaping a house in the air with her hands. "Like the stand that Flor and I used to have in the tianguis. A house, an inviting place, for people to come in and eat warm food that reminded them of where they came from, out of bowls like the ones that Flor painted, on top of tablecloths that I had embroidered."

The restaurant had always been something special and different for Jade, a treat. But it had served another purpose for the others in the barrio, the regulars, the people who had grown up in places like San Juan de las Jacarandas and ached for a place that felt like home.

A wind whooshed outside and Jade looked up to see it breathe through the leaves of the two big oaks in the backyard, coaxing some of the leaves off their branches and sending them fluttering delicately to the ground.

She looked back at Abuela, who had closed her eyes. Jade wasn't supposed to tire her out too much; she needed to rest. Jade still wanted to know so much—about Tía Flor's paintings and the colors she used, about the jade bracelet—but it would have to wait.

"Do you want the bread, Abuelita?" she said.

"No, gracias, Chalchihuite," said Abuela.

Jade picked up the tray and headed to the door. When she was in the doorway she said, "Gracias, Abuelita."

Abuela gave a little smile and a hum, and Jade stepped out into the hallway and closed the door.

Katerina was in the kitchen when she got there with the tray. Jade set it down and offered her sister the slice of bread that Abuela hadn't eaten.

Katerina grabbed the bread and took a bite. Jade watched her and recognized the feeling of comfort that came over her sister as she relished its soft-yet-chewy consistency. Jade took a bite of her own bread and they stood like that for a moment, not saying anything, and eating the bread.

"Thank you, Sissy," Katerina said suddenly, and she pulled on Jade's skort and leaned into her leg.

Jade reached down and smoothed her hair, running her fingers down the loose braid that her dad had hastily made that morning. Their mom was still away, but at least they had each other and this bread and a house that felt like home.

17

Even though only two days had passed since the attack, Coach Jackson insisted on having practice. Jade was glad to ride in her red jeep again with the other girls. She thought maybe if she ran hard and fast, she could forget the dark clouds of smoke, the creased worry stamped on her mother's face on TV.

The team did their warm-ups on the field. Perhaps this was one of those *before* things that were important to hold on to.

Before sending them off to do any laps or sprints, Coach Jackson clapped her hands together, and said, "All right, Bobcats, the meet is next week! How are we going to beat them?"

"Run fast!" said Samantha.

"Absolutely. But what if they run faster? What if you're right up next to a Christ Savior girl, and she's gaining on you, maybe even starting to go a little faster than you—what do you do?"

"Focus on your personal best," said Emily. "Just do your best."

"That's right. Do your best. And what's the main thing, the number one thing, to remember?"

"Keep your head in the race!" they all chanted, except Jade, who was hearing this for the first time.

"Exactly," said Coach Jackson. "Keep your head in the race. Never give up. Never think, *Oh, I'm losing, I'll stop trying.* NO!" She yelled it. "No giving up! And remember, you might have a PR right now, but that could change in the race. Those of you who ran last year know, it's different when it's real, when it's not practice. Just give it your best, all the time. Find your rhythm, and keep it up. And at the end, go for it! Just *run*! What's that number one rule again?"

Jade joined in this time as they all shouted, *"Keep your head in the race!"*

She remembered what Abuela had said about Tío Efraín, how he had already determined to make the goal before he made it.

"All right, good," said Coach Jackson. "It's going to be at Stone Mountain on Thursday afternoon. If you have people coming to watch—parents, brothers, sisters, whoever—you can tell them that the finish line is going to be right under the Confederate memorial. Okay?"

Jade's teammates nodded.

Stone Mountain rang a bell, but Jade had never heard anything about the Confederate memorial. They didn't have things like that in Chicago. Wasn't Stone Mountain the place Devon and Shannon had been talking about the other day after practice? They had said something about a laser show. What *was* this place?

"All right, two laps on the long loop, let's go!" said Coach Jackson.

Jade dashed off with the team toward the forest. She focused on the trees ahead, on finding her rhythm, like

Coach Jackson had said. For some reason it felt a little harder today, like her insides were sluggish.

When they were cooling down and walking back to the locker room, Jade took big gulps from her water bottle and asked Chloe, her breaths still heavy, "So, what's this Stone Mountain?"

"It's a fun place," said Chloe. "They have a little train you can ride around it. My dad likes to take me and Nikos there sometimes when he comes to see us."

"Hmm," said Jade. It sounded like some kind of amusement park.

She wondered if Nikos would be at the meet. She knew she shouldn't care, but she couldn't help thinking that she wasn't sure she wanted him to see her all sweaty at the end of the race, wisps of hair flying in every direction.

"Apparently, it's not technically a mountain, but they call it that," Chloe went on. "It's all rock. Granite, I think. There's a Native American festival there every year."

"What?" said Jade.

"Yeah, I think it was a sacred place for the people who lived here," said Chloe, "Before"—she made a sweeping gesture across the field, the general landscape.

Jade nodded. *Before.* She suspected it might still be sacred for some people, something they held on to. And now it was a place for laser shows and . . . a Confederate memorial?

"But what about this Confederate memorial?" she asked Chloe.

"I don't really know why it's there," said Chloe. "But you can't miss it. It has—Emily, who does it have?"

"What?" said Emily, coming over to them. They were almost at the locker room now.

"The memorial on the side of Stone Mountain."

"Oh," said Emily, rolling her eyes. "I feel like it's Robert E. Lee and a couple of other guys. They're all like"—she stuck her chest out and made herself rigid—"on their horses. I'm pretty sure the KKK had something to do with it."

"What!" said Jade. She thought of the people who had held the mountain sacred for generations, how terrible it must be to have a scene like that, with Confederate "heroes" blasted into the precious stone.

They were at the locker room now, and suddenly Jade realized she really needed to pee. She had drunk half her water bottle in one go, and it must have gone straight through her.

She made for one of the stalls, closed the door quickly, and sat down to let it flow. *Ahhh*. She put her head in her hands and rubbed her forehead. She was very tired. Tired from running, from thinking about this mountain, from watching her mom on TV, and not knowing when she would be home.

She looked between her fingers and saw something red. She lowered her hands. It was a wet, red circle on her white underwear, getting darker as she watched it.

Not this. Not now. Her mom wasn't even around to help her. She did the only thing that came to mind, which was to stuff her underwear with toilet paper. When she came out of the stall, the girls had all left, except Chloe.

"You okay?" said Chloe, as Jade washed her hands.

"Yeah," said Jade. "I just—my period started, apparently?" she said.

"Oh, gotcha," said Chloe. "Weird, isn't it?"

"Super weird," said Jade. "I had no idea it was happening until I went to pee. What if it starts one day and I don't notice, and it bleeds through my shorts?"

"Yeah, I'm terrified of that, too," she said.

Jade smiled. She remembered how Chloe had been at the museum.

"What do you have going on now, toilet paper?" said Chloe.

"Yeah."

"Here." Chloe unzipped a pocket of her backpack and pulled out a pad wrapped in pink flowery packaging. She handed it to Jade. "Do you know what to do with it?" she said.

"Um, I think so?" said Jade. She went back to the stall, and luckily it was super simple.

"You good?" said Chloe, from outside the door.

"Yep!" said Jade. "I feel like I'm wearing a diaper but at least I won't bleed everywhere!"

Chloe laughed.

"Thank you," said Jade, when she got out of the stall.

"No problem," said Chloe. "Welcome to the club."

Jade laughed. All she wanted was for things to go back to normal, to be able to go pee without having to worry that *this* might happen. But at the same time, a part of her was glad it had happened. She wanted to feel just a little closer to being a grown-up woman, especially now that she was dealing with grown-up things in a way she hadn't before. Still, she would have preferred to suddenly get big boobs or something, instead of a red spot on her underwear.

"I'm going to have to tell my dad," she said as they walked out of the gym, realizing it as she said it. "My mom's still not home yet."

"Oh god, I'm sorry," said Chloe. "*That's* going to be awkward. He's picking us up, right?"

Jade nodded.

The blue sedan pulled up soon after they joined the other girls on the curb. The front window rolled down and Jade drew in a breath. "Mom!" she said, and she felt herself smile wider than she had in weeks.

Her mom opened the door and stepped out, and Jade rushed into her warm embrace. She was a little embarrassed to let the other cross-country girls see her like this, but mostly she was just happy to see her mom. She hugged her tight and buried her face in her shoulder.

"You managed to come home," she said, pulling away a little.

"I did," said her mom. She was holding Jade's shoulders and beaming at her. "I got on a plane first thing this morning. They shut down the airways again right after I landed. I was lucky to get out." She was still wearing her flying clothes, but her blouse was untucked and her hair was loose from its shape. She looked tired like she had on TV, but not quite as worried. "It's so good to see you, honey," she said. "Chloe!" she said, noticing her. Jade stepped away. "Good to see you, too!"

"Hi, Mrs. O'Callaghan!" said Chloe.

"Oh my god—are you the person on TV?" said Shannon. A few gasps followed.

"Wait—Jade. Your mom is *Sol O'Callaghan?*" said Caitlyn. "Oh my god, *hi*, Mrs. O'Callaghan!"

A chorus of "Hi, Mrs. O'Callaghan!" rose up from the girls on the curb. Jade didn't know what to do with all the attention so she turned away from it, but her mom smiled and waved like she was already used to it.

Jade climbed into the back seat and Chloe followed her. Katerina was already there, in her Daisies uniform.

"Mommy's back!" said Katerina.

"I know!" said Jade.

"And—guess what," said Katerina.

"What?"

"Mommy told me this time she's staying."

The relief hit Jade like a warm ray of sun.

As they pulled out of the parking lot, it didn't matter anymore that airplanes were grounded again, that she was dead tired from practice, that she had started bleeding out of nowhere. Her mom was home.

"How was practice?" her mom asked when they were on the road.

"Hard," said Jade. "But I like it."

"You do like it?" Her mom looked pointedly at her in the rearview mirror.

"Oh yeah," said Jade. "I almost wish it were every day," she said.

"Every day?" said Chloe. "That'd be a lot."

"Well, I don't know about every day . . . but, Mom?" she said.

"Hmmm?"

"Um, are you—how are *you*?" she said. She wasn't sure she had ever asked her mom that before.

Her mom said nothing for a bit, the car swallowing up the band of highway in front of it.

"I'm okay," she said at last. "I'm just glad I'm back. Glad to be with you girls." She smiled into the rearview mirror, and it was a tired smile, but it put Jade at ease.

After they dropped Chloe off, Jade said, "Mom, I have to tell you something when we get home." She remembered what her mom had said when she had taken one of her razors, that she shouldn't hesitate to ask her for something like that.

"What is it, honey?" said her mom.

Jade didn't want to say it with Katerina there. For one thing, her sister would want to know all about it, and for another, she was likely to go telling everyone, *My sister got her period!* without having the faintest clue what that meant.

But her mom was looking at her insistently in the rearview mirror, and the last thing Jade wanted to do was to make her more worried for no reason. So she said, "I got my—" and stopped.

"You got your what?"

"Um, my—it started?" she said.

"Oh!" said her mom, getting it. Her eyes went wide for a second, but then she looked relieved. "Let's talk when we get home. Are you good right now?"

"Yeah, I'm good," she said.

Her mom smiled again, almost to herself this time.

As they pulled into the driveway, her dad came out to greet them. He was walking easy now, a little sway to his step.

"How are my girls?" he said as they got out of the car.

"Mommy's here!" said Katerina.

"That's right!" he said. "How about you, Jade? How was practice?"

"Pretty good," she said. "There's a meet next week."

"Oh, is there?" said her mom.

"I've got it on the calendar," her dad said, turning to her mom. More quietly he said, "I was just about to put some coffee on—do you want some?"

"Yes, please," she said, giving him a peck on the lips. "You make the best coffee."

Inside, her mom stepped out of her flats and motioned for Jade to follow her. She led Jade down the hall and through her parents' bedroom to their bathroom. The blue-gray tecolote on her mom's dresser watched them as they passed by, into the big bathroom with the two sinks and the shiny silver faucets and the granite countertop.

"When did it start—today?" her mom said, opening the bathroom closet and handing Jade a package of pads from it. The package was pink and flowery like the wrapper on the one Chloe had given her.

"Yeah, right after cross-country," she said, taking it. "Chloe gave me a pad."

"Thank god for Chloe," her mom said.

Jade smiled. Thank god for Chloe indeed.

"And how do you feel?"

"Fine? Like . . . maybe my insides feel a little weird, but that's it." She had thought it might be more awkward to talk about this, but her mom was being very matter-of-fact about it all.

Her mom nodded. "I know we talked about this before, but it's all theoretical until it actually happens," she said. "You'll shed blood for a few days, you'll have to keep changing your pads, and then it'll be gone—until next month. It's a *good* thing. It means your body is working properly."

Jade nodded and looked down at the package of pads. She wanted to be grown-up about this, but what if she wasn't ready? What if she forgot one day and just went about her life and then it leaked through—and onto something?

Her mom took her by the shoulders and looked her in the eyes. "Look, Jade," she said, "I know it's disconcerting, and it's annoying, and you *are* going to forget, and you *are* going to have to learn to remember—"

"—so I don't bleed all over my pants?" said Jade.

"Yep. It's a pain. But you're going to be fine. It's just part of growing up."

"Yeah," said Jade. "I know."

Her mom patted her shoulders and let go.

Jade thought of Chloe's chic leather purse. Before she had known what was inside, she had thought it was just an accessory to match her boots. "Does this mean I get to wear a purse now?" she said.

"Yes," said her mom, with a smile. She walked over to a wall of pegs in the bedroom where she hung her bags and scarves. "Which one do you want?" she said.

"Really?" said Jade.

"Well, not to *keep*, just for now," she said. "We'll get you your own purse soon. This is just for the meantime."

Jade scanned the purses. They all looked so professional—*too* professional. But one was different. It was small and off-white—the color of a corn husk—and it was embroidered with a blue-green hummingbird that was drinking nectar from the yolk-yellow center of a red flower.

"Did Abuela make this?" she said, taking it in her hand.

"Yes," said her mom. "You can have that one, actually. I never wear it."

"Are you serious?"

She nodded.

Jade pulled it off the hook and ran her thumb over the soft, bright ridges of thread. If getting her period meant she got to wear this purse, then it was totally worth it.

"Thank you," she said.

"Coffee's ready!" her dad called from the hall.

Her mom perked up at his voice and her face softened. As she headed out of the bedroom, the cinnamony smell of her dad's coffee floated past her mom and swirled into the room.

Jade headed to her own bedroom to put away the bright hummingbird purse and the garish pink package of pads. She laid the purse on her bedspread and stuffed the pads under the sink in her bathroom.

When she came back out to the living room, Abuela was in the recliner, sitting up straighter than before, and her mom was on the couch with her legs crossed toward Abuela.

Jade's dad came in from the kitchen with a steaming cup of coffee for her mom. He had served it in one of the mugs with the raised colored vines dotted with berries. Jade squeezed onto the couch beside Katerina and her mom.

Her mother took a first sip and let out a loud groan, like she was exhaling the pent-up stress of weeks. Her whole body seemed to relax, and at last the creases on her forehead began to smooth.

Jade knew she was still sweaty, but even so she leaned against Katerina. Abuela smiled at the three of them, and there was no crookedness in her smile this time. Jade, Katerina, and her mom made a sandwich on the couch, pressing against one another as the earthy scent of coffee rolled over them.

When she got out of the shower, Jade felt renewed. She changed into a comfy T-shirt and sweat pants and stretched out on the bed with her green notebook and her pencils. This time she made sure to get out her nicer pencils that her grandma had given her, not just her old ones that she always used. Graphite pencils for outlines and shading, with points of varied resistances that were stamped along their sides: H, HB, 2H. Colored pencils with soft points that were easier to blend.

The hummingbird purse lay before her on the bed, and the tin of watercolors sat on her desk within reach. She left the clay pot that held the precious green ink in its spot on her bookshelf, protected by the ceramic lid with the playful painted rabbits. Jade wanted to paint soon with the watercolors and the green ink—but not just yet. She still didn't feel ready. First, she wanted to use her pencils to draw the outlines of what she was holding in her head, thoughts and images that she felt the need to get out and onto the page. It was only by drawing them that she could make sense of how they flowed together, how they were connected.

Mortimer curled up beside her and pretended not to be interested in what she was about to draw. "I got my period today," she told him quietly, ruffling the fur on his neck. He meowed and let himself be petted, waving his tail back and forth. "Does that mean I'm different now?" she said. "Does it mean I'm not a kid anymore?" Mortimer closed his eyes and purred as she stroked his back.

Jade pressed her face into his warm fur for a moment. "I still kind of want to be a kid," she confided to him in a whisper. Mortimer just went on purring.

She pulled her face away from the comforting warmth and turned the pages of her notebook back to her first drawing of watery hills. She still couldn't fill in everything, but she could fill in more, after what her mom and Abuela had told her.

The ridge of the spiral binding that sliced her map in two down the middle looked more than ever to Jade like a gash. A canyon, perhaps, or an insurmountable mountain pass. But of course, the picture continued, the journey pressed on, from one side to the other.

She drew a volcano by the watery hill of San Juan de las Jacarandas. The volcano that the mirror was made from.

It bubbled just slightly at the top with fiery lava and smoke that she blurred with the flat edge of her soft graphite pencil. She sketched a hummingbird and a rabbit, trying to capture the animated essence of the hummingbird on the purse and the rabbits on the lid of the green ink on her bookshelf. She wanted to be able to draw animals as vibrant and lively as the ones Abuela embroidered—and that Tía Flor painted, if it was Tía Flor who had painted these rabbits. She would have to ask Abuela.

She feathered blues and grays together to draw three owls on a tree near the Casa Azul, the ones her mother had told her about. She drew curling tongues for speech like the ones Itztli had painted beside Moctezuma, to stand for whatever it was the tecolotes had told her mother, whatever guidance they had given her.

At the entrance to the Casa Azul she added the praying Mary in blue that Abuelo had carved.

And rolling along the footprints between the Casa Azul and the house in Atlanta, she drew a disc that was a mirror and also a soccer ball.

She contemplated her work. The smell of carne picada and corn frying on the comal filtered in under the door. She breathed in slow and deep, closed her eyes. She had missed her mom's cooking so much.

When she opened her eyes, she thought maybe it was time to try her hand at painting. She may have reached the limit of what she could do with the colored pencils.

But the afternoon was turning to evening, and if she wanted to keep drawing, she would have to turn on the overhead light. And she knew that what she wanted to draw could only be done in the slanting, natural light of the sun.

She would have to wait for another day. She sighed and carefully put her pencils away. Slowly, she stood and gently lifted the lid from the pot of green ink on the bookshelf. She rocked the pot in her hand just a little, to make sure the ink was still good. It was.

"Jade, will you come set the table?" her mom called from the hall.

"Coming!" she said.

As she covered the pot again and headed out the door, her eye caught the hummingbird on the little purse. She swore it shot her a coquettish look, its wings a whir, about to take flight.

18

Over the next few days Jade waited for the light to be right so she could paint. A spate of overcast days and a few drizzles of rain made the situation less than ideal.

Remembering to bring the hummingbird purse every time she went to the bathroom at school took some getting used to. Sometimes she forgot and had to come back to class to get it. She liked wearing the purse, slung crossways over her torso. It was something pretty that she got to wear, separate from the uniform. But she also worried that everyone knew why she was wearing it.

On Sunday afternoon, the clouds chased each other away and the sky finally cleared. At last, the light was right for painting.

The house was sleepy after lunch and the sun was still high but just beginning to angle itself. The bright light spilled onto Jade's bed where she sat by her window, hugging her knees. Mortimer nuzzled against her calves and settled himself on the covers to take in the sun.

Her bedroom felt cramped; she wanted to paint like Itztli, out in the full force of the sun, where cushions and walls didn't swallow up its rays.

Opening her desk drawer, she took out her sketchbook with the good paper for painting and ran her fingertips over the first page. The paper was satisfyingly thick, porous, and soft, like it was just waiting to be inked with paint. She put the sketchbook in her backpack along with her green notebooks, a few of her nice graphite pencils for outlining, and her tin of watercolors. The inkpot she would carry separately, so it wouldn't break or spill.

Just as she was ready to head out, she decided to bring the mirror with her, to see its smoky shadows dance in the unfettered light of day. She remembered what her mom had said, that it was made of lava turned black glass that had rolled and thundered out from the volcano overlooking the town where Abuelo and Abuela grew up. Jade would paint that volcano today.

She emptied the hummingbird purse and slid the mirror into it. Slipping the purse on crossways over her shoulder, she headed out into the backyard barefoot so the grass could tickle her toes.

Outside, the neighborhood was weekend quiet. The squirrels jumped around for nuts like the yard was theirs, and a sparrow splashed joyfully in the birdbath. Jade chose a patch of grass free of shadows and seated herself cross-legged on the ground near the birdbath facing the pines and the forest beyond them. She laid her tools out in a neat semicircle in front of her. She thought of how Itztli's pens and paintbrushes and inkpots were laid out carefully before he began his artwork. She wanted to be just as prepared.

Now it felt right to paint. The sun was strong but not harsh, and the only shadows near her were those painted on the undersides of leaves, whose green surfaces shone in a million different hues. She would capture those greens.

Her worn, ruled notebook opened easily to the spread with the watery hills as Jade laid it out on the ground. Cool blades of grass nudged her toes as she bent over the fresh white paper in her lap with her sharpened pencil and began to draw a version of what had come before. A detailed drawing with more control, an enhancement of what were once just sketches. The work absorbed her; she drew her long and short and curved and swelling lines with fierce precision, hardly blinking.

She drew not in order of time, but in order of how the story came to her. The final touch was the Casa Azul. She penciled curls of smoke that rose up from the hearth, the breath let off by the warm kitchen fire that had drawn so many into the restaurant. The restaurant was also, of course, a watery hill—a life-giving place. A place for people to feel at home, even if home was far away, and they had been torn from it. Below the restaurant, Jade drew swirls within swirls of water, swelling into one another.

Now it was time for the color. She popped open the tin of watercolors for the first time since she had gotten it as a present.

It was just as nice a set as she remembered. The colors were arranged in solid, inviting rectangles nestled in niches. They weren't the primary tones of her colored pencils. The yellow had an amber tint, and the red had a touch of earth like the clay that Itztli had uncovered when he drew in the stream bank. The blue was as dark and brilliant as one of her mother's suits. The rectangles were so perfectly unmarred that Jade hesitated again, like she had when she first saw them under her grandma's Christmas tree, to moisten them with one of the brushes in the set.

She had forgotten to bring any water. She looked up at the birdbath—a simple stone bowl sitting on a wire stand. She reached for it and set it down on the grass. Yes, this would do.

She pried a fine-tipped brush out of the set and dipped it in the birdbath, trying to hold it lightly but firmly in her fingers, the way she had seen Itztli do. The tight, flame-shaped bristles loosened and spread like hair in a bathtub. She pressed them against the stone to let the water out.

And she went for it.

She wet the blue first, marking the first shallow divot in the perfect rectangle to release the paint. She painted the water of the watery hills blue; she bathed the agave fields gently with blue. Rinsing her brush in the bowl, she switched to the red and colored the kitchen fire of the Casa Azul, the lava of the volcano, and the brick of the house in Atlanta. She tried out almost all the colors on the hummingbird near the town. With minuscule flicks of her wrist she feathered the colors into one another.

She kept coming back to the Casa Azul and the blue paint. She played with the color as she filled the restaurant in with designs, diluting the paint to the blue of a cloudy sky and using the tip of her brush for accents as delicate as embroidered threads.

The water of the watery hill of the Casa Azul wasn't supposed to be just blue; it needed to be green, too, to echo the shifting earthy and bright tones of the jade beads on Abuela's bracelet. It had to evoke the gentle hues she saw in the rushing creek water in the golden afternoons beneath the trees when Itztli told his stories.

She didn't even consider using the green that came in the set of watercolors.

It was time for Itztli's green.

She removed the lid with the rabbits from the inkpot, cleaned her brush, and dipped it in the green paint, stirring it a little. This paint was thicker and heavier than the watercolors. When she pulled out the brush, making sure the bristles were coated but not dripping, she held it above the swirls of water beneath the Casa Azul the way she would hold a pencil, as if she were about to write as much as draw.

The blue she had painted the water with was drying fast in the sun, settling into a hue that was pretty but pale. She washed a thin, translucent layer of green paint over the blue, holding the brush lightly. The paint scintillated on the page, as if capturing bits of sun, and as it dried, the colors melded to a subtle turquoise.

An immense satisfaction began to settle into Jade. The colors she envisioned in her head were taking form on the page.

She kept painting with sure, wavy strokes, like Itztli had when he painted the bend in the stream on the bark. She became bolder with the green, tracing deeper, darker veins through the water to get that forest-water green that she was aiming for. She painted right up next to the curved pencil lines, the fine tip of her brush nosing at their edges like a cat coaxing a ball of thread to roll and unwind.

"Te pareces a Flor."

Jade jerked her head up. It was Abuela. She had come out—on her own, apparently—and Jade hadn't noticed at all.

Abuela was leaning forward against her walker, smiling down at Jade. How she had gotten down the back steps on her own, Jade didn't know. She must be feeling much better if she was able to do that.

"Abuela, do you want to sit?" she said. It was all Jade could think to say. She couldn't shake the shock of seeing Abuela there, in front of her. Her mind was still half with the water and the colors and the lines. She laid down her things and got up from the ground. She couldn't just leave Abuela standing there. She wished she had noticed earlier that she was out here so she could have helped her down the steps.

Jade went over to her. Abuela was trying to sit on the built-in seat on her walker, but it was wobbling around. Jade found the brakes and halted it, then held under Abuela's elbow with one hand and steadied her back with the other, as Abuela shuffled into position and carefully lowered herself to the seat. The sun was in her eyes a little, and Jade shifted the walker just slightly, so that the light and warmth would bathe her, but at a different angle. The sun was lower now; soon it would start to kiss the tops of the trees.

"Crystal said it would do me some good to sit out in the sun," said Abuela. "Ah . . ." She turned her palms skyward as she settled in. "The sun feels like a hug." She closed her eyes, and her lids were wrinkled half-moons the color of unfiltered honey. "Keep painting, Chalchihuite," she said, opening her eyes a little.

Jade shook her head. There was no way she could go on painting right now. That was a sacred thing that she had to do alone, in the quiet. She could finish later. Besides, she didn't always get to spend time with Abuela when she was feeling this well.

Jade sat down again and leaned back on her arms, this time facing Abuela. "What was that you said?" she asked.

"That you remind me of Flor," said Abuela.

"How so?" said Jade, flattered.

"She was always like that when we were girls, her eyes close to the page, drawing designs with thin, thin lines and forgetting about the world." She gave a little laugh.

Jade smiled. She reached over and set the paintbrush aside to put the lid back on the inkpot so it wouldn't dry out.

"You even have her hair," said Abuela.

"What?" That made no sense to Jade. Her hair was the color of dry grass in winter, and today she had pulled it back in a pouf of a ponytail to get it out of her face.

"Yes, the very same," said Abuela. "Flor used to tie it back like that, too, when she was working. It was a different color, of course, when she was your age."

"Oh," said Jade. It hadn't occurred to her that she could have the same hair as someone on her mom's side of the family, if the color came from the other side. But now that she thought about it, it didn't seem strange at all.

"Your hair is beautiful," said Abuela.

"Oh—thank you," said Jade. No one had ever told her that. "You really think so?" Lately she mostly thought of her hair as something she had to deal with, something she needed to keep under control.

"Of course!" said Abuela. "Do you know how many people wish they had hair like yours?" she said. "With natural waves, and all that body—and *personality*."

Jade smiled and almost believed it. Maybe she *did* have pretty hair after all. There was no doubt in her mind that Tía Flor did. In fact, in the only photo she knew of Tía Flor, she had one side of her dark hair pulled up from her forehead in a barrette, and otherwise it hung around her shoulders in a regal mane. Tía Flor held her head high in that picture, in a way that didn't leave any room for you to look at her and think her hair was anything *other* than beautiful. Maybe Jade just had to learn to hold her head that way.

"Flor painted those rabbits, you know," said Abuela, pointing to the ceramic lid.

"Oh!" said Jade, looking at the lid. "I was wondering if she had! The rabbits are so . . . *alive*." She paused. "That lid is from . . ." She trailed off, not fully wanting to confess that she had taken it from the elaborate teapot in the china cabinet.

"Lo sé," said Abuela, with a smile. *I know.* "That was a wedding gift from Flor."

"And the teacups, too?" said Jade, thinking of the matching rabbit teacups on the high shelf in Abuela's house.

"That's right," said Abuela. "Of course, it was hard to take much with us when we moved to the States, but I managed to take the cups, wrapping them in my clothes and packing them carefully in my suitcase. Your mother brought back that teapot after we returned to bury Ernesto. Flor had kept it safe, and she wanted us to have it. I told Sol she could keep it—I didn't want another thing in my house that would remind me of lost times. I have enough of those already."

Jade looked at the leaping rabbits again and thought of Tía Flor painting them with a fine brush—maybe a brush like hers—with sure strokes, making a gift for her sister.

"That must be a special color," said Abuela. She was pointing to the inkpot.

"Yes, it's—how did you know?" said Jade.

"Flor used to do that, too," she said. "She kept all her special colors in jars in her room, and she would open their lids every once in a while and stir them and talk to them, like they were her pets. She bought them at the tianguis when the traveling sellers came through. People who gathered the colors from far away, who knew where to find the plants, the stones, the insects, how to crush and boil and mix them into paints. She bought colors from Mexico that had been used for centuries, and colors from other parts, too. She had blues from China, reds from Mexico . . . colors from all over.

"I used to make so much fun of Flor," Abuela went on, smiling. "Sometimes she would spend a whole month's earnings on her colors. But Flor got the last laugh! Because one day she bought dyes for me, too, not just paint, and when I tried those dyes on my threads—oh! You should have seen those colors." She shook her head.

Abuela was fiddling with the jade bracelet on her wrist. Rubbing one of the beads between her fingers, a small one streaked with sandy gold, the same way she did when she rubbed the beads of her rosary. Jade bit back the urge to ask her about it. She trusted that Abuela would tell her about it in her own time.

Abuela's face brightened and she pointed at the hummingbird purse, apparently seeing it for the first time.

"I haven't seen that in years!" she said. "*Those* are the dyes, Chalchihuite. See the red of the flower? How it hasn't faded at all? That red is made from tiny insects that live on nopales. Very hard to get."

Jade gathered the purse into her lap and studied the flower. "It's beautiful, Abuelita," she said.

"That purse was meant for Flor."

"Oh," said Jade, holding it out a little away from her.

"But I'm glad you have it," said Abuela. Jade relaxed. Abuela was playing with a different bead on her bracelet now. "I made it for her a long time ago, and meant to send it to her for her birthday. But Sol liked it too much."

"But—my mom told me she never wears it!" said Jade.

"Oh, I'm not sure she ever actually used it," said Abuela. "She just *liked* it. She kept it hanging from her closet door, where she could see it when she was falling asleep. She was about your age."

Apparently, there were still plenty of things her mother wouldn't tell her. Not outright, at least. Her mom had so freely let her have the purse, but maybe it hadn't been so easy for her to give it up after all. Or maybe she had actually wanted Jade to have it.

"Well, *I* want to wear it everywhere," said Jade. "I love it, and I want people to see it."

"That's good," said Abuela. "I want you to wear it. I want you to show off to everyone what artists we are."

"We?" said Jade.

"Yes, we," said Abuela, and the sunlight danced in her eyes. "We, my sister, my mother and I—and her mother before that, who made the finest papel picado you've ever seen. And your grandfather, Ernesto, and his brothers, the finest wood carvers and sculptors in the state of Jalisco. We all took the traditions—the old ones, and the new ones—and we made what we could of them. We made art."

Jade let it sink in. She saw her family anew, as a family of artists. Of *course* they were. Their house was full of art, and she had grown up with art all around her. She just wouldn't have thought to name it that.

"And you, Chalchihuite. You are an artist, too. Just like Flor." She was looking straight at Jade, as though she wanted to make sure she understood.

Jade said nothing. Her, an artist, too? She looked at Abuela, then at her painting. The sun was beginning to wash the colors with a hint of gold.

She *wanted* to be an artist. She acknowledged this to herself perhaps for the first time. She wanted to use all the best colors and tools to make her pictures. She wanted to master the art of inking the page, the myriad brushstrokes Itztli used that were like so many steps in a dance. She wanted so much to be an artist like Itztli. A painter of stories. Of *her* story.

Maybe she *was* an artist, if Abuela said so. A warm thrill fluttered through her chest.

"And we must not forget the artists in our family who tamed the hardest material," Abuela went on. "The ones who made it bend to their wishes, and whose works are still with us, after all these years. The stone carvers."

"Stone carvers!" said Jade. "We have stone carvers in our family?" She remembered the carved jade stones in the museum, and what Itztli had said about how the jade carvers were revered in his time.

She leaned forward. Abuela ran her fingers over the jade bracelet again, caressing the beads. This time not absently, but like she was paying attention to the little stones themselves. Was she going to tell her their secrets, at last?

"These chalchihuites are from long, long ago," she said.

"Chalchihuites?" said Jade. It was the first time she had heard her name—the one her abuelos and Itztli called her—when clearly they were not calling her name.

"Sí, chalchihuites," said Abuela. "Como tú."

Jade got it. Of course.

Chalchihuite.

Jade.

"These bracelets have been in our family for ages," said Abuela. "Flor has one, too. They help me remember things. They hold so many memories. Some I know, some I only know the shadows of, and some I don't know at all. But they are with me always. What my mother told me, and her mother told her, is that they were made by artists in our family who were held in such high esteem, they were summoned by Moctezuma himself."

Jade felt her eyes nearly pop out. The stones on Abuela's bracelet had been in the palace of Moctezuma? In the same city where Itztli had gone to learn about his father, and to paint in the old ways?

"Is that true?" said Jade.

Abuela laughed softly. "That is what my mother told me," she said, a playful smile on her lips. It was just the way Itztli would answer her.

"Can I see it?" she said, standing up.

"Por supuesto," said Abuela. She slipped the bracelet off her wrist and held it out to her.

Jade took the polished beads in her palms with reverence. The stones were warm, and their weight surprised her. She marveled that Abuela wore these on her slender wrist all the time. There was nothing fancy about the beads that she could put her finger on, but their beauty was exceptional, especially up close like this. Some were tinged with blue and shone turquoise, some had spectacular amber veins, and some were a green as deep as the thickest part of the forest. One even had a note of pink running through it. They had been thoughtfully chosen and cleft from the mother stone, then carved and polished with the utmost skill and care. Jade remembered what Itztli had told her, that sometimes beads like these carried the breath of the dead.

She handed the bracelet back to Abuela and watched her slide it back onto her wrist where it belonged.

"Gracias," said Jade.

Abuela nodded. "Now, what's in that purse?" she said. Her smile made Jade think she already knew the answer.

Jade scooped the purse up from the grass. She stroked the hummingbird's wings for a moment before she opened it, her fingers slightly jittery. She couldn't believe the moment was finally here, when she was going to learn the story of the obsidian mirror, the story her mother had only told her pieces of.

She pulled the mirror out. Its black sheen flashed in the sun. She handed it to Abuela and watched her turn it over in her hands and pet it fondly. They were clearly old acquaintances.

"I sewed this into a secret pocket in my skirt when Ernesto and I came to the US," said Abuela. "I thought, even if someone stops us and steals everything—they can't have this. Because my mother gave it to me, and her mother before her, and her mother before her, and so on, back and back and back."

"Did someone in our family make this, too?" said Jade.

"Yes," said Abuela, "so I'm told. One of the most revered obsidian carvers. You may have noticed that it's no ordinary mirror."

"It's for sure a funny mirror," said Jade. "The reflection is weird, and it changes all the time, and sometimes I feel like all I'm seeing are smoky lines."

"This mirror can show you who someone is," said Abuela.

Jade listened carefully. That wasn't exactly what most mirrors did.

"Do you just have to know how to use it?" she said. "How to look at it?"

Abuela shook her head. "It's not about that. You may look into it and think you see something, but this mirror can play tricks on you."

Jade nodded. She had learned that already, the many times she had tried to penetrate beyond the smoke, to uncover its secrets, but the wispy haze had taunted her. The mirror had never fully let the smoke clear. And yet she nearly always wanted to keep looking, because she had the sense that at any moment, the haze might lift.

"The mirror will only show you who a person is once you truly know the person," said Abuela. "And you only truly know a person when you have listened, and listened well, to what they have to tell you."

Jade drew in a breath. It wasn't as simple as staring hard at the mirror or angling it the right way against the light. It took more than that to get it to reveal its secrets.

"Abuela," she said. "What about—your own reflection? Does the mirror show you who you really are, too?"

"Yes, Chalchihuite," she said. "But only once you are in tune with who you are, when you have listened deep within yourself."

Abuela handed the mirror back to Jade. Jade slipped it solemnly back into the purse, wondering how it was possible to listen deep within yourself, to get in tune with who you were. Was it something that you had to do on your own? Maybe that was part of what the guides were for.

She was about to ask Abuela more, but Abuela said, "Oh! I think I've about had enough sun for today! Chalchihuite, will you help me . . . ?"

"Of course!" said Jade. She hastily slung the purse across her body and helped Abuela up from the seat, holding on to her until she was steady on her walker. Jade walked her to the back steps and up to the landing, then held the door and stood on the stoop until Abuela had shuffled her way in. Right when Abuela was inside, an impulse seized her, and she pulled the mirror out of the purse and angled it just slightly toward Abuela so she could see her reflection in it.

The smoke cleared on the black stone for just a moment, and there it was. A spritely, long-eared rabbit, leaping happily into the house.

Jade stared. The mirror had never shown her anything before besides strange shadows and oddly proportioned reflections. But there, in the mirror just now, she was certain she had seen Abuela.

19

All week Jade couldn't stop thinking about the rabbit. When she was sitting in pre-algebra, when she was running to beat her PR in cross-country as Coach Jackson pushed them harder and harder, or when she was walking through the Wildcat Trail. Often when she was in her room doing homework, she reached over to her dresser drawer and drummed on the wood with her fingertips, thinking of the mirror she kept there. If it could show her who Abuela was, what else could it tell her? And what did it mean that Abuela was a rabbit?

Somehow it made complete sense to her that Abuela was a rabbit, though she couldn't quite put her finger on why. Maybe it made sense because Abuela had a liveliness to her that was like a rabbit bounding across the yard. Or perhaps it was because she could picture Abuela as one of those mother rabbits she saw sometimes at the edge of the backyard, sitting an arm's length from her kid rabbit, her long ears pricked up for danger even as she left the little one plenty of space.

Had Abuela met any rabbits when her mother gave the mirror to her, many years ago? And had they guided her into becoming who she was now?

Jade hadn't tried it yet, but she was pretty sure she knew what she would see in the mirror if she held it up to her mother. She would certainly see a tecolote, a vigilant owl who took in everything from a high branch and who swooped sedately, dressed always in blue-gray elegance.

If the mirror had brought Itztli to Jade, as her guide, did that mean she was a jaguar?

Jade barely dared to hope that this was true.

Every night that week after dinner, Jade took the mirror out and peered into it, only illuminating it with the moon's rays and the dusty Atlanta sky that was always faintly pink even on the darkest nights. She wanted the mirror to tell her for sure who she was.

But the milky surface billowed with impenetrable clouds, and the mirror never answered.

Each night Jade sighed and stowed the mirror once again. Abuela had said that you had to be in tune with who you were for the mirror to show you your reflection. Apparently, she wasn't quite there yet.

Jade's mom filled up the space that she had left empty while she was gone. It was as though a familiar warmth that had gone missing was spreading itself through the house once more. They ate salsa and tortillas again, and her mom's shiny work pumps claimed their home in the foyer. Her dad's shoulders were more relaxed when he picked her up from cross-country, and Abuela spent entire evenings in the recliner in the living room, chatting with Jade's mom, who sat on the couch going through documents on her computer.

The TV was on sporadically, when Katerina wasn't likely to see it. It was a reminder that not all was warm and well in the world. The newspeople began to talk differently about the events of last week that had shaken everything and kept Jade's mom in New York for too long. The words they used no longer conveyed just splashes of directionless fear. Instead, the enemy now had names. *Hijackers. Terrorists.* Nineteen bearded faces flashed on the screen one by one. Every man on the news wore a tiny American flag pinned to his suit stuck in a shiny, immobile billow. It wasn't just the *Twin Towers* or the *Pentagon* or the *White House* that had been under attack—it was *America under attack*, they repeated over and over again.

On Wednesday after a particularly intense cross-country practice, Jade flopped down on her bed and gazed out at the trees. If anyone was going to help her sort out who she was, and what part she was supposed to play in this quickly changing world where the grown-ups did their best to harness their fear and give it direction, it would be Itztli.

She decided to go find him.

She wanted to bring the mirror with her this time. She didn't move yet, though. As much as she wanted to get up and go into the trees, she wanted to let her soft bed hug her sore muscles just a minute more. On top of the dresser, her mom had laid out her uniform for the meet tomorrow—a black-and-gold tank top with matching shorts that had arrived in the mail. It looked a lot better than the outfits Jade still wore to practice; with everything going on, she hadn't even asked her mom about getting new running clothes.

Practice had been especially rough today. Coach Jackson had shouted herself hoarse urging them on. She was determined that they win against Christ Savior. The other girls, too, were getting riled up about the Christ Savior girls. *They're so mean, such cheaters,* Caitlyn had said today in the locker room, and Chloe and everyone else had voiced their agreement. Jade had joined in, too, just so she could feel like she was one of them, like she was really part of the team.

She looked back at the trees. For a moment she thought she saw Itztli's spotted hide at the edge of the pines. Was he waiting for her?

She sprang up, retrieved the mirror, and tucked it into her hummingbird purse. Slipping the purse over her shoulder, she headed to the back door. Her mom was busy with Abuela, and her dad was helping Katerina start a new puzzle in the living room. Jade stepped out into the golden afternoon and walked, sure-footed, into the trees.

She didn't see Itztli at first, but she knew he was here. She felt her senses sharpen as she walked, the way they sometimes did when she ran. Her bare feet seemed to know more than she did, and she found the creek easily, feeling through the green and brown thorniness of the forest. She stood at the outer curve of the bend with one hand resting on her purse and the mirror inside it.

Itztli was wearing his fur when he emerged from the trees on the other side. He leapt lightly down to one of the stones that poked their heads up from the rushing water, and, in a continuous movement, jumped from stone to stone, off down the stream.

Jade understood that she was supposed to follow. She held tight to the purse and stepped down onto the first stone. It felt a little slippery, but her toes found their hold. She watched Itztli and did her best to move like him, springing lightly from stone to stone. She wished she had a tail for balance.

Itztli didn't take her far; he stopped at the top of a miniature waterfall, a step in the stream that the water raced over in polished curves. The stream widened here and the sunlight came in stronger. To the side stood a great old oak tree with infinite twisting branches, the one her dad had pointed out to her when he had told her and Katerina about the plants along the Wildcat Trail. Its muddy roots formed a good part of the stream bank, gripping down into the water with tenacity.

"She's beautiful, isn't she?" said Itztli.

He was a man again, leaning on his staff on the side of the stream, gazing toward the great oak. Jade thought he looked sadder than usual. She stepped out of the water onto the side of the stream across from where Itztli stood to get a good look at the tree. The intricate, sinuous pattern of the overlapping branches was indeed a sight to behold. She wondered what Itztli saw in the tree that made his eyes shine so sad, with more than just the glint of the sun.

"It *is* beautiful," she told him. She wanted to ask him why he had called the tree "she," but the shine standing in his eyes made her hesitate.

Itztli leaned heavily on his staff and lowered himself to sit cross-legged on the ground, and Jade mirrored him on her side of the stream. Itztli's mouth and jaw were tight as he sat, and it looked to Jade that he must be biting back pain. The pain of old, old, impossibly old age. The way he moved as a man, he looked far more frail than Abuela did—especially now that she was recovering so well. If Jade were in Itztli's place, she thought, she would want to spend as much time as she could as a jaguar, strong and lithe.

"I am glad you have come, Chalchihuite," said Itztli. Jade smiled, hearing her name. "These are troubling times," he went on. "I have a great deal to tell you. But first, tell me, why have you come this time?"

Jade considered this. She had come because she didn't know what to make of the attacks last week, and the explanations on TV weren't helping. It wasn't so much that she wanted to understand what was happening or why—it was that she wanted to know how she was supposed to act now, in a world that felt new and the same all at once, where the rules weren't yet clear.

And of course she had also come because she wanted to know more about the mirror in her purse that could show you who a person was, deep inside. And she wanted to know how she could find that out herself—who she was deep down—and *be* that.

She took a deep breath and did her best to put it into words. "I came because I want to ask you—how do you live after a big change, when you don't even know yet what *after* will look like?" She was thinking of the attacks, but also about her period. So much had changed since they moved here, she couldn't even name all the changes. *She* had changed, too—but she wasn't quite sure how. "I also wanted to ask you, how do you figure out who you really are?" she said. "You told me last time that you would tell me how you learned you were jaguar. Will you tell me now?"

To Jade's surprise, Itztli chuckled. "You have many questions, Chalchihuite," he said, "and I will get to them all. But first, let me tell you this. It is okay not to know exactly who you are. It takes a lifetime and a little bit more to figure that out. It does not flash for you all at once, like lightning. No, no. You find it out gradually, in a series of little epiphanies—moments of wonder and sudden understanding—when you realize something that you've always known, but that you didn't know you knew. It comes like armpit hair—not all at once but little by little."

It was Jade's turn to laugh now. Armpit hair? She hadn't expected that from Itztli. Her laugh came out a little nervous, too, because she had just started sprouting soft little tufts of hair on her armpits not long ago, and it was something so private she could hardly even imagine talking to Chloe about it.

Her laughter subsided, got lost in the chattering rush of the stream. There was something comforting in Itztli's words. She didn't have to know it all right now. She thought of the moment when she'd seen the carved jade beads in the museum and felt a resonance with them, those small, polished stones with pictures etched into them. It was as if something had shifted inside her that she couldn't quite name. It must have been one of those "little epiphanies."

"You may not know *all* of who you are for a long time," Itztli went on. "But to reach deep inside yourself to your innermost core and release the strength of will coiled there, at the very center of who you are—that you can do anytime. And it can be particularly helpful to do this when times are stormy. You must simply learn how."

"How?" said Jade.

Itztli smiled, and Jade was glad to see the familiar playful glint return to his eyes. "I can help you," he said. "But in the end, it is you who must find out for yourself."

She took another deep breath and tried to summon her patience. She was sure she would learn some interesting things today, but she was also certain that she wouldn't leave with the answers to all her questions.

Itztli reached over and extracted from among the roots of the tree the book with the wooden binding that he had painted last time—the amoxtli—and his fine reed pen.

Jade paid close attention. She didn't want to miss anything Itztli drew.

He opened the amoxtli and laid the accordion-folded pages across his lap, his arms spread wide. The figures he had painted—the island city, the ships, the seated king Moctezuma, the bird with the mirror for a head—seemed to undulate with the movement of the paper. His arms weren't wide enough to open the pages out completely, and it didn't look like he was trying to. He left his painting half folded in jagged hills and valleys.

In a quick, practiced motion, he flipped the book over, and the upturned blank white pages, still in sharp triangles, made Jade think of the steps of a temple, with their alternating light and shadow.

He collapsed the book so that just one white page was showing, and propped it against one of the sturdy roots of the great, sinewy oak tree. With his reed pen, he began to draw.

Jade tried to figure out if it was a person or a beast that he was drawing. Even as he added more and more detail to the figure, Jade saw both at once. It was a spotted creature with a furry hide and pointed claws—or was it a man lifting a blade, his stance ready to fight?

"This was my father," said Itztli.

"The jaguar warrior," said Jade.

Itztli nodded and kept drawing. He was outlining the large fangs of the jaguar's head, and Jade realized that the man—Itztli's father—was *wearing the jaguar's skin*. His head, his angular face in profile, emerged from the jaguar's maws, the fangs encircling him, menacing not him, but instead whoever was his foe. Dressed in the jaguar, Itztli's father was more than a man—he was a man *and* he was the animal.

Jade shuddered to think of wearing a dead animal like that. But the way Itztli had drawn it, the jaguar looked very alive. It was as if he and the man were one. The head of the jaguar reminded Jade of the jaguar head she had seen carved on that jade bead in the museum. Its eyes were awake and determined; if Jade were to color them, she would paint them in bright and fiery hues of red and gold.

"My father proved himself to be jaguar with his prowess in battle and sharpness of wit. Through his courage, speed, and skill in hitting the mark, he earned the honor of charging into battle wearing the suit and crown of the jaguar, the prince of all the animals," said Itztli.

"But *you're* jaguar, too," said Jade. "How did you learn that? You're not a warrior."

"No, not at all!" said Itztli, shaking his head and laughing softly. "I am terrible with an atlatl—give me a spear and chances are, I'll hurl it backward." He laughed heartily now, throwing his head back. "No, I am jaguar in a different way." He tapped his drawing with his finger. "Being jaguar doesn't just mean being able to run fast, or being able to destroy with precision," he said. Jade listened carefully. "It doesn't just mean being strong and powerful. Being jaguar means being able to *discern*." He looked at Jade, and she had never felt his gaze so sharply as now. "It means being able to see in the darkness, past the smoky mist," he said. "And it means having the courage, the confidence in yourself, to face down whoever tries to get in your way. It means charging forward and showing yourself in all your strength and splendor, even when they try to strip you of your fangs, even when they try to tell you that you're not who you know you are. *That* is what it means to be jaguar."

He tossed the reed pen high into the air, where it flipped and flipped and flipped, up into the trees, and when it fell he caught it easily with one hand, his fingers already poised to draw again.

Jade's heart was beating fast, like she had just sprinted. Itztli made it sound and look so easy to be jaguar—to shed your fear and dress yourself in courage. She wanted to be like that. She wanted to be jaguar. And she knew that even though Itztli made it seem easy, there was no way that it could be.

"You wanted to know how to figure out who you are," said Itztli. "I found out when people questioned me. When the people of Tenochtitlán who did not respect me said, *You are Purépecha. You do not belong here.* When the Spanish painters said, *You are Mexican. You are not a real painter.* And when a Spanish judge once told me, upon seeing my work in an amoxtli that told the history of the Mexica, *What nice drawings. How lovely it would be if you had a true history.* That is how I learned I was jaguar, Chalchihuite. When I learned to stand up for myself in those moments, to tell them, *No, you are wrong. I belong here. I am a painter, and these are our histories.*"

Jade was stunned, and angry. Angry because of the terrible things these people had said to Itztli. Stunned because now, as he repeated them to her, he controlled his anger, overcame it, and retained that monumental calm that he always carried with him.

"How can you be so calm about it?" she said. "Those are such awful things to say! To hear!"

Itztli set his reed pen down in front of him and locked his fingers together. "It is not enough to be angry," he said slowly. "It is not enough to simply lash out. The jaguar has pinpoint precision, like the tip of a pen." He tapped the point of the reed pen lightly with one finger, his hands still interlaced. The pen pressed into the pad of his fingertip like one of Mortimer's teeth when he wanted to nip but not quite bite. A thin trickle of black ink leaked onto the pad of Itztli's finger.

He pulled his finger away and went on. "The jaguar jumps, sprints, and pounces only when necessary," he told her. "And when that is done, the jaguar lets the calm roll in once more, like the smooth, glassy surface of a lake after a storm. Your standing-up fur lies back on your skin, and you walk slowly and deliberately through the forest. But you always keep an eye out for what might come next, even in the darkest night, and you're always ready to spring again."

When Jade had first seen Itztli, he'd looked so fearsome in his russet fur and powerful, clawed paws. She always recognized, in his jaguar form, the fiery energy he carried within him. But she had learned that he was every bit as measured and reserved in his royal fur as he was in his plain white tunic.

"Itztli, how do you do it?" she said. "How do you have so much control?"

"It takes practice," he said, smiling. "Like anything."

Jade reached for her purse. She wanted there to be a shortcut, a way to figure it all out at once. "Itztli," she said. "My abuela told me that this mirror can show you who a person truly is." She slipped the mirror out of the purse and held it lightly in her palm. On its curved surface she saw the water and the sky and Itztli all at once. In the smooth black reflection, Itztli was a jaguar, sitting patient but alert, his tail wrapped around him. But when she looked up, he was still a man, sitting cross-legged on the other side of the creek.

His eyes brightened, and Jade thought she saw the reflection of the smoky mirror in them.

"At last, you have brought the tezcatl!" he said. "And it is so much more beautiful than I had imagined."

Jade sat up straighter. Itztli knew about the mirror.

She looked back down at the stone. The tezcatl. It had clouded over.

She held it out to Itztli over the stream. "Do you want to see it?" she said.

"Yes, Chalchihuite, thank you," he said, reaching for it with his dark, wrinkled fingers. He took the stone in both his weathered hands and sat for a moment, looking intently into it. He had it angled slightly toward her. He gave a delighted little laugh and looked up at Jade.

"What did you see?" said Jade eagerly.

Itztli shook his head.

"You're not going to tell me?" she said.

"You must find out on your own who you are," he said, and held the mirror out to her again. "Take good care of your tezcatl," he said. "There are few as nicely made as this one."

Jade took the mirror back and slipped it into her purse again. "My tezcatl," she whispered, patting the hummingbird.

"Your tezcatl showed me what I already knew," said Itztli. "That's what it does."

Jade nodded. That's what Abuela had told her. She had hoped that Itztli would tell her something more.

She waited. The way Itztli was rocking back and forth slowly, almost imperceptibly, as if he were a plant swaying in a gentle wind, she knew he had more to say.

"One of the first stories that Don Martín told me when I arrived in Tenochtitlán and he took me in," said Itztli, "was about the god who could see into people's hearts. The god who used a mirror, a tezcatl, to do this. The god named Tezcatlipoca—Smoking Mirror."

Jade sat still, listening as closely as she could.

"Don Martín took me out to the lake at sunset to tell me this story," Itztli went on. "We looked out over what was left of the lake, and the water was smoking. A fine, lacy mist rose up and disappeared into the night." He extended his hand over the stream, and his fingers danced over it, mimicking the steam rising from the lake. "Behind that," he continued, "the volcano was smoking, too. It was as if the lake and the fire-bellied mountain were reminding us of what lay just below the surface, reminding us that beneath its calm lay a ferocious force that could leap up at any moment."

Itztli's hand glided smoothly just above the surface of the happy stream.

"Don Martín told me that there were five Suns, five great eras. There were many gods, and some of them ruled over the different eras. One was Quetzalcoatl, the Feathered Serpent, and one was Tezcatlipoca."

"Smoking Mirror," said Jade.

"Exactly. Tezcatlipoca ruled over the First Sun—the first era. But his brother Quetzalcoatl wanted to rule, and so they fought. You know how siblings fight."

Jade laughed.

"But when the gods fight"—Itztli pointed to the sky—"we all know it."

Jade looked up at the sky. Cottony clouds were approaching, and some of the more distant ones were dark as shadows.

"For weeks there were fearsome storms. Endless water poured down from the clouds where the brother gods were fighting," Itztli went on. "The earth began to break open. Deep underground fissures yawned and shook the ground, and the fiery insides of volcanoes gurgled up and raced down the mountainsides. At last, Quetzalcoatl dealt a thunderous blow that threw Tezcatlipoca out of the sky. The God of the Smoking Mirror fell into the sea with a great splash."

Itztli splashed his hand into the creek with unexpected force, sending the water leaping up.

"A calm began to take hold over the earth again," he went on. "The fight was over." Already the stream was flowing placidly into itself again, healing over the spot where Itztli had disturbed its current. "The earth stopped shaking and the rains stopped battering the land," he said. "The volcanoes ceased their raging indigestion, and the red lava racing from their entrails slowed and cooled to black. It was the beginning of the Second Sun."

Peace was still possible in the end, Jade thought, even after all that fighting of the gods, the brothers, overhead, and the chaos they had caused. Destruction that the earthlings could do nothing about, except watch.

She closed her eyes and slipped her toes into the stream to feel some of that cosmic calm that Itztli was talking about. The cool current made room for her toes, massaging them gently, before continuing on.

"When everything was very still," said Itztli, "Tezcatlipoca leapt up out of the sea and let out a great roar. The celestial fall and the terrific splash had made him jaguar."

Jade snapped open her eyes. She had just started to settle into the calm of the stream water flowing over and around her toes.

"You see," said Itztli, "when the brothers stopped fighting, the calm took hold, and that was good. But the God of the Smoking Mirror refused to be vanquished, refused to be buried beneath the sea. And so he rose up and roared, made himself heard, as if to say, *I am here. You can't get rid of me.*" Itztli spread his arms wide. "That is the spirit of the jaguar," he said.

As Jade watched him, the light struck his bright, dark eyes in such a way that they flashed amber, like his eyes when he was jaguar.

"Itztli," said Jade. "Do you feel like you're jaguar—are you jaguar—right now?"

Itztli smiled and nodded slowly, bringing his hands down. "Of course, Chalchihuite," he said.

Jade looked up at the great oak tree with the twisting branches beside Itztli. She wondered what it must feel like to be that in tune with who you were, all the time.

"But how does that work?" she said. "How are you jaguar—even while you're human?"

"It works like this," said Itztli. "I am jaguar in the way I listen. I try to be silent and attentive. I am jaguar in the way I paint stories. I try to draw carefully with the fine lines of my reed pen, but also dash broad strokes across the page when necessary."

Jade nodded, doing her best to listen quietly and intently.

"But there are many, many ways to be jaguar, and many ways to paint stories, and to keep memories," Itztli went on. "I learned that in Tenochtitlán. I met tradesmen who came from the north and sold pottery with designs I had never seen before, and turquoise beads and pendants carved in ways that pushed the bounds of what I thought was possible. Some were just pretty, but some held within them customs and memories that the Spaniards hadn't stamped out—and I wanted to know more."

Jade waited, her toes still dangling in the quiet water. She realized this was one of those moments when Itztli wanted to tell her something, and wanted her—maybe even *needed* her—to listen.

"So I set out on a pilgrimage of sorts," he said. He took up his reed pen again and drew footsteps out from the jaguar man he had drawn. Was that still his father? Or was it also Itztli? Was it perhaps also Tezcatlipoca, the God of the Smoking Mirror?

"I walked north, and I learned the ways of the people there. I kept walking, for months, following a trail of corn and pottery and carved stones. I wanted to learn everything I could. Each time I saw a new design, I asked where it was from, and I walked to that place. And everywhere I went, the people fed me corn, and the corn made me feel at home wherever I was." He drew a cornstalk with its curled leaves peeling out in perfect symmetry.

"Is that how you got here?" said Jade.

Itztli nodded. He drew a large hill now that looked a lot like a watery hill, but with a wider curve to it.

"At length, I came to Stone Mountain," he said.

"I have a race there tomorrow!" said Jade.

"Ah!" said Itztli. "So you will run there, on the ancient ground. It is miles tall and miles wide—the largest granite stone in all the world to rear its head up from the ground. Ages ago, the granite, hot in the womb of the earth, cooled to smoky gray."

"Wow," said Jade. Tomorrow she would run in the shadow of that giant rock that had once bubbled deep inside the earth.

"It was a meeting place," said Itztli, "a place where the roads met." He drew the crossroads at the base of the mountain. "And it was there that I met my beloved."

Jade sat still. The way he said it, she knew: Whoever his beloved was, he had lost her.

Itztli was looking up toward the great oak tree now. At first Jade thought that he was simply lost in thought, remembering his beloved, but in fact he was looking intently *at* the tree. He had called it "she."

"My beloved Chesequah made cooking bowls and jars from the red clay of these parts," he said, still looking up at the tree. "She etched them with spirals that looked like eddies, and she rolled corncobs gently across the clay while it was still soft and supple, stamping the red earth with the food we cannot do without—the food of my childhood." He looked back at Jade. "I took one drink from her jug, and that was it for me," he said, smiling. "I fell madly in love."

Jade smiled, and remembered Abuela's story of how Abuelo had proposed marriage because of a handkerchief. She was sure there was a lot Itztli wasn't telling her—just like there was a lot Abuela hadn't told her—but that was okay. She knew that if she waited and listened, she would hear whatever it was Itztli *did* want to tell her.

"We were happy together," said Itztli, looking back at the tree. He set down his reed pen and reached out to touch the trunk affectionately. "We lived in a house that was a hill built from the earth. And soon, she was expecting a child. Our child. Every day I covered her belly with kisses, wild with the idea."

The clouds were getting closer now, and the heavier, darker ones were beginning to crowd out the white tufty ones.

"Our happiness was short-lived," said Itztli, lowering his eyes. "She died when she went into labor. The baby was stillborn." Itztli interlaced his hands again and studied them.

"But before she died," he said, "I held her hand, and I told her all the stories I knew. All the stories my mother had told me, and all the stories that Don Martín had told me. It was all I could do. We both knew she would soon be gone." He looked up at Jade. "She told me something before she died. She said, *Itztli, we will always be together. Honor my memory, tell our story, and I will be with you always.*"

Jade sucked in her breath. Itztli was doing that now, telling her their story.

Itztli began to stand up, in pained, slow-motion movements. Jade put her hand out instinctively across the creek, but Itztli did not accept the help. He leaned on the tree for support and pushed himself up with his staff.

"I came here to the deepest part of the forest that I could find in these parts," he said. "And the most beautiful, happiest stream within it. And I planted this oak in honor of my beloved because the oak shelters us, and where I come from, it forms a bridge to a divine world beyond this one. It lets us speak with the gods, and I wanted them to know about her."

Jade remembered the oaks in Itztli's bark painting in her room, the trees sheltering the gods as they whispered to the humans in their sleep. Itztli had told her then about the oaks, and how their wood fed the fires that glowed for the gods in the temples.

"This oak is also for our little one, who we lost," said Itztli, patting the tree. "And it is for my father, who died fighting as a jaguar. And for my mother, who died battling the pestilence that boiled and consumed her body."

Jade looked at the twisted branches of the oak. She wondered how long it must have taken for the spindly little green shoot of a tree to thicken and twist out in all these different directions. She thought of how it sprouted and shed its leaves year after year—it must have been doing that for a very long time.

"I have been here since then, tending to this tree, protecting it. I have seen so much in these years, Chalchihuite. I have seen Spaniards come and Spaniards leave, Englishmen come and Englishmen stay. I have seen great houses built, and people enslaved and made to work the land, their hands scarring into maps of suffering and desire and broken memory. I have seen terrible wars. I have seen betrayal. I have watched invaders steal away the lands of my beloved's people, piece by piece. I have watched her people fight for their homeland. I have watched the descendants of the invaders force her people out of their homes, force them to walk west to unknown places. This oak is for them, too—for all those who did not survive the trek, or who died fighting for their land."

Itztli leaned against the tree now, as if weighed down by the heft of his own words. Its trunk cradled his slight form.

"All this time the forest has gotten smaller and smaller," he said. "But here we remain."

Jade thought of the construction site at the high school, and near Chloe's house. How mounds of clay-red dirt replaced what trees must have stood there.

"And I need *you*," said Itztli, pushing away from the tree trunk and suddenly standing upright, touching his staff only lightly, as if he barely needed it. "I need you to keep my stories, my child. And you have come—your tez-catl has led us to this moment."

Jade took this in. Her obsidian mirror hadn't just brought Itztli to her as her guide, then. It had also brought her to Itztli, to listen to and care for his stories.

Itztli picked up the amoxtli and folded it shut. "You have listened, Chalchihuite, and you have watched with avid eyes," he said. "And you have learned well. I knew you would."

He held the amoxtli out to her over the water.

Jade hesitated. The book was so precious. How could she take it?

"My child," said Itztli, and his tone was pleading in a way that Jade had never heard before.

She sank her toes into the soft silt and tiny pebbles of the creek and stood up, the water swirling around her ankles. She took the wooden book in her hands, feeling its heft, the weather-worn grain of its covers.

"Are you sure?" she said. "But—you haven't finished it."

Itztli shook his head. "You can finish it," he said. "You have what it takes. I have waited all these years for you. You must take it now."

Jade brought the book in close, pressed it to her chest, and nodded. "Yes, Itztli," she said. She thought she understood. If the world was going to hold together despite its brokenness, she had to keep the stories alive. "I will paint your stories as well as I can, and I will tell them, and I will keep them alive," she said. "I promise." It was a big promise to make, but Itztli trusted her, and she knew she had to do it.

Tiny raindrops began to ping on the surface of the stream, and Jade started to feel them, fine but insistent on her hair. If she wasn't careful, the book would get wet.

Itztli gave her a sad, satisfied smile. "Thank you," he said. And then, behind the fine, misty rain, he was a jaguar again.

Jade watched him climb the oak easily, swishing his tail for balance. He reached one of the tallest limbs of the tree and stood perched there, his golden fur a radiant beacon in the subdued hues of the rainy forest. There, on the high branch, he let out a great, resounding roar that filled the woods.

Jade hugged the book to her chest and listened as she watched him, blinking against the rain. It was a roar of anguish, but also of triumph. A roar that resonated with something deep inside her.

The rain began to come on thick now. She sprinted back to the house, Itztli's roar echoing in her ears. Just as she entered the back door, the water came down hard and began pounding the windows.

Back in her room, Jade set the amoxtli down on her bed and watched the storm. The rain fell in thick slanting sheets and the pines bent and swayed in the wind.

Perhaps the gods were fighting overhead. Perhaps they were crying, letting out their sobs in great, heaving water-falls that washed loudly over the earth.

A flash of lightning lit the backyard and left it dark again. A thunderclap broke over the neighborhood, a deafening crack and a bellow that sounded like it could rip the universe.

Jade looked down at the wooden amoxtli. *You can finish it,* Itztli had said. *You have what it takes.*

20

Jade still had the amoxtli spread open on her bed as she watched the storm when she heard her mother's voice behind her.

"What a storm," she said. "I thought I heard a roar a while ago—but maybe it was just thunder."

Jade turned and saw her mom in the doorway wearing slippers, her hair relaxed. She stepped in slowly, watching Jade as if for permission this time.

Jade didn't stop her. She was actually grateful for her company in the midst of all this thunder and thrashing trees, and the wind that sometimes whistled strangely as it whipped around the corners of the house. Jade looked down at the floor—she had tracked in mud again with her bare feet as she raced in from the rain.

"Sorry—I'll clean that up," she said.

Her mom nodded but didn't seem too concerned about it. She stepped closer to the bed and looked at the amoxtli, taking in what Itztli had painted there. Jade waited to see what she would say. Did she know what it was?

"The mirror works, doesn't it?" her mom said softly after a little while, not taking her eyes off the painted pages.

"Well—yes," said Jade, and with relief she realized that this was one of those moments when her mother was opening up and this kind of conversation could happen.

Lightning brightened the room for a moment, but the thunder didn't come right away. It rolled in a few seconds later.

"I . . . met my guide," said Jade.

Her mom looked up at her, a little smile on her lips. "I'm glad," she said. Her gaze drifted to the hummingbird purse that Jade still had strapped to her side, the obsidian mirror bulging inside it. Only a few drops of rain had fallen onto the fabric; Jade had managed to get inside just in time.

Jade pulled the mirror out. "It *does* work," she said. "But it still won't show me who I am. Abuela told me that I have to be in tune with myself, and then it will show me."

"That's right," said her mom. "But you'll see your reflection soon enough." She gave Jade's shoulder a squeeze.

"Okay," said Jade, deciding to trust her. She slipped the mirror back into the purse. She noticed that her mom was looking with softened features at the embroidered bird, as if she were contemplating an old friend.

"How do you feel about the race tomorrow?" her mom said.

Jade was startled. With everything her mom had to worry about right now, she was surprised that she remembered.

"Um—I think I feel good about it," she said. "I'm excited, actually. I mean, we've been practicing, but now it'll be for real, you know?" She was looking forward to testing herself in the high-stakes context of the race, seeing how fast she could run when it really mattered.

"You'll be great," her mom said. "I'll be there."

"Really?" Jade had sort of expected that only her dad would come, considering the mountain of work and worry her mom was under these days.

"Of course!" her mom said, and her smile got wider, like she wanted to make sure Jade knew she was truly looking forward to it. "All three of us will be there—me, your dad, and Katerina."

Jade felt a smile break across her face. Her family cared. They would all be there tomorrow to cheer her on. Somehow, she felt like that would make all the difference.

The rain had let up a little now, and was falling straight and steady instead of slanted. Her mom glanced at the amoxtli again, then patted Jade lightly on the shoulder and left the room.

The sizzling smells of dinner floated down the hall and through the house. Jade wiped up the mud she had tracked in, and when the storm subsided enough that it was safe to shower, she went to wash herself of the intense day. She used her mom's razor to shave her legs, slowly and carefully this time so she wouldn't miss any spots or nick herself. As she stepped out and changed into her nightclothes, a deep, satisfying tiredness came over her. She would probably sleep well tonight, which was good because then she would run better tomorrow.

She sank into the couch in the living room beside the recliner where Abuela was dozing. The TV was on low but Jade could still hear it. The anchorwoman was saying something about how there was a renewed debate over racial profiling in the wake of the attacks on the Pentagon and the World Trade Center. She had a legal expert on to talk about it, a balding man with one of those shiny little American flags pinned to his suit.

"You know, it seems to me that after these attacks we've seen, it's going to be more difficult now to make the argument in court that racial profiling isn't effective," the man said.

"But is it legal?" the anchorwoman pushed back, her face stony. "Is it constitutional?"

"Well, in terms of legal precedent, in 1976, the Supreme Court ruled that there was no violation of the constitution in a case in which a Mexican man was arrested . . ."

Jade felt something rise up in her chest, like bile or a foul burp. She switched off the TV and stared into the black screen. Abuela shifted a little but got still again.

How dare anyone question someone just because of how they looked? Jade had never really wanted to believe that people treated her mom badly in the airport sometimes, but she knew it was true. She couldn't understand why anyone would think it was okay to be suspicious of someone—maybe even *arrest* them—just because they looked like they were Mexican.

Itztli had learned he was jaguar when people questioned him. When they said awful things to him. That was what it meant to be jaguar—to be able to rein in your anger, to know when to lash out, and when to muster all your strength and remain calm.

She took a deep breath, trying to be like Itztli. She couldn't change what that man said on the TV. All she could do was focus on her race tomorrow, and run as fast as she possibly could. She wanted to show everyone that she was part of the team. And she wanted to represent her family—all of them—including Tío Efraín, who had run so fast and scored so many goals.

The smell of dinner was strong now and seemed to stir Abuela from her reverie. She blinked a few times and opened her eyes.

"Ya es hora de cenar, ¿no, Chalchihuite?" she said. "Qué hambre . . ."

"Sí, Abuela," said Jade, standing to help her up from the recliner.

As she guided Abuela to find her grip on the walker, Jade wondered if she would ever see Itztli again, or if today had been the last time. After all, he had given her the amoxtli. Perhaps his roar had been his farewell. She didn't want that to be true.

She shook the thought from her head. Dinner was on the table now—her dad's meat and potatoes with her mom's corn and zucchini. There was even some happy orange flor de calabaza mixed in with the zucchini. Katerina ran into the dining room, drawn by the smell, and they all sat down to the hearty weekday feast.

The light came in strong when Jade's alarm woke her up the next morning. As her vision cleared, she saw that Mortimer was standing up on his hind legs with his paws on the window, peering through the blinds. The crack he made with his paws let the daylight in.

"What is it, Morty?" she said, yawning. She pried him away from the window and pulled up the blinds, squinting.

The cat squirmed in her arms and jumped to the window-sill, pressing his whiskers to the glass.

And then she saw it. Two huge, bulbous roots stared back at her. "Oh man," she said. The roots belonged to the two great oaks in the backyard that, until yesterday, had stood like tall twins overlooking her dad's flower beds. The trees had pulled up part of the earth with them as they fell; raw, red mud clung to their roots. The spot in the landscape and the sky where they used to stand looked strangely empty.

The yard was strewn with the crisscrossed remnants of the storm. The pines had stayed upright but looked wind-swept, and many of their clusters of long green needles had tumbled to the ground. It was a minor miracle that the two oaks had fallen toward the pines, away from the house. If they had fallen the other way, they would have crashed directly into Jade's bedroom—or Abuela's—while they slept.

Jade scooped Mortimer up and held him to her for comfort. The might of the storm was hard to wrap her head around. The cat nuzzled his head against her chin for a moment, then gave a little squeak and jumped down toward the door.

"Mom!" Jade called, getting off the bed and opening the door. Mortimer bolted down the hall to the kitchen. "Dad!" she called down the hall. "Have you seen this?"

Katerina came in first and wriggled onto Jade's bed in her polka-dotted red pajamas. Standing on her knees as she looked out the window, she said, "Whoa! It's so sunny now. Look! You can see all the way to the forest!"

"What is it, honey?" Jade's mom said as she came in, already dressed for work. "Oh my," she said, seeing it. Her

eyes widened and she made the sign of the cross, something she almost never did.

"Holy . . . ," her dad said, walking in behind her. He was
holding his toothbrush aloft, fresh toothpaste capping the
bristles.

"Do you think it was just all that wind?" her mom
asked him.

"That, and the ground got so soft, with all that rain," her
dad said, leaning closer to the window. "The sky was just
dumping gallons last night—the soil had no time to absorb
it. These southern thunderstorms are serious business."

"Thank god those trees fell that way," her mom said.

Thank all the gods, Jade thought.

Her dad took a deep breath and nodded, over and over
again. At last he rubbed his eyes and said, "We'll have to
call the tree people and get that seen about." Her mom
started to make a sound but he stopped her and said, "I
got it, Sol, I'll take care of it." She nodded. "Before your
race," he added, turning to Jade.

Jade took a deep breath, hearing him say it. A steadiness took hold of her. Despite the storm, despite the trees
down, her family was still going to be there for her today.

"We're gonna watch Sissy win!" said Katerina, throwing her hands up.

"Shhhh," said Jade, smiling. "Don't jinx it!"

The Wildcat Trail was textured with muddy leaves and
damp pine needles as Jade walked to school with Katerina
and her dad. With each step her leather uniform shoes
sank a little into the earth. She peered through the trees

and caught sight of the great twisty oak that Itztli had shown her yesterday, standing just as before. It was impossible for that tree to go down, she thought, even with a storm like this. Its roots were too tightly anchored into the ground.

When she got to homeroom, Chloe came up to her and said, "Are you ready for this afternoon?" Her eyes were big, her mascara thick.

"I guess so?" said Jade. "Are you?"

Chloe dropped her voice to a whisper. "I always get so nervous at meets," she said.

"Really?" said Jade. "But you're so fast! Why would you get nervous?"

"It's different when it's a race, you know?" she said. She looked around to make sure no one was listening, then added, "I always throw up at the end. It's super gross, and it's so embarrassing. And then I get worried that I'm going to throw up and it's going to be awful—"

"Chloe," said Jade, putting her hands on Chloe's shoulders. She tried to give her friend some of the steadiness her family had given her this morning. "*I'm* the one who's supposed to be nervous," she said. "It's my first race! *You're* going to be fine. Promise. Even if you puke."

Chloe laughed, and Jade let her arms drop. She held out her pinky, and after a moment, Chloe curled her own pinky into hers. *Promise.*

When the last bell rang and school let out, Jade headed into the bathroom with the other cross-country girls to get changed. Coach Jackson had said it would be easier if they changed now, before they got to the course at Stone Mountain.

It was the first time Jade had put on the black-and-gold tank top and matching shorts. The top was stamped with ssm in blocky gold letters—Saint Stephen Martyr—and it was just loose enough to let some wind through. Gold lines like the white ones on Coach Jackson's blue tracksuit ran up the sides of the black shorts. They were way shorter than the ones Jade wore for practice. She wasn't used to seeing so much of her pale legs exposed like that. She was glad she had shaved.

As they were about to leave, Jade caught sight of herself in the mirror. The black-and-gold pattern was sleek. Perfect for running. She liked how she looked in these colors, in these clothes. She hoisted her backpack on and headed for the door, her feet feeling bouncier than usual in her sneakers. When she got outside to the parking lot and Coach Jackson's red jeep, she felt that in this outfit, she was ready for anything.

In their excitement the girls talked over one another the whole way. The highway stretch was longer this time— Stone Mountain was a little ways away. Jade got caught up in the chatter as much as she could, but she also took in the changing landscape outside the window.

A few lanes were blocked off where a tree had fallen. And a crop of flags had sprouted on the cars. Little ones flapped like terrified fishes against hoods, and billowing

Old Glories were fixed on bumper stickers with UNITED WE STAND stamped across them in cursive letters.

Jade sat back against her seat and wondered what that slogan really meant. Who was the *we*? And who did it leave out?

She thought of the man interviewed on TV last night. Clearly, some people *were* left out.

Again she felt the anger rise within her. It was hard to let go of.

The song came on—their song. Jade knew all the words by now. Her heart began to race as Coach Jackson turned up the volume. Jade did her best to give herself over to the excitement, to the feeling like she was one of these girls, part of this team. Right now, she wanted to be part of a *we*. They all belted along, and when they got to the chorus, Jade and Chloe did a duet of sorts, with Jade calling and Chloe giving a full-throated answer, and they all put their hands up in the air. The throaty fullness of Chloe's voice never ceased to surprise Jade. She made it seem so easy to sound like Beyoncé.

Jade felt better—freer—by the end of the song. "Just run like you sing," she whispered to Chloe.

Chloe gave her a funny look, but then she said, "Okay," and nodded like she had taken it to heart.

Coach Jackson took the exit for Stone Mountain, and they wound through the tall pines. At last they arrived, and Jade saw the great gray arch of the massive stone. She got down from the jeep and saw the Confederate carving high up on the mountainside. From this far away, it didn't look as big as she had imagined. It was a squarish oval blasted out of the smooth granite, with three men inside it riding horses and looking ahead. From the chest down, the horses faded to striated stone clouds of nothing, like the sculptors had grown tired of it.

She thought of the crossroads Itztli had drawn at Stone Mountain on the amoxtli. So many people had passed through here. She thought of all the things he told her he had seen in this land. The pottery textured with corncobs, the people forced from their homes, the people forced to work, to scar their hands. This giant carving that was dwarfed by the enormity of the mountain itself recorded nothing of that story. It told another, different one, and only half-heartedly. But it had left a scar on the mountain nonetheless.

Coach Jackson led them to the meadow that marked the beginning of the course. The grass here was wilder than the buzz-cut, crisp green grass of the track field. Coach Jackson pointed out the entrance to the trails and showed them on a big sign where they would be running today. One big loop through the forest at the foot of the mountain.

Shannon, Devon, and Samantha arrived, and Coach Jackson led the team through some warm-up stretches and told them to conserve their energy.

"What's the number one rule?" Coach Jackson asked them.

"*Keep your head in the race!*" they all replied.

Some families were beginning to gather. Jade kept an eye out for hers, but didn't see them yet. She wasn't exactly nervous; she just felt like there was something tense and coiled inside her that she needed to release. She wanted to just run already.

The Christ Savior girls arrived together on a bus. It didn't seem to Jade like they were all that different from the girls on her own team. They wore their hair in the same high ponytails, and their uniforms were similar, only blue and white. All this time practicing, Jade had been running to do her best, or to keep up with the other girls, or to feel like part of the team. Now it was time to pull together as a team, and win.

The two teams stood apart from each other, the girls on each team eyeing the girls on the other. No one greeted anyone, except the coaches, with a no-nonsense handshake and brief, perfunctory smiles.

Chloe's face brightened and she waved toward the sidelines. Jade turned and saw that Chloe's mom and Nikos had arrived and were approaching from a distance. Nikos was wearing jeans and a black Saint Stephen Martyr T-shirt with an angry bobcat on it.

Jade's heart gave a little jump at the sight of Nikos. He looked great in black. She couldn't help but wonder what he thought of her now, in her racing clothes. She hoped he would notice how awesome she looked—because she knew she looked great.

She turned away from Nikos and back toward her team. It was time to concentrate, time to win. That mattered more than anything else right now.

Her mom's voice called out her name behind her. She turned and saw her family, the three of them, approaching.

"Good luck, Sissy!" Katerina called.

Jade smiled and waved. "Thank you!" she answered, and a surge of extra energy pulsed through her. They had her back.

"It's time," Chloe said to her quietly.

Jade turned back to the race. The runners were getting into position, and Jade took her stance. She concentrated to the fullest, trying to stay in tune with her legs, to keep them moving, ready to spring to action.

"Ready—Set—"

The whistle blew, and Jade dashed off through the slapping mud, Chloe by her side.

It was harder than ever to pace herself. She quickly figured out who the fastest runner on the other team was: a tall, pale girl with a straight, dark ponytail that flapped in the wind like the furious tail of a galloping horse. Jade kept her eye on her and stayed level with her as best she could. She wasn't going to let her get ahead, she told herself. But the girl's legs were impossibly long—there was no way this was fair. This girl looked like she could be in high school already.

Jade knew that if she was going to help her team win, if she was going to show everyone that she belonged, if she was going to honor Tío Efraín and all the strong and determined people in her family, she was going to have to control herself, conserve her energy, and find her rhythm and stick to it, like Coach Jackson always said. She remembered what Itztli had told her, that being jaguar meant knowing exactly when and how to strike, that it meant having control over your emotions, your actions. If she was going to win the race, she needed to have control. She would let go of the anger that she was still holding. She would harness and direct her energies, and *run*.

The ground was wet and squelchy, and her sneakers were getting slathered in rust-colored mud that slapped at the backs of her calves. The mud made it even harder to find her rhythm. She concentrated on her feet, her body, the sound of her footsteps—and there it was, *there* it was, her rhythm that she marked with the beat of her feet on the ground.

Her tank top fluttered in the swift mountain breeze. Pines flanked one side of the trail; on the other side rose the granite surface, the sun sparkling off the ancient stone. Jade breathed in time with her quick, even steps that were faster than the pace she usually kept.

The speedy girl on the other team was getting ahead now. The runners were starting to spread out. These Christ Savior girls really did run fast.

It was the last stretch now, and it was uphill.

Jade picked up her pace. Now was the time for her team to gain on Christ Savior and overtake them.

But the Christ Savior girls had picked up their pace, too. Jade ran faster and faster, as fast as she thought she could, panting hard, her calves burning. Chloe sped nearby.

Jade focused even more than before. She had to make it count now. She tried to let it all fall away, all except what was essential. She smelled the wet ground, the fresh pine needles. She heard each breath, each pounding step, of the racing girls. She saw distinctly the stone carving far up ahead on the side of the mountain, each chiseled detail of it. She felt a fierce power rise up within her, felt the wet grass between her toes, felt the ground give way beneath her paws, felt the breath of the mountain wind enter her lungs as she bared her fangs and raced along the ground . . .

The finish chute was approaching. The rope to funnel them in single file was at the height of her eyes, of her ears, of her sensitive whiskers. All her muscles burned but she let out a roar and it propelled her forward and she passed the tall, fast girl, and she was first to cross the finish line, first to stumble out into the wide-open meadow at the foot of the towering, scarred mountain.

Jade's legs kept moving as she came back to her normal self, slowed down. There were her sneakers, her pale knees, her black-and-gold shorts. She held her sides, the places where it hurt to breathe. She had just unearthed a part of herself that she had always known was there, but never had the strength to dig up from her core—until now.

She panted and watched as the rest of the girls crossed the finish line. Chloe, then the Christ Savior girl with the dark ponytail. Their red-brown footprints mixed on the grass. She counted the runners from each team.

Barely able to speak, she said to Chloe, "We—we won, didn't we?"

Chloe nodded, slowed, and puked onto the grass. She did it like a pro, wiping her mouth with the back of her hand and standing up straight afterward. She held her other hand up and gave Jade a high five. "You were an animal out there," she said.

Jade grinned, because it was true in more ways than one. And because on some level Chloe, who knew her so well, had also sensed it. "You were awesome, too," she said.

"That's my girl!"

Jade turned. It was her dad. He and her mom and Katerina were running toward her. Katerina gave her a great big hug that nearly toppled her over and her dad put a water bottle in her hand. Her mom came up and squeezed her tight, sandwiching Katerina between them. Jade drank up and did her best to hug back and not fall over.

She closed her eyes and let herself be loved. She knew it for sure, now—she didn't even need the mirror to tell her. She knew what it would show her.

She was jaguar.

She opened her eyes. The girls on her team were high fiving one another, and the Christ Savior girls were starting to line up behind them, getting ready to shake hands in defeat. Coach Jackson looked happier than Jade had ever seen her. Jade wanted to go and be with them. But before she headed into the circle of celebration, she stood there just a second more, letting the mountain breeze cool her, and her family hold her.

21

Crisp-smelling mounds of wood chips took the place of the wide holes that the trees had torn out of the yard when they fell. As Jade walked past these small hills the next morning, heading into the Wildcat Trail with Katerina, she thought the soft rise of the wood chips made the raw earth wounds look like inviting beds.

She felt great. The force that had surged within her yesterday at the meet still pulsed inside her, only more faintly now. But she knew it was still there. It wasn't going away.

She wanted so much to tell Itztli about it. To tell him that she understood now—or thought she did—what it meant to be jaguar. She had a feeling that she still had a lot to learn.

As she walked through the path that was still soft from the rain, she noticed some plastic orange ribbons tied here and there to some of the bigger trees. She had never seen them there before. She saw more and more of them as they neared the end of the trail and the parking lot. Their slick brightness and the way they slapped against the thick trunks when a breeze came through felt decidedly out of place among the gentle greens and browns of the waking forest. The ribbons unnerved Jade, and she made sure not to let any of them touch her as she walked past. But as she and Katerina stepped out into the parking lot, the thrill that had stayed with her since yesterday overtook her once more, and the little orange ribbons left her mind completely. She couldn't wait to see the cross-country girls again in homeroom, and celebrate with them.

Caitlyn nearly knocked her over in a big hug when she walked in, and Emily came up right after. Jade had never felt this close with her teammates, and a smile stamped itself across her face and stayed there. Chloe walked in and belted their song, and they all put their hands up like the song told them to.

Coach Jackson motioned for them to quiet down, but her smile was as big as Jade's.

Jade glided through the rest of the day as if on skates. Her locker clicked open for her on the first try every time, the equations in pre-algebra immediately made sense when Ms. Colby explained them, and people kept passing her the ball when they played soccer in PE. She and Chloe made a goal together, dribbling back and forth as they ran, with Chloe making the final kick that scored, the ball hammering into the back corner of the net. And maybe she was imagining it, but Jade felt like the guys were paying more attention to her today. When the last bell rang and she headed out to the sunny breezeway with the cross-country girls, untucking her shirt as she went, she was pretty sure Benjamin was watching her, and he tripped for a second before recomposing himself with a little flick of his brown hair.

But when she looked out across the parking lot toward the forest, what she saw made her backpack suddenly feel heavy, as if a rough speed bump had risen up in the smooth course she had been riding along all day. A yellow bulldozer sat at the edge of the parking lot beside the trees, right beside the entrance to the Wildcat Trail. She remembered the little plastic ribbons from this morning, and the same uneasiness spread within her again.

"Jade, are you okay?" said Chloe. "You just got—really quiet all of a sudden."

"Oh. Yeah," said Jade. "Do you see that?" She pointed her chin toward the bulldozer.

"Yeah," said Chloe. "What do you think they're going to do? You live right behind there, right?"

"Right," said Jade. "I don't know what they're going to do. But I don't like it." The machine was monstrous and metallic against the soft and sinuous contours of the trees.

Katerina came out of the elementary school building and Jade said goodbye to Chloe, Caitlyn, and Emily. Jade held Katerina's hand firmly as they walked into the Wildcat Trail.

"Sissy, that's a bulldozer," said Katerina, pointing to it as they entered the trail. Jade was pretty sure she had learned this word from *Bob the Builder*. "Why is it here?"

"I don't know," said Jade, squeezing her sister's hand more tightly. "But I don't think it has any business being here."

This time the orange ribbons strangling the trees reminded Jade of the tails of garish Halloween ghosts that people sometimes decorated their houses with. She tried not to guess what the bulldozer was going to do. This forest was too precious, these trees too old. There was no way anyone could take down this forest.

Her dad was in the backyard walking pensively among the mounds of wood chips when Jade and Katerina came out of the Wildcat Trail. He got home early on Fridays sometimes. When he saw them, he waved and said, "What do you girls think we should plant where these trees were? I want to make them into flower beds."

"That's cool," said Jade. She did like the idea, but she had more pressing matters on her mind. "Dad, there's a bulldozer parked outside the Wildcat Trail at school," she said.

Her dad lifted his eyebrows, then frowned and crossed his arms.

Just then, a loud rumble started up. The sound chafed against Jade's entire being—it was mechanical, insistent, and monstrous. She watched her dad's eyes go wide as he looked toward the trees. Katerina pressed her hands to her ears and squeezed her eyes shut.

Jade's heart began to pound, almost as loud as the bulldozer engine. She felt the energy rise within her that had surged inside her the day before, at the race. It propelled her to run, to do everything she could to stop this from happening, to keep that giant metal beast away from these precious trees.

She slid her backpack to the ground and ran.

She ran back through the Wildcat Trail, kicking up mud as she did so, racing past the last kids who were headed home. Barely any time passed before she neared the other end of the trail. The awful noise grew, and it was sharper, higher.

A strip of yellow tape now cordoned off the last stretch of the trail up ahead. Beyond it, the bulldozer was barreling into the forest like a tank—she could feel it. This close, the ground shook. The thunderous rumble sent tremors up Jade's legs through the soles of her feet as she kept running, running toward it.

Panting hard, her feet pounding the ground, Jade saw the blinding yellow of the bulldozer up ahead. Its ravenous teeth scraped low along the ground, tearing up monkey grass by the roots and wrecking stalks of hollyhock and ironweed. Jade kept running, her eyes widening all the while, the wind sharp on her eyes, and watched it dig into the base of a skinny tree with determination and tear it up from the ground, sending dirt spraying off the unearthed, spindly roots. The machine raised its fanged metal maw before coming back down for more, its corners dripping fresh red soil and grass.

"*Itztli!!!*" she screamed, and she dashed into the yellow tape so forcefully that she took it with her, tearing it from the trees where it was stuck at either end.

"Jade!"

It was her dad, calling to her from behind.

Jade wanted to keep running, but she willed her legs to slow, to stop. She remembered how glad she had been to hear her dad's voice yesterday, when she won the race, how much strength her family had given her when she had felt like falling over. She leaned over and held her knees, her hair falling into her face. Through the curtain of hair she could still see the yellow bulldozer advancing, its wheels imprinting their grotesquely even pattern on the forest floor, trampling and flattening it.

When she caught her breath, Jade looked back and saw her dad running toward her, a frightened look on his face. Immediately she felt bad, sorry that she had scared him, running like this.

The great rumble shook the ground even harder now. The bulldozer was getting dangerously close to her.

She ran back, directly into her father's arms.

"I'm sorry, Dad," she said into his chest. "I'm sorry I scared you. It's just—I don't want them to mess up this forest." She kept her face in his chest and her eyes closed, hoping that way the tears wouldn't come.

"Sh-sh-sh-sh-sh," he said, like he used to do when she was a little kid and got upset. "I don't want them to destroy this forest either," he said, rubbing her back. "But running toward a bulldozer is not going to help. There are other ways to fight this."

Jade pinched her eyelids shut and willed back her tears. She wasn't sure what he meant by that, but she was glad her dad saw that it *was* necessary to fight this.

"Let's go home," he said.

Jade nodded and finally pulled away.

The loud cracks and whines and grumbles of the bulldozer accompanied them as they walked home. Jade's dad spoke loudly over the noise so she would hear him. "It looks like they're just preparing the ground right now," he said.

Jade looked up at him in surprise. *Just preparing the ground?* This didn't seem like "just" anything to her—it looked and felt pretty drastic.

"But those markers," he continued, pointing to a few of the ribbons tied to some of the bigger trees, "it looks like they want to take down some of the big trees, too. And that—*that* we can't let happen." His voice was raised now not only to be heard, but also in anger, the words coming out almost as a shout, his face reddening. This forest meant a lot to him, too.

When they got to the backyard, Katerina was standing near the back stoop, her eyes wide.

"You okay, bug?" her dad said, hurrying toward her and scooping her up.

"Yeah," said Katerina. "I stayed right where you told me to." She looked over his shoulder at Jade. Jade retrieved her backpack from the spot by the birdbath where she had dropped it and went to join them. She wanted to be close to them right now.

"That's good," Jade's dad said to Katerina as he carried her up the steps. He set her down on the stoop and opened the door just as Jade caught up to them.

As they walked inside, Jade thought about what her dad had said, that there were other ways of fighting this. It wasn't so different from what Itztli had told her, about how it was important to know when and how to strike, and to be able to control your anger. She figured that, with practice, this would get easier, but maybe it would always be hard. It looked like it was hard for her dad to contain himself right now.

Of course her dad was angry, too, she thought, reaching into the fridge for two string cheeses—one for Katerina and one for her. The forest trees sheltered their home, filtered the sunlight, and cast a welcoming shade on their backyard and her dad's plants.

The forest was also Itztli's home. And the home of the oak with the twisted branches by the stream where he kept alive the memory of his beloved. The forest was so many things.

Jade peeled open one of the string cheeses and held it out to her sister. Katerina took it silently, looking up at her. As their dad headed into the living room, Jade shrugged off her backpack and leaned against the kitchen counter to eat her own string cheese. She and Katerina ate their snacks side by side in the kitchen, saying nothing, the muffled mechanical snarl of the bulldozer whining outside.

The noise was much more tolerable inside the house, far from the parking lot. Jade stayed in the living room, away from the backyard and the forest, and tried to concentrate on her pre-algebra homework. Katerina pattered back and forth through the house, leaving a trail of plastic toy animals as she went. Abuela was in her room resting, with Dolores keeping her company. Dolores emerged a few times, her eyebrows knit. When she passed through the living room carrying something for the laundry, she asked Jade, "What *is* that noise? It won't stop! It doesn't let Doña Luz rest properly!"

"It's a bulldozer in the forest by the school," said Jade. It made her angry all over again to know that the noise was disturbing Abuela's rest. She tried not to think about how much destruction the bulldozer was wreaking, how far into the forest it might have gotten by now. She just hoped it didn't get very far.

"Ah!" said Dolores, raising her eyebrows, then frowning like her dad had done. She wadded up the piece of linen in her hands more tightly. "But—are they allowed to chop down that forest?"

"No," said Jade's dad, walking into the room. "I'm pretty sure they're not allowed." He said it loudly—almost too loudly—as if by declaring it he would make it true. Jade hoped it was. Dolores nodded slowly and headed off to the laundry room, and Jade wondered what the forest meant to her.

Her dad went to the back door in the kitchen. She heard him curse quietly, indistinctly.

Her dad never cursed. Hearing it made the muscles of Jade's back tense up between her shoulders.

At last the noise of the bulldozer stopped. The end of it came like a bodily relief, a release from the tension that had been building ever since the incessant din had started. It had only been a couple of hours, but it felt like it had been longer. Jade's mom wasn't even back from work yet.

"I'm not going to let them cut down any more trees, if I can help it," her dad announced, coming into the living room. "It's not right—they didn't alert the neighbors. I'm going to talk to the neighbors about this, and we're going to do something about it."

All at once she needed to know how bad the damage was. Had the hungry jaws of the machine disturbed the place where Itztli told her his stories? Or the place where the creek dipped in a short waterfall beside the twisty old oak?

She shut her math book and ran to the back door.

"I'm going to go see what they've done!" she called to her dad, and without waiting for an answer, she headed out the door and into the Wildcat Trail.

The trail was still the same familiar path. The sounds were perhaps a little different—the squirrels and birds were squeaking a bit more than usual, as if in alarm over the ruckus they had just endured. As Jade approached the place where she had torn down the yellow caution tape, she began to see what the bulldozer had done. It had upturned and flattened what it could of a rectangular section of the forest near the parking lot. The ground there was a turbulent sea of crisscrossed twigs, thin logs that had been snapped at odd angles, papery flower petals smushed into the dirt, and leaves that lay crushed and muddied on the forest floor. The biggest trees that the bulldozer was no match for still stood, the orange ribbons flapping around their waists.

Air filled Jade's lungs as she saw that Itztli's oak was still standing. The oak with the twisty branches, the oak he had planted to honor those he loved. From where she stood on the trail, she could see its curly branches and leaves silhouetted against the afternoon sky. It rose like a wizened warrior, ancient but firm, beside the freshly splintered branches and the uncovered red clay that lay exposed like an open wound. It stood just inside a rough line that marked where the bulldozer had stopped. As if intimidated by the great tree, the machine had halted before it and retreated.

Jade stepped lightly off the trail, feeling like she could breathe again. The oak was still there. Maybe Itztli was around here, too. She headed for the bend in the stream where Itztli painted and told his stories. She needed to find him.

When she arrived, the rushing creek water was darker and creamier than usual, carrying away leaves and forest debris. Already, though, it looked to Jade like it was beginning to flush itself out, like it was in the process of cleansing itself of this mess.

Where was Itztli?

She looked around, but she saw no flash of gold, heard no faint rustle of leaves stirred by padded feet.

Jade's heart began to beat faster again. She tried to remain calm and breathe as deeply as she could as she walked along the edge of the stream toward the tree. Maybe he was there. She did her best to step slowly and deliberately, fighting the urge to run and make her steps keep pace with the rising rhythm of her heartbeat. She kept her senses pricked, her eyes, ears, and nose searching for anything to let her know that Itztli was here.

When she got to the place where the great oak stood on the other side of the creek, she leapt across the stream to where it was. She was briefly proud of herself for that leap— she felt almost as graceful as Itztli in his jaguar form. She put a hand on the trunk of the old tree, just above the ugly ribbon they had tied around it, and the grooved bark beneath her palm felt like a thick hide with a thousand wrinkles.

But where was Itztli?

Jade's heart was really pounding now, and there was nothing she could do to slow it down this time.

"Itztli!" she cried out.

A white-tailed rabbit hopped up onto what was once the leafy top of a small tree. It saw Jade and stood still for a moment, looking at her with one big, dark eye, then hopped away over the freshly angular brush, its white tail popping.

Jade spun on her toes, dancing an anxious pirouette on the side of the stream, and scanned the landscape for any sign of Itztli.

The wind creaked the limbs of the old oak tree, and it sounded like an ancient sigh. Jade looked up at its swaying branches, which stretched like curved fingers over the landscape. Its lacy leaves fluttered in the sun.

Jade nuzzled closer to the tree for comfort, to try to slow her heart. She walked around the wide trunk, drinking in the shade of its branches, patting it with her hands. When she found the knot in the orange ribbon they had tied around it, she slipped her finger into the plastic creases and undid it, releasing the trunk. She stuffed the orange plastic into the waistband of her skort to get rid of later, and kept walking, closing the circle around the tree. She stepped lightly, reverentially, over and between its firm, strong roots.

As she came back around to the creek side of the tree, she felt something against her ankle, hard but soft at the same time. Her foot was in a crevice between two of the roots that plunged toward the creek. Curious, she crouched to see what was there.

The V of the roots made a small dome on the stream bank. They sheltered a hollow that resembled a tiny room with a pointed entrance, like the door to a chapel. Inside, something was wrapped up neatly in a cloth bundle. Jade reached in and pulled the bundle out carefully. Even before she had pulled it out completely, she heard the clink of ceramic and felt the familiar roundness through the cloth that was just the same roundness of the inkpot Itztli had given her. Could this be the rest of his inkpots? Had he left them for her to find, knowing she would come here?

Holding the bundle carefully in her hands, Jade sat back against the trunk of the tree and crossed her legs beneath her. Now she was facing across the stream, to the side where she had sat so many times to listen to Itztli's stories and watch him paint. She kept her hands as steady as she could and unwrapped the bundle. The cloth was a soft but strong cotton that appeared to be the same material as Itztli's tunic.

Inside it were indeed three inkpots, and Jade placed them gently on the ground beside her among the roots of the tree. The powders to make the inks shimmered inside them—the obsidian black, the brilliant blue, and a deep red that Jade hadn't seen before.

The bundle held two more things, too: Itztli's reed pen, with its elegant tip, and his paintbrush, with its vanishingly fine bristles. Jade stared at the two implements on the cloth, unable to bring herself to touch either of them. These were Itztli's tools—how could she possibly handle them?

The realization hit her, and it was clear now. Perhaps she had known it before, but she hadn't been able to bring herself to accept it. Itztli wanted her to have his tools. He wanted her to have his pen and his paintbrush that he wielded with such fierce dexterity. He wanted her to draw and paint with them, to carry on what he had taught her. It was an incredible honor, and one that Jade wouldn't have dared to dream of. But she wanted to accept it. She wanted to paint stories with them.

But there was another part of the realization, too, like the opposite side of a coin, and this one was harder to accept.

He was gone.

For the second time this afternoon, Jade felt tears well up. She squeezed her eyelids shut and tried to will them back, but she felt them, hot and insistent, begin to leak out anyway. She wiped them away with the backs of her hands but they kept coming. She tried to take deep breaths but they came out shallow and sniffly. She leaned her head back against the tree for support, for comfort, and felt her face contort as she gave in to soft little sobs and the tears ran slow and steady down her face.

At last she took a deep, snorty breath and opened her eyes. Her vision was still blurry from the tears but she blinked them away and looked at the pen and the paintbrush.

Itztli wanted her to have them, to use them. *You have what it takes,* he had said.

She reached out her hand and hovered it above the pen. Carefully, reverentially, she took it into her palm and curled her fingers around it, the way she had seen Itztli do. The wood was cool and smooth against her fingertips.

She held the pen in the air, its point poised before an imaginary page.

Slowly, she set it back down on the cloth and picked up the paintbrush. The tool to add the color to her drawings. The brush that Itztli had used so many times, flicking it with his deft, sure strokes. Its weight felt perfect in her hand.

She laid the paintbrush back down on the cloth and set the inkpots back on it, too. She was about to wrap the bundle back up again when she saw something else glinting in the little hollow under the roots. Leaning closer, she saw four dried corn kernels—red, white, yellow, and blue—arranged like a star on the ground and shining brilliantly in the afternoon sun that slanted toward it like a golden finger pointing to them. Jade reached into the crevice and pulled them out. They shone like finely cut jewels in her palm, and they made her think of the dried corncobs of many colors that Abuela decorated her stoop with in the fall.

When Itztli had come here, he had followed a trail of stories, art, and corn. On his travels the corn was what had always made him feel at home. Jade wondered where these seeds had come from, and how long he had had them. Had he kept them with him all along his travels, the way Abuela kept the mirror with her on her journey to Chicago?

She placed the corn kernels delicately onto the cloth as well. They were Itztli's last gift to her. She didn't quite understand what they meant, but she hoped that in time she would.

She wrapped the bundle back up carefully, knotting it the way Itztli had. Clutching the bundle to her, she stood up.

Before she left, she turned to the great old tree. The waning light came gold and slanted now through its leaves. She pressed her free palm to the wrinkled bark and leaned her forehead against its trunk. "Thank you," she whispered. "Thank you for everything." She said it to the tree because she couldn't say it to Itztli anymore.

As she walked back to the Wildcat Trail and made her way back home, Jade held the bundle close to her chest. Itztli had given her such a great honor—and such a great responsibility. She hardly knew if she was up to it. But this was no time for doubting; Itztli had trusted her, and she trusted Itztli.

Her mom was waiting for her in the backyard beside the entrance to the Wildcat Trail. She was still wearing her work clothes. She must have arrived home not long ago.

"Honey," she said, stretching out her arms, her voice soft.

"Mom," said Jade, and the word came out high and cracking. She threw herself into her mom's embrace, taking care not to crush the bundle, and she was crying for real now, loud, heaving sobs, and her tears were making a big wet spot on her mother's blouse. Itztli was gone, and if anyone would understand what that meant, it was her mom.

Her mother held her and rubbed her back and let her cry.

At last the embrace soothed Jade somewhere deep inside her, and her sobs subsided to little sniffles. A warmth spread from her chest out to the ends of her limbs.

"Thanks, Mom," she said, pulling away at last, her voice thick and goopy with snot.

"Here." Her mom offered her some tissues from her purse.

Jade took the tissues and blew her nose loudly, grossly, with her free hand, the cloth bundle tucked under one arm. She took a deep breath, glad she could breathe more easily now without her nostrils all stopped up. She shoved the tissues into the waistband of her skort beside the orange ribbon to throw away.

"Mom, my—um—guide—is gone now," she said.

"Oh, Jade," she said. Her mom looked her in the eye and Jade could tell that she got it, how difficult that was. "And—it's terrible what they're doing to the forest," Jade went on.

"Yes, your dad told me," said her mom. "But there's no way we're going to let them destroy that forest."

Jade let out a breath, relieved. The O'Callaghan family wasn't going to let this happen.

"Jade, I know you lost someone special," her mom said. "But your guide gave you many things, right?" Her gaze drifted to the cloth bundle, then back to Jade again.

"Yes," said Jade, sniffling. It was true—Itztli *had* given her so many things. He had given her his stories, his drawings, his paintings. He had given her his inks—including that precious green paint—and he had given her the amoxtli. And now, he had entrusted her with his very own paintbrush and reed pen.

And he had shown her what it meant to be jaguar.

She remembered the promise she made to Itztli the last time she saw him. *I will paint your stories,* she had told him. *I will keep them alive.* She knew deep down that now she had everything she needed to do this.

"Let's go inside," her mom said softly, putting a hand on her back. "Abuela's up now. She wanted to know where you were."

A smile sneaked itself across Jade's lips and she nodded. It was nice to know that Abuela had asked about her. "Yeah," she said. "Let's go inside." Right now all she wanted was to be around people who understood her, without her having to explain.

They walked in the door and Mortimer nuzzled up to Jade's shins. He petted her legs with his tail, and together they walked to her room.

Jade set the bundle down carefully on her desk. Before she talked with Abuela, she needed to see something. She turned to her dresser and pulled the obsidian mirror out from where it lived now inside the hummingbird purse, nestled among her clothes. She sat cross-legged on her bed with the mirror, facing out the window at the line of pines at the edge of the yard, and the forest beyond that. Mortimer settled himself in her lap and watched the mirror, too, with his yellow-green eyes. She tilted the polished face of the mirror toward the forest and peered into the reflection in the stone. Amid the smoky veins the trees grew and shrank to odd proportions on the convex surface. Jade kept looking, trying to channel the energy and power she had felt yesterday, and had still felt this morning.

And then she saw him in the mirror—the regal jaguar, bounding lightly through the forest from tree to tree.

Jade lowered the mirror and smiled out at the pines, despite everything. She had his tools, she had his stories, and she had the forest. And as long as she had these things, Itztli would never really leave her.

22

As sunset began to overtake the backyard, Jade arranged the corn kernels Itztli had given her into a star on her bookshelf, the way she had found them. The last sparks of day made them glow bright and colorful, as if lit from within.

She unwrapped the cloth bundle on her desk and spread Itztli's tools on the soft white cloth. The opened-out bundle released into her room the smells of the forest—the moist scent of dirt by the stream bank, the fresh perfume of newly sprouted leaves, the sharp odor of pine bark.

These tools were hers now, but she could hardly think of them that way. To her, they would always be Itztli's tools.

She wanted to share some of this with Abuela. She wanted to let her know that she understood the mirror better now, that it had done for her some version of what it had done for so many in her family, for generations. She wanted to share the loss that she felt today, but also the many things that made that loss bearable. Like these colors that Itztli had left her.

The red ink powder intrigued her the most. She scooped the jar up carefully. Holding it firmly in her hands, she carried it to the living room, where Abuela was waiting for her in the recliner.

"Chalchihuite, your father told me about the forest," Abuela said when she saw her, leaning forward slightly. "He told me they didn't get very far today, though. How do you feel about it?"

"I'm okay," said Jade, grateful for the question. "I'm glad they didn't destroy much more. And I hope they don't get any farther than they did today." She settled into the couch beside Abuela, holding the ink jar in her lap. She cupped it with both hands, the way she had seen Abuela hold her té de manzanilla sometimes.

"You have another color," said Abuela, eyeing the inkpot.

"Yes," said Jade. "I wanted to show it to you."

"Let me see," said Abuela, holding out her hands.

Jade placed the jar in her hands and watched Abuela close her fingers around it to get the feel of it and bring it close to her face so she could see it better. After inspecting it, her brow pensive, she balanced it on her lap, holding on to it with her good hand, and dipped the fingers of the hand that the stroke had weakened inside the narrow lip. Her hands held surprisingly steady as she did this, and Jade resisted the urge to help her.

When Abuela brought her fingers out again, the tips were tinted vermilion. She rubbed her thumb and fore-finger together, and the crushed powder shone with an even brighter luster, an even more brilliant shade of red. It was a red as full and potent as the red on the cushions she had embroidered, and the red on the feathers of the hummingbird that shimmered on the purse that was now Jade's.

"Nocheztli," said Abuela, and excitement vibrated in her voice as she contemplated the red on her fingertips. It sounded like a word that Itztli would have said.

"Nocheztli," Jade repeated.

"Sí, o grana cochinilla," said Abuela.

"Is that the red you told me about before?" said Jade. "The one made from the insects that live on the nopales?"

"Exacto," said Abuela. "The very one. This was the red that made me convinced about Flor's hunt for all the right colors. At first I thought she was too obsessed, going after all these colors, when she could just use the cheaper, synthetic ones. But then I saw this red, and I tried it out on the threads for my bordados, and she never had to try to convince me again." She was smiling now at the inkpot, rubbing her thumb over the clay. "One day soon, when I am feeling strong enough, I will show you how to make it into paint or dye, depending on what you need," she said, looking at Jade. "I will show you what Flor and I learned in San Juan de las Jacarandas."

"Yes, please!" said Jade, smiling.

"Ten," said Abuela quietly, and she held the jar out for Jade to take again. When Jade reached out and took it, she could still feel the warmth where Abuela's hands had held it.

"Um, Abuela?" she said.

"Yes?"

"The mirror is how I got this red," she said.

"I see," said Abuela, and she was smiling softly again, and her smile was perfectly aligned, with not a hint of the droop from the stroke.

Jade looked back down at the jar and the red powder inside it. She could feel something stirring inside her, preparing itself to leap. Now she knew what it was, of course. It was her jaguar self stirring, waving its tail slowly across the ground, twitching its whiskers in preparation to roar.

"I know it's hard to see the forest like that, Chalchihuite, with some of the trees down, and all that," said Abuela. She reached out to touch Jade's arm, and her grip was light but firm. "But I want you to know something."

"What's that?" said Jade.

"No se puede enderezar un árbol ya caído," said Abuela. *You can't make a fallen tree stand up straight.*

"I know," said Jade, looking down. She knew she needed to be tough, to get through this, to overcome the loss. She needed to be strong like she had been when Abuelo died and she had learned to go to the house that he and Abuela had shared and still feel the warmth that went on living there.

"Pero ya verás cómo retoñarán," said Abuela. *But you'll see how they sprout back.*

Jade looked back up at Abuela, surprised, and saw that she was smiling. Her hand was warm and comforting on Jade's arm. Jade put a hand on top of hers, too, and they sat like that for a while, the grays of dusk filtering into the room, and the warmth from Abuela's hand spreading through Jade and calming her.

After their easy Saturday breakfast the next morning, Chloe called and asked for Jade. "You just seemed really upset by the bulldozer yesterday," she said. "Do you want to come over?"

"Yes," said Jade, nodding emphatically into the receiver. She could think of no better way to spend the morning than with Chloe.

Chloe came out the door of the town house as soon as Jade's dad pulled up. Jade barely said goodbye to her dad and dashed out of the car. She wanted to get lost in one of her long conversations with Chloe, the ones where they talked about all sorts of things and she felt like Chloe *got* it.

Chloe's house was cozy like Jade remembered it. Chloe's mom and Nikos were out, so they owned the place, at least for the next few hours. Chloe went to the fridge and got out a teacup with Saran Wrap over it.

"I saved it for you," she said, putting it in the microwave.

As the microwave started, Jade began to smell the warm cinnamon and vanilla of the rice pudding that Chloe's mom had made the first time she came here. The Friday special for the restaurant.

"It smells amazing," she said to Chloe.

Chloe smiled, her eyes wide in agreement, and nodded. When the microwave dinged, she took the steaming cup out and offered it to Jade with a spoon. Jade took the cup and said, "Aren't you going to have some too?"

"That's all that's left," she said. "You have it."

Jade hovered the spoon hesitantly over the rice pudding, then dug in. There really was only enough for one person. It made her feel special, knowing that Chloe had saved it for her and not just eaten it herself. That was impressive. "Mmm!" she said, tasting it. "Oh my god, thank you," she said, with her mouth still full.

Chloe laughed. "Of course! Let's go to my room."

Jade nodded and swallowed. She scraped the spoon against the bottom of the cup—it was all gone now. After setting the cup in the sink, she followed Chloe upstairs, already feeling better.

"So," said Chloe, sitting on her bed and patting the space beside her for Jade to sit. "That forest means a lot to you."

"Yeah," said Jade, sitting down beside her slowly. She remembered how her mom had told her the story about meeting the owls, how she had kept some things private. She felt that way about meeting Itztli, and learning, eventually, that they both were jaguar, that they shared that. That was *her* story, which she could choose to tell or not to tell.

"You know," said Jade, "when you lose someone . . ."

Chloe nodded, listening.

Jade started again. "Chloe, you told me that you feel like you know your grandparents because of the stories your parents told you about them. You said you know your grandma because your mom still sings her songs."

Chloe nodded. "Yes." She reached for the worn teddy bear on her pillow, in what looked like an unconscious, instinctive gesture. "Did your grandma ever tell you what you wanted to know?" she asked.

"Yeah, she did," said Jade. "There's still a lot I don't know—and probably won't ever know—but my abuela told me some . . . surprising things. She told me more about the place where she and my abuelo grew up, where they come from, and it sounds like this amazing, colorful place . . ." Jade shook her head, thinking of what Abuela had told her about the tianguis, and about how she and Tía Flor became artists, following a long tradition of artists in the family. "And I'm so glad she told me all that. But there's also—" She let out a sigh, trying to figure out how to say it. "My abuelo is gone," she said. "And Abuela can tell me some things, but not everything. My abuelo told me all these stories when I was little, and I thought maybe I would be able to fill in all the pieces and put the stories back together again, but actually, what I have left of them is still just—what I remember of them." She looked at Chloe. "Does that make sense?" she said. "Like I have my abuela's stories, and I have what I remember of Abuelo's stories, but in the end there are still these big holes." She stretched her arms out wide as if to encircle an imaginary hole the size of an uprooted tree.

"Yeah, I think that makes sense," said Chloe. "Some things are just lost forever. Or you can only have them in bits and pieces." She was playing with the ears of her teddy bear. It looked incredibly soft and well-loved.

Jade nodded. She thought about how Itztli was gone, and she realized it felt a little like losing Abuelo all over again. But as with Abuelo, he had left her with stories and memories that she would always have, if only in bits and pieces, as Chloe said.

Jade watched as Chloe pulled the teddy bear to her chest and kept petting the top of its head. It had a balding spot from where she had petted it so much this way. Jade wondered what lost things or people Chloe might be thinking of right now.

"What's its name?" said Jade, nodding toward the bear.

"Charlotte," said Chloe.

"Oh!" said Jade. Charlotte. The city where Chloe had lived before coming to Atlanta.

"Reminds me of being a little kid, you know." Chloe said it almost as if she were talking to the bear.

They were silent. Chloe kept stroking the top of Charlotte's head. After a moment she gave the bear a quick kiss and tossed it back onto the pillow. "Let me show you something," she said.

Chloe got up and opened a drawer in her desk. She drew out a purple spiral-bound notebook. "This is where I keep Yia Yia's songs," she said. "These are the songs that my mom still sings. Most of them are ones that my yia yia came up with herself." She opened the notebook and laid it out on top of the bed. Jade stood up to look at it.

The lyrics in Greek were penciled across the ruled pages and looked like poems. Jade couldn't read them at all, couldn't even sound out the words because they were written in Greek letters, but still she recognized Chloe's handwriting.

Some pieces were missing in the song-poem on the page that Chloe was showing her. Blank spaces where her writing stopped, before picking up again.

Chloe pointed to one, her fingernail filling up the empty space. "That's where there's a part that my mom has forgotten," said Chloe. "That's where she just hums—*hmm-hmm-hmm!*—until she gets to a part that she remembers. It's not always the same part that she forgets or remembers, so sometimes I go back and fill something in, when I hear her singing new lyrics. But sometimes she sings something completely different from what she sang the last time, and then I don't know which version to put down." She pointed to a line that was really two lines squeezed one on top of the other. "There are always parts missing, and I'm probably never going to get the whole song," said Chloe. "But, you know, I guess I think it's worth it to get down what I can of it."

"Totally!" said Jade. "You should sing it, too!"

Chloe looked down at the notebook, rubbed the corner of one of the pages.

"You're—an amazing singer," said Jade.

"My mom says I have my yia yia's voice," said Chloe, not looking up from the notebook.

"Well, I didn't know your grandma, but if that's true, then she must have been an incredible singer."

Chloe's lips broke into a smile at last. "You know, I sing these songs to myself when no one's around," she said, looking up at Jade.

"Can I hear some?" said Jade.

Chloe laughed, then said, "Yeah, sure," and Jade could tell that she was actually excited to sing for her.

Chloe opened her closet and kicked away her muddy cross-country sneakers and a bag of laundry. She stooped to take out her record player, set the turntable on her desk, and bent around to plug it in.

"I can show you all this because my mom is out," said Chloe. "Otherwise . . ." She shook her head.

Jade watched Chloe go back to the closet and rummage around behind some clothes in the back. She brought out a glossy, square cardboard cover with a woman on it who was dressed in a fluttery ball gown with her arms outspread, as if she were about to fly. Chloe tilted it on its side and slid the black vinyl record out and placed it carefully on the turntable. She flipped through the pages in her purple notebook on the bed, until she found what she was looking for. She did all this with the concentrated seriousness of a performer readying her stage.

"You know, my parents used to be in love," she told Jade, looking directly at her.

Jade didn't know what to say. She knew that neither she nor Chloe understood very much at all about romantic love. But Jade knew that her own parents were in love, and she trusted that Chloe had known that, too.

"They used to dance," Chloe went on, grabbing the karaoke mic from her boom box. Jade sat back down on the bed to watch. She felt like she was a spectator in a show, like there should be a spotlight on Chloe now, telling the story of the song before she sang it. "They would wait until they thought Nikos and I were asleep," Chloe went on. "This was in the old house in Charlotte. And they would put on these old Greek ballads, and they would dance. Nikos and I used to watch through the crack in the door. They would dance so slow, so lovingly. And the music was so romantic. I thought there was nothing more beautiful in the whole wide world." She said this last part into the mic, even though it wasn't turned on, and Jade could hear the music beginning to take over her voice as she said it.

Chloe looked straight at her now, her mascara-painted eyes deep and dark. "But then one day, my mom came home by herself from the restaurant we had there, and she got out all the records and she threw them one by one into a black trash bag. She looked at each one, made sure she knew what it was, and then she threw it away. I watched her do it. She had this look on her face while she did it, like she was determined not to be sad. I'm pretty sure she didn't know I was there."

"Did you ever find out why she did that?" said Jade, quietly.

"I don't know," said Chloe, and she looked out over Jade, as if she were addressing a large audience that was just beyond the window. "Mom would never tell me. Dad either. All I know is—after that, they fought all the time, like I told you. And they never danced again." She looked back at Jade. "It was like the world broke in two," she said.

Chloe switched on the record player. She picked up the needle and held it just above the revolving vinyl. "This is a song that my yia yia used to sing, and that my parents used to dance to. It's not one of the ones she wrote. It was one of the only songs she sang that was popular enough for there to be a recording of someone singing it." She let down the needle gently. There was a static beat, another. And then the song began.

Strings swelled, and a chorus of woodwinds. They rose and fell in chords that were unfamiliar to Jade. The rhythms were sad, but left room for hope. Chloe closed her eyes and took a deep breath, then opened her mouth to sing.

Chloe's voice, warm and brassy, melded with the voice on the recording. Jade had never heard her sing so beautifully. The tones of the voices—Chloe's and the recorded one—were strong and determined, amid the sorrow they conveyed. Chloe's eyes flicked over to the notebook every once in a while for the words. Her face was as expressive as a diva's on a movie screen. Jade watched and listened and tried to get what she could from the sounds of the song, not understanding any of the words.

Chloe began to sway, stretching her arms out like the woman on the record cover, and moving her hips a little. She motioned to Jade, and Jade stood up from the bed and put her arms out, too, let her body sway to the rhythm of the strings and Chloe's voice. Jade closed her eyes and let her body move as it wished, her feet, her legs, her hips, her torso, her head—her body that she felt more and more comfortable in every day. She and Chloe twirled around the room, Chloe singing low and sad into the microphone, and the black vinyl turning round and round.

Jade's mom picked her up a few hours later, after she and Chloe had raided the fridge for some delicious leftovers— spinach pastry triangles and a piece of roasted lamb with yogurt sauce from a Tupperware container. Her belly full and content, Jade climbed into the passenger seat and waved goodbye to Chloe from behind the window as they drove out of the parking lot.

"We were able to find out some things about the plans for the forest," her mom said when they were out on the road.

"Oh yeah?" said Jade. She was impressed but not particularly surprised that her parents had been able to get information so quickly—after all, this was the kind of fact-finding that her mom did for a living. She always had to get to the bottom of a story.

"It's a developer," her mom said evenly. "They want to build more houses. They bought up the lot without the neighborhood knowing. None of the neighbors are happy about it," she added, glancing over at Jade.

The forest meant a lot to many people, it seemed.

"Turns out they don't have a permit," she said, and there was pride in the way she shifted her shoulders and her grip on the steering wheel. "So, they have no right to clear any trees or to build. That means we have a case. I think it'll be pretty hard for them to keep going with their plans, now that the cat is out of the bag."

"You really think they won't do anything else?" Jade allowed herself to hope.

"Yep, I really think so," said her mom. "I don't think they want a CNN reporter on their tail."

Jade laughed and sat back against her seat. "I bet!" she said.

When they drove up to the house, her dad and Katerina were digging in the flower bed by the mailbox in the front yard. Katerina looked like she was having fun making a tiny mountain of dirt beside the garden with her little red shovel. Abuela had brought her walker out to the front yard, too, and she was sitting on it near the entrance of the house, taking in the sun.

When Jade and her mom got out of the car, her dad took off his gardening gloves and sauntered over to her mom, and they gave each other a smooch.

"We're gonna win this one," her dad said, squeezing her mom's arm. Turning to Jade, he said, "Can you believe these guys didn't even have a permit?"

"Mom told me!" said Jade.

Her dad shook his head. "There's no way they would give them one either. Some of those trees they want to cut down are historic. If they were in the garden where I work, they would have plaques beside them that said, 'Tulip Poplar. Tallest one for three hundred acres. Beech. Oldest one in town.' No way they can take these trees down. And we're going to make these guys replant what they've already destroyed," he added, glancing at her mom. She was smiling and gave him a little scratch on the back near his shoulder, before heading toward Abuela and the house.

"That would be great," said Jade. She thought about what Abuela had said last night, that the trees they had managed to clear would grow back. Of course, *those* trees would never come back. The new ones would be different, echoes of the old.

She thought about the two big piles of wood chips in the backyard where the great oaks had been and how her dad wanted to turn them into sunny flower beds.

At once it hit her—what to do with Itztli's corn kernels.

"Dad," she said. "Can you help me plant some corn in one of those new gardens in the backyard?" She knew as she said it that this is what Itztli would have wanted—to have the corn flower and multiply, to have it bear colorful fruit that could be ground into masa and eaten. The corn that for him meant home, that had brought comfort to him on his journey. He had planted the great twisty oak in honor of his beloved, in honor of his mother, in honor of his father, and she would plant this corn in honor of him.

"Corn?" said her dad. He scratched his chin, which he hadn't yet shaved today. "Now that's an idea," he said. "There's plenty of sunlight now. It would remind me of home."

Jade thought of the endless tall cornfields on the drive to her grandma's house in Nebraska. Corn meant home to lots of people.

"We'll have to wait till next summer, though," he said, "or else it'll freeze."

"That's fine," said Jade. She could wait. The kernels that Itztli had given her would decorate her bookshelf until then.

As she headed into the house, she stopped to greet Abuela. "Hola, Abuelita," she said. "How are you feeling?"

Abuela lifted her palms to the sky. "¡De maravilla!" she said. "The sun has been cradling me. It's a gorgeous day. Perfect for painting, don't you think?" She smiled up at Jade.

Jade smiled back and thought about it. She looked out at the yard, the neighborhood. The light was indeed just right for painting this afternoon.

"Your gift is too great, too precious, Chalchihuite," said Abuela.

Jade looked back at her, gave Abuela her full attention.

"Do you think I made that purse just by looking at it?" Abuela went on. Her dark eyes sparkled at her in the sun. "It takes practice, to be able to make what you want, how you want it."

The jade bracelet glinted on Abuela's wrist. It must have taken years of practice to make those beads just right, too, Jade thought. If she wanted to paint stories as lively and colorful as Abuela's embroidered hummingbird and Tía Flor's painted rabbits, and as enduring as these radiant stones on Abuela's wrist, she was indeed going to need to practice.

"You're right," said Jade.

"Por supuesto," said Abuela, playful. *Of course.*

Jade laughed and went in, heading for her room. She went straight to her bookshelf and touched her finger to the spine of the amoxtli, and beside that, the edge of her sketchbook from her grandma where she had begun the painting of her family's watery hills. The light streamed in strong onto the bookshelf now.

If she was going to paint, she was going to need the mirror. She pulled the hummingbird purse out of her dresser and ran her fingers along the brightly embroidered stitches, especially the red threads that had been dyed with nocheztli. The black mirror flashed in the light from the mirror as she pulled it out.

"Sissy, can I see your corn seeds?"

It was Katerina, standing in the doorway, still carrying her little red shovel. The tip of it shed a dusting of dirt on the floor.

"I want us to grow lots of corn so we can make it into tortillas and eat them," Katerina added.

Jade smiled and laughed. She set the mirror down carefully on top of the purse on her dresser. "I want that, too," she said. She scooped the colorful kernels up from her bookshelf and sat on her bed. She patted the spot beside her, and Katerina let the shovel clatter to the floor and climbed up next to her.

Jade held the seeds out to her sister in her palm. "Here they are," she said. "They're very special."

Katerina leaned close. "Can I touch them?" she said.

"Yes," said Jade. "Just be very careful."

Katerina reached out and gently touched the kernels one by one with the tip of her index finger.

"Will you help us plant them next summer?" said Jade.

Katerina looked up at her and nodded very seriously. "Yes," she said. "But, Sissy, why are these seeds so special? Where did you get them?"

Jade closed her hand over the kernels and stood up to set them back carefully on the bookshelf by Itztli's blue-and-white painting. She coaxed the colorful seeds back into the star shape they were in when Itztli left them for her.

How could she answer Katerina's questions? How could she explain what Itztli had told her, and what she had learned about how to listen well, how to take in what her elders told her and carry their words with her as best she could?

The only way she could answer Katerina was by telling stories. Itztli's stories, but also Abuela's stories. The only way she could explain why the seeds were so special was if she told her how corn had sustained Itztli on his long journey to the home of his beloved, how these were his last gift to her after he gave her the bark painting and the precious green ink and the amoxtli—and the gift of showing her how he painted, how he made stories come to life, how he carried on the memory of those he loved.

The seeds were so special for all these reasons and because Itztli had made her see that, yes indeed, she was jaguar, but the only way to truly be in tune with her jaguar self was to listen. And Abuela had given her so many precious things to listen to, about San Juan de las Jacarandas, about Abuelo and his wooden creations, about the artists in their family and how Tía Flor had tracked down the most vibrant pigments to paint her pottery with.

She wanted to tell her sister all these things. But not yet, not now. She was still too little. One day, though, she would understand.

Jade sat back down on the bed beside Katerina. "I will tell you all about it when you're old enough," she said. "I promise."

"You promise?" said Katerina, looking up at her. Her eyes were big.

"I promise."

Katerina was silent for a moment, holding the gaze with her big eyes. "Okay, Sissy," she said at last. "Just don't forget."

"I won't," said Jade, and she gave her a squeeze. Katerina hugged her back, then almost immediately squirmed free and scooted herself down from the bed, apparently content. She grabbed her little shovel and skipped out the door, leaving a fine line of dirt in her trail.

Something flashed across the surface of the mirror on Jade's dresser just as her sister bounded out. Jade glanced and caught the reflection of her sister just in time. It was a dainty ladybug, lifting her tiny wings, and taking flight.

Jade smiled and shook her head. Of course.

She turned back to the bookshelf and the notebook with her painting and Itztli's amoxtli. She pulled them both out and placed them on her bed in the pool of sunlight from the window. They were hers to finish, both of them. And Jade had a feeling there would be many more stories to listen to, to paint—and to *tell*. Because the stories wouldn't be complete when she was done painting them. They would only be complete once she *shared* them. And she would share them with Katerina.

She opened her sketchbook to the painting she had begun of her family's stories. The colors had dried and set on the porous page. Itztli's green was brightly fixed in jade tones in the water and on the hummingbird she had drawn. But the watercolor paints her grandma had given her shone brightly, too, and the blue of the Casa Azul sent a calm through her, like the calm she used to feel when she walked into the restaurant as a kid.

Seeing how harmoniously Itztli's green fit with the colors from her grandma, how well the jade hues complemented the watercolor tones, Jade thought that maybe if she was going to paint Itztli's stories and the stories of her family, it was okay if she didn't paint them exactly the way Itztli would. She could mix colors, styles, paints, and stories. Wasn't that what her family's stories—and Itztli's—were anyway? A mix of colors and lines and memories and ways of being?

She had wanted so badly to paint just like Itztli. To hold his reed pen and his paintbrush in her hands, to match his masterful strokes. He had shown her how to hold the brush firmly but lightly at the same time, how to make painted people seem to stir on the page. She wanted to practice these techniques until she mastered them, until she breathed into her figures some of that spirited force that animated his paintings. In the end, though, what she painted would not be what Itztli would have painted. It would be her own.

Perhaps Itztli had come to know this about his own painting when he was learning the old tlacuilo ways in Tenochtitlán. Maybe then he had felt something like what Jade was feeling now—a sense that the old stories could never be told and painted in quite the same way again, but they could still be told, just in a different way now, borrowing from other stories and ways of painting, mixing them together like inks to make new colors, new drawings, new stories.

That is just one way to tell the story, Itztli had said. *Others will remember it differently. I may even tell it differently myself.*

Jade ran her finger over the blank spaces in her painting and thought of the blank spaces in the lyric-poems in Chloe's notebook. Chloe could have given up and left the songs unwritten. Instead, she recorded them, and her mom hummed along through the forgotten parts, until she got to where she knew the words again.

That's what Jade's painting would be like. She would paint the stories with the memories that she *did* have. She would give them color the way she knew how.

She opened out the amoxtli, unfolding its accordion pages. Mortimer stepped delicately between her sketchbook and the amoxtli, his fur shining in the sun. Itztli's detailed figures reminded Jade of each stroke of his reed pen, and the dashes of blue paint gleamed brightly as if they'd never dried. The pages Itztli had left blank were an invitation, and she would fill them in soon, and finish the amoxtli. But first, she needed to practice, like Abuela said, so that when the time was right, she would bring to the page everything that she had learned, and all the mastery that she could summon.

Carefully she set aside the clay jars with the ink powders. Soon she would learn to mix them into ink, but today, she would stick with the jade green that evoked the forest and the creek like no other green.

On top of the cloth she began to pack her bundle— Itztli's bundle—with tools. Itztli's reed pen and his paintbrush with the fine, fine tip. Her grandma's watercolors, which no longer daunted her. As she reached into the desk drawer for the watercolors, her fingers found a small glass bottle of black ink—another untouched gift from her grandma, from her college days in Switzerland. This was it—the black ink she would need to outline her figures before she livened them with color. She set it on the cloth, too.

And of course, she couldn't forget the mirror. Her smoking mirror, her tezcatl. She needed it to give her strength. To remind her of the people who came before her, and of the God of the Smoking Mirror who roared to life as jaguar from the deep expanse of the sea. She slipped the smooth stone back into the hummingbird purse and strapped it on.

Satisfied, she knotted the bundle and placed it carefully inside her backpack, along with her nice sketchbook and the amoxtli, and hoisted it on. She gathered the precious pot of green ink with the rabbit lid close to her chest. Armed with her instruments, she felt prepared, the way she had when she put on her black-and-gold uniform before the race. Her tools and her paints and her memories kept her company as she walked out to the backyard.

She sat down cross-legged in the grass, facing the forest. The sun was just beginning its afternoon slant. As she spread her sketchbook and her bundle before her, she thought of how she would paint the stories she wanted to keep and tell. When she thought about her family's stories, she thought of Itztli's stories. In both sets of stories, there were watery hills along the way that people made into a home. There were fierce women like Abuela and Itzpapalotl, the Obsidian Butterfly goddess, who bravely left their homes. There were artists who drew from the old ways and the new. And there were people who had fallen in love across languages and across great swaths of land.

She wanted to paint it all.

She unscrewed the top to the little glass bottle of black ink. Taking the reed pen in her hand, she willed her movements to be steady and sure, like the steps of the jaguar. She dipped the tip into the obsidian-black ink and touched it to the page to draw an ear of corn beside the watery hill of her house.

The tip of the pen stroking the paper and traveling along it focused her mind. As she inked the fine kernels and the wispy silks, she could scarcely believe it. She was holding Itztli's reed pen and drawing, in the style of the old tlacuilos, but also in a manner that was all hers. The ink flowed smooth and controlled beneath her fingers. One day soon, she would checker the kernels with vermilion.

She wanted to make the corn and the house come alive with color, and she wanted to paint with the green again. A thrill pulsed through her as she set down the reed pen and took Itztli's paintbrush between her fingers. She dipped its soft bristles in the jade-green ink, and began to color the forest that curled like a cat around her house.

A surge of energy, now familiar, rose inside her. The green bloomed dark and rich on the page, and the sun flashed, warm and golden, through the pines.

A Note on Research

This book is a work of fiction informed by a great deal of research. In writing this novel, I consulted many sources, and curious readers may wish to consult some of them as well. The following are the main sources.

I drew inspiration for many of Itztli's paintings and stories from works of art and documents from the pre-Columbian and colonial eras of Mexico. Among these is Friar Bernardino de Sahagún's sixteenth-century *General History of the Things of New Spain*, also known as the *Florentine Codex*, compiled in collaboration with Indigenous artists and writers and available through the World Digital Library. Diana Magaloni Kerpel examines the *Florentine Codex* in *The Colors of the New World: Artists, Materials, and the Creation of the Florentine Codex* and in her online exhibition, "Visualizando la nueva era. Los ocho presagios de la conquista de México en el *Códice Florentino*." Barbara Mundy's article "Mapping the Aztec Capital: The 1524 Nuremberg Map of Tenochtitlan, Its Sources and Meanings" offers a compelling reading of the map of Tenochititlán that was printed with Hernán Cortés's second letter on the conquest of Mexico, available through the World Digital Library. The sixteenth-century Spanish soldier Bernal Díaz del Castillo describes the fall of Tenochtitlán in his *Historia verdadera de la conquista de la Nueva España*. Selections of his history are available in English in *The History of the Conquest of New Spain by Bernal Díaz del Castillo,* edited by Davíd Carrasco.

Cave, City, and Eagle's Nest: An Interpretive Journey through the Mapa de Cuauhtinchan No. 2, edited by Davíd Carrasco and Scott Sessions, analyzes a map of the origin and migration story of the people of Cuauhtinchan, or the "Place of the Eagle's Nest." I focused in particular on essays by Florine G. L. Asselbergs, Elizabeth Hill Boone, and Keiko Yoneda. Angélica Jimena Afanador-Pujol's *The Relación de Michoacán (1539–1541) & the Politics of Representation in Colonial Mexico* examines a document representing Purépecha history.

Other works I consulted include *Daily Life of the Aztecs* by Davíd Carrasco and Scott Sessions; *Stories in Red and Black: Pictorial Histories of the Aztecs and the Mixtecs* by Elizabeth Hill Boone; *Ancient Maya Art at Dumbarton Oaks,* edited by Joanne Pillsbury, Miriam Doutriaux, Reiko Ishihara-Brito, and Alexandre Tokovinine; the online Nahuatl Dictionary through the University of Oregon, edited by Stephanie Wood; and essays by Nicholas J. Saunders, Elizabeth Baquedano, and Michael E. Smith in *Tezcatlipoca: Trickster and Supreme Deity,* edited by Baquedano.

These are good places to start if you want to know more about Tenochtitlán, the old tlacuilo ways, or jade stones carved long ago.

Acknowledgments

My deep gratitude goes to my immensely thoughtful, insightful, and generous editor, Meghan Maria McCullough, for believing in this book, for really *getting* it, and for guiding me to tell the story it needed to tell. This book would not be what it is without her.

I cannot imagine a better home for this book than Levine Querido. From the beginning I've known my story and I were in good hands. Gracias to everyone in the stellar team there who worked to bring this book into being, especially Arthur A. Levine, Antonio Gonzalez Cerna, and Irene Vázquez.

I deeply appreciate Anne Heausler's and Johanie Martinez-Cools's work to bring this text to its most polished form.

Thank you to Molly Mendoza for her beautiful cover art that captures Jade and her story so imaginatively, and to Jonathan Yamakami for his creative and discerning eye for style and design. My gratitude goes to Freesia Blizard for supervising this book's production. It is an honor to have this book presented physically and visually with such care.

Many thanks to the sales team at Chronicle Books for ushering this story into the hands of readers.

I am grateful to the staff and faculty of Madcap Retreats in partnership with We Need Diverse Books, as well as the Hambidge Center, for welcoming me into quiet forests and the fellowship of creative minds. Hambidge brought me to Olivia Tarcov and Courtney Young, whose companionship as writing buddies in New York I greatly appreciate.

Thank you to my writing professors, Amy Hempel and Bret Anthony Johnston, for sharing their wisdom and spurring me to have confidence as a writer. I am indebted to all the teachers who encouraged me to write, especially my fifth-grade teacher Ms. Sonia Campbell, who taught me how to make narrative into story, and who made writing and publishing books feel like an achievable dream.

Thank you to Lauren Gunderson, who first published my writing and helped me imagine myself as an author.

I am grateful to everyone who fed my curiosity and taught me about Indigenous Mexican art and stories. Davíd Carrasco and Lisa Trever nourished my interest in Mesoamerican history and culture, which I explored under the supervision and encouragement of Joanne Pillsbury at Dumbarton Oaks Library and Collection. Anna Deeny and Nenita Ponce de León Elphick helped me hone my writing and understand the resonances of Latin America's past in our present. Vicente Ferrer taught me the basics of the Nahuatl language, and Seth Kimmel and Alessandra Russo challenged me to think through the nuances of how we know what we know about the past of this continent.

The support of friends and family made this book possible. To Karen Stolley and David Littlefield I will always be grateful. Noni Carter's encouragement marked a pivotal moment. Thank you to the dear friends who had faith in me always: Elizabeth McCormick, for so thoughtfully encouraging my writing; Lucy Fleming, for being an early, longstanding, and inspiring partner in imagination; Anna Rose Gable, for all those games of "Let's pretend;" Molly Lindberg, for her enthusiasm and careful listening; and Carson Evans, for always being there, on the other end of the line—and for her fine photography. Thank you to everyone who, at some point during this journey, celebrated with me, got excited with me, and was there for me. I cherish you all.

My deepest gratitude goes to my parents, Hugo Méndez Ramírez and Vialla Hartfield-Méndez. In a house filled with books and art, they gave me the most beautiful and adventurous childhood I could imagine—bilingual, multicultural, and full of poetry. My father has always known I was a writer, and he spurred me to heed that existential flame, even when I didn't quite dare. My mother gave me music and rhythm, so essential to story; helped me hand-make my very first books; and is my most trusted reader. My parents supported me even in their own grief, when my Abuelo, Grandma, and Abuela passed away during the pandemic. I thank them for their love, for their trust, and for all the moments we've shared over a good meal, under the watchful gaze of a bright-eyed tecolote.

Some Notes on This Book's Production

The art for the jacket was created by Molly Mendoza in Procreate using an iPad Pro and Apple Pencil. The digital inkwork and watercolor effects were achieved using MaxPacks Procreate brushes from the Comics and Watercolor brush packs respectively. The artwork was composed using multiple layers, with the sketch and color comp layers acting as the underpainting for the piece.

The body text was set in Freight Text Pro, designed by Joshua Darden for The Freight Collection in 2005. The display text was set in Spirits, designed by Alfonso Garcia for Latinotype, an independent Chilean type foundry established in 2008. It was composed by Westchester Publishing Services in Danbury, CT.

Production was supervised by Freesia Blizard
Book design by Jonathan Yamakami
Edited by Meghan Maria McCullough

LQ

LEVINE QUERIDO